INTERNATIONAL

BLACK BOX

AMOS OZ

Translated from the Hebrew by
NICHOLAS DE LANGE
in collaboration with the author

VINTAGE INTERNATIONAL
VINTAGE BOOKS   NEW YORK
A DIVISION OF RANDOM HOUSE, INC.

First Vintage International Edition, March 1989

English translation copyright © 1988 by Nicholas de Lange

All rights reserved under International and Pan-American Copyright Conventions. Published in the United States by Random House, Inc., New York. Originally published in Hebrew as *Kufsah shehorah* by Am Oved Publishers, Ltd., Tel Aviv. Copyright © 1987 by Amos Oz and Am Oved Publishers, Ltd., Tel Aviv. This translation originally published, in hardcover, by Harcourt Brace Jovanovich, Inc., in 1988.

Library of Congress Cataloging-in-Publication Data
Oz, Amos.
Black box.
(Vintage international)
Translation of: Kufsah shehorah.
I. Title.
[PJ5054.09K8413 1989]   892.4′ 36   88-40376
ISBN 0-679-72185-1 (pbk.)

Manufactured in the United States of America
10 9 8 7 6 5 4 3 2 1

ACKNOWLEDGMENT

I am grateful to William Jovanovich
and the Colorado College community
for providing me with a peaceful year in which I could write
the major part of this novel.

But you, you knew the night is still and silent,
And I alone remain alert and brood.
I am the only victim of your weeping:
The beast has fixed his eye on me to be his only food.

At times I shudder suddenly and tremble,
I wander, lost, and panic drives me wild:
I hear you calling me from all directions,
I feel like a blind man being tormented by a child.

But you, you hid your face. You did not stop me,
With pigeon's blood and darkness in your tears,
Entangled in the dark, remotely sobbing,
Where memory or sense or understanding disappears.

From "Weeping" by Natan Alterman

BLACK
BOX

Dr. Alexander A. Gideon
Political Science Department
Midwest University
Chicago, Ill., U.S.A.

Dear Alec,

If you didn't destroy this letter the moment you recognized my handwriting on the envelope, it shows that curiosity is stronger than hatred. Or else that your hatred needs fresh fuel.

Now you are going pale, clenching your wolfish jaws in that special way of yours, so that your lips disappear, and storming down these lines to find out what I want from you, what I dare to want from you, after seven years of total silence between us.

What I want is that you should know that Boaz is in a bad way. And that you should help him urgently. My husband and I can't do anything, because Boaz has broken off all contact. Like you.

Now you can stop reading, and throw this letter straight on the fire. (For some reason I always imagine you in a long, book-lined room, sitting alone at a black desk, with white snow-covered plains stretching away beyond the window opposite. Plains without hill or tree, dazzling arid snow. And a fire blazing in the fireplace on your left, and an empty glass, and an empty bottle on the empty desk in front of you. The whole image is in black and white. You too: monkish, ascetic, haughty, and all in black and white.)

Now you crumple up the letter, humming in a British sort of way, and shoot it accurately onto the fire: what do you care about Boaz? And, in any case, you don't believe a word I'm saying. Here you fix your grey eyes on the flickering fire and say to yourself: She's

1

trying to pull a fast one again. That female won't ever give up or let be.

Why then am I writing to you?

In despair, Alec. Of course, when it comes to despair, you're a world authority. (Yes, naturally, I read—like everybody else—your book *The Desperate Violence: A Study in Comparative Fanaticism*.) But what I am talking about now is not your book but the substance of which your soul is fashioned: frozen despair. Arctic despair.

Are you still reading? Feeding your hatred of us? Tasting *schadenfreude* like expensive whisky, in small sips? If so, I'd better stop teasing you, and concentrate on Boaz.

The plain fact is that I haven't the faintest idea how much you know. I shouldn't be the least bit surprised if it turned out that you knew every detail, that you have instructed your lawyer, Zakheim, to send you monthly reports about our lives, that you've been keeping us on your radar screen all these years. On the other hand, I wouldn't be astonished to discover that you don't know anything at all: neither that I've married a man called Michael (Michel-Henri) Sommo, nor that I've had a daughter, nor what's become of Boaz. It would be just like you to turn your back with one brutal gesture and cut us once and for all out of your new life.

After you kicked us out, I took Boaz and we went to stay with my sister and her husband in their kibbutz. (We didn't have anywhere else to go, and we didn't have any money, either.) I lived there for six months and then I came back to Jerusalem. I worked in a bookshop. Meanwhile Boaz stayed in the kibbutz for another five years, until he was thirteen. I used to go and see him every three weeks. That's how it was until I married Michel, and ever since then the boy has called me a whore. Just like you. He didn't come to see us once in Jerusalem. When we told him our daughter (Madeleine Yifat) was born, he slammed the phone down.

Then two years ago he suddenly turned up one winter's night at one o'clock in the morning to inform me that he was through with the kibbutz, and either I send him to an agricultural high school or he'll go and "live on the streets" and that'll be the last I'll hear from him.

My husband woke up and told him to get out of his wet clothes, eat something, have a good wash, and go to bed, and tomorrow morning we'd talk. And the boy (even then, at thirteen and a half, he was a good bit taller and broader than Michel) replied, as though he were crushing an insect underfoot, "And who are you, anyway? Who asked you?" Michel chuckled and answered, "I suggest you step outside, chum, calm down, change the cassette, knock on the door, and come in all over again, and this time try to act like a human being instead of a gorilla."

Boaz turned toward the door. But I put myself between him and the doorway. I knew he wouldn't touch me. The baby woke up and started crying, and Michel went off to change her and warm some milk for her in the kitchen. I said, "All right, Boaz. You can go to agricultural school if that's what you really want." Michel, standing there in his underwear holding the baby, who was quiet, added, "Only on condition you say 'sorry' to your mother and ask nicely and then say 'thank you.' What are you, anyway, a horse?" And Boaz, his face contorted with that desperate loathing and contempt he's inherited from you, whispered to me, "And you let that *thing* fuck you every night?" and immediately afterward he stretched his hand out and touched my hair and said, in a different voice, which wrings my heart when I remember it, "But your baby's quite pretty."

Then (thanks to the influence of Michel's brother) we got Boaz into Telamim Agricultural High School. That was two years ago, at the beginning of 1974, not long after the war that you—so I was told—came back from America to take part in as commander of a tank battalion in the Sinai, before running off again. We even gave in to his request not to go and visit him. We paid the fees and kept quiet. That is to say, Michel paid. Well not exactly Michel, either.

We did not receive so much as a single postcard from Boaz during these two years. Only alarms from the headmistress. The boy is violent. The boy got in a quarrel and smashed open the night

3

watchman's head. The boy disappears at night. The boy has a police record. The boy has been put on probation. The boy will have to leave the school. This boy is a monster.

And what do you remember, Alec? The last thing you saw was a creature of eight, long and thin and sandy, like a cornstalk, standing silently for hours on end on a stool, leaning on your desk, concentrating, making model airplanes out of balsa for you from do-it-yourself booklets you brought him—a careful, disciplined, almost timid child, although even then, at the age of eight, he was capable of overcoming humiliations with a kind of silent, controlled determination. And in the meantime, like a genetic time bomb, Boaz is now sixteen, six foot three and still growing, a bitter, wild boy whose hatred and loneliness have invested him with astonishing physical strength. And this morning the thing that I have been expecting for a long time finally happened: an urgent telephone call. They have decided to throw him out of the boarding school, because he assaulted one of the women teachers. They declined to give me the details.

Well, I went down there at once, but Boaz refused to see me. He merely sent word that he didn't want "to have anything to do with that whore." Was he talking about the teacher? Or about me? I do not know. It turned out that he had not exactly "assaulted" her: he had uttered some sick joke, she had given him a slap in the face, and he had instantly given her two in return. I pleaded with them to postpone the expulsion until I could make other arrangements. They took pity on me and gave me a fortnight.

Michel says that, if I like, Boaz can stay here with us (even though the two of us and the baby live in one and a half rooms, for which we are still repaying the mortgage). But you know as well as I do that Boaz won't agree to that. That boy loathes me. And you. So we do have something in common, you and I, after all. I'm sorry.

There's no chance that they'll take him at another vocational school, either, with his police record and the probation officer on his back. I'm writing to you because I don't know what to do. I'm writing to you even though you won't read this, and if you do, you won't reply. At the very best you'll instruct your lawyer Zakheim to send me a formal letter begging to remind me that his client still denies paternity, that the blood test did not produce an unambiguous result, and that it was I who at the time adamantly opposed a tissue test. Checkmate.

Yes, and the divorce released you of any responsibility for Boaz and any obligation toward me. I know all that by heart, Alec. I have no room for hope. I am writing to you as though I were standing at the window talking to the mountains. Or to the darkness between the stars. Despair is your field. If you like, you can treat me as a specimen.

Are you still thirsting for vengeance? If so, I am hereby turning the other cheek. Mine, and Boaz's too. Go ahead, hit as hard as you can.

Yes, I will send you this letter, even though just now I put the pen down and made up my mind not to bother; after all, I've nothing to lose. Every way ahead is blocked. You have to realize this: even if the probation officer or the social worker manages to persuade Boaz to undergo some kind of treatment, rehabilitation, aid, a transfer to another school (and I don't believe they'd succeed), I haven't got the money to pay for it.

Whereas you've got plenty, Alec.

And I have no connections, whereas you can get anything fixed up with a couple of phone calls. You are strong and clever. Or at least you were seven years ago. (People have told me you've had two operations. They couldn't tell me what sort.) I hope you're all right now. I won't say more than that, so you won't accuse me of hypocrisy. Flattery. Bootlicking. And I won't deny it, Alec: I'm still prepared to lick your boots as much as you like. I'll do anything you ask of me. And I mean anything. Just so long as you rescue your son.

If I had any brains, I'd cross out "your son" and write "Boaz," so as not to infuriate you. But how can I cross out the plain truth? You are his father. And as for my brains, didn't you make up your mind a long time ago that I'm a total moron?

I'll make you an offer. I'm prepared to admit in writing, in

5

the presence of a notary, if you like, that Boaz is the son of anyone you want me to say. My self-respect was killed long ago. I'll sign any bit of paper your lawyer puts in front of me if, in return, you agree to give Boaz first aid. Let's call it humanitarian assistance. Let's call it an act of kindness to a totally strange child.

It's true; when I stop writing and conjure him up, I stand by these words: Boaz *is* a strange child. No, not a child. A strange man. He calls me a whore. You he calls a dog. Michel, "little pimp." He calls himself (even on official documents) by my maiden name, Boaz Brandstetter. And the school we had to pull strings to get him into, at his own request, he calls Devil's Island.

Now I'll tell you something you can use against me. My in-laws in Paris send us a little money each month to keep him in this boarding school, even though they have never set eyes on Boaz and he has probably never so much as heard of their existence. And they are not at all well off (they're immigrants from Algeria), and they have, besides Michel, five more children and eight grand-children, in France and Israel.

Listen, Alec: I'm not going to write a word about what happened in the past. Apart from one thing, something I'll never forget, even though you'll probably wonder how on earth I know about it. Two months before our divorce, Boaz was taken to Shaarei Zedek Hos-pital with a kidney infection. And there were complications. You went without my knowledge to Dr. Blumenthal to find out whether, if necessary, an adult could donate a kidney to an eight-year-old child. You were planning to give him one of your own kidneys. And you warned the doctor that you would make only one condition: that I (and the child) should never know. And I didn't until I made friends with Dr. Adorno, Blumenthal's assistant, the young doctor you were planning to sue for criminal negligence over Boaz's treat-ment.

If you are still reading, at this moment you're probably going even whiter, snatching up your lighter with a gesture of strangled violence and putting the flame to your lips (because your pipe isn't there) and saying to yourself all over again: Of course. Dr. Adorno.

Who else? And if you haven't destroyed the letter already, this is the moment when you destroy it. And me and Boaz too.

And then Boaz got better and then you kicked us out of your house, your name, and your life. You never donated any kidney. But I do believe that you seriously intended to. Because everything about you is serious. That much I will grant you—you are serious.

Flattering you again? If you want, I plead guilty. Flattering. Bootlicking. Going down on my knees in front of you and hitting my forehead on the ground. Like the good old days.

Because I've got nothing to lose and I don't mind begging. I'll do whatever you command. Only don't take too long, because in a fortnight they throw him out on the street. And the street is out there waiting for him.

After all, nothing in the world is beyond you. Unleash that monster of yours, your lawyer. Maybe with some string pulling they'll take him into the naval college. (Boaz has a strange attraction to the sea; he has had ever since he was a small child. Do you remember, Alec, in Ashkelon, the summer of the Six-Day War? The whirlpool? Those fishermen? The raft?)

And one last thing, before I seal this letter: I'll even sleep with you if you want. When you want. And any way you want. (My husband knows about this letter and even agreed that I should write it—apart from the last sentence. So now if you feel like destroying me, you can simply photocopy the letter, underline the last sentence with your red pencil, and send it to my husband. It'll work like a charm. I admit it: I was lying when I wrote earlier that I have nothing to lose.)

And so, Alec, we are now all completely at your mercy. Even my little daughter. And you can do anything you like to us.

Ilana (Sommo)

———

Mrs. Halina Brandstetter-Sommo London
No. 7 Tarnaz Street 18.2.76
Jerusalem, Israel

EXPRESS

Dear Madam,

Your letter of the 5th inst. was forwarded to me only yesterday
from the United States. I shall refer to only a small part of the
matters you chose to raise therein.

This morning I spoke on the telephone with an acquaintance
in Israel. Following this conversation the headmistress of your son's
school telephoned me on her own initiative. It was agreed between
us that the expulsion is canceled and his record will simply carry a
warning. If, nevertheless, your son prefers—as is vaguely hinted in
your letter—to transfer to a cadet school, I have reasonable grounds
for supposing that that can be arranged (via my lawyer, Mr. Zakheim). Mr. Zakheim will also convey to you a check in the sum
of two thousand dollars (in Israeli pounds and in your husband's
name). Your husband will be asked to acknowledge in writing receipt
of this sum as a gift to you on account of hardship, and not in any
sense as a precedent or as an admission of any obligation on our
part. Your husband will also be required to give an assurance that
no further appeals will be forthcoming from you in the future (I
hope that his indigent and very extended family in Paris is not
planning to follow your example and demand pecuniary favors from
me). Over the remaining contents of your letter, including the gross
lies, the gross contradictions, and the simple common, or garden,
grossness, I shall pass in silence.

[*Signed*] A. A. *Gideon*

P.S. I am retaining your letter.

———

Dr. Alexander A. Gideon   *Jerusalem*
London School of Economics   27.2.76
London, England

Dear Alec,

As you know, last week we signed on the dotted line and received the money from your lawyer. But now Boaz has left his school and he has been working for several days in the central market in Tel Aviv with a wholesale greengrocer who is married to one of Michel's cousins. It was Michel who fixed him up with the job, at Boaz's request.

This is how it happened: After the headmistress told Boaz the news that he was not going to be expelled, but only cautioned, the boy simply picked up his kit bag and disappeared. Michel got in touch with the police (he has some relations there), and they informed us that they were holding the kid in custody in Abu Kabir for possession of stolen goods. A friend of Michel's brother, who has a senior position in the Tel Aviv police, had a word with Boaz's probation officer on our behalf. After some complications we got him out on bail.

We used part of your money for this. I know that was not what you had in mind when you gave it to us, but we simply don't have any other money: Michel is merely a nonqualified French teacher in a religious state school, and his salary after deduction of our mortgage payments is barely enough to feed us. And there is also our little girl (Madeleine Yifat, almost three).

I must tell you that Boaz hasn't the faintest idea where the money for his bail came from. If he had been told, I think he would have spat on the money, the probation officer, and Michel. As it was, to start with he flatly refused to be released and asked to be "left alone."

Michel went to Abu Kabir without me. His brother's friend (the police officer) arranged for him and Boaz to be alone together in the office at the police station, so they could talk privately. Michel said to him, Look, maybe you've somehow forgotten who I am.

I'm Michael Sommo and I'm told that behind my back you call me your mother's pimp. You can say it right to my face if it'll help you let off steam. And then I could come back at you and tell you you're off your rocker. And we could stand here swearing at each other all day, and you wouldn't win, because I can curse you in French and in Arabic and you can barely manage Hebrew. So when you run out of swearwords, what then? Maybe better you should get your breath back, calm down, and make me a list, what exactly it is you want from life. And then I'll tell you what your mother and I can give. And then we'll see—perhaps we can strike a deal.

Boaz replied that he didn't want anything at all from life, and the last thing he wanted was to have all sorts of people coming along asking him what he wanted from life.

At this point Michel, who has never had it easy, did just the right thing. He simply got up to go and said to Boaz, Well, if that's the way it is, the best of luck, chum. As far as I'm concerned, they can put you in an institution for the mentally retarded or the educationally subnormal, and that's that. I'm off.

Boaz tried to argue; he said to Michel, So what? I'll murder someone and run away. But Michel just turned around in the doorway and answered quietly: Look here, honey child. I'm not your mother and I'm not your father and I'm not your anything, so don't go putting on a show for me, 'cause what do I care about you? Just make your mind up in the next sixty seconds if you want to leave here on bail, yes or no. For all I care, you can murder whoever you like. Only, if you can, just try to miss. Good-bye.

And when Boaz said, Hang on, Michel knew at once that the boy blinked first. Michel knows this game better than any of us, because he has seen life most of the time from the underneath, and suffering has made him into a human diamond—hard and fascinating (yes, in bed too, if you must know). Boaz said to him: If you really don't care about me, why did you come all the way from Jerusalem to bail me out? And Michel laughed from the doorway and said, Okay, two points to you. The fact is I actually came to see close up what sort of a genius your mother had; maybe there's some potential in the daughter she had by me, as well. Are you coming or aren't you?

And that's how it happened that Michel got him freed with your money and invited him to a kosher Chinese restaurant that's opened recently in Tel Aviv and they went to see a movie together (anyone sitting behind them might have got the idea that Boaz was the father and Michel the son). That night Michel came back to Jerusalem and told me the whole story, and meanwhile Boaz was already fixed up with the wholesale greengrocer from the market in Carlebach Street, the one who's married to Michel's cousin. Because that's what Boaz told him he wanted: to work and earn money and not be dependent on anyone. So Michel answered him then and there, without consulting me: Yes, I like that, and I'll fix it up for you this very evening right here in Tel Aviv. And he did.

Boaz is staying now at the Planetarium in Ramat Aviv: one of the people in charge there is married to a girl who studied with Michel in Paris back in the fifties. And Boaz is rather attracted by the Planetarium. No, not by the stars, but by the telescopes and by optics.

I am writing this to you with all the details about Boaz with Michel's consent. He says that since you gave the money, we owe it to you to let you know what we're doing with it. And I think you'll read this letter several times over. I think you also read my first letter several times. And I enjoy thinking about the fury I've caused you with these two letters. Being furious makes you masculine and attractive, but also childlike and almost moving: you start to waste an enormous amount of physical effort on fragile objects like pen, pipe, glasses. Not to smash them but to master yourself and to shift them two inches to the right or an inch to the left. This waste is something I treasure, and I enjoy imagining it taking place now, as you read my letter, there in your black-and-white room, between the fire and the snow. If you have some woman who sleeps with you, I admit that at this moment I am jealous of her. Jealous even of what you are doing to the pipe, the pen, the glasses, my pages between your strong fingers.

To return to Boaz: I'm writing to you as I promised Michel I would. When we get the bail money back, the whole sum you presented to us will go into a savings account in your son's name. If he decides to study, we'll finance his studies with this money. If he wants to rent himself a room in Tel Aviv or here in Jerusalem, despite his young age, we'll rent him one with your money. We won't take anything from you for ourselves.

If you agree to all this, you don't have to answer me. If not, let us know as soon as possible, before we've used the money, and we'll return it to your lawyer and manage without it (even though our finanacial situation is pretty bad).

One more request:

Either destroy this letter and the previous one, or—if you have decided to use them—do it now, right away, don't keep dithering. Every day that goes by and every night is another hill and another valley that death has captured from us. Time is passing, Alec, and both of us are fading.

And another thing: You wrote to me that you responded to the lies and contradictions in my letter with silent contempt. Your silence, Alec, and your contempt too make me suddenly fearful. Have you really not found in all these years, in all your travels, anyone who could offer you a single crumb of gentleness? I'm sorry for you, Alec. What a terrible business: I'm the one who did wrong, and you and your son are paying the full penalty. If you like, scrub out "your son" and write Boaz. If you like, scrub out the whole lot. As far as I'm concerned, don't hesitate, just do anything that'll relieve your suffering.

Ilana

———

Mr. Michel-Henri Sommo   *Geneva*
No. 7 Tarnaz Street   7.3.1976
Jerusalem, Israel

REGISTERED POST

Dear Sir,

With your knowledge—and, as she herself claims, with your encouragement—your wife has recently seen fit to send me two long and rather perplexing letters which do her no credit. If I have succeeded in penetrating her vague language, there are indications that her second letter is also intended to hint to me about your pecuniary shortcomings. And I will wager that you, sir, are the puppet-master who lurks behind her demands.

Circumstances make it possible for me (without any special sacrifice on my part) to come to your assistance once again. I have instructed my lawyer, Mr. Zakheim, to transfer to your bank account an additional contribution of five thousand dollars (in your name, in Israeli pounds). If this does not suffice, either, I must ask you, sir, not to address me again via your wife and in ambiguous terms but to inform me (through Mr. Zakheim) of the final and absolute sum you require to solve all your various problems. If you will be good enough to specify a reasonable sum, you are likely to find me ready to go some way toward meeting you. All this on condition that you do not bother me with inquiries into my motives for giving the money, or with effusive expressions of gratitude in the Levantine style. I, for my part, naturally refrain from pronouncing any judgment on the values and principles which permit you to demand and to accept financial assistance from me.

> *With all due respect,*
> A. A. *Gideon*

—

13

To Mr. Manfred Zakheim   *By the Grace of G-d*
Zakheim & di Modena, Lawyers   *Jerusalem*
36 King George Street   *13th of II Adar, AM 5736 (14.3.76)*

LOCAL

Respected Sir,

Following our telephonic conversation of yesterday: we require *in toto* a sum of some sixty thousand dollars U.S. to pay off our mortgage and construct an additional room and a half, and another like sum to settle the future of the son and likewise that of the little girl, amounting in all to one hundred and eighty thousand dollars U.S. There is requested further a contribution in the sum of ninety-five thousand dollars U.S. toward the purchase and renovation of Alkalai House in the Jewish Quarter of Old Hebron (a Jewish property that was seized by force by Arab rioters during the 1929 riots, which we are now attempting to repossess, not by violence, but by paying the full market price).

Thanking you in anticipation for your trouble, sir, and with deep respect to Dr. Gideon, whose scientific writing has inspired admiration in our country and increased the honor of the Jewish people among the nations, and with all good wishes for a happy Purim,

Yours faithfully,
Ilana and Michael (Michel-Henri) Sommo

———

A GIDEON HOTEL EXCELSIOR WEST BERLIN

ALEX PLEASE ENLIGHTEN ME IMMEDIATELY IS IT BLACKMAIL SHOULD I PLAY FOR TIME SHOULD I INVOLVE ZAND AWAITING INSTRUCTIONS MANFRED

———

SELL PROPERTY ZIKHRON YAAKOV IF NECESSARY ALSO BINYAMINA
ORANGE GROVE PAY THEM EXACTLY ONE HUNDRED THOUSAND
CHECK HUSBANDS BACKGROUND SOONEST CHECK BOYS CONDITION
SEND PHOTOCOPY DIVORCE PAPERS RETURNING LONDON END OF
WEEK ALEX

———

Ilana Sommo   20.3
7 Tarnaz St.
Jerusalem

Ilana,

You asked me to think about it for a day or two and let you
know my opinion. You know as well as I do that whenever you ask
for someone else's opinion, or advice, what you are really asking
for is their approval for something you have already done or decided
to do. Never mind—I've decided to write anyway, to clarify for
myself how it was that we parted on bad terms.

The evening I spent with you last week reminded me of the
bad old days. I was in a panic when I got home. Even though on
the surface everything was as usual, apart from the rain that didn't
stop all night. And apart from Michel, who was looking tired and
gloomy. He spent an hour and a half putting up those bookshelves,
with Yifat passing him the tools, and at one point when I got up
to help him by holding two uprights for him, you mockingly suggested from the kitchen that I should take him back to the kibbutz
with me because his talents are wasted here. Then he sat at his desk
in his flannel pajamas and dressing gown, marking his students'
exercise books in red ink. He marked exercise books all through the
evening. In a corner of the room the kerosene heater glowed, Yifat
played for a long time on the straw mat with the toy lamb I'd bought
her at the bus station, there was a concerto for flute with Rampal
on the radio, you and I sat in the kitchen whispering to each other,

15

and on the surface we were having a quiet family evening together. Michel was withdrawn, and you didn't address more than twenty words to him the whole evening. Nor to Yifat or me, if it comes to that. You were all wrapped up in yourself. When I told you about the children being ill, about Yoash's new job in the plastics factory in the kibbutz, about the executive committee's decision to send me to take a course on cooking for special diets, you were only half listening; you didn't ask a single question. It didn't take me long to realize that, as usual, you were waiting for me to finish my trivial report before moving on to your own fateful dramas. That you were waiting for me to ask. So I asked. But I didn't get an answer. Michel came into the kitchen, spread margarine and cheese on a piece of bread, made himself a cup of instant coffee, and promised that he wouldn't disturb us, and that he would soon go and put Yifat to bed, so that we could carry on our conversation without interruption. When he'd gone, you told me about Boaz, about your two letters to Alex, about the two payments he made you, and about Michel's decision "to demand from him this time every last penny he owes," on the assumption "that perhaps the so-and-so is finally beginning to acknowledge his sins." The rain hammered on the windows. Yifat fell asleep on the mat, and Michel managed to put her pajamas on her and get her into bed without waking her up. Then he put the television on softly, so as not to disturb us, watched the nine o'clock news, and quietly went back to his marking. You peeled vegetables for lunch the next day, and I helped you a little. You said to me: Look here, Rahel, it's no good your judging us, you in your kibbutz, you've no idea what money is. And you said: I've been trying to forget him for seven years. And you also said: In any case, you can't understand. Through the door I could see Michel's curved back, his hunched shoulders, the cigarette he'd been clutching all evening, forcing himself not to light it because the windows were closed, and I thought to myself: She's lying again. She's even lying to herself. As usual. Nothing changes. But the only thing I said to you when you asked me to tell you what I thought was something like: Ilana, don't play with fire. Be careful. You've had enough already.

To which you replied angrily: I knew you'd start going on at me.

I said: Ilana, if you don't mind, I wasn't the one who brought the subject up in the first place. And you said: But you made me. So I suggested we stop. And we did, because Michel came back into the kitchen, jokingly apologized for trespassing on the "women's quarters," washed and dried the supper things, and told us in that scorched voice of his about something he had seen on the news. Then he sat down with us, made a joke about "Polish tea," yawned, asked after Yoash and the children, absentmindedly stroked both our heads, apologized, went to pick up Yifat's toys from the mat, went out on the veranda for a smoke, said good night and went to bed. You said: After all, I can't forbid him to meet Alex's lawyer. And you said: To secure Boaz's future. And without any obvious connection you added: Anyway, he's present all the time in our lives.

I said nothing. And you, with suppressed loathing, called me dear old clever, normal Rahel, and added: Only, your normality is an escape from life.

I couldn't contain myself. I said: Ilana, every time you use the word *life* I feel as though I'm in the theater.

You took offense. And cut the conversation short. You made up a bed for me, gave me a towel, and promised to wake me at six, so I could catch the bus for Tiberias. You sent me to bed and went back to the kitchen to sit alone and feel sorry for yourself. At midnight I went to the bathroom. Michel was snoring softly, and I saw you sitting in the kitchen in tears. I suggested you go to bed, I offered to sit with you, but when you said, in the second person plural, You leave me alone, I decided to go back to bed. The rain didn't stop all night long. In the morning, before I left, while we were having our coffee, you whispered to me to think quietly for a day or two and let you know my thoughts. So I tried to think about what you had told me. If only you weren't my sister, it would be easier for me. Still, I made up my mind to write to you that in my opinion Alex was a disaster for you, and Michel and Yifat are everything you have. As for Boaz, you ought to leave him in peace now, because any attempt to "hold out a maternal hand to him" will only increase his loneliness. And his distance from you. Don't touch him, Ilana. If there's any necessity to get involved again, leave Michel to take care of it. And as for Alex's money, like everything else to do with him, that money has a curse on it. Don't risk gambling away everything you've got. That's my feeling. You asked me to write, so I have. Try not to be angry with me.

Rahel

All the best from Yoash and the kids. Give a kiss to Michel and Yifat. Be good to them. I've no idea when I'll be in Jerusalem again. We're having rain the whole time too, and a lot of power cuts.

—

Dr. A. A. Gideon   *Jerusalem*
16 Hampstead Heath Lane   28.3.76
London NW 3, England

My dear Alex,

If you think the time has come for me to go to hell, just send me a four-word telegram, "Manfred go to hell," and I shall be on my way right away. But if, on the other hand, you've decided to take a look at a psychiatric ward from the inside, then would you please mind doing so alone, without me. I won't get any kick out of it.

In accordance with your instructions and against my better judgment, yesterday I unfroze our citrus grove near Binyamina (but not the Zikhron Yaakov property: I haven't quite taken leave of my senses yet). In any event, I can realize about one hundred thousand U.S. at twenty-four hours' notice for you and hand it over to your lovely ex-wife's husband, provided I have your final instructions to that effect.

However, I have permitted myself not to finalize the deal yet, so as to leave you an opportunity to change your mind and cancel your whole Father Christmas act without suffering any loss as yet (apart from my commission).

At least could you kindly let me have urgently some convincing evidence that you haven't gone stark, staring mad: please excuse, my dear Alex, my caustic language. The only thing I've got left to do in the fine situation you've put me in is to send you a nice letter of resignation. The trouble is that I'm somewhat fond of you.

As you are well aware, for some thirty years your remarkable father shortened my life, before and during his sclerosis and even after he had already forgotten his own name and my name and how to spell Alex. And no one knows better than you do how hard I worked for five or six years to arrange for you to be appointed sole trustee of all his property, and without three-quarters of it disappearing in inheritance tax or senility tax or some other Bolshevik siphon. The whole exercise brought me—I shall not attempt to hide it from you—a measure of professional satisfaction, a fine apartment in Jerusalem, and even a bit of fun, for which I have paid, it would appear, with an ulcer. But if I had imagined then that in ten years' time Volodya Gudonski's one and only son would suddenly start dispensing fortunes to Les Misérables, I wouldn't have made those titanic efforts to transfer the whole damn dowry intact from madman to madman—for what?

Allow me to inform you, Alex, that the slice that you are intending to hand to that pocket-sized zealot comes, at a rough calculation, to seven or eight percent of everything you own. And how can I be sure that tomorrow you won't have another brainstorm and decide to parcel out the rest between the Home for Unmarried Fathers and the Shelter for Battered Husbands? And, if it comes to that, why should you give him money at all? Just because he deigned to marry your secondhand ex-wife? Or as emergency aid to the Third World? Or perhaps it's reparations money for discrimination against Orientals? And if you have gone completely crazy, perhaps you wouldn't mind making one tiny effort more: Go crazy at a slightly different angle, and leave all your property to my two grandchildren. I'll arrange it for you without taking any commission. Surely we Germans have suffered here at least as much as the Moroccans have? Didn't you despise us and trample all over us, you the Frenchified Russian aristocracy from the region of North Binyamina? And don't leave out of the calculation, Alex, the fact that my grandchildren will invest your fortune in the development of the country! Electronics! Lasers! At least they won't squander it on restoring ruins in Hebron and turning Arab shithouses into synagogues! For I have to inform you, my dear Alex, that your beloved Mr. Michel-Henri Sommo may be a little man, but he's a great zealot. Not a noisy zealot, but of the latent variety: soft-spoken, polite, and ruthless. (See, when you can spare a moment, the chapter in your excellent book entitled "Between Fanaticism and Zealotry.")

I checked Mr. Sommo out yesterday. Here in my office. He earns barely two thousand six hundred pounds a month, of which he contributes a quarter each month to a small national religious splinter group, roughly three fingers to the right of the Greater Israel Movement. Incidentally, you might have thought your dazzling wife, after trying out every fifth man in Jerusalem, had settled in the end for some Gregory Peck—well, it turns out that this Mr. Sommo begins (like the rest of us) on the ground, but he terminates abruptly at five foot three or thereabouts. In other words, he is a good head shorter than she is. Perhaps she bought him cheap, by the yard.

And so this African Bonaparte appears in my office wearing permanent-press slacks, a check jacket a little large for him, curly-haired, uncompromisingly clean-shaven, drenched in radioactive after-shave, sporting gold-rimmed spectacles, a gold watch on a gold watch chain, and a red-and-green necktie fastened with a gold tie-clasp, and on his head—as though to dispel any possible misunderstanding—a small skullcap.

It transpires that the gentleman is far from stupid. Particularly when it comes to money, or to manipulating guilt feelings, or to armor-piercing hints at all sorts of powerful relations he has strategically located in the municipality, the police, his party, and even in the revenue department. I can promise you almost for certain, Alex my dear, that one day you will see this Sommo sitting in Parliament and firing long, devastating patriotic salvos at do-gooders like you and me. So perhaps after all you should be watching out for him, instead of financing him?

Alex. What the hell do you owe them? You, who drove me mad during your divorce, in the best tradition of your deranged father, making me fight like a tiger to make sure she didn't get a penny out of you, not a roof tile of the villa in Yefe Nof, not even the pen she was eventually forced to sign the papers with! It was only reluctantly that you agreed she could keep her underwear and a few pots and pans, as a special favor, and even then you stubbornly insisted on recording that this was "an *ex gratia* concession."

So what's come over you all of a sudden? Tell me, is somebody threatening you with something by any chance? If so, tell me all about it at once. Treat me like a family doctor. Send me a quick signal—and then you can sit back and watch me making mincemeat of them for you. It'll be a pleasure.

Listen to me, Alex: The fact is, there's no reason for me to get involved with your lunatic schemes. I've got a nice juicy case on the launching pad right now (concerning the property of the Russian Orthodox Church), and what I make from that, even if I lose it, is worth approximately twice the widow's mite you have made up your mind to donate as a Passover gift to North African Jewry or the Association for Aging Nymphomaniacs. Go fuck yourself, Alex. Just give me my final instructions, and I'll hand over whatever you like, whenever you like, to whomever you like. To each according to his greed.

Incidentally, the fact is, Sommo does not whine greedily. On the contrary, he speaks very nicely, in soft, rounded tones, with a smiling, didactic refinement, like a Catholic intellectual. These people have apparently undergone, on the way from Africa to Israel, a thoroughgoing refit in Paris. Outwardly he seems almost more European than you or me. In a nutshell, he could give Emily Post a few lessons in polite behavior.

I ask him, for example, if he has any notion why Professor

Gideon is suddenly handing him the keys to the safe. And he smiles at me mildly, a sort of "come on, now" smile, as if I have put a truly childish question to him, beneath his dignity and mine, refuses to take one of my Kents and offers me one of his own Europas, but deigns—possibly as a gesture of Jewish solidarity—to accept a light from me. And he expresses his thanks and shoots me a sort of sharp look, which his gold-rimmed spectacles magnify like the look of an owl at midday: "I am sure Professor Gideon could answer that question better than I can, Mr. Zakheim."

I contain myself and ask him whether a gift of the magnitude of a hundred thousand dollars does not at the very least arouse his curiosity. To which he replies: "Indeed it does, sir," and shuts up like a clam. I wait for maybe twenty seconds for him to say something more before giving in and inquiring whether he has by chance any theory of his own on the matter. To which he replies calmly that, yes, he does indeed, but that, with my permission, he would prefer to hear my own theory.

Well, at this juncture I determine to fire at point-blank range; I put on the grim Zakheim face I use in cross-examinations, and shoot, with little pauses for added effect between the words: "Mr. Sommo. If you don't mind, my theory is that somebody is putting strong pressure on my client. What you and your friends would call 'hush money.' And I am tempted to discover as quickly as possible who, and how, and why." That ape, unabashed, smiles a sweet, sanctimonious smile at me and replies: "His sense of shame, Mr. Zakheim; that's the only thing that's putting pressure on him." "Shame? On account of what?" I ask, and the answer is ready on the tip of his honeyed tongue even before I've finished asking: "For his sins, sir." "What sins, for example?" "Putting others to shame, for example. Putting people to shame in Judaism is tantamount to shedding their blood."

"And what are you, sir? Are you the tax collector? The bailiff?"

"Me?" he answers, without batting an eyelid. "My role is a purely symbolic one. Our Professor Gideon is a man of letters. He has a world-wide reputation. He is enormously respected. One might say admired. The only thing is, until he has put right what he has done wrong, all his good deeds count for nothing. Because they are built on sin. Now he is smitten with remorse, and it would seem that he is finally beginning to seek the path to repentance."

"And you are the keeper of the gate of repentance, Mr. Sommo? You stand there and sell tickets?"

"I married his wife," he says, fixing me, like a projector, with his eyes magnified three times in the lenses of his spectacles, "I healed her shame. And I also watch over his son's footsteps."

"At a price of one hundred dollars a day times thirty years, cash in advance, Mr. Sommo?"

And so, at last, I managed to ruffle his calm. The Parisian patina shattered and the African fury erupted like pus.

"Mr. Zakheim, with all due respect, you earn for your merry japes more money in half an hour than I have seen for all my labors. Kindly take note, Mr. Zakheim, that I did not ask to receive a penny from Professor Gideon. He was the one who offered. And it was not I who asked for the present meeting with you, sir. You asked to meet me. And now"—the little teacher suddenly got to his feet, and I had a momentary feeling that he was about to pick up a ruler from my desk and rap my over the knuckles; without offering his hand, barely concealing his loathing, he ejaculated—"and now, with your kind permission, I shall put an end to this conversation because of your malicious and indecent insinuations."

And so I hastened to appease him. I effected what you might call an "ethnic withdrawal." I put the blame on my impossible Germanic sense of humor. I begged him to be kind enough to ignore my unsuccessful joke and consider my last words as unsaid. And I immediately expressed an interest in the financial contribution he had sought from you toward some zealot monkey business in Hebron. Here he adopted an impassioned didactic air as, still standing on his short legs and with field-marshal-like gestures toward the map of the country on the wall of my office, he favored me with a free (apart from my time, which in any case you pay for on his behalf) mini-sermon on the subject of our right to the land, etc. I shall not weary you with matters we both know ad nauseam. The whole thing was embellished with Biblical quotations and allusions, and simplified, to boot, as though he thought me somewhat slow on the uptake.

I inquired of this miniature Maimonides whether he was aware of the fact that your political views happened to be more or less at the other end of the spectrum, and that all these lunatic schemes for Hebron were diametrically opposed to your publicly stated position.

He retained control of himself this time too. (I tell you, Alex, we shall hear more of this mad mahdi!) He replied patiently, in honeyed tones, that in his humble opinion "Dr. Gideon is currently undergoing, like so many other Jews, an experience of purification leading to intimations of repentance which will soon bring about a general change of heart."

At this point—I shall not try to conceal it from you, my dear Alex—it was my turn to lose my European patina and to explode at him: What, in heaven's name, gave him the idea that he knew what went on in your mind? How could he have the nerve, without even having met you, to decide for you—perhaps even for all of us—what is going on or what is going to go on in our hearts, even before we know it ourselves?

"Surely Professor Gideon is attempting even now to expiate the sins that stand between man and man. That is the reason why you invited me here to this meeting in your office, Mr. Zakheim. So why should we not take advantage of the occasion to open up, by means of this donation, a way to expiate the sins that divide man from the Almighty?"

And he was not content to leave until he had taken the trouble to explain to me the inherent ambiguity of the Hebrew word for *blood*, which can also mean *money*. *Ecce homo*.

My dear Alex, I hope that you have been duly infuriated on reading this account. Or, better still, that you had a good laugh and changed your mind about the whole business. That was the reason I took the trouble to reconstruct the whole scenario for you.

How does the little preacher put it? "The gates of repentance are never closed." So repent you at once of your strange idea and send the pair of them to hell.

Unless there is something in that old intuition of mine, which whispers to me that somebody somehow has got wind of some embarrassing detail, and this devil—or whoever is hiding behind him—is using it to threaten and blackmail you so as to use your money to buy his silence (and also the ruins of Hebron). If that's the way of it, I implore you once more to give me the slightest signal and you'll see how elegantly I defuse their explosive device for you.

Meanwhile, following the instructions in your telegram, I put a small private investigator onto Sommo (our old friend Shlomo Zand), and I attach the report. If you take the trouble to read it attentively, you will no doubt realize that if it comes to intimidation, we also have something to go on, and we can easily persuade the gentleman in question that two can play at that game. Just give me the go-ahead, and I'll send Zand to him for a nice little tête-à-tête. I guarantee that within ten minutes it'll be all quiet on the eastern front. You won't hear another cheep out of them.

So there are three documents enclosed with this letter: (a) Zand's report on Sommo; (b) Zand's assistant's report on the boy B. B.; (c) photocopies of the decision of the Rabbinical Court in the matter of the termination of your marriage and of the decision of the District Court on your lovely's claim against you. I have underlined the important parts for you in red. But do try not to forget that the whole business ended more than seven years ago, and that now it is no more than ancient history.

So much for what you asked me to do in your telegram. I hope that at least you are pleased with me, because I'm not at all pleased with you. I await further instructions, in my usual humble way. Just don't go mad, for God's sake.

Your very anxious
Manfred

PERSONAL ZAKHEIM JERUSALEM ISRAEL

YOU HAVE EXCEEDED YOUR AUTHORITY PAY THE HUNDRED
PRECISELY INSTANTER AND STOP PESTERING ME ALEX

———

A GIDEON NICFOR LONDON

IVE PAID RESIGN FROM HANDLING YOUR AFFAIRS AWAIT IMMEDIATE
INSTRUCTIONS ON TRANSFER OF YOUR PAPERS YOU ARE STARK
STARING MAD MANFRED ZAKHEIM

———

PERSONAL ZAKHEIM JERUSALEM ISRAEL

YOUR RESIGNATION NOT ACCEPTED TAKE A COLD SHOWER CALM
DOWN AND BE A GOOD BOY ALEX

———

A GIDEON NICFOR LONDON

MY RESIGNATION STANDS GO TO HELL ZAKHEIM

———

PERSONAL ZAKHEIM JERUSALEM ISRAEL

DONT LEAVE ME IM MISERABLE ALEX

———

IM LEAVING THIS EVENING ARRIVE AT NICHOLSONS EARLY MORNING
JUST DONT DO ANYTHING STUPID IN THE MEANTIME YOURS
MANFRED

———

To Michael Sommo
Tarnaz 7
Jerusalem

Hello Michel. Look Ill come strate to the point with you—I
need a lone. Im working hard for your brother in law Abram Abu-
dram, Im shifting crates of vegtibles all day. You can check with
him that Im OK. Im happy too because he treats me fare and pays
daily and even gives me two meals a day. Thanks for fixing it up.
The lone is to by materials to build a do it yourself telescop. Your
friend Janin (Mrs. Fuks) as you no also fixed me up as a night
watchman (with acomodation) at the Planetarium for nothing. I
mean they dont pay me and I dont pay them. But if Im good enough
at optikal equipment that Im getting the hang of and theyve got a
vacancy their even going to pay me a little. The outcome is I havent
hardly got any expenses, only incom. But I want to start on the
telescop rite away and the price is 4000 pounds so Im asking you
to lend me 3000 (Ive already got 1000 put away). Ill pay you back
300 a month out of my pay, assuming you dont want any interest.
If you cant or its just dificult for you forget it never mind. In the
meantime I havent killed anyone yet. The only thing Im asking is
dont let the woman know anything about it. To you personaly and
the little girl all the best. Thanks

Boaz B.

———

For Boaz Brandstetter
Via Abraham Abudarham
The Wholesale Market
Carlebach Street, Tel Aviv

By the Grace of G-d
Jerusalem
First intermediate day of Passover
(16.4.76)

Dear Boaz,

I received your letter and I was very sad that you did not come for Seder Night in accordance with our invitation. But I respect the agreement between us, according to which you can do whatever you like as long as you do it uprightly and in the sweat of your brow. You didn't come—so you didn't come. Never mind. Whenever you want to come, just come. Abram phoned and said you were excellent. We also received very positive greetings from you via Mrs. Janine Fuchs. Well done, Boaz! I was almost the same age as you when I arrived in Paris with my parents from Algeria, and I worked hard as an apprentice to an X-ray technician (he was my uncle) so as to earn a little money. By the way, unlike you, I only worked in the evenings, because during the day I was studying at the lycée. And it is interesting to compare that I once asked this uncle for a loan for the purpose of purchasing a Larousse dictionary that I needed badly (but he refused).

Which brings me to your request. I enclose postal orders to the value of IL 3000. If you need any further sums, and if you specify a positive purpose, we shall be only too happy to try to comply. As for the interest you mentioned, as a matter of fact I should not be opposed to your repaying the money with interest, but not now, Boaz, but many years from now, when you are rich in commandments and good deeds and also materially (and before then I hope you'll learn to write without mistakes!!). Meanwhile it would be best for you to continue putting some savings aside. You listen to me, Boaz.

In one respect I was obliged to break your request: your mother knows about the money I am enclosing herewith. That's because we have no secrets from each other, and with all due respect to you I am not prepared to do any secret deals with you, however worthy the purpose. If this does not meet with your approval, don't accept the money. I shall close now with warm regards and all good wishes for the festive season.

Yours,
Michael (Michel)

———

To Michael Sommo
Tarnaz 7
Jerusalem

Hello Michel and thanks for the lone. Ive bought the equipment and Ive already started to put it together slowly. Bruno Fuks from the Planetarium (Janin's husband) is helping me a bit. He's a good guy. He knows about optics and he doesnt preech. Its my opinion, and dont laugh, that everyone should no one thing very well and do it very well and not tell other people what to do and how to do it. Then therd be a lot more satisfaction in the country and a lot less personal problems. I dont care that much about your wife nowing about the lone I just dont want any complecations with her. With you its difrent. Tell me how did you manage to by the dictionery you needed in Paris? Thanks again and kiss the pretty little girl from me Boaz. PS Anyway Ill start repaying your money slowly starting as from next month. Its your money, right?

Boaz B.

———

Boaz Brandstetter
% A. Abudarham
Wholesale Market
Carlebach St., Tel Aviv

By the Grace of G-d
Jerusalem
23 Nisan 5736 (23.4.76)

Dear Boaz,
Since you asked, I have a responsibility to reply. The money is not mine; it is your father's. If you come up to Jerusalem for the Sabbath, or for another Sabbath, we'll gladly tell you all we know about this business (apparently there are some aspects we have not

been informed about). Your mother and sister join me in this invitation. Stop being a mule, Boaz, just come and that's that. We're planning to build an extension to the flat soon, comprising two extra rooms (toward the backyard) and one of them is for you for whenever you want it. But even before then we always have room for you. So don't be a child, come for next Sabbath. In my opinion your pride is always pulling you in the wrong direction. I believe, Boaz, that the difference between a child and a man is that a man does not wastefully spill his seed or his pride but keeps them for the right moment, "until it is pleasing," as the Good Book says. And you're not a child any more, Boaz. I mention this analogy both in connection with your refusal (so far) to come home, and in connection with your generally stubborn attitude toward your mother, and also to hint to you not to react childishly to the information I have just given you concerning the source of the money. After all, I didn't have to tell you, did I?

Which brings me to the second question you asked in your letter: how did I buy the Larousse in Paris when I was your age after my uncle refused to let me have a loan? The answer is simply that I did not buy it until a year later, but that uncle lost on the spot a cheap and willing assistant, because I felt so insulted by him that I left him and took a job cleaning stairs (after school!). It was in 1955, and you could say that I was definitely a mule. In any case I was still a child. I shall sign off now with friendly good wishes,

Yours,
Michel

P.S. If you really insist on repaying me the loan right away, in monthly installments, I have no objection. I'm actually rather impressed! But in that case let's be quite clear that interest is out of the question.

Three documents enclosed with letter from M. Zakheim, lawyer, of Jerusalem, to Dr. A. Gideon in London, dated 28.3.76:

ITEM A.: Report by Shlomo Zand (private investigator) of S. Zand, Private Investigations Ltd., Tel Aviv, on the case of Michel-Henri (Michael) Sommo. Drawn up on instructions from Mr. M. Zakheim of Zakheim & di Modena, Lawyers, Jerusalem, and handed to the client on 26.3.76.

Dear Sir,

Since we received your instructions on 22.3 and we were requested to effect a very rapid check and convey our report to you within a few days, the present material is not to be considered a full and thorough investigation but merely as preliminary findings, hastily collected. We would however point out that the material does provide a basis for various lines of investigation, including some that are potentially sensitive. If I am asked to continue working on this file, I could expect to submit a comprehensive report within a month or thereabouts.

Your instructions comprised the collection of information on the background of MHS and also on his present mode of life, including the professional, financial, and family aspects. Our partial findings were as follows.

GENERAL BACKGROUND

MHS was born in Oran, Algeria, in May 1940. Parents' names Jacob and Sylvie. The father worked in Oran as a tax collector until 1954, when the family moved to a suburb of Paris. (Three brothers and one sister, all older than MHS, had previously emigrated to France and raised families of their own. The eldest brother lives in this country.)

MHS was a pupil at the Lycée Voltaire until 1958 and subsequently studied French literature at the Sorbonne for two years. He did not complete his studies and holds no academic degree.

During this period he became associated with groups of the Betar movement in Paris (under the influence of his eldest brother) and also became an observant Jew (apparently under the influence of another brother, who underwent a return to religion and is still active in religious Zionist education in Paris).

MHS gradually abandoned his studies at the Sorbonne and devoted himself instead to Hebrew and Jewish studies. By the time he emigrated to Israel he had already mastered the Hebrew language. In late 1960 he emigrated to Israel and for a few months he worked as a construction laborer for a religious contractor in Petah Tikva. He then applied to the Police College and was accepted (apparently with the help of one of his relatives), but he left in the middle (we have been unable to ascertain the background), and went to study at the Sacred Lamp Yeshiva in Jerusalem. But he did not persevere with his studies here, either, and in the years 1962–1964 he supported himself through a part-time job as an usher at the Orion Cinema while he endeavored, unsuccessfully, to complete his course in the French Culture Department at Hebrew University. During this period he lived in a laundry room on the roof of the block of flats where his brother-in-law's brother lived in Talpiyyot. In 1964 he was permanently exempted from military service (reserve duty in the town major's unit), in consequence of a kidney disease with complications.

Since 1964 he has worked, first as an assistant teacher and subsequently as a regular teacher (nongraduate) of French in the Isaac's Tent Religious State High School for boys in Jerusalem. Since his marriage in 1970 to Ilana (Halina) Gideon nee Brandstetter he has been living in a one-and-a-half-room flat at No. 7 Tarnaz Street, Jerusalem. This flat was purchased with the help of members of his family in Israel and France, on a ten-year mortgage with monthly repayments, of which roughly half has now been repaid.

FINANCIAL SITUATION

MHS earns IL 2550 per month from his job. The wife does not work. Additional sources of income: private lessons (some IL 400 per month), plus a regular allowance from his parents in

Paris (IL 500 per month). Principal expenses: IL 1200 monthly mortgage repayments on the flat; IL 500 per mo. to keep his wife's son Boaz Brandstetter at the Telamim Agricultural High School (until three weeks ago); monthly donation of IL 650, payable by standing order at the Talpiyyot branch of the Bank Leumi, to the Jewish Fellowship Movement. He is frequently in arrears on his bills (electricity, water, tax), but is always punctilious about paying the mortgage, the school fees, and the donation.

FAMILY AFFAIRS

Married (since 1971) plus one daughter, almost three (Madeleine Yifat). The wife was previously married to the well-known scholar Professor A. Gideon, now living in the USA (marriage dissolved). In accordance with a decision of the Rabbinical Court and following a lawsuit between the two parties in 1968, there is no financial liability on either side. MHS and his wife lead a respectable married life. They keep a kosher home, observe the Sabbath, and so forth, and their way of life could be described as traditional or moderately religious (they do not refrain from going to the cinema, for example).

We found no evidence of romantic ties outside the marital bond on the part of either MHS or his wife. Information is, however, available (although it goes beyond your brief to us) concerning apparent entanglements on the part of Ilana Gideon-Sommo from the time of her previous marriage. There is also information about her son Boaz's being on probation since May 1975 (see the report by our agent A. Maimon, submitted to you at your request with this report). The relations of the boy Boaz with MHS and his wife are not good (for some years now he has refused to visit them in Jerusalem). On the other hand, relations between MHS and his extended family (cousins, in-laws, etc.) are very close.

POLITICAL LIFE

Here we had no difficulty in finding plentiful information. MHS's views are close to the right. His eldest brother and other members of his family are known activists in the Herut Bloc (some of them in the National Religious Party). MHS has been at various times a paid-up member of both the aforementioned parties, albeit intermittently. In 1964 he was one of the organizers of a group of North African intellectuals and students in Jerusalem under the name *Moledet* (Fatherland). The group split on financial and ideological grounds and went out of existence in 1965. On the eve of the Six-Day War MHS was very active in propaganda and signature-gathering against the wait-and-see policy of the Eshkol government and in favor of taking the military initiative against Egypt and the other Arab countries.

Immediately after the Six-Day War MHS volunteered for an active role in what later became the Greater Israel Movement, specializing in propaganda and demonstations. In 1971 he suddenly left the movement. Shortly afterward he made a great show of handing in his membership card to the NRP. In 1972 he was among the founders of a group called Jewish Fellowship, most of whose members are young immigrants from America and Russia. MHS still serves on the executive committee of this organization. After the Yom Kippur War it was involved in demonstrations against the troop disengagements in the Sinai and the Golan Heights, and also in attempts to purchase land illegally from Arabs in the area around Bethlehem. MHS was twice interviewed by the police in connection with his activities for this organization (in October '74 and again in April '75), but he was not charged. So far as we can ascertain, MHS was not personally involved in any violent act of lawbreaking. He had a dozen letters published in the two evening newspapers in which he urged a policy of encouraging the Arab population to leave the country and the occupied territories peaceably and through financial inducements.

In conclusion we shall cite a detail that seems to us particularly significant, and that hints apparently at an important item of information we have not yet managed to track down: In December of last year (four months ago) MHS applied to the French Embassy in Tel Aviv for the restoration of his French nationality (which he had voluntarily relinquished in 1963) side by side with his Israeli nationality. His application was turned down. Immediately afterward, on the tenth of December last, he went to Paris and stayed there four days only (!). It is not clear what the purpose of his trip was or who paid for it. Not long after his return, his French nationality was indeed restored, with a speed that indicates beyond all doubt a departure from the normal procedures. We did not succeed in ascertaining what lay behind this episode.

As already stated, we consider the report now before you a partial and nonexhaustive effort, owing to the severe time limit imposed upon us by yourselves. We shall be happy to place ourselves at your disposal should you be interested in further investigation either of this or of any other matter.

[*Signed*] *Shlomo Zand*
S. Zand Private Investigations Ltd., Tel Aviv

ITEM B: Report of Albert Maimon (private investigator) of S. Zand Private Investigations Ltd., Tel Aviv, on the case of the youth Boaz Brandstetter. Drawn up on instructions from Mr. M. Zakheim of Zakheim & di Modena, Lawyers, Jerusalem, and submitted to the client on 26.3.1976.

Dear Sir,

Following your instructions we put in hand a rapid search (one working day) and established that the aforementioned, son of Mrs. I. Brandstetter-Sommo of Jerusalem and unknown father, voluntarily left the Telamim Agricultural High School on 19.2.76, on account of general unsuitability and long-standing and repeated disciplinary problems, for an unknown destination. Two days later, on 21.2, he was arrested at the Central Bus Station in Tel Aviv and questioned concerning dealing in stolen property (he already has two previous records for similar offenses, and has been on juvenile probation since May 1975). The following day, 22.2, he was released on the surety of Mr. Michael Sommo of Jerusalem (his mother's husband) and apparently with some internal connivance within the police. Since then, he has been employed by a relative of Mr. Sommo in the wholesale vegetable market in Tel Aviv, apparently in contravention of the law on employment of minors. At present BB is living on the premises of the Planetarium in Ramat Aviv on the invitation of one of the people in charge, and he is described as "volunteer night watchman." BB is not yet sixteen (born 1960), but looks much older (to go by my personal impression, I would have put him at eighteen at least: physically very big and exceptionally strong). As far as I could ascertain, he is not making any social connections at present. Of his social life at the time when he was studying at Telamim College I received contradictory assessments. There is no further significant information. Please let us know if there are any specific questions you would like us to investigate for you.

[Signed] A. *Maimon, Investigator*
S. *Zand Private Investigations Ltd., Tel Aviv*

ITEM C: The parts underlined in red pencil by Mr. Zakheim in the material he enclosed with his letter to A. A. Gideon in London dated 28.3.76.

1. From the decision of the Rabbinical Court in the case of the divorce suit of A. A. Gideon versus Halina Brandstetter-Gideon, Jerusalem, 1968: ". . . we therefore find that the wife committed adultery, on her own admission . . . she therefore forfeits her *ketubah* and maintenance. . . ."

2. From the decision of the Jerusalem District Court, 1968: "As for her claim for maintenance for herself and her small child . . . because of the father's insistence that he is not the child's father . . . in the light of the inconclusive results of the blood test . . . this court advised the parties to undergo a tissue test . . . the wife declined to undergo this test . . . the husband also declined to

undergo a tissue test . . . the wife withdrew her claim for maintenance for herself and the child . . . the court therefore strikes out her claim, both parties having declared that henceforth they have no further demands on each other."

———

Dr. Alexander Gideon   *Jerusalem*
Political Science Department   *19.4.1976*
Midwest University
Chicago, Ill., U.S.A.

Distant Alec,

I am writing to you again to your Illinois address in the hope that some secretary will take the trouble to forward my letter to you. I do not know where you are. The black-and-white room, your empty desk, the empty bottle, and the empty glass surround you always in my thoughts like the capsule of a spacecraft in which you are constantly moving from continent to continent. And the fire burning in the grate, lighting up your monkish body and your greying, balding head, and the deserted snowfields you can see from your window stretching away until they fade into the mist. Everything as in a woodcut. Always. Wherever you are.

So what do I want this time? What more can the fisherman's wife ask the golden fish to give her? Another hundred thousand? Or a palace of emerald?

Nothing, Alec. I have no request. I am only writing so as to talk to you. Even though I already know all the answers. Why you have such long ears. And why your eyes are flashing and sparkling at me. And why such sharp teeth.

There's nothing new, Alec.

At this point you can crumple the letter up and throw it on the fire. The paper will flare up for a moment and then vanish to another world, a tongue of flame will stretch up and die down as though kindled by an empty passion, a fine charred strip will take off and flutter around the room, perhaps to land at your feet. And you will be alone again. You can pour yourself a whisky and celebrate your victory, all alone: there she is, groveling at my feet. She has lost interest in her African discovery and now she is begging for mercy.

Because apart from malicious glee you have never known any other joy in your life, wicked, solitary Alec. So read this and rejoice. Read this and laugh silently to the moon at the end of the snow at your window.

This time I am writing to you behind Michel's back. And without telling him. At ten-thirty he switched off the television, went around the flat systematically turning out the lights, covered the child, checked that the door was bolted, put a sweater around my shoulders, wrapped himself up in a blanket, glanced at the evening paper, muttered something, and fell asleep. Now his spectacles and his cigarettes are on the desk next to me, his gentle breathing blends in with the ticking of the brown clock, which was a present from his parents. And I am sitting at his desk and writing to you, and so I am sinning both against him and against our child. This time I cannot even use Boaz. Your son is all right: your money and Michel's wisdom extricated him from trouble. The friends of the Sommo family got his police record closed. Little by little Michel is finding his way toward Boaz. Like making a way through a thicket. Can you believe it? He managed to make Boaz come and see us here in Jerusalem last weekend, and several times I could not help laughing at the sight of my tiny husband and my giant of a son competing with each other all day for the favors of the little girl, who seemed to be enjoying the contest and even fanning the flames. When the Sabbath was over, Michel made us all a salad with olives and hot peppers, hamburgers and fried potatoes, and asked the neighbors' son to baby-sit so we could go to the second show at the cinema.

Does this rapprochement complicate your strategy? I'm sorry. You have lost a point. How did you put it to me once? When the battle is at its height there is no more sense in the initial briefings.

In any case, the enemy now knows about the briefing and does not act in accordance with it. That's how it happened to you that Boaz and Michel are almost friends now, while I watch and smile: for instance, when Michel climbed up on Boaz's shoulders to change a light bulb on the veranda. Or when Yifat tried to put Michel's slippers on Boaz's feet.

Why am I telling you all this?

In fact we ought to have gone back to our established silence. From now to the end of our days. To accept your money and say nothing. But there is a will-o'-the-wisp that persists in flickering over the marsh at night, and neither of us can take our eyes off it.

If despite everything you have decided to go on reading these pages, if you have not shot them onto the fire burning in your room, I suspect that at this moment your face is wearing that mask of contempt and arrogance that suits you so well and gives you an air of arctic strength. The frozen ray at the touch of which I melt as though under a spell. Right from the start. I melt and hate you. I melt and give myself to you.

I know: from the letter you are holding in your hands right now there is no going back.

But then, my two previous letters would be enough for you, if you want to destroy me.

What have you done with my previous letters? Are they in the fire, or in the safe?

As a matter of fact, there's hardly any difference.

Because you do not trample to death, Alec, you sting. Your poison is fine and slow; it does not slay at once but destroys and dissolves me over the years.

Your prolonged silence: For seven years I tried to withstand it, to exorcise it with the noises of my new home. And in the eighth year I have given in.

I was not lying to you when I wrote you my first and second letters in February. All the details I brought to your knowledge about Boaz were accurate, as Zakheim has no doubt already confirmed to you. And yet, it was all a lie. I was deceiving you. I was setting a trap for you. In my heart I was perfectly certain, from the very first moment, that it was Michel who would rescue Boaz from his troubles. Michel, not you. And so indeed it turned out. And I knew from the very first moment that Michel, even without your money, would do the right thing. And at the right time and in the right way.

And I knew this too, Alec: that even if the Devil made you try to help your son, in fact you would not know what to do. You would not even know where to begin. You have never in your whole life known how to do something on your own. Even when you made up your mind to propose to me, you couldn't go through with it. Your father had to ask me for you. All your Olympian wisdom and all your titanic powers always begin and end with one thing— your checkbook. Or else with transatlantic telephone calls to Zakheim or to some government minister or general from your old gang (and they, in their turn, call you when the time comes to get their sons into some prestigious college or to fix themselves a nice cushy sabbatical year).

And what else can you do? Spread charm or icy fear with your air of drowsy condescension. Classify historic zealots. Send thirty tanks charging across the desert to crush and trample Arabs. Dispatch a woman and a child with a cold knockout. Have you ever managed, at any time in your life, to arouse a single smile of joy on the face of a man or a woman? To wipe a tear from any eye? Checks and phone calls, Alec. A small-time Howard Hughes.

And indeed it was not you, but Michel, who picked Boaz up and found a place for him.

So, if I knew in advance that it would turn out like that, why did I write to you?

You'd better stop here. Have a little pause. Light your pipe. Let your grey glance roam a little over the snow. Emptiness meeting emptiness. Then try to concentrate and read what follows with the same surgical severity with which you analyze a text by a nineteenth-century Russian nihilist or a virulent patristic sermon.

My real motive for writing those two letters to you in February was a desire to place myself in your hands. Do you really not understand? It's not at all like you to have your enemy in the center of your sights and to forget to pull the trigger.

Or perhaps I wrote to you like a beautiful damsel in a fairy story sending to the faraway knight the sword with which he can slay the dragon and set her free. There, now that predatory smile of yours is spreading on your face, that bitter, fascinating smile. Do you know, Alec, I'd like to dress you up one night in a black robe and put a black cowl over your head. You wouldn't regret it, because it's an image that excites me.

Or perhaps I reckoned anyway that you could somehow help Boaz. But much more than this, I wanted you to send me the bill. I was longing to pay.

Why didn't you come? Have you really forgotten what you and I can do to each other? The fusing of fire and ice?

That was a lie too. I knew you wouldn't come. I shall now remove my last veil: the real truth is that even in my most lunatic longing I never forgot for an instant what you are. And I knew that I would never receive a punch from your fist or an order to report. I knew that the only thing I would get from you would be an arctic gust of pale, deathly silence. Or at most a spit of venomous contempt. No less, but no more, either. I knew that it was all lost.

And yet I have to admit that your spit when it came stunned me completely. Of all the thousand and one things I might have anticipated, it never occurred to me that you would simply pull out the plug and drown Michel in money. This time you've left me reeling. That's what I always loved. There's no limit to your devilish talent for invention. And from the puddle you've rolled me into, I offer you myself fouled with mud. That's what you always loved, Alec. That's what we both loved.

So, nothing is lost after all?

There is no going back from this letter. There never will be. I am deceiving Michel just as I deceived you so many times for six of the nine years of our marriage.

A born harlot.

Yes, I knew you would say that, with your oceanic wickedness glimmering like the northern lights in the depths of your grey eyes. But no, Alec. You are mistaken. This deceit is different: every time I deceived you with your friends, with your superiors in the army, with your pupils, with the electrician or the plumber, I was always trying to approach you by deceiving you. It was always you I had in my mind. Even when I was screaming aloud. Especially then. As it is written in letters of gold above the Holy Ark in Michel's synagogue: I have placed the Lord before me always.

And now it is two o'clock in the morning here in Jerusalem, Michel is curled up fetuslike between the sweat-soaked sheets, the smell of his hairy body mingles in the warm air with the smell of pee that comes from a pile of the child's sheets in a corner of the cramped room, a hot dry wind comes from the desert through my open window and blows hatefully in my face. I am in my nightdress, sitting at Michel's desk surrounded by exercise books, writing to you by the light of a hunchbacked table lamp, with a demented mosquito humming overhead and distant Arab lights looking back at me from the other side of the wadi, writing to you out of the depths and by so doing deceiving Michel and deceiving my child in an entirely different way. In a way that I never deceived you. And deceiving him precisely with you. And deceiving him after years in which not the faintest shadow of a lie has passed between us.

Am I going out of my mind? Have I gone mad like you?

My husband Michel is a rare man. I have never met anyone like him. "Daddy," I call him, ever since before Yifat was born. And there are times when I call him child, and hug his thin, hot body as though I were his mother. Even though in fact Michel is not only my father and my child but above all my brother. If we have some sort of life after we die, if we ever get to some world where lies are impossible, Michel will be my brother there.

But you were and remain my husband. My lord and master. Forever. And in the life after life Michel will hold my arm and lead me to the bridal canopy to my marriage ceremony with you. You are the lord of my hatred and my longing. The master of my dreams at night. Ruler of my hair and my throat and the soles of my feet. Sovereign of my breasts my belly my private parts my womb. Like a slave girl I am in thrall to you. I love my lord. I do not want to be set free. Even if you sent me away in disgrace to the ends of the kingdom, to the desert like Hagar with her son Ishmael, to die of thirst in the wilderness, it would be thirst for you, my lord. Even if you dismissed me from your presence to be a plaything for your servants in the dungeons of the palace.

But you have not forgotten, my solitary evil Alec. You cannot fool me. Your silence is transparent to me, like tears. The spell I cast on you gnaws you to the bone. In vain do you hide in a cloud like a barren deity. There are a thousand things in the world that you can do a thousand times better than me—but deception is not one of them. No, in that department you don't come up to my knees, and you never will.

"Your honor," you said to the judge before the verdict was given on our case, in your drowsy, indifferent voice, "it has been demonstrated here beyond all possible doubt that this lady is a pathological liar. Even when she sneezes it is very dangerous to believe her."

That's what you said. And as you said it a sort of dirty chuckle ran around the chamber. You smiled faintly and didn't look in the least then like a cuckolded husband whose hundred horns made him the laughingstock of the whole town. On the contrary, at that moment you seemed to me higher than the lawyers, higher than the judge on his dais, higher than yourself. You looked like a knight who has killed a dragon.

Even now, after seven years, at nearly three o'clock in the morning, as I record the memory of that moment, my body reaches out for you. Tears fill my eyes and there is a kind of shivering in the tips of my nipples.

Well, Alec, have you read? Twice? Three times? Did you get a thrill? Is it over? Have I just managed to make a single sapling of joy sprout in the wilderness of your loneliness?

If so, the time has come for you to pour yourself a fresh whisky. Fill a new pipe. Because now, Mister God of Vengeance, you are going to need your little whisky.

"Like a knight who has killed a dragon," I wrote a moment ago. But don't be too quick to celebrate. Your arrogance is at least premature, sir: for you are the crazy knight who slew the dragon and then turned and slew the damsel and finally dispatched himself as well.

In fact, you are the dragon.

And this is the delightful moment for me to reveal to you that Michel-Henri Sommo is much better than you are even in bed. In everything to do with the body, Michel has had perfect pitch since birth. At any moment he can always offer me, in plenty, what my body still does not know how much it yearns to receive. To hold me spellbound for half the night with voyages of love back and forth between the shores of pleasure, like a leaf caught by the breeze, through meadows of patient grace, through cunning and longing, through dappled forests and turbid rivers and pounding seas to the point of fusion.

Have you crushed your whisky glass yet? Say hello from Ilana to your pen, your pipe, your reading glasses too. Wait, Alec. I haven't finished yet.

As a matter of fact, it's not just Michel. Almost all of them could give you a lesson or two. Even that albino boy who was your driver in the army. Chaste as a lamb and perhaps barely eighteen, guilty, terrified, meeker than a blade of grass, all atremble, his teeth chattering, almost pleading with me to let him off, almost bursting into tears, and suddenly starting to spurt even before he'd managed to touch me, and letting out a howl like a puppy dog, and yet, Alec, at that moment that boy's baffled eyes gave me such a pure glow of gratitude, of wonderment, of dreamy adoration, as innocent as the singing of angels, that he made my body and heart shudder more than you ever managed to do in all our years together.

Shall I tell you what you are, Alec, compared to the others I've had? You are a bare, rocky mountain. Just like the song. You're an igloo in the snow. Do you remember Death in *The Seventh Seal*? Death winning the game of chess? That's you.

And now you get up and destroy the pages of my letter. No, this time you don't tear them carefully into pedantic squares, but throw them in the fire. And perhaps when it's all over you sit down again and start hitting your grey head against the black desk top; the blood spills from your hair into your eyes. And so at long last your grey eyes run. I hug you.

A fortnight ago, when Zakheim handed over to Michel your amazing check, he saw fit to warn Michel with the words: Bear in mind, sir, that two can play at that game. I quite fancy that little sentence, and I'm inclined to send it to you now by way of wishing you good night. You will not liberate yourself from me, Alec. You won't succeed in buying your freedom with money. You won't turn over a new leaf.

And by the way, your hundred thousand: we are grateful. The money is in good hands, never fear. Your wife and son are in good hands too. Michel is extending the flat and we'll all be able to live here. Boaz will make Yifat a slide and a sandbox in the garden. I shall have a washing machine. We'll have a stereo set. We'll buy a bicycle for Yifat, and Boaz will have a telescope.

I'll close now. I shall get dressed and go out alone into the dark empty street. I'll walk to the mailbox. I'll send you this letter. Then I'll come home and get undressed again and wake Michel and hide myself away in his arms. Michel is a simple, tender man.

Which is more than one can say about you. Or about me, my love. We are both, as you know, despicable, rotten creatures. And that is the reason for the hug that the slave girl is sending now to the faraway marble dragon.

Ilana

———

To Boaz Brandstetter   *By the Grace of G-d*
% Fuchs   *Jerusalem*
4 Lemon St.   *2nd of Iyyar 5736 (2.5.76)*
Ramat Hasharon

Greetings Boaz, thou perverse and rebellious donkey!

Don't think I'm calling you names because I've suddenly seen red. I actually fought hard against my baser instincts and delayed writing this letter until I caught you this morning on the telephone and also heard with my own ears your version of what happened. (I couldn't come to see you because your mother was taken ill, and in my opinion that was also because of you.) Now that we have spoken on the phone I can tell you, Boaz, that you are still an infant and not a man. And I'm beginning to be afraid that you are never going to grow into one. Maybe your destiny is to grow up into a hotheaded hoodlum. Maybe the time you hit that teacher in Telamim and when you beat up the night watchman were not just unfortunate episodes but a warning sign that we are going to have a mule growing up in our midst. Although "growing up" is hardly the right phrase in your case—it might be better if you stopped growing like some sort of beanstalk and matured a bit for a change.

Now tell me something, if you don't mind: did it have to happen just two days after you'd stayed with me for the Sabbath? After we had all tried so hard (yes, you too) and we'd begun to feel that after all we are a family. Just when your sister had started getting used to you and we were so thrilled by the teddy bear you brought her? Just when you had given your mother a little hope after all the suffering you'd caused her? Tell me, have you gone raving mad?

I have to tell you that if you were my own son or my pupil I would not have spared you the rod—on the face and on the bottom too. Although on second thought I'm not so sure in your case. You might have hit me with a vegetable crate as well.

So perhaps after all we made a mistake when we rescued you from that institute for juvenile delinquents. Perhaps that would have been the most natural place for a customer like you. I understand very well that what happened was that Abram Abudarham gave you a little kick after you were insolent. And permit me to put down in writing that I consider he was quite justified (even though personally I don't hold with kicking).

But what do you think you are? Tell me. A duke? a prince? So you got a little kick because of your big mouth, so what? Is that a sufficient reason to start hitting people with crates? And who did you hit? Abram Abudarham, a man of sixty, who for your information suffers from high blood pressure! And after he'd taken you on to work for him, even with your two police records and the third one, which Inspector Almaliah and I barely managed to have closed for you? What are you? Tell me. An Arab? A horse?

I nearly went mad when you told me on the phone that you really did hit Abraham with a crate because he gave you a tiny kick for being insolent. You may be my wife's son and my daughter's brother, but you're not a human being, Boaz. Scripture says: "School a youth according to his way." And my interpretation is this: So long as the youth follows the right way he should be schooled gently, but if he makes a mess of himself, then he deserves everything he gets! What, are you above the law? Are you the president?

Abraham Abudarham was your benefactor and a kindhearted man, and you repaid his kindness with wickedness. He invested a lot in you, and you let him down, and you also let me down and Inspector Almaliah too, and your mother has been ill in bed for three days now because of you. You have let down everyone who has had anything to do with you. As it is written in Scripture: "And he looked to make grapes, and it made sour grapes."

Why did you do it?

Now you don't answer. Very nice. All right, so I'll tell you why: because of arrogance, Boaz. Because you were born big and handsome like a demigod and you were given a lot of strength of arm, and in your stupidity you think that strength is for hitting people. Strength is for self-discipline, you ass! For mastering your baser instincts! To take all the buffetings that life has in store for us and to keep advancing quietly but firmly along the path that we have decided to follow, that is to say, the straight and narrow. That's what I call strength. Smashing someone's head in—any plank or rock can do that!

That is why I said to you above that you are not a man. Certainly not a Jew. Perhaps it would really suit you to be an Arab. Or a gentile. Because to be a Jew, Boaz, is to know how to stand up to adversity and to practice self-mastery and to keep on treading our ancient path. That is the whole Torah on one leg: self-mastery. And also to understand very well why life has buffeted you, and to learn a lesson from it and always to improve your ways, and also to accept the just decrees of fate, Boaz. Abraham Abudarham, if you think about it for a moment, treated you like a son. Admittedly, a stubborn and rebellious son. And you, Boaz, instead of gratefully kissing his hand, you bit the hand that fed you. Take note, Boaz: You disgraced your mother and me, but first and foremost you disgraced yourself. It seems as though you will never learn humility now. I am just wasting words on you. You refuse to be taught.

And shall I tell you why? Even if it hurts you to hear it? All right, I'll tell you. Why not. It's all because you've got it fixed deep down in your head that you're some kind of prince or something. That you have noble blood flowing in your veins. That you were born and bred a dauphin. Well let me tell you something, Boaz, man to man, even though you are still a thousand miles short of being a man, nevertheless I'll lay all the cards on the table.

I do not have the honor to know your dear, famous father, nor do I hanker after that honor. But this I can tell you straight: that your father is neither a duke nor a king—unless he is the King of Villains. If you only knew to what shame and misery he reduced your mother, how he humiliated her and impugned her honor and drove you yourself out from his presence like a loathsome offspring!

So it is only right that now he has remembered to pay something as recompense for sorrow and disgrace. And right too that I should have decided to overlook our self-respect and accept his money. And have you perhaps asked yourself why I decided to accept his tainted money? For you, you ungrateful donkey! To try to raise you up onto the straight and narrow path!

Now listen carefully to why I'm telling you all this. Not to make you hate your father, Heaven forbid, but in the hope that you will choose to follow my example rather than his. Learn that in me pride and humanity are expressed through mastery of the baser instincts. I accepted money from him instead of killing him. That is my honor, Boaz: that I overcame my sense of humiliation. As it is written: "Whoever effaces his own honor, his honor is never effaced."

I am continuing this letter to you in the evening, after an intermission to give two private lessons and get the supper ready and look after your poor mother, who is ill because of you, and then I watched the news and "Second Glance" on the television. I deemed it right to add something here about my own life, following on what I wrote about self-control and mastering the baser instincts. Without going into what we suffered, Boaz, in Algeria in our time, first from the Arabs as Jews and later in Paris from the Jews as Arabs and from the French as *pieds noirs*, if you happen to know what that means, I mention purely and simply what I myself have been through in this country and still go through because of my beliefs and opinions, my appearance and my origins; if you knew, you might realize perhaps that to get a little kick from a good, dear person like Abram Abudarham is really the equivalent of a caress. The trouble with you is you've been spoiled. You wouldn't understand, anyway. I've been accustomed since the day I was born to get real, authentic kicks three times a day, and I've never raised a crate against anyone. And the reason for that is not just to fulfill the commandment "Thou shalt love thy neighbor as thyself," but first and foremost because I tell you that man must learn to accept suffering with love.

And are you prepared to hear something else from me? In my opinion it is better to receive a thousand sufferings than to cause even one, Heaven forbid. No doubt the Almighty has a few black marks in his ledger against the name of Michael Sommo too. I won't deny it. But among my black marks you won't find any item under the heading Caused Suffering. No—not that. Just ask your mother. Ask Abram, after you ask him nicely to excuse and forgive you. Ask Mrs. Janine Fuchs, who knows me well from way back when we were still in Paris. While as for you, Boaz, who were gifted with physical size and beauty and wonderful skills and the outward appearance of a prince, you have already started to follow your father's tainted path: arrogance, cruelty, and wickedness. Causing suffering. Violence. Even though in fact I made up my mind not to say a single word to you in this letter about the terrible sufferings you have been causing your mother for several years, so that now

49

she is sick because of you—because as I see it you are still unworthy to be talked to about suffering. Apparently you are simply still too young. At least until you can get up and show like a man that you have some shame in your heart.

And if you have decided to be a second edition of your dear father, then you can go and burn in Hell. Forgive me for those words. I didn't intend to write them. But a man should not be judged in his sorrow, as it is written. In fact I want to say exactly the opposite: that I am praying for you, that you will not burn in Hell. Because, it's the truth, Boaz, I have a fondness for you.

So much for the preamble, and now for the main part of my letter. The following is written on behalf of myself and your mother. Both of us.

1. You will go at once to Abram and ask him to excuse and forgive you. That's the first thing.
2. As long as the Fuchs family, Bruno and Janine, agree to have you stay in the shed in their backyard—why not, you can stay with them. But from now on I'm paying them rent. Out of your father's reparation money. You shall not live there for nothing. You are not a beggar and I am not a welfare case.
3. It is a top priority with me that you should go now to learn the Torah and a trade at a college in the liberated territories (your spelling is worse than a seven-year-old's). But this is something we definitely don't want to impose on you. If you like, we'll arrange it for you. If you don't, we won't. We have a saying about the Torah: "Its ways are ways of pleasantness." Not ways of compulsion. As soon as your mother is well again I'll come and see you for a chat and we'll see? Maybe you'll agree? But if what you want is to study optics, just tell me about the course or, better still, show me a prospectus, and I'll pay. From the fund I mentioned earlier. And if by any chance you want to look for another job, come here to Jerusalem, live at home, and we'll see what we can fix up for you. Only, no crates.

4. All this on the assumption that from now on you are going to mend your ways.

Yours sadly and anxiously,
Michel, Yifat, and Mother

P.S. Please note, on my word of honor: If there is so much as one more tiny act of violence on your part, Boaz, even your mother's tears won't help you with me any more. You will walk your evil way on your own and go to your fate without me.

The Sommo Family
7 Tarnaz Street
Jerusalem.

Hi. I got your long letter Michel and I foned sorry to Abram even tho Im not sure who should say sorry to who. Also I left a note to say thanks a lot to Bruno and Janin Fuks before I went out. When this letter reaches you Ill be at Sea already on board ship. As far as Im conserned forget me. Despite the fact I quite like Yifat from the two times I visited you and I quite admire you to Michel even if you nag sometimes. As for you Ilana Im sorry for you becos it would be much better for you if youd never had me.

With Thanks,
Boaz

To Ilana and Michel Sommo   8.5.76
7 Tarnaz St.
Jerusalem

Michel and Ilana: When Michel rang yesterday and asked if Boaz had turned up here I must have been too stunned to grasp what had happened. And the line was so poor I could hardly hear.

I didn't manage to understand the story of the to-do that Boaz was involved in. This morning I tried to call you at your school, Michel, but it was impossible to get through. That's why I'm writing these lines, which I'll send to you with the treasurer of the kibbutz, who's going to Jerusalem tomorrow. It goes without saying that I'll let you know at once if Boaz suddenly turns up here. But the fact is I don't think he will. I'm optimistic and I believe that in the next few days you'll get some sign of life from him. It seems to me that his need to disappear and break off contact does not spring from the particular incident in Tel Aviv. On the contrary, the latest complication, like its predecessors, perhaps springs from the urge to distance himself from the two of you. From all of us. Naturally I'm not writing this note just to calm you and to recommend that you sit back quietly and wait—it's vital to go on looking for him in every way possible. But nevertheless I'd like to share with you my feeling—and perhaps it is only a feeling, an intuition—that Boaz will be all right and will eventually find his niche. Of course he is liable to get mixed up over and over again in little troubles here and there, but during the years he was living here in the kibbutz I could observe his other, more positive, side, a solid mental element of decency and clear logic. Even if it's a different kind of logic from yours or mine.

Please, believe me: I'm not writing this just to encourage you at a difficult time, but because I'm convinced that Boaz is simply not capable of doing anything really bad, either to others or to himself. Let us know at once, via the treasurer who is bringing you this note, if you want Yoash or me or both of us to get a few days' leave and come to be with you.

Rahel

—

To Professor Gideon
Via Mr. Zakheim, Lawyer
36 King George

By the Grace of G-d
Jerusalem
9th of Iyyar 5736 (9.5.76)

LOCAL

Dear Sir,

I the undersigned had sworn a solemn oath to have no further dealings with you, whether for good or ill, whether in this world or the next, on account of what is written in the Book of Psalms, Chapter 1, Verse 1. "Happy is the man who has not walked in the counsel of the wicked nor stood in the way of sinners nor sat in the sitting of the scornful." The reason for my hereby breaking my oath is that it is a matter of life or death. Perhaps even, Heaven forbid, two lives.

A. Your son Boaz. As you are aware from reading his mother's letters, the boy has already gone slightly off the rails once or twice, and I have tried to get him back on the straight and narrow. Two days ago we received a phone call from the dear family Boaz was staying with: he has disappeared. I went there immediately with all the speed I could muster, but what could I do? And then this morning we had a sign of life from him, a short letter to say that this time he is running away to work on board a ship. And this after he was mixed up in more devilment.

For reasons that someone like you, sir, would be unable to understand, I decided not to remove my supervision from him and I instantly pulled some strings to make sure that he would be sought on every ship, whether Israeli or foreign, that was about to leave. To my regret there is no certainty that the searches will produce a positive result: it is possible that the boy is not at sea at all, but on dry land, wandering around somewhere in the country. That is why I have decided to turn to you, despite everything, to ask that you should also do something in the direction of offering help, on account of the great wrong you did him and his mother. For a scholar like yourself I imagine that a hint is sufficient, that you will understand that we are not asking for money, but that you should act urgently (perhaps by means of circles that are close to you). I mention this so as to avoid a repetition of the unpleasantness of the recent past, when my wife requested your help with the boy's difficulties and you did not stir a finger to help but instead you perhaps tried to silence your conscience with money that you sent us without being asked. This is on the assumption that even someone like you has such a thing as a conscience. Perhaps I am still too naive.

B. My wife Ilana Sommo. She is now on her sickbed in consequence of Boaz's pranks. Yesterday she admitted to me that she had sent you without my knowledge another personal letter, following your financial payment. As you might imagine I was very angry with her, but I immediately withdrew my anger and forgave her because she had owned up and especially because suffering atones for sins. And Mrs. Sommo is someone who has suffered exceedingly, thanks to you, Mr. Professor.

Naturally, for my part, it did not occur to me to investigate what she put into these letters (such a thing would be beneath my dignity), but she of her own accord told me that you had not replied to her. In my opinion, by your silence you are adding insult to injury. Don't worry, I won't read what you write to her, not only from religious scruples but because I consider you, sir, to be tainted. Maybe she will forget a fraction of the suffering you caused her if you write her a letter explaining why you treated her so badly and apologizing for all your sins. Without that, all your money was given in vain.

C. The money. You, sir, sent me from Geneva on the seventh day of March an arrogant and even insolent letter, telling me to take the money and stop my mouth and not say thank you. Well, take note that it never even occurred to me to say thank you! Thank you for what? Because you deigned to remember very belatedly to pay a small part of what fairness and justice demanded you should give to Boaz and Mrs. Sommo, and in fact also to our little daughter? It would seem that there is no limit to your impudence, sir. As it is written: a brazen brow.

From the size of the sum you saw fit to send (one hundred and seven thousand U.S. dollars in Israeli pounds in three unequal installments) I understood that the contribution to the redemption of Alkalai House in Hebron had been summarily abandoned. I shall nevertheless take advantage of this unfortunate occasion to urge you once again to contribute without delay the sum of one hundred and twenty thousand U.S. dollars to this sacred cause: here too there may be an element of life-saving, as in the previous two items, albeit in a broader sense. As stated above, were it not a matter of life and death, I would not be communicating with you for good or for ill. I shall explain this below. According to our faith there is a connection between your wrongdoings and Boaz's troubles together with his mother's sufferings. It is possible that your repentance and your contribution will arouse the divine compassion for the boy and he will return safely. There are rewards and punishments, there is divine justice, even if I am unworthy to presume to understand its workings, or why your sins should be visited on this woman and child. Who knows? Could it be that some day your own son may be privileged to dwell in Hebron beneath the very roof we intend to redeem from alien hands by means of your donation, and in this way justice will be redressed, and He Who sitteth in Heaven will laugh? As Scripture saith, "The wind goes round," and it is written, "Cast your bread upon the waters for in the fullness of days you shall find it again." And perhaps this donation will serve to counterbalance your sins when your day comes to stand before a Judge before Whom there is neither laughter nor levity. And remember, sir, that there you will have no lawyer and your plight will be parlous.

Which leads me to stress, in conclusion, that I am obliged to send this letter through your lawyer, Mr. Zakheim, for reasons not of my choosing, since Mr. Zakheim simply refuses to let me have your address, and I will not ask my wife because I do not want to tell her about this letter—her nerves are strained enough even without that.

I wish hereby to complain about Mr. Zakheim's conduct. It would appear that he has in his head some cheap film about threats and blackmail, a thriller with Michael Sommo in the role of Don Corleone of the Mafia or something of the sort. If such a thing had come from someone else, I would not pass over it in silence. But from Mr. Zakheim's name I presume that he or his family came to us from the Holocaust. To Jews who come from the Holocaust I forgive everything: Mr. Zakheim may have undergone experiences that have made him morbidly suspicious, especially against someone like myself with my national outlook and with my origins, not to mention my religious observances. As it is written, He sees the shadows of mountains as mountains.

I have therefore resolved to forgive your lawyer. But not you, sir. For you there is no forgiveness. Perhaps if you faithfully fulfill each of the three items of this letter, to wit, the search for the boy, the apology to the lady, and the donation for the Redemption of the Land, perhaps then the Almighty will exercise His compassion. At the very least they will see that you have something on the credit side.

With best wishes on the occasion of the Festival of our Independence,

Michael Sommo

ENCLOSURE

Dear Alex,

Just a couple of lines. I am passing you the enclosed sealed envelope from your diminutive successor. I'll wager that he is asking you for money again. He probably thinks he's managed to establish direct contact with the government printer. If by any chance you decide this time to have the Temple rebuilt at your expense or just to pay a bonus to the Messiah's donkey, do it without me, if you don't mind. I'll convert to Islam and that will be an end to it.

I gather from Sommo that the juvenile colossus has run away again: not that I understand how they can manage to lose such an obelisk every time. But there's nothing to worry about, they're sure to find him in a day or two in the Central Bus Station selling goods spirited off a ship, as happened last time he disappeared.

By the way, I happened to catch sight of your old jalopy in Ben Yehuda Street the other day. It looks as though the gent is keeping her well serviced: she looks pretty good for her mileage, especially bearing in mind how many times she's changed hands.

Which is more than one can say about you, Alex: I was rather alarmed at the way you looked when we met last time in London. Take yourself in hand and stop trying to find trouble.

Your ever faithful
Manfred

SOMMO TARNAZ 7 JERUSALEM

ZAKHEIM HAS INSTRUCTIONS TO FIND BOY LETTER DISPATCHED SOON TO LADY AS REQUESTED YOULL HAVE ANOTHER FIFTY THOUSAND IF YOU AGREE TO ARRANGE TISSUE TEST FOR BOY ILL TAKE PARALLEL TEST SIMULTANEOUSLY HERE IN LONDON ALEXANDER GIDEON

Mr. Manfred Zakheim, Lawyer   14.5.76
Messrs. Zakheim & di Modena
King George 36
Jerusalem

Dear Mr. Zakheim,

My ex-husband has informed us by cable that he has asked you to help me to find my son, who has apparently run away to sea. Please do whatever you can, and do let me know the moment you discover anything. My ex-husband mentioned in his cable a tissue test for Boaz for the purpose of establishing paternity. As I told you on the telephone this morning (and you asked to have it from me in writing) I withdraw my opposition of seven years ago to such a test. The only problem now is to find the boy and convince him to agree to have the test that his father is asking for. And that won't be easy. Please, Mr. Zakheim, explain to my ex-husband that I am withdrawing my opposition to the test without any connection to the sum of money he mentioned in his cable. In plain words, he doesn't have to give us a penny more. On the contrary, I am delighted that the request for a test came from him this time. At the time of our court case, as you will recall, Mr. Zakheim, I opposed a test—but he did not agree to be tested, either.

If he would like to make a donation to the cause my present husband mentioned, let him do so without any reference to the question of the test. Simply tell him that as far as I'm concerned it's perfectly all right now. The main thing is, Mr. Zakheim, I beg of you, if you have any information about where the boy is, let us know, even if it's in the middle of the night.

Yours gratefully,
Ilana Sommo (Gideon)

—

To Mrs. Sommo   *Hampstead, London*
                                         15.5.76

PRIVATE
To be delivered personally by Mr. M. Zakheim

Dear Mrs. Sommo,

Zakheim is exerting himself to recover your lost property. Even though I imagine it is not easy for him to compete single-handed with the hordes of Sommos who have doubtless already been summoned to the hunt by the tribal drums. One way or another, I imagine that before this letter has reached its destination there will be a sign from Boaz. Incidentally, it almost makes me feel sad: which of us has never dreamed of disappearing without trace?

Yesterday I received a letter from your husband. It seems he has experienced some sort of a theophany; a heavenly voice has ordered him to rebuild the walls of Jericho, and at my expense moreover. And as part of his master plan to build the heavenly Jerusalem he commands me to repent at once, starting with apologies and explanations to you. Followed, apparently, by breast-beating and self-mortification.

And I thought naively that our relations had already been amply explained in two rabbinical lawsuits and before the District Court, and that any further expatiation would be invidious. As a matter of fact, I was under the impression that you were the one who owed me an explanation. And indeed there can be vaguely discerned in your letters a veiled attempt to expound your present condition, including details about the bedtime exploits of Mr. Sommo. I have no interest in this matter (although your description is quite well written; perhaps a trifle too literary for my taste). Moreover, the feelings that my person does or does not continue to arouse in you do not affect me one way or the other. I should be glad if both of you would stop bidding so energetically for my contributions: I am neither the Bank of England nor a sperm bank. On the other hand, you have not touched on the only question that exercises me: Why did you choose at the time to resist the tissue test so violently? If it had transpired that I was the biological father, it would obviously have been much harder, if not impossible, for me to win the case. To this day I have not succeeded in comprehending this. Did you suspect that I would be shown not to be his father? Did you suspect that I would be shown to be his father? Is there the slightest doubt who his father is, Ilana?

And what has made you suddenly change your mind now and agree to the test after all? That is, if you really have changed your mind. And if you haven't changed it again since.

Is it really only the money? But there was money then too. And you fought for the money then too. And lost. And rightly so.

I repeat my suggestion: You can have another fifty thousand dollars (and I don't care what good cause it's for—it could be for the conversion of the Pope for all I care) once the test has been done, and irrespective of its outcome. Even though

Zakheim maintains that I have gone clean out of my mind. According to his decisive logic, from the moment I promised you in the cable that you would receive the money irrespective of the outcome of the test, you held all the cards, and I handed you my head on a gold platter with my own hands. Thus spake Zakheim.

Is he right?

Are you prepared to explain to me now why you let yourself and Boaz down in court by opposing the test instead of demanding it? What more did you have to lose that you had not already lost, one way or another? Did you have any doubt about the outcome of the test? Or did you deliberately and maliciously prefer to lose everything and be thrown out on the street with the child, just to inject a doubt into me?

And now you have the gall to write to me that I do not trample to death, I sting. Is this some kind of sick joke? You have another offer on the table now from the retired dragon: If you give me a straight answer to the question why you opposed a test of paternity in 1968 and why you agree to one now, I undertake to name Boaz my heir. And also to send you another fifty thousand by return mail. In point of fact, if you give me an answer, the test will be unnecessary. I renounce it in exchange for a convincing answer to my one and only question.

If, on the other hand, you choose to go on weaving your tissue of lies, we might as well break off all contact again. And this time it'll be forever. You have already fed me enough lies for a whole regiment of cuckolds. You won't manage to lie to me again. And by the way, what sort of explanations does your husband expect me to give you when you have admitted yourself in the presence of three rabbis that you managed while we were married to each other to sleep with a whole army?

Either way it might be better for us to break off contact. What more do you want from me? What have I got to give apart from money? Have you got a sudden craving to gorge yourself on dragon steak and fries? Why have you come along to disturb our cemetery suddenly after seven years?

Let it be. I am living alone. Quietly. I go to bed every night at ten o'clock and slip into a dreamless sleep. I get up at four every morning to work on an article or a lecture. All passion is spent. I even have a walking stick, which I bought in an antique shop in Brussels. Men and women, money, power, and fame—they all leave me cold. From time to time I take a little stroll among ideas and concepts. I read a couple of hundred pages every day. I bend down and pluck a quotation or a footnote here or there. That's the way it is, Ilana. And while we are on the subject of my life, although your poetic descriptions with the spacecraft and the snow and so forth are actually quite pretty (that was always your forte), it so happens, for your information, that in fact I have central heating, not a fireplace. And outside the window there is no snow (it is May, after all), but just a little garden, a neat English lawn with a forsaken wooden bench, a weeping willow, and a grey sky. And anyway I'll be back in Chicago soon. As for my pipe and my whisky, I've been forbidden to drink or smoke for more than a year now. If you really care about my changing my will, if your husband is hankering after a few more tens of thousands, all you have to do is give me a straight answer to the one and only question I am putting to you. Just remember this: One more lie and you two will get nothing more out of me. Not a word and not a penny. Ever. Now I shall sign off with the new name you have given me:

Alec, the solitary rogue

——

Dr. A. Gideon   *Jerusalem*
% Mr. M. Zakheim   *24.5.76*

Dear solitary rogue,

Today we had a postcard from Boaz. He is somewhere in the Sinai, he won't say where, but according to the card he is "working and earning good money." For the time being we have not managed to locate him. Apparently even your omnipotent Zakheim has failed.

On the other hand, you managed in your letter to hurt me and even to alarm me. And not in the poisonous bits, but when you said that you are not allowed to smoke or drink. Please write and tell me what happened. What operations did you have? Write and tell me the whole truth.

You put two questions to me: Why did I not agree when I brought the lawsuit against you that the three of us should undergo a tissue test? And am I still opposed to such a test? The answer to the second question is that I am not. Only that now it's really a matter for you and Boaz. If it's truly important to you, try to persuade him to have the test. But first of all go and find him. Go yourself; don't send Zakheim and his detectives.

I am wasting my words. You are hiding in your lair and you won't come out.

The answer to your first question is that seven years ago I did very much want to get some maintenance money out of you and also some of the property, but not at the cost of handing Boaz over to you. I am astonished that you, with your international brains, couldn't understand that at the time.

As a matter of fact, I am not astonished.

The reason I opposed the tissue test was that my lawyer explained to me that if the test showed that you were the father, and after you had forced me to admit to adultery, the Rabbinical Court, and any court of law, would give you custody of the child. I was convinced that you hated us so much that you would not hesitate to take Boaz away from me and leave me a little money in his place. And Boaz was only eight years old at the time.

That is the whole secret, sir.

The simple truth is that I did not want to win the case and lose the child. I was hoping to get some maintenance out of you, because I didn't have a cent, but not at the cost of giving up Boaz. That was the reason I exercised my right to oppose the test, which would have shown that your son was your son.

The truth is, we both lost. Boaz belongs only to himself, and perhaps he is a stranger to himself as well. Just like you. My heart gasps when I think of the tragic similarity between you and your son.

And if only you had given me then even a tenth of the money you have started to shower on us now, I could have brought Boaz up at home with me. And things would have been somewhat less bad for both of us. But that was precisely the motive that made you take everything away from me. Even now you wouldn't have given us a cent if you hadn't been shaken to death when I told you how Michel is winning his way into the child's affections and how Boaz, in his undemonstrative way, apparently likes Michel. Incidentally, I don't give a hoot if Michel goes on believing naively that you have suddenly turned penitent and begun, as he would put it, to mend your ways. But you can't fool me, Alec: you didn't give us the money to make amends, but to destroy. Poor Alec, it was all for nothing that you tried to run away. That you acted the remote deity. Hiding in your cloud and trying to open a new chapter. You were even less successful than I was. It was all for nothing that we kept silence for seven years, the two of us. Did you put on the black robe? The cowl over your head? Let's go on. I'm ready.

But write me the whole truth about your health. The weeping willow and the grey sky at your window have suddenly started to disturb me.

Wait just a minute, Alec. After all, this is a game for two. Now it's my turn to ask you a question: Why did you accept my refusal? And in fact why did you also refuse a tissue test? Why didn't you fight at least as hard for Boaz as you fought to defeat me in the lawsuit? Why didn't you fight for him so as to be able to annihilate me? And why have you only now thought of offering us a fortune so that the test should take place? It's your turn not to lie. I'm waiting for an answer.

Ilana

———

To Ilana Sommo   *London*
                                                      2.6.76

By hand of M. Zakheim

Because I couldn't, I didn't want to, take Boaz away with me.
I didn't know what to do with him. If I had agreed to a test, they
would have attached the boy to me by a court order. What would
he have become if he had grown up with me?

That is the answer to your question.

What does it say at the end of our decree? "Henceforth they
have no further demands on each other."

And meanwhile Zakheim and the detectives have managed to
find Boaz. That is to say, I did and Sommo didn't. How does your
saint put it? "Kindly make a note." It turns out he's working on a
glass-bottomed tourist boat at Sharm al-Sheikh and really is doing
quite well for himself. I gave Zakheim instructions on the phone
to leave him alone. I am relying on your husband to have enough
sense to do likewise and not try to interfere. Perhaps you could
suggest to him that he put Boaz down as my contribution to the
redemption of the liberated territories and send me a stamped receipt?

Have you let him read my letters? I presume he insists on his
right to read them before you and perhaps even to censor them here
and there. Yet it is equally possible that he honorably refrains from
peeping at his wife's mail and secretly prodding around in her
drawers. A third possibility would be that he reads every word fur-
tively while you are out of the house, and afterward swears on the
Bible that he trusts his wife not to have any sinful thoughts, Heaven
forbid, and that he considers her correspondence sacrosanct. A
fourth possibility is that you will swear that he doesn't read my letters
even though you really do let him read them. Or that you'll tell
me he does and actually not let him. Cheat him with me, cheat
me with him, cheat us both with each other, or cheat us both with

the milkman. With you, anything is possible. Everything, Ilana, except for one thing: for me to know who you really are. I would give all I have to know. But all I have is money, and money, as you wrote to me, will not help. Checkmate.

And while we are on the subject of money, write and tell me how much more you need. Do you really want me to give him a donation for the redemption of Hebron? I don't care. I'll buy him Hebron. And then I'll buy him Nablus. When is his birthday? In exchange I shall ask you to reveal to me the secret of this paragon. How did he manage to win and hold you? I have authoritative assurances from two private investigators that you have apparently never betrayed him (if we leave out of account the love ticket you sent me with a price tag of a hundred thousand dollars on it, which is enough to put us both into the *Guinness Book of World Records* for the highest price ever paid for a screw that never happened). Incidentally, in his latest (for the time being) demand for payment, your Maher-Shalal-Hash-Baz hints that I it was who "reduced you to sin." Such stories are apparently common currency in the background from which he comes. It is not difficult for me to imagine what you have told him about our life together. Stories of Beauty and the Beast.

What do you see in him? What does Boaz see in him?

"A bitter, wild boy," you wrote to me, whose hatred has given him "astonishing physical strength." I remember the way he used to sleep at night: all huddled up in a heavy blanket pulled up over his fair hair like a cub dug into a hole. I remember the candy bed in the garden. The graveyard for butterflies. The maze and the amusement park he made for the tortoise. His tiny hands on the steering wheel of my car. The tank battles we fought on the rug, and how he washed my pipe out once with soap and water. How he ran away into the wadi after one of your suicides. And how I came home one night and found a green lighter, not mine, on the kitchen table and started to punch you and suddenly he appeared in the kitchen in his spaceman pajamas and asked me quietly to stop because you were weaker. When I said to him, "Get into bed," and went on hitting you, he picked up a little potted cactus and threw it at me, and it hit me on the cheek and I let go of you and grabbed hold of him in a frenzy and beat his golden head over and over again against the wall. I had my pistol in my pocket and I could have fired at the two of you that night and then put a bullet in myself. In fact I did, and, ever since, the three of us have been a dream.

I want you to know that in all these years not a month has gone by without my receiving a report on you and Boaz from Zakheim and the detectives. And everything I know, including his violence, I like a lot: this tree is growing a long way from the rotten apples. We don't deserve him, either of us. Neither of us deserves anything, apart from a bullet in the brain. Perhaps it's only your black devil who deserves something. To be buried in the Patriarchs' Tomb in his Hebron. And the sooner the better.

What did you see in him, Ilana? What does Boaz see in him?

If you give me a convincing answer, you'll get the promised check.

Your sudden concern for my health (or your eagerness for an inheritance) is, as usual, touching. But please don't exaggerate: I'm still on the map. Despite those operations. But without the whisky and the pipe, so that from your poetic arsenal only the pen and the spectacles remain, and it is true that I sometimes move them an inch to the left or two inches to the right on my desk. Just as you described in your letter. Although I do not smash glasses or throw things on the fire. Instead of your snow and the empty glass and the empty bottle, you can use the weeping willow outside my window. The black and white are fine, as long as you employ the idea with restraint and not in your usual overexuberant style.

I will nevertheless pour myself a tot of whisky now, before I sample the cure you prescribed for me, to bang my head against the corner of the desk until the pain stops.

Your
Dragon

—

GIDEON NICFOR LONDON

BOAZ HAS TURNED UP HERE REQUESTS FROM YOU FIVE THOUSAND
DOLLARS FOR PURCHASE OF GLASSBOTTOMED BOAT TO SET UP OWN
BUSINESS SHARM ALSHEIKH PLUS ONE THOUSAND TO BUILD
TELESCOPE THERE FOR TOURISTS HAVE REPLIED NEGATIVE FOR
YOUR INFORMATION MANFRED

—

PERSONAL ZAKHEIM JERUSALEM ISRAEL

GIVE IT TO HIM IDIOT ALEX

—

GIDEON NICFOR LONDON

NOW HES ASKING FIVE THOUSAND FOR APARTMENT IN OPHIRA ZANDS
MEN HAVE DISCOVERED HE IS LIVING AT A GAS STATION THERE
WITH TWO SWEDISH GIRLS ONE FRENCH DITTO AND A BEDOUIN
HAVENT GIVEN A PENNY YOU HAVE NO CASH HERE AND I HAVENT
MANAGED TO REALIZE PROPERTY GO HAVE YOUR HEAD EXAMINED
MANFRED

—

PERSONAL ZAKHEIM JERUSALEM ISRAEL

MANFRED DO ME A FAVOR MAKE ME A LOAN AGAINST THE ZIKHRON
PROPERTY AND GIVE HIM WHAT HES ASKING TELL HIM ITS THE LAST
TIME ALEX

—

GIDEON NICFOR LONDON

LOAN REFUSED MANFRED

PERSONAL ZAKHEIM JERUSALEM ISRAEL

YOURE FIRED ALEX

———

GIDEON NICFOR LONDON

THANK GOD FOR THAT TELL ME WHO TO HAND PAPERS OVER TO
ZAKHEIM

———

PERSONAL ZAKHEIM JERUSALEM ISRAEL

YOUR RESIGNATION NOT ACCEPTED YOU ARE A BEAST ALEX

———

GIDEON NICFOR LONDON

CARRYING ON ON CONDITION YOU DISCONTINUE SOCIAL ASSISTANCE
TO NEEDY OF GREATER ISRAEL INCLUDING NEGATIVE REPLY TO
BOATS AND APARTMENTS IN SHARM DO YOU THINK YOU ARE DMITRI
KARAMAZOV OR KING LEAR MANFRED

———

PERSONAL ZAKHEIM JERUSALEM ISRAEL

OK RASPUTIN CALM DOWN I SURRENDER FOR TIME BEING ALEX

———

Mr. M. H. Sommo   7.6.1976
7 Tarnaz St.
Jerusalem

BY REGISTERED POST

Dear Mr. Sommo,

You are hereby warned not to address any further requests/
demands for financial favors, whether directly or through your wife
or through your wife's son, to my client Dr. A. A. Gideon, additional to the *ex gratia* payments you have already received from
him.

Permit me hereby to draw your attention to the fact that my
client has authorized me by cable to veto absolutely any transfer of
funds extracted from him by means of emotional or other pressure.
In plain words, you had better get it into your head that if there is
anything else you want, there is no point in pestering Dr. Gideon,
personally or via your relations. Try addressing yourself to me, and
if you behave properly you will find me responsive. For your own
good, sir, I suggest you bear in mind that we possess all the information we require to deal with any difficulties that may arise on
your part in the future.

> *Your obedient servant,*
> *M. Zakheim*
> *Lawyer and Business Manager*

———

Mr. M. Zakheim, Lawyer   *By the Grace of G-d*
Mr. Zakheim & Mr. di Modena   *Jerusalem*
36 King George   *13th of Sivan 5736 (10.6.76)*

LOCAL

Esteemed Mr. Zakheim,

First of all my respectful greetings to you on the occasion of
the Festival of Shavuot!

Heaven forbid that you should think that I have any complaint or grievance against you. As it is written, "May He Who protects the simple protect me from suspecting the righteous or from casting aspersions." On the contrary, I think that you do your job of acting for Professor Gideon as well as possible. Likewise I appreciate the efforts you made on our behalf to renew contact with Boaz, apologize for any distress that has been caused you, thank you for your trouble, and express my confidence that your virtuous actions will stand you in good stead.

Nevertheless, and with all due respect, you will forgive me for finding myself under the necessity to observe, in response to your letter, that you are disqualified from acting as an intermediary between me and my family and Professor Gideon. This is for the simple reason that you are completely identified with the other party, and quite rightly so as long as he is paying you for your pains. So, as it is written, "no to your sting and no to your honey," Mr. Zakheim. If Professor Gideon should come to be persuaded out of the goodness of his heart to make a donation toward the rebuilding of the Land, with all due respect you have no right of veto or *locus standi*, you do not belong in the picture, and I'll thank you to step out of it.

On the other hand, if you decide that you would also like to contribute something toward our holy sacred cause, your contribution will be most welcome and will be accepted with appreciation and without too close a scrutiny.

Moreover I have made a note of your explicit hint about the material that you claim to have assembled against us. I was not unduly impressed, however, for the simple reason that we have nothing to hide. As it is written, "Who shall ascend into the hill of the Lord? or who shall stand in his holy place? He that hath clean hands, and a pure heart; who hath not lifted up his soul unto vanity," etc. Your explicit hint can only embarrass you, Mr. Zakheim. And I for my part, obedient to the command "You shall take no vengeance nor bear any grudge," have decided to overlook it and consider it as though it never existed.

My dear Mr. Zakheim, I should have thought that you, as

someone who came here perhaps from the Holocaust, would be the first to wish to strengthen the state and consolidate its borders. Without, save the mark!, assailing the honor or property of the Arab inhabitants. I should like to propose you for membership in our organization, the Jewish Fellowship Movement (I enclose a prospectus with full details). What is more, Mr. Zakheim, by virtue of the legal prowess you have displayed in the service of Professor Gideon, I have the honor to offer you hereby the position of legal representative of the Movement, either on a voluntary basis or in return for full and proper fees.

Moreover I hereby request you to accept the position of private property manager for me and my family, in light of the fact that with God's help, and with your own deeply welcome help, part of the plundered property has been restored to us, and I am confident that the rest will come as well.

I am prepared to pay you for your trouble at the usual commission and a little over. We could even operate on a partnership basis, Mr. Zakheim, since I am intending to invest a good deal of money through our organization in certain business enterprises connected with the redemption of the liberated territories. A partnership between us should bring ample rewards to both parties, besides rewards for the State of Israel and the Jewish people. As it is written, "Will two walk together if they have not agreed?" My proposal, therefore, is that you should come over to our side, without of course abandoning your client Professor Gideon. Please think about this seriously. There is no urgency about replying. We are accustomed to waiting and do not believe in haste.

Professor Gideon may represent the achievements of the past, but it is my conviction that the future belongs to us. Take thought for the future, Mr. Zakheim!

> *Yours with great respect and in Jewish solidarity,*
> *Michael (Michel-Henri) Sommo*

Rahel Morag   11.6.76
Kibbutz Beit Avraham
Mobile Post, Lower Galilee

Dear normal Rahel,

And yet I still owe you a line or two. I didn't answer you before
because I was up to here in Boaz's problems. No doubt you've put
on your understanding-forgiving-Rahel look, and in your elder-sister
tone you're remarking to yourself that I haven't been concerned
about Boaz but, as usual, about myself. After all, ever since we
were children you were always the one to save me from my crazes.
"My dramas," to use your term. And you'll start feeding me a stew
of that applied psychology you picked up from your child-care course.
Until I go out of my mind and scream: Leave me alone! And then
you'll smile at me sadly, refrain as usual from taking offense, keep
quiet, and let me reach by myself the realization that my outbursts
only exemplify what you have been wise enough to diagnose already.
That tolerant, pedantic wisdom of yours—which has infuriated me
all these years, until I almost choke with rage and explode and insult
you, thus giving you a perfect opportunity to forgive and also
reinforcing your constant anxiety about my condition. Aren't
we a perfect team, the two of us? You see, I only meant to
write you a couple of lines to thank you—you and Yoash—for
being willing to drop everything and come to Jerusalem to help.
And look what came out. Forgive me. Even though if it
weren't for my dramas, what connection would there be between
the two of us? And where would you send your salvos of crushing
kindness?

As you know, Boaz is okay. And I am trying hard to calm
down. Alec's lawyer hired some investigators, who discovered that
he was working on some sort of tourist boat on the Sinai coast and
didn't need any of us. I managed to persuade Michel not to go
to him in the meantime. You see, I accepted your advice to leave
him alone. As for your other advice, to forget Alec for good and to
refuse his money, don't be angry if I tell you you don't understand

a thing. Give my regards and thanks to Yoash and kisses to the children.

Your intolerable
Ilana

Best wishes to all of you from Michel. He is starting to extend the flat with the money we got from Alec. He's already got permission to add two rooms on the back, into the yard. Next summer you'll be able to come and stay with us for a break, and I'll be on my best behavior.

———

From world-wide press reviews of *The Desperate Violence: A Study in Comparative Fanaticism* by Alexander A. Gideon (1976).

"This monumental work by an Israeli scholar sheds new light—or, rather, deep shade—on the psychopathology of various faiths and ideologies from the Middle Ages to the present day. . . ."

Times Literary Supplement

"A must . . . an ice-cold analysis of the phenomenon of messianic fervor in both its religious and its secular guise . . ."

New York Times

"Fascinating reading . . . vital for an understanding of the movements that have shaken and still shake our century . . . Professor Gideon describes the pheomenon of faith . . . any faith . . . not as a source of morality but as its precise opposite. . . ."

Frankfurter Allgemeine Zeitung

"The Israeli scholar maintains that all world-reformers since the dawn of history have actually sold their souls to the devil of fanaticism. . . . The fanatic's latent desire to die a martyr's death on the altar of his idea is, in the author's view, what enables him to sacrifice

73

the lives of others, sometimes of millions, without batting an eyelid.
. . . In the fanatic's soul, violence, salvation and death are fused
into a single mass. . . . Professor Gideon bases this conclusion not
on psychological speculations but on a precise linguistic analysis of
the vocabulary which is characteristic of all fanatics of all ages and
of all positions in the religious and ideological spectrum. . . . This
is one of those rare books that force the reader to re-examine himself
and all his views fundamentally and to seek within himself and his
surroundings manifestations of latent sickness. . . ."

New Statesman

"Ruthlessly lays bare the true face of feudalism and capitalism. . . .
With great skill he exposes the Church, Fascism, nationalism, Zion-
ism, racism, militarism, and the extreme right. . . ."

Literaturnaya Pravda

"You sometimes have the feeling as you read that you are looking
at a painting by Hieronymus Bosch. . . ."

Die Zeit

———

To Dr. A. Gideon   Jerusalem
Via Mr. M. Zakneim   13.6.76

Dear Monk,

If only you had given me a hint seven years ago, at the trial,
that you were not plotting to take advantage of my admitting adultery
to take Boaz away from me I should have had no reason to object
to the paternity test, which in any case would have been unnecessary. How much suffering could have been spared if you had only
said two words then. But what's the point of asking a vampire how
he can drink fresh blood?

I am doing you an injustice. You forfeited your son because
you wanted to spare him. You were even intending to donate a

kidney to him. Even now you could photocopy these letters of mine and send them to Michel. But something interferes with your hatred. Something whispers to you like wind in dry grass, interrupting the arctic silence. I can remember you with your friends having the usual ritual Friday-night argument: your long legs stretched out under the coffee table, your eyes only half opened, the rough sun-tanned skin of your arms, your pensive fingers slowly kneading some absent object. For the rest, a motionless fossil. Like a lizard watching an insect. Your glass precariously balanced on the arm of your chair. The din of voices in the room, the arguments, the counter-arguments, the cigarette smoke—they all seem to be happening a long way below you. Your best white shirt, starched and neatly pressed. And your face sealed in contemplation. And all of a sudden, like a viper, you dart your head forward and spit into the conver-sation: "Just a minute. I'm sorry. I must have missed something." The din of the argument fades instantly. And you scythe through the discussion with a sentence or two, cut across the positions from a sharp, unexpected angle, demolish the point of departure, and conclude with, "Sorry. Carry on." Then you settle back into your disconnected position. Indifferent to the silence that you have gen-erated. Letting someone else formulate in your name the conclusion that might possibly be implied by the question you have put. Slowly, sheepishly, the argument warms up again. Without you. By then you are completely engrossed in a solemn study of the ice cubes in your glass. Until the next interjection. Who was it who warped your mind and made you see compassion as weakness, gentleness and sensitivity as shameful, love as a sign of effeminacy in a man? Who was it who banished you to the snowy steppes? Who was it who corrupted a man like you into obliterating the stain of his compassion for his son, the shame of his longing for his wife? What a grim horror, Alec. And the crime is its own punishment. Your monstrous suffering is like a thunderstorm behind the mountains at dawn. I hug you.

Meanwhile the Hebrew edition of your book is all the rage here now. Your picture stares out at me from every newspaper.

Except that the picture is ten years old at least. It shows your face as lean and concentrated, with your military sternness stretched the width of your lips, as if you are about to give the order to fire. Was it taken when you left the regular army and went back to the university to finish your doctorate? As I look at it the arctic brilliance flashes opposite me out of the grey cloud. Like a spark trapped in an iceberg.

Ten years ago. Even before you finished building the house that looks like a castle in Yefe Nof, from the money that Zakheim managed to extract for you from your father, who was already disappearing into the distance toward the steppes of his melancholy, like an old Indian heading for the happy hunting ground.

We were still living in our old flat in Abu Tor, with that rocky yard and its pine trees. And I remember particularly the rainy winter weekends. We would stay in bed till ten o'clock, battered and exhausted from the cruelty of our night, almost tolerating each other, like a pair of boxers between rounds. Almost leaning on each other. Punch-drunk. When we emerged from the bedroom we would find Boaz already awake. He had dressed himself two hours earlier (with his shirt buttoned up wrongly and with odd socks) and would be sitting in academic earnestness at your desk, with your lamp lit in front of him, your pipe in his mouth, drawing instrument panels of spaceships on one sheet of paper after another. Or an airplane crashing in flames. Sometimes cutting out for you a pile of wonderfully neat rectangular little cards, his contribution to your doctorate. Or for the Armored Corps. It was before the period of the balsa airplanes.

Outside it was raining gloomily, persistently. The wind dashed the rain against the tops of the pine trees and the rusty iron shutters. Through the streaming window the yard seemed to have been drawn with a Japanese brush: pine needles trembling in the mist with droplets of water trapped at their tips. In the distance, between blocks of cloud, domes and minarets floated as though also joining the caravan that was rolling with the thunder eastward toward the desert.

When I went to the kitchen to get breakfast ready I discovered that Boaz had already laid the table for three. Red-eyed you and I would avoid looking at each other. Sometimes I would fix you with my eyes as though I were hypnotizing you, only so you would not be able to look at me. And the child, like a social worker, would act as intermediary for us, asking me to pour you more coffee, you to pass me the cream cheese.

After breakfast I would put on that blue woolen dress, comb my hair and make my face up, and sit down with a book in the armchair. Except that the book would almost always stay open upside down on my lap: I could not take my eyes off you and your son. You would sit together at the desk, cutting out, sorting, and pasting pictures from your *Geographical Magazine*. You worked in almost total silence, the child skillfully guessing your wishes; passing you just at the right moment scissors, paste, penknife, even before you could ask for them. As though you were practicing some ritual together. And all in deep seriousness. Apart from the hum of the kerosene heater, there was no sound to be heard in the flat. And occasionally you would unconsciously lay your strong hand on his fair hair, and dirty it with glue. How different was that purposeful masculine silence from the desperate silence that came down on you and me the moment the last spasm of desire left us. How I trembled to see the touch of your fingers on his head, and compared it with the nocturnal rage they had bestowed on me a few hours earlier. When did we see Death winning at chess in *The Seventh Seal*? Where were the frozen tundras that gave you the vicious strength to disown that child? Where do you draw the frozen power from to compel your fingers to write the words "your son"?

And at the end of those Saturdays, at the close of the Sabbath in the twilight between rain showers, even before we had put Boaz to bed, you would suddenly stand up, angrily pour yourself a quick brandy, down it in one gulp without screwing up your face, deliver a couple of violent pats on your son's back, as if he were a horse, roughly shrug on your coat, and hurl at me from the doorway: "I'll be back on Tuesday evening. Try to evacuate the zone before then if you can." Then you would go out, closing the door with a sort of desperate self-control beyond all slamming. Through the window I would see your back disappearing into the gathering darkness. You have not forgotten that winter. In you it goes on and on, but growing ever greyer, moss-covered, sinking into the ground, like an old tombstone

If you can, try to believe me when I say that Michel does not read your letters. Even though I have mentioned to him that we are corresponding through Zakheim. Don't worry. Or perhaps I should write: Don't hope?

Despite your denial, I still see you sitting at your window with a vista of snowfields, brilliant plains without tree, hill, or bird, stretching away until they merge with masses of grey fog, all as in a woodcut. All in the heart of the winter.

Whereas here, meanwhile, the summer has arrived. The nights are short and cool. The days are blazing, dazzling like molten steel. Through the window of my room I can see the three Arab laborers that Michel has hired digging trenches for the foundations of the extension that Michel is building with your money. Michel himself works with these laborers every day when he gets home from school. He doesn't need a contractor, since he was once a builder himself, the first year after he came to Israel. Every couple of hours he takes some coffee out to them and exchanges jokes and sayings with them. His brother-in-law's nephew, who is an official in the City Council, got us our building permit early. A cousin of his friend Janine has promised to do the electrical wiring for us, and to charge us only for the materials.

On the other side of the fence are two fig trees and an olive. Beyond them begin the steep slopes of the wadi. And you can see on the other side of the wadi the Arab quarter, half suburb and half village, a flock of little stone houses clustering around a minaret. Before dawn the cocks call to me from there insistently, as though trying to seduce me. At sunrise goats bleat, and sometimes I manage to hear the bells of the herd going off to nibble on the edge of the desert. A whole battalion of dogs bursts at times into a barking that is dulled by the distance. Like the ashes of old passions. At night their barking descends to a strangled howling. The muezzin responds with his own wailing, guttural, unbridled, consumed with veiled longings. It is summer in Jerusalem, Alec. Summer has come and you have not.

But Boaz has turned up—the day before yesterday. As if nothing had happened. And his manner was almost joking: "Hi, Michel. Ilana. I've come to eat up your Yifat. But first of all, here, little one, eat these sweets so that you'll be sweeter for me to eat." A Bedouin Viking, sun-scorched, smelling of sea and dust, his shoulder-length hair white-hot, like burnished gold. He already has to stoop when he comes through the doorway. He turns and addresses Michel with a deep bow, as though of reverence, as though performing deliberately and consciously a ritual gesture of respect. Whereas for Yifat he went down on all fours, and she, a dark-skinned monkey, climbed up and clung to his limbs until she could touch the ceiling. And dribbled a sticky mess from the candy he had given her into his hair.

Boaz brought with him a skinny, silent girl, who was neither pretty nor ugly. A math student from France, a good four years older than he is. Michel, after investigating her background and discovering that she came from a Jewish family, calmed down and suggested that they stay the night on the carpet in front of the television. For greater security he left the light on in the shower and the door between us and them wide open, so as to insure "that Boaz doesn't get up to any nonsense in my house."

What brings Boaz here? It appears that he turned to Zakheim and asked for a sum of money for purposes you know. For some reason Zakheim decided to tell him about the hundred thousand you gave Michel, but refused to give Boaz so much as pocket money. Some sort of sly scheme which I can't decipher is apparently brewing inside his devilish shaven skull, and that's why he suggested to Boaz that he come and see Michel "and claim what is rightfully yours."

Perhaps you are also a party to this plot? Perhaps it's your very own? Is it just obtuseness that always prevents me from anticipating your next blow, even when it is just about to hit me? Surely Zakheim is merely a kind of exuberant operetta puppet in which you sometimes choose to conceal your grim fist.

Boaz came to suggest nothing less than to take Michel into partnership in some business to do with tourist boats in the Red Sea. That was why he came up to Jerusalem. He needs, as he puts it, a preliminary investment, which, he is sure, he will recover in a few months. While he was talking, he dismantled a matchbox and made Yifat a sort of camel on chicken's legs. This child is you: enthralled, I watched his fingers recklessly squandering rivers of strength just to refrain from breaking a matchstick. Such a dazzling waste, at the sight of which I was nearly filled instantly with an overwhelming physical envy of his French dropout.

On hearing the offer of a partnership Michel stood up and, as usual, did the right and fitting thing at the most appropriate moment. That is to say, he suddenly climbed onto the window sill and opened up the box of the roller blind to dismantle and reassemble the screw and so release the blind, which was stuck. Then he remained standing on the window sill, and thus was able to talk to your son *de haut en bas*, as though from the bridge of a ship. Michel explained to Boaz dispassionately, without either losing his temper or in any way softening the blow, that there was nothing to talk about, neither loans nor investments, and that even if Boaz was "the epitome of wisdom, like King Solomon in his day, still the Sommo family will not finance either the harem or the ships of Tarshish." And he also nailed Boaz with the verse "in the sweat of your brow you shall eat your bread."

But immediately afterward he got down from his launching pad and went to the kitchen and made Boaz and his friend regal hamburgers, fried potatoes, and a virtuoso salad. And in the evening he asked the neighbors' boy to baby-sit Yifat again and took the two of them and me out to the cinema and afterward for ice cream. It was only when we returned home, close to midnight, that Boaz summoned up enough courage to ask Michel whose "that money from America" was. Michel, who symbolically had not got down for an instant from his pedestal, replied calmly: "The money is your mother's, your sister's, and yours in three equal parts. But for the time being you and Yifat are still minors as far as the law is concerned, and naturally as far as I am too. Meanwhile your mother is responsible for the two of you and I am responsible for her, so go and tell that to Mr. Zakheim, and tell him to stop boring us all. As for you, Boaz, even if you grow to be taller than the Eiffel Tower, for me you will still have the status of a minor Eiffel Tower. If you want to study, that's another matter altogether: just say so, and the money's yours. But to waste money that you didn't earn on fishes and tourists and girls? That I won't finance, even if it is happening in the liberated Sinai. That money is intended to make you into a human being. Now if by any chance you have an urge to hit me over the head with a vegetable crate, go ahead, Boaz; there's one under Yifat's bed."

Boaz listened and said nothing, merely spread that thoughtful smile of his on his mouth, and his regal, tragic beauty filled the room like an aroma. He did not stop smiling even when Michel changed over to French and plunged into a lengthy conversation with the girl student. I am fascinated by the way my husband and your son, out of the depths of contempt and humiliation, are silently fond of each other. Be careful, sir: your victims are only too likely to make common cause against you. And I get a thrill out of your jealousy, which no doubt has just made you purse your lips like wire. And close by an inch or two the space between your spectacles and your pen on your desk. But don't touch the whisky again: your illness is outside the rules of the game.

This morning some friends of Michel's, skullcapped Russians and Americans, came in a van and took Michel and Boaz and his friend for a trip around Bethlehem. So I am here by myself, writing to you on pages torn out of an exercise book. Yifat is at the nursery. She looks like Michel but with a sort of comical exaggeration, as though she had been specially made to be a parody of him: she is thin, curly-haired, has a slight squint, and is obedient, even though she is given to occasional tantrums. But most of the time she radiates shy friendliness, which she lavishes indiscriminately on objects, animals, and people, as though the world were waiting to receive grace and favor from her tiny self. Almost since the day she was born Michel has addressed her as "Mademoiselle Sommo." He pronounces it "Mamzelle," and she responds by innocently calling him *mamzer*, "bastard."

Did you know, Alec, that Michel has decided to leave his job as a French teacher at the end of the year? To leave the school and also give up his private lessons? He has dreams of dealing in real estate in the territories, of a political career, following in the footsteps of a brother he hero-worships. Not that he tells me much about it. Your money has changed his life. It may not be what you had in mind, but it happens sometimes that even a dragon produces some noble result, fertilizes a plot of land that will one day yield crops.

At eleven o'clock I have to go to the Café Savyon, to give this letter to Zakheim at a secret rendezvous. As you have instructed. Even though Michel knows. And Zakheim? He is thrilled. He comes to these meetings arrogant, stylish, and deadly. Wearing a sporty jacket with a bohemian silk scarf around his neck, his Tatar shaven head gleaming and perfumed, his fingernails carefully manicured, the effect spoiled only by the clumps of black hairs sprouting from his nostrils and ears. Time after time he manages to break down my resistance and force a coffee and cake on me. And then he starts to ooze extravagant compliments, double entendres; sometimes he even touches me accidentally, and hastens to apologize with veiled eyes. By our last meeting he had advanced as far as the flower stage. Not a whole bunch, of course, just a single carnation. I forced myself to smile and to sniff the bloom, which smelled of Zakheim's scent rather than its own. As if it had been soaked in it.

You ask what I saw in Michel. And I have to admit it: I was lying again. And I am taking back that tale about Michel the virtuoso lover. So meanwhile you can relax. Michel is all right in bed, and he's trying hard to go on improving. I even found a handbook in French that he had hidden from me in his toolbox. I'm sorry if I've taken away one of your instruments of mortification. I'll let you have others, even sharper ones. Michel and I met a year or so after the divorce. He used to come to the bookshop where I was working, and he used to wait for me, browsing among the magazines until the shop closed. Then he used to take me to a cheap restaurant, to the cinema, to public discussion groups. After the film we sometimes walked mile after mile through the empty night streets of south Jerusalem—he did not dare to invite me up to his room. Perhaps he was ashamed of his lodgings in the laundry room on the roof of a house belonging to one of his relatives. And he would shyly describe his views and plans to me. Can you imagine a bashful ego trip? Even to put his arm through mine was beyond his courage.

I waited patiently for nearly three months, until I had had enough of the sidelong hungry-but-well-trained-dog looks he kept giving me. Finally one night I grabbed his head and kissed him in a back street. So we began to kiss occasionally. But he was still apprehensive about my meeting his family and about my reaction to his partial piety. I liked his timidity. I tried not to put pressure on him. When several more months had passed, and the winter chill had turned our strolls to martyrdom, I took him to my room, undressed him like a child, and folded his limbs around me. Nearly an hour passed before he managed to relax a little. And after that I still had quite a struggle before he showed signs of life. It transpired that the little he knew he had learned as a youth in Paris from girls who were apparently as frightened as he was. And perhaps, despite his denials, in some paupers' brothel. When I let out a little sigh, he was terrified and began to murmur: *Pardon*. And then he got dressed, went down solemnly on his knees, and desperately asked for my hand in marriage.

I became pregnant after our wedding. Another year passed after the baby was born before I managed to teach him how to wait for me. How to wean himself from behaving like a bicycle thief whenever he made love. When he finally succeeded in wringing from me for the first time the sound that you can draw out of me even by mail, Michel resembled the first astronaut to land on the moon: his modest, ecstatic pride made my heart tremble with love. The next day, in a transport of enthusiasm, he did not go to school but borrowed some money from his brother to buy me a summer dress. He even bought me a little electric mixer. And in the evening he cooked me a regal four-course meal, complete with a bottle of wine. He did not stop plying me with little treats and favors. Since then he has slowly improved and sometimes manages to get a clear sound.

Have you relaxed, Alec? Did the vampire's smile appear like a crack between your lips? Are your fangs shining white by the light of the flickering fire? Is the grey malice capering behind the cold stare? Wait. We haven't finished yet. You have never reached and never will as far as Michel's feet. The silent respect, Alec, the shy flicker of gratitude with which he defers to my body before love and after it, the dreamy glow that spreads over his face at night: like a humble restaurant violinist who has been permitted to touch a Stradivarius. Every night, as though this were the first time in his life, his fingers explore my body, surprised by a blow that never falls. And afterward, by the light of the bedside lamp when he gets up to fetch me my nightie, his myopic eyes tell me in fervent silence that the regal favors that I have undeservedly bestowed upon him exceed his humble deserts. A wavering, spiritual glow, like a prayer, lights up his brow from within.

But what can a scaly, bone-plated dragon like you understand of grace and kinship and tenderness? You have never had anything, and you never will have, besides your torture dungeons. Which my flesh longs for. Your tropical hell. The steamy jungles bubbling wih warm decomposition, and glowing dimly in the half-light filtering through the foliage where the oily rain rises from the earth that simmers with fat wanton marrow, catches in the dense treetops, and spills back again, melting, from the treetops to the mud and to the rotting roots. After all, I was not the one who got up and ran away. It was you who smashed it all up. I was prepared to carry on, and I still am. Why did you divorce me? Why did you bring me to the heart of darkness and leave me and run away? And you are still hiding from me in your black-and-white room. You will not return. You are paralyzed by fear. You exhausted, feeble male, hiding, trembling, in your hole. Is the dragon really so shabby? Such a floppy, sloppy dragon? A vampire stuffed with rags? Write and tell me where you are. Tell me of your doings. And the truth about your health.

Weeping Willow

———

To Mr. M. Zakheim, Attorney   *Tel Aviv*
Zakheim & di Modena   *18.6.1976*
36 King George St.
Jerusalem

Dear Mr. Zakheim,

Following your telephone request earlier this week I flew to Sharm al-Sheikh for a few hours and checked out the story. My assistant, Albert Maimon, also succeeded in tracking the youth and discovering his whereabouts up to two days ago. The report is as follows:

During the night of 10th to 11th June the tour boat on which BB has been working lately was stolen from the civilian anchorage at Ophira. The same night, at two o'clock in the morning, the boat was discovered abandoned not far from Ras Muhammad, after apparently being used by Bedouin smugglers to transport drugs (hashish) from the Egyptian coast. The patrol that discovered the boat set off in pursuit of the smugglers. At five o'clock (dawn on 11 June) a young Bedouin by the name of Hamed Mutani was arrested. He was living with BB at a gas station, together with three young women from abroad. The Bedouin resisted arrest (he denies this) and I have reason to believe that he was beaten up on the spot by the police and the military (they deny this). BB got involved in the incident, and with the help of a tire attached to a rope he went berserk and injured nine soldiers and five members of the Ophira police force before he was eventually overpowered. He was arrested and charged with obstructing a lawful arrest. BB's version, as it was taken down at the police station, is that it was those conducting the arrest who employed violence against his friend the Bedouin, who was acting, as was BB, in "self-defense." The Bedouin was released after a few hours, once his interrogators were convinced that he had had nothing whatever to do with either the theft of the boat or the smuggling.

After less than twenty-four hours, during the night of 11th to 12th June, BB succeeded in breaking down the wall of the prefabricated structure housing the police station and escaped. The officer on duty at the time believes that the youth is still wandering around in the desert, and may have taken shelter with the Bedouin. It was in this direction that the Ophira police continued to search for him. As mentioned above, investigator Albert Maimon of our staff (who submitted a brief report on BB to you on a previous occasion) turned in a completely different direction (MHS) and indeed quickly obtained positive results. The youth BB stayed until two days ago in a rented apartment in Kiryat Arba, near Hebron, inhabited by a group of five unmarried religious men of American and Russian origins. These young men are attached to a small right-wing organization calling itself Jewish Fellowship. As you are aware, MHS is also associated with this cause.

In accordance with our legal responsibility, we communicated this discovery to the police. But meanwhile the youth disappeared again. That is the extent of the information in our possession. (Invoice enclosed.) Please inform us promptly if you wish us to continue working on this case.

[Signed] *Shlomo Zand*
S. Zand Private Investigations Ltd., Tel Aviv

———

A GIDEON HILTON AMSTERDAM

ARE YOU STILL INTERESTED IN MY SELLING PROPERTY ZIKHRON
I HAVE PURCHASER ON EXCELLENT TERMS ADVISE PROMPT
ACTION AWAITING INSTRUCTIONS MANFRED

PERSONAL ZAKHEIM JERUSALEM ISRAEL

NEGATIVE ALEX

———

GIDEON GRANDHOTEL STOCKHOLM

TRIED TO REACH YOU BY TELEPHONE THIS IS UNREPEATABLE OFFER
CALL IMMEDIATELY FOR DETAILS NOT LONG AGO YOU WERE
PRESSING ME TO SELL WHATS THE MATTER WITH YOU MANFRED

———

PERSONAL ZAKHEIM JERUSALEM ISRAEL

I SAID NEGATIVE ALEX

———

GIDEON NICFOR LONDON

BOAZ IN TROUBLE AGAIN POLICE LOOKING FOR HIM YOU MAY
REQUIRE FUNDS URGENTLY PURCHASER IS WILLING TO PAY NINE
HUNDRED IMMEDIATELY IN WILLIAM TELL SALVO TO YOUR ACCOUNT
IN MAGIC MOUNTAIN THINK CAREFULLY MANFRED

———

PERSONAL ZAKHEIM JERUSALEM ISRAEL

GIVE BOAZ MY ADDRESS SO HE CAN CONTACT ME DIRECT AND STOP
NAGGING ALEX

—

GIDEON NICFOR LONDON

THE DEVIL KNOWS WHERE BOAZ IS WHAT ABOUT ZIKHRON PROPERTY
STOP CHANGING YOUR MIND EVERY FIVE MINUTES OR YOULL END
UP LIKE YOUR FATHER MANFRED

—

PERSONAL ZAKHEIM JERUSALEM ISRAEL

GIVE ME A BREAK ALEX

—

SOMMO TARNAZ 7 JERUSALEM ISRAEL

INFORM ME IMMEDIATELY WHATS UP WITH BOAZ DO YOU NEED MY
HELP WIRE ME AT NICFOR LONDON ALEXANDER GIDEON

—

DOCTOR GIDEON C/O NICFOR LONDON

EVERYTHING IS ALL RIGHT NOW WE GOT THE NEW POLICE RECORD
CLOSED TOO ONCE HE UNDERTOOK TO STUDY AND WORK IN KIRYAT
ARBA DONT NEED ANY FAVORS WHAT ABOUT YOUR DONATION
MICHAEL SOMMO

—

Dear Weeping Willow,

I got back here this morning after my term in London and a few lectures in Holland and Sweden. Just before I left London I got your long letter, which dear old Zakheim forwarded to me. The letter with the juices and the jungles. I read it in the plane somewhere over Newfoundland. Why did I divorce you? That's your question this time. We'll deal with that in a minute.

But meanwhile I hear that Boaz has struck again. And that Sommo has come to the rescue again. I'm beginning to like this fixed pattern. My only reservations are about the bill that he'll be sending me soon no doubt, together with interest.

Has Boaz started to grow side locks yet? Is he going to live with the religion freaks on the West Bank? Has Sommo given him a choice between a pioneering settlement and a reform school? That's just fine. If I know Boaz, it won't be long before the settlers start cursing Sommo and the day they agreed to take on our skull-smasher.

My answer to your question is: No, I shall not come to see you, except perhaps in dreams. If you had pleaded with me to stay far away from you, to have pity on you and not sully with my presence your pure new life with your humble restaurant violinist, who is playing on your Stradivarius, I might just have come running. But you are imploring me, Ilana. The thick smell of your desire, the smell of figs that were picked too long ago, reaches all the way here. Although I won't deny that I am astonished at your efforts to avoid your fixed habit and write a letter without any lies in it. It's nice that you're working on yourself. We can carry on for a while.

I owe you an answer to your simple, cunning question: Why did I divorce you seven and a half years ago?

Well done, Ilana. Ten points for putting the question. I'd like to put it in the newspapers, on television even: "Rahab rides again— sleeps with three divisions then wonders why she's been divorced. Says: All I really wanted was to come out all right in the end."

I'm evading the issue. I'll try to find an answer for you. The sad thing is, my hatred is starting to go. It's getting thin and grey, just like my hair. And apart from my hatred, what have I got left? Only money. Which is also being gradually drained out of my veins into Sommo's tanker. Don't interfere with my death, Ilana. For seven years I was slowly sinking into the fog, and all of a sudden you swooped down on me to wreck my death as well. You attacked without warning with your fresh troops while my tired old tanks are silent, without fuel or ammunition. Perhaps even starting to rust.

And in the middle of this assault you have the nerve to write to me that grace and tenderness and compassion exist. The murderess starts chanting psalms to elevate her victim's soul?

Did you happen to notice the motto from the New Testament that I chose as the epigraph for my book. I borrowed it straight from Jesus, who remarked at one moment in one of his inspired moods: "Those who live by the sword shall die by the sword." Which did not prevent that delicate zealot from raising his voice on another occasion and roaring: "Do not think I came to bring peace to the world; I did not come to bring peace but a sword." And the sword ended up by eating him as well.

What will you do with your sword once you have felled the dragon? Will you present it to Gush Emunim, the scabbard to Mazkeret Gideon and the blade to Tel Alexander, those two great West Bank settlements that will be built with my money?

But surely the sword you wrenched from my grasp will wilt and fade and melt between your fingers. The blade will turn into a jellyfish. And in the strategic reserve, fresh and ready for the fray, fueled with deadly hatred and armed to the teeth with my arctic malice, Boaz Gideon is waiting for you. Your pincer movement, your plot to team Boaz up with Sommo so as to outflank me, will end badly for you. Boaz will gobble up Sommo and you will be left with nowhere to flee to, face to face with my killer child, who can slay a thousand men with the jawbone of an ass.

I ask myself why I did not follow your good advice, why I didn't throw your first letter, like a live scorpion, straight into the fire, as soon as I read the opening sentence? Now I don't even have the right to resent you: after all, you generously offered me in advance the way to avoid the trap you were laying for me. You did not fear for a moment that I would get out of the net. You recognized an insect that was out of its mind at the smell of a female in heat. I didn't have a chance. You are stronger than I am, in the same ratio as the sun is stronger than snow. Have you ever heard of carnivorous plants? They are female plants that can exude a scent of sexual juices over a great distance, and the poor insect is drawn from miles away into the jaws that are going to close around it. It's all over, Ilana. Checkmate. As after a plane crash, we have sat down and analyzed, by correspondence, the contents of the black box. And from now on, in the words of our decree, we have no further demands on each other.

But what will your victory give you?

Thousands of years ago a certain man of Ephesus looked at the fire burning in front of his eyes and proclaimed: "Its victory will be its destruction." What will you do with the sword when you have wiped me out? What will you do with yourself? You will be extinguished pretty damn quick, Madame Sommo. You will age. You will put on a lot of weight. Your golden hair will grow dull. You will have to bleach it a ghastly peroxide blond. As long as you don't take to wearing a head scarf. You will have to drown the smells of your degenerating body in deodorants. Your breasts will fill with fat, and your dazzling bosom, as usually happens to Polish matrons, will rise up to meet your chin. Which for its part will lengthen and go halfway to meet the bosom. The nipples will become pale and bloated, like drowned corpses. Your legs will swell. A network of varicose veins will spread from hip to foot. The corsets in which you will be obliged to contain your cascades of flesh will groan fit to burst as you fasten them. Your posterior will become beastlike. Your vulva will flap and stink. Even a virgin soldier or a retarded youngster will flee from your charms as from the wild advances of a female hippopotamus in heat. Your tame party hack, little Monsieur Pardon, will trail around after you in a dazed state, like a puppy dog after a cow, until he stumbles on some lively girl student who will effortlessly pull him out and extricate him, thankful and out of breath, from under the mountain lying on top of him. And so the episode of your Saharan carnival will finally come to an end. A lover who knows neither laughter nor levity is getting closer and closer to you. Perhaps for you he will put on his black robe and cowl as you asked.

I stopped writing to you and stood at my high window (on the twenty-seventh floor of an office building by the lakeside in Chicago, built of glass and steel and somewhat resembling a ballistic missile). I stood there for about half an hour looking for a truthful and lethal answer to your question: mate in three moves.

Try to picture this man, if you can, thinner than you remember and with much less hair, in dark blue corduroy trousers and a red cashmere sweater. Even though in principle, as you say, he is in black and white. Standing at the window with his brow pressed against the glass. The eyes in which you detect an "arctic malice" search the outside world where the light is fading. And his hands are in his pockets. Clenched. Every few minutes he shrugs his shoulders for some reason and hums in a British sort of way. A coldness passes through his bones. He shudders, removes his hands from his pockets, and clasps his shoulders with his arms crossed. This is the embrace of those who have nobody. And yet, for all that, a tight-coiled animal element still endows his silent standing by the window with some characteristic of inner tension: as though flexed to leap back like lightning and anticipate his assailants.

But there is no reason for tension. The world is red and strange. A strong wind blows off the lake and dashes clumps of fog against the silhouettes of the tall buildings. The dusk light pours over the clouds, the water, the nearby towers, an alchemical quality. A transparent orange hue. Opaque and yet transparent. Not a single sign of life can he spy from his window. Apart from millions of salvos of foam capering on the surface of the lake, as though the water had rebelled and tried to convert itself into another substance altogether: slate, for example. Or granite. Every now and again the wind erupts and the windowpanes chatter like teeth. Death appears to him now not like a hovering threat, but like an event that has been going on for some time already. And here is a strange bird being swept toward his window with spasmodic flapping, describing circles and loops as though trying to sketch an inscription in space: perhaps the wording of the answer to you that he is looking for? Until all of a sudden it comes rushing toward the glass and almost bursts in his face as he realizes at last that it was not a bird at all but just a sheet of newspaper trapped in the claws of the wind. Why did we part, Ilana? What took hold of me and made me suddenly extinguish the furnaces of our hell? Why did I betray us? An empty evening is falling violently on Chicago. Lightning flashes of white-hot iron bluster from horizon to horizon like flares, and now convoys of thunder are starting to roll in the distance, as though my tank battles are pursuing me here all the way from the Sinai. Has it ever occurred to you to ask yourself how a monster mourns? The shoulders heave in a rapid, compulsive rhythm, and the head extends forcefully forward and downward. Like a dog coughing. The belly is seized by frequent cramps, and the breathing becomes a hoarse gurgling. The monster chokes with rage at the fact of being a monster and writhes in monstrous spasms. I have no answer, Ilana. My hatred is dying and my wisdom is expiring with it.

As soon as I came back to my desk to continue writing to you, there was a power cut. Just imagine: America—and power cuts! After a moment of blackness, the emergency lighting came on: pale, skeletal neon, looking like moonlight on chalk hills in the desert. The most electric moments in my life were spent in the desert, charging and trampling under my tracks all that lay in my path, smashing with my gunfire whatever displayed signs of life, raising columns of fire and smoke, causing clouds of dust to billow up, shaking the whole world with the roar of thirty engines, inhaling like an intoxicating drug the smell of scorched rubber, the stench of charred flesh and burning metal, leaving behind me a trail of destruction and empty shell cases, and at night, hunched over a map, devising clever stratagems by the light of the dead moon, shedding its silver over the dead chalk hills. To be sure, I could have answered you with a burst of machine-gun fire: I could have said, for example, that I threw you out because you had started to rot. Because your carryings-on, even with apes and he-goats, had begun to get boring. Because I had had enough. Lost interest.

But we had agreed to dispense with lies. After all, all these years I could sleep only with you. All my life, in fact, because I was a virgin when I met you. When I take into my bed some little admirer, pupil, secretary, interviewer, you appear and intrude yourself between us. If ever you forget to turn up, my sleeping partner has to help herself out. Or make do with an evening of philosophy. If I am a demon, Ilana, then I am a genie, and you are my bottle. I've never managed to escape.

Nor have you, for that matter, Lady Sommo. If you are a demon, I am *your* bottle.

I read in Bernanos that unhappiness is a source of blessing. To this Catholic honeydew I replied in my book that all happiness is basically a trite Christian invention. Happiness, I wrote, is kitsch. It has nothing in common with the *eudaimonia* of the Greeks. Whereas in Judaism the whole idea of happiness does not exist; there isn't even a word corresponding to it in the Bible. Apart, perhaps, from the satisfaction of approval, a positive feedback from God or your neighbor: "Blessed are the undefiled in the way," for instance. Judaism recognizes only joy. As in the verse "Rejoice, O young man, in thy youth." Ephemeral joy, like the fire of the cryptic Heraclitus, whose victory is its destruction, joy whose converse is wrapped up in it and in fact actually makes it possible.

What is there left of all our joy, yours and mine, Ilana? Only perhaps joy at the other's misfortunes. Embers of a dead fire. And here we are, puffing on those embers from halfway around the globe in the hope of fanning a momentary flicker of malice. What a foolish waste, Ilana. I give in. I'm ready to sign a document of capitulation here and now.

And what will you do with me? Of course. There is no other way. Nature herself decrees that the routed male be enslaved. He is castrated and made to serve. He shrinks to the size of a Sommo. So you will have two of us: one to worship you and sweeten your nights with his religious passion, the other to finance these spiritual nuptials. What should I write on the next check?

I'll buy you both whatever you want. Ramallah? Bab Allah? Baghdad? My hatred is dying and in its place I am falling under the spell of my father's impetuous generosity. He intended to leave his fortune, at the end of his days, to build homes for consumptive poets on top of Mount Tabor and Mount Gilboa. I shall use my money to arm both sides in the battle that will erupt one day between Boaz and Sommo.

And now I shall tell you a story. A sketch for a romantic novel. An opening for a *tragedia dell'arte*. The year is 1959. A young major in the regular army brings his intended to meet his almighty father. The girl has a Slavic face, sexy in a dreamy way, but not particularly beautiful in the accepted sense. There is something beguiling in her expression of childlike surprise. Her parents brought her here from Lodz when she was four. They have both died on her. Apart from a sister in a kibbutz, she has no family left in the world. Since leaving the army she has earned her living as a copy editor for a popular weekly. She is hoping to publish some poetry.

And this morning she is visibly worried: what she has heard about the father does not bode well. Her personality and background are certain not to be to his liking, and she has heard alarming stories about his fits of rage. She sees the meeting with the father therefore as a sort of fateful interview. After some hesitation, she decides to wear a shiny white blouse and a flowery spring skirt, perhaps to emphasize the surprised-little-girl effect. Even her hussar, magnificent in his starched uniform, appears a little tense.

And at the gateway to the estate between Binyamina and Zikhron Yaakov, pacing up and down on his gravel path and fingering a fat cigar as though it were a gun, Volodya Gudonski, the great dealer in land and importer of iron, awaits them. Tsar Vladimir the Terrible. Among the many stories circulating about him they tell how, when he was still a pioneer in charge of stone quarries, in 1929, he killed three Arab brigands by himself, with a sledge hammer. And they tell how he was the lover of two Egyptian princesses. And they also tell how, after he had embarked on his import business and made a small fortune out of his dealings with the British Army, it once happened that the High Commissioner at a reception affectionately called him a "clever Jew," and the Tsar, on the spot, roared at the High Commissioner and challenged him to a fistfight in the middle of the party, and when the man declined called him a "British chicken."

The hussar and his intended were greeted on their arrival with iced pomegranate juice and then taken on a long tour of inspection of the length and breadth of the estate, whose fields were worked by Circassian laborers from Galilee. And there was an ornamental pool with a fountain and goldfish, and a rose garden with a collection of rare varieties imported from Japan and Burma. Zeev-Benjamin Gudonski talked without stopping, lecturing with picturesque enthusiasm, wooing, as though overflowing with whimsical exaggeration, his son's fiancée. Cutting and handing her whatever flower her eyes lighted upon. Clasping her shoulders in an expansive gesture. Jokingly kneading her fine shoulder blades. Bestowing upon her the honorary rank of thoroughbred filly. His deep Russian voice waxed enthusiastic over the elegance of her ankles. And suddenly he demanded with a roar to be shown her knees at once.

Meanwhile the Crown Prince was firmly and absolutely deprived of the right of speech for the whole duration of the visit. He was not permitted to utter a single cheep. What alternative did he have, therefore, but to grin like an idiot and occasionally relight the cigar that had gone out in his father's mouth. Even now, in Chicago, as he writes down for you his memories of that day, seventeen years later, he suddenly has the feeling that that idiotic grin is spreading over his face again. And a ghostly breeze blows on the embers of his hatred for you, because you were so thrilled to join in the tyrant's game. You even, with peals of schoolgirlish laughter, repeatedly exposed your knees to his gaze. An enchanting blush colored your cheeks as you did so. Whereas I must have been as pale as a corpse.

Next the young couple was invited to a meal in the dining room, where French windows afforded a view of the Mediterranean from the top of the escarpment of Zikhron. Christian Arab servants in tail coats served pickled fish with vodka, consommé, meat, fish, fruit, cheese, and ice cream. And a regular caravan of glasses of steaming tea straight from the samovar. Every refusal or apology provoked bellows of titanic rage.

As evening came on, the Tsar, in the library, still determinedly strangled at birth any sentence that the cowed prince tried to speak: the father was busy up to his ears with the *krassavitsa*, and must not be disturbed. She was asked to play the piano. Requested to recite a poem. Examined in literature, politics, and art history. A record was placed on the phonograph and she was obliged to dance a waltz with the tipsy giant, who trod on her toes. To all these challenges she responded readily, good-humoredly, like someone trying to please a child. Then the old man began to tell rude jokes of the spiciest variety. Her face reddened, but she did not deny him her rippling laughter. At one o'clock in the morning the dictator finally fell silent, grasped the tip of his bushy mustache between brown finger and thumb, closed his eyes, and fell fast asleep in his armchair.

The couple exchanged glances and gestured to each other to leave him a note and depart: they had not planned to spend the night there. But as they were leaving on tiptoe, the Tsar leapt from his place and kissed the beauty on both cheeks, and then, lengthily, on her mouth. And delivered a stunning clap on the back of the neck to his son and heir. At half past two he called Jerusalem, woke a dazed Zakheim from a sweet conspiratorial dream, and bombarded him with instructions to purchase an apartment in Jerusalem for the young couple first thing in the morning and to invite "the world and his wife" to the wedding, to take place "ninety days from yesterday."

And we had only gone to see him so that he could meet you. We had not yet discussed the question of marriage. Or if we had, you had spoken and I had hesitated.

To our wedding, which did indeed take place three months

later, he actually forgot to come: he had found himself a new mistress in the meantime and had taken her to the Norwegian fjords for a honeymoon. As he regularly did with his new mistresses, at least twice a year.

One bright morning, a short time after our wedding, when I was away on brigade maneuvers in the Negev, he turned up in Jerusalem and started to explain to you delicately, almost sheepishly, that his son—to his great sorrow—was merely a "bureaucratic spirit," whereas the two of you were "like a pair of trapped eagles." And therefore on his bended knee he implored you to consent to spend with him "just one magical night." And he immediately swore to you by all that was precious and holy to him that he would not touch you with so much as his little finger—he was no villain— but would merely listen to your playing and your reading of poems and go for a walk with you in the mountains around the city, concluding with the view of the "metaphysical sunrise" from the top of the YMCA tower. When you refused him, he called you a "little Polish shopkeeper" who had lured his son into your "clutches" with your "tricks," and he took his presence elsewhere. (During those nights you and I had already started to excite ourselves by playing at threesomes. Even if at that time we had not yet advanced beyond the realm of the imagination. Was the Tsar the first third man in your fantasies? The first lie you told me?)

When Boaz was born, for some reason Volodya Gudonski was staying in northern Portugal. But he managed to send a check from there to some dubious Italian firm, which dispatched to us an official certificate testifying that somewhere in the Himalayas there was a Godforsaken peak that would henceforth and forevermore be named on all maps "Boaz Gideon Peak." You must check to see if the piece of paper still exists. Perhaps your messiah will found a settlement there. And in 1963, when Boaz was two or three years old, Volodya Gudonski decided to become a recluse. He sent his army of mistresses scattering to the four corners of the globe, Zakheim he tortured like a Scythian, and us he adamantly refused to see even for a brief audience—he considered us to be degenerates. (Had he noticed something from his exalted throne? Did he nurse some suspicion?) He shut himself away within the four walls of his estate, hired a couple of armed guards, and devoted his days and nights to learning Persian. And then astrology and the Doctor Feldenkreis Method. Doctors hired by Zakheim he sent packing like dogs. One day he upped and dismissed all his workmen with a wave of the hand. Since then the orchard has gradually been turning into a jungle. One day he upped and sacked the domestic servants and guards as well, leaving himself only one old Armenian to play billiards with him in the cellar of the dilapidated house. Father and the Armenian slept on camp beds in the kitchen and lived on canned food and beer. The door from the kitchen to the rest of the house was secured with a crossbeam and nails. Branches of the trees in the garden began to grow through the broken upstairs windows into the bedrooms. Plants and bushes grew in the ground-floor rooms. Rats and snakes and night birds nested in the corridors. Creepers climbed up the two staircases, reached the first floor, ramified from room to room, penetrated the ceiling, pushed up a few roof tiles, and so found their way out to the sunshine again. Eager roots sprouted between the decorated floor tiles. Tens or hundreds of pigeons requisitioned the house for their own use. But Volodya Gudonski chatted in fluent Persian to his Armenian. He also discovered the weak point in the Feldenkreis Method and burned the book.

One day we risked our lives, defied his Biblical curse, and went to see him, the three of us. To our great surprise he received us gladly and even tenderly. Large tears rolled down his new beard, a Tolstoyan beard that covered his Brezhnevian features. He addressed me in Russian, using an expression that can best be translated as "foundling." He used the same expression in speaking to Boaz. Every ten minutes he would drag Boaz down to the cellar, and after each of these excursions the boy would return clutching a present of a coin from the time of Turkish rule. You he called "Nusya," "Nusya maya," after my mother, who died when I was five. He bewailed your pneumonia and blamed the doctors and himself.

Finally he roared at you with his last strength that you did away with yourself deliberately, just to torment him, and therefore he would leave his "fortune" to build a home for starving poets.

And indeed he began to scatter his wealth in all directions: rogues and charlatans swarmed around him, demanding donations to funds to make Galilee Jewish or the Red Sea blue. Not unlike what has been happening to me recently. Zakheim worked away patiently, discreetly, at transferring the property to my name. But the old man summoned up the strength to fight back. Twice he sacked Zakheim (and I hired him). He set up a panel of lawyers. He paid for three dubious professors to come from Italy and sign an attestation of sanity for him. For nearly two years the property went on leaking. Until Zakheim managed to get him taken in for observation and eventually committed. And then he changed his tune again and wrote and signed a detailed will in our favor, together with a short, melancholy letter in which he forgave us and asked our forgiveness and warned us against each other and implored us to have pity on the child, and signed it with the words "I bow down in awe before the depth of your afflictions."

Since 1966 he has been living in a private room in a sanatorium on Mount Carmel. Silently staring at the sea. Twice I went to see him, but he did not recognize me. Is it true, as Zakheim tells me, that you still visit him occasionally. What for?

It was with his money that we built the villa in Yefe Nof. Even though the abandoned castle between Binyamina and Zikhron is still registered in my name. Zakheim maintains that its value has reached a peak, and begs me to sell quickly, before the fashion changes. Perhaps I should leave it all for some scheme? To drain the Huleh Marshes? Or to paint the Black Sea white? Or to rescue stray dogs? In fact, why not to Boaz? To Sommo? To both of them? I shall compensate your Sommo for everything: his color, his height, his humiliation. I shall give him a belated dowry. I have nothing to do with my property. Or with the time I have left.

Or perhaps I won't leave it to anybody just yet. On the contrary, I'll come back. I shall move into the crumbling kitchen, remove the beam from the door leading to the rest of the house, and slowly restore it. I shall mend the broken fountain. Restock the pool with goldfish. I shall establish my own settlement. Perhaps we shall run away there, the two of us? And live like a couple of pioneers in the crumbling building? In your honor I shall dress in black robes and put a cowl over my head.

Only write and let me know what you want.

I am left owing you an answer: Why did I divorce you? Among the papers on my desk is a note in which I wrote that the word *ritual* comes from the Latin *ritus*, which means something like "right condition." Or perhaps "fixed habit." As for *fanaticism*, it may possibly come from *fanum*, meaning "temple" or "place of worship." And what of *humility*? *Humility* comes from *humilis*, which comes, it seems, from *humus*, "earth." And is there humility in the earth? Apparently anyone can come and do whatever he feels like doing to it. Dig and plow and sow. But eventually it swallows all its masters. Standing there, eternally silent.

You have the womb—you have the advantage. That is the answer to your question. I never had a chance and that was why I ran away from you. Until your long arm reached me in my hideaway. Your victory was child's play. From a range of twelve thousand miles you managed to score a bull's-eye on an empty abandoned tank.

Ten to midnight. The storm has died down a little but there is still no regular power. Perhaps I'll call Annabel, my secretary, and wake her up. I'll tell her to get the Scotch out and make me a light supper. I'll tell her I'm on my way. She is a divorcee, about thirty, embittered, diminutive, bespectacled, ruthlessly efficient, always dressed in jeans and chunky sweaters. Chain-smokes. I'll call a taxi and in half an hour I'll be ringing her bell. The moment she opens the door I'll shock her with a hug and proceed to crush her lips with mine. Before she can collect herself I'll ask her to marry me and demand an instant reply. My famous name, plus my aura of grim manliness, plus the smell of battlefields that clings to me, plus my property, minus love, plus the growth that has been removed from my kidney, in return for her stunned consent to bear my surname and look after me if my illness gets worse. I'll buy her a sweet house in one of the delightful suburbs, on condition that we share it with a mentally disturbed giant of sixteen, who will have permission to invite girls home without any obligation to leave a light on in the shower or inspection doors open. The ticket will be sent to him in Hebron tomorrow morning. Zakheim can worry about the rest.

It's no good, Ilana. My hatred is peeling away from me like old plaster. By the neon light in the room, with the lightning falling into the lake in the darkness, I do not have it in my power to thaw the cold in my bones. In fact, it's extremely simple: when the electricity was cut, the heating also stopped working. And so I got up and put on a jacket. But no improvement was apparent. My hatred is being dashed from my clasp like the sword from the hands of Goliath after the pebble sank into him. This is the sword you will lift and kill me with. But you have nothing to boast about: you slew a dying dragon. Perhaps you will get the credit for putting me out of my misery?

Just now there was a hoot outside in the darkness. Because the darkness outside is complete, apart from a thin line of radioactive purple on the horizon. A hoot from the outer darkness where according to Jesus there is "howling and gnashing of teeth." Was it a boat? Or a train arriving from the prairies? It is hard to know, because the wind is frenziedly whistling a single, sharp high note. And the power is still off. My eyes ache from writing in this mortuary light. I have here in my office a bed, a closet, and a small bathroom. But the narrow bed, between two metal file cabinets, suddenly frightens me. As though there is a corpse laid out on it. Surely it is only the clothes I unpacked in a hurry when I got back from London this morning.

There is that hooting again. This time nearby. So it wasn't a boat or a train, but the plaintive siren of an emergency vehicle. An ambulance? A police car? There's been a crime in one of the neighboring streets. Somebody is in big trouble. Or is there a fire—a building on fire and threatening to take its neighbors and all the neighborhood with it? Has a man decided he's had enough and jumped from the top of a skyscraper? Someone who lived by the sword dying by the sword?

The emergency lighting sheds its pallor on me. It is a ghostly mercury light, the kind used in operating theaters. I loved you once and there was a picture in my brain: You and me on a summer's evening sitting on the veranda of our home facing the Jerusalem hills and the child playing with bricks. Sundae glasses on the table. And a newspaper that we are not reading. You are embroidering a tablecloth and I am making a stork from a pine cone and slivers of wood. That was the picture. We weren't able. And now it's late.

Your Vampire

———

(Note delivered by hand)

Dear Mr. Zakheim, I shall hand you this note at the end of our meeting today at the Café Savyon. I'm not going to go on meeting you. My ex-husband will have to find another way of getting his letters to me. I can't see why he doesn't send them by mail, as I shall do from now on. I am writing this note only because it would be difficult for me to tell you to your face that you disgust me. Every time I have had to shake hands with you I have felt as if I were holding a frog. The shady "deal" that you hinted at, in connection with Alex's inheritance, was the last straw. Perhaps the fact that in the past you were a witness to my misfortune has unsettled you completely. You did not understand my misfortune and even today you understand nothing. My ex-husband, my present husband, and perhaps my son too, know and understand what happened then, but you do not, Mr. Zakheim. You are on the outside.

Ilana Sommo

Despite everything, I would do what you want if only you could find a way of bringing him back to me. And because of his illness it is urgent.

Mr. Michael Sommo   *Jerusalem*
Isaac's Tent Religious State High School   5.7.1976
Jerusalem

My dear Mr. Sommo,

I am in receipt of yours of 13 Sivan. I delayed replying so as to learn your proposals. Meanwhile we have succeeded by a combined effort in getting our elephant through the eye of the needle. It would not occur to me to compete with you on your home ground, but I wonder if my memory can be deceiving me about the city of Kiryat Arba, or is it somehow connected with giants even in the Bible? You did an excellent job with our young hero. (I gather that his new police record has been closed through internal intervention.) I take my hat off to you. Would it be possible to make use of your magical powers again on other occasions? With talents and contacts such as yours, it is not you who should hire my humble services— as you suggested in your letter—but perhaps the other way around?

Which brings me straight to the body of your letter and to our very fruitful telephone conversation of yesterday. I confess unashamedly that I have no special feelings about the Territories, etc. It is possible that I should be inclined, like you, simply to swallow them whole were it not for the Arabs who live there. And I can do without them. I therefore perused respectfully the prospectus for your organization that you kindly enclosed with your letter. Your plan is to pay each Arab in full for his land and property and give him a one-way ticket at our expense. The aspect that strikes me as problematical is, naturally, the multiplication of, let us say, twenty thousand dollars by two million Arabs, give or take a billion dollars or so. To finance this migration we would have to sell the whole of the state, and would still get into debt. Is it really worth selling the State of Israel to buy the Territories? Surely instead of that we could simply do a swap: we can go up to the cool sacred mountains, and they can take our place on the damp coastal plain. They might agree to that of their own free will.

With your permission I shall dwell for another brief moment on the notion of exchanging the coastal plain for the mountains. To my regret it would appear that our dear Dr. Gideon has changed his mind about selling his property in Zikhron Yaakov. Even though it is possible that in the near future he will change it back again. Recently it has proved rather hard to gauge his state of mind. Mr. N. of Paris will therefore have to gird himself with patience. You see, my friend, Zakheim's long nose sniffs into everything: from certain delightful persons it has become known to me that Mr. N., who at one time was your friend in the Betar youth movement in Paris and who over the years has built up an empire in women's clothing, is the holy ghost that begat, with your collaboration, the Jewish Fellowship Movement. Between you and me, Mr. Sommo, I am also aware of the fact that it was our very own Mr. N. who financed your semisecret trip to Paris last spring. Moreover, I am also aware that the purpose of your trip was to negotiate on behalf of your organization with a certain Christian religious order, whose headquarters are in Toulouse, concerning some land belonging to the aforementioned order and situated to the west of Bethlehem, on the West Bank. And again, it was the same tireless Mr. N. who exerted himself to arrange for the restoration of your French citizenship, so as to give you a legal basis for a transaction that Mr. N. himself, for understandable reasons, preferred not to be involved with in any formal sense. You see, my friend, this transaction fascinates me too. The robed gentlemen from Toulouse are not prepared to sell you their God's little acre in the Holy Land, but they will apparently agree to exchange the fields of Bethlehem for an ample building with appropriately ample lands attached in a central location within the pre-1967 borders. No doubt for missionary purposes. All this seems perfectly logical to me. While the readiness of Mr. N. to finance such a deal I accept as a fact. So far, all well and good. We would be able to complete the triangle Bethlehem-Toulouse-Zikhron admirably were it not for the volatile state of mind of our learned friend. I shall endeavor to soften him up to the best of my modest abilities and to the advantage of all the parties concerned.

And in the meantime my advice is as follows: Out of both ethical and practical considerations it is preferable for me not to undertake to manage your private affairs or to represent your organization. Which relieves you of the obligation to pay me any fee. On the other hand, I shall be delighted to advise you gratis on any matter on which you may decide to rely on my modest talents. (And with your permission I shall commence with the suggestion that you have one or two decent suits made: from now on you are, after all, a highly respected man of property, and liable to be even more highly respected in consequence of the tragic aspects of the Dr. Gideon episode. Provided of course you know how to take a hint here and there.) Your public position too contains the seeds of great and wonderful things, Mr. Sommo; it is possible that the day is nigh when you will be called to higher spheres.

But the matter of dress is, of course, peripheral. The substance of my hopes I pin on the meeting I have arranged for Monday between you and my son-in-law, the industrialist Zohar Etgar, of Herzlia. (Zohar is married to my only daughter, Dorit, and he is the father of my two grandchildren.) I have no doubt, Michel—if you will permit me to address you by this name—that you will find him to be a young man after your own heart. Recently he has been planning, like you, to move into land. And by the way, Zohar, even more than I, is inclined to bet on a change of government within the next two years. Such a change is bound to entail the opening up of exciting new horizons in the Sinai, the West Bank, and the Gaza Strip for forward-looking men like ourselves. I am certain that the two of you, my son-in-law and you, will bring abundant advantages to one another: your wealth and good connections will be worth their weight in gold in the aftermath of the aforementioned change, while Zohar's energy will be directed into promising channels.

As for me, as I have said I will continue to keep an eye on things from Dr. Gideon's angle. I have reason to hope that I will soon be able to bring you glad tidings concerning the property in Zikhron. Provided we gird ourselves with patience and trust one another.

In conclusion I am compelled to touch on a somewhat delicate point. I will do so with extreme brevity. An intensive correspondence has evolved between your good wife and her former husband. This correspondence strikes me as, to say the least, puzzling: in my humble opinion no good will come of it to any of the parties. Dr. Gideon's illness is likely to drive him into unexpected behavior. His will in its present disposition is rather positive from your point of view (you will appreciate that I am unable to expatiate on this point). This matter opens up numerous avenues for future collaboration between your good self and my son-in-law. Whereas the renewed contacts with the lady are liable to upset the applecart, not to mention other avenues implied in this liaison, which are not compatible with good taste from your point of view. Women, my dear Michel, are in my humble opinion very much like us in certain respects, but in others they are astonishingly different. And I am referring to those respects in which the most stupid woman is cleverer than the cleverest of us. Therefore if I were you I would keep a sharp lookout. I shall take my leave of this embarrassing topic with the age-old words with which you closed your esteemed letter: *"verb. sap."*

> *With hopeful good wishes,*
> *Yours admiringly,*
> *Manfred Zakheim*

P.S.: Contrary to the supposition expressed in your letter, I do not have the honor to be numbered among the survivors of the Holocaust. My family brought me to this country in 1925, when I was a child of ten. This in no way detracts from my admiration for your perspicacity. M. Z.

—

Sommo Family
Tarnaz 7
Jerusalem

Hi Michel and Ilana

Everythings fine with me here in Kiryat Arba and I havent got
into trubble with anybody. But you no Michel your not rite? Even
tho I respect you and Im not forgetting all the favors youve done for
me every time Ive been in trubble but thats just the problem. I
never hit anyone only when Im rite—not 99 percent rite but 100
percent rite. Even then I dont always hit them, mostly I just drop
it. Thats how it was that time with the teacher in Telamim when
I was rite and the same the time with Abram Abudaram and the
time with the cops in Sharm. I was always in the rite and I still got
into trubble and you really saved me, only every time you want to
run my life for me do this dont do that like if I wasnt rite and like
if I had to pay you back all the time for the things Ive done wrong
that I havent done wrong at all. Your not rite Michel.

You really saved me from reform school but only on condition
I agreed to Kiryat Arba because theres an optics workshop here thats
OK for me but the rest of it isnt OK at all. The religious studies
Im not intrested in at all and as for girls you never see them here.
Well only in the distance. The men do try to be nice (some of
them) and to do favors all very nice but why me all of a sudden?
What am I a religion freak or something? I dont like the way they
talk about the arabs here behind there backs (some of them). OK
maybe its true once an arab always an arab so what? They could
say the same about you once Michel always Michel so what? Thats
not a reason to look down on people or to make fun of them. Im
against making fun of people. And Im against you looking after the
money that belongs to me and Ilana the money from America and
running my life for me. You run Ilanas life to but thats her problem.
Do you think your G-d Michel?

Now I supose youll rite me that Im biting the hand that feeds
me but youre hand never fed me nothing Michel. All the time Im

working and earning money. The money that youve got is mine and that means Im feeding you! I want to ask you too favors that you give me some money and permission from the police to leve hear and if you want to no were to? the truth is I dont no. So whats rong with wandering round some before you decide were to settle down. Didn't you wander round in Algiers and France and Israel before you decided? The candy rappers in the envelope are for Yifat take care not to crumpel them and tell her there from me Boaz. Hi Ilana dont worry about me. Please tell him to pay me some of my money and fix it up for me to leve hear so as I dont get into more trouble for hitting people.

Thanks Boaz B.

———

To Boaz Brandstetter (% Schulvass)   *By the Grace of G-d*
Ancestral Homeland Street 10   *Jerusalem*
Kiryat Arba   *13th of Tammuz 5736 (17.7.76)*

Dear stubborn and rebellious wise-guy Boaz!

More than anything else I am pleased with your progress in the optical department and because you are earning your keep honorably and participating in the rebuilding of the Land and going from strength to strength and even volunteering as night guard two nights a week. All this is on the credit side. Well done. But on the debit side, my heart bleeds at your slackness in your studies. We are the People of the Book, Boaz, and a Jew without Torah is worse than a beast of the field.

Your letter was very poor (a) in its spelling and style and (b) in its content. Like a backward child's! The reason I say this, Boaz, is precisely that I am very fond of you. Otherwise I would long ago have let you go to hell and there's an end of it. It would appear that you are even more of an ass now than you used to be, and all you've learned from your troubles is how to go looking for more trouble. As it is written: "Though you should bray a fool in a mortar yet his foolishness will not depart from him" (Proverbs 27:22). Wisdom, Boaz, does not go according to weight or bulk; otherwise Og the giant king of Bashan would be considered by us the wisest of men.

I have done a lot for you, far beyond what I had to, and you know that, but if you have made your mind up to leave Kiryat Arba and to go and do what is evil in the sight of the Lord, then let's see you, go ahead, who's stopping you? What, have I bound you with a chain? Please yourself. Go. We'll see how far you get with the spelling of an Arab and the hooliganism of a gentile. You've already passed your bar mitzvah, thank God, and so you're no longer subject to our authority. So why not? Go ahead, follow in the footsteps of your dear father and see what happens. Only don't come running to Michel for relief and deliverance. Deliverance I can understand, but you have the cheek to ask me for relief as well? And since we are on the subject of relief, in other words the money that you so unwisely mentioned in your letter, that money really and truly does belong to your mother, you, and Yifat in three equal parts, and you Boaz shall receive your share from me in full when you are twenty-one and not a day sooner. If your dear father had wanted you to have the money right away, who was to prevent his giving the check straight to you, instead of to me? So it would seem that despite everything he knew what he was doing, more or less, and he gave me the responsibility over you. And if you don't like it, please feel free to turn to him and lodge a complaint against me.

In general, as far as I am concerned, Boaz, you can do whatever you like, you can even turn into an Arab if you are on their side. Only do me a favor and don't try to teach me what an Arab is. I grew up among them and I know them well. You may be surprised to hear me say that the Arab is fundamentally very positive, he has many noble characteriestics, and in his religion there are many fine things that were taken straight from Judaism. But bloodshed is very deeply ingrained in their tradition. What can we do, Boaz? It is just as the Bible says about Ishamel: a wild man, whose hand is against every man and the hand of every man is against him. In their Koran it is written: the faith of Muhammad by the sword. And in our Torah it is written: Zion shall be redeemed by justice. That's the whole difference. Now you choose which of the two suits you better.

For the last time I urge you to take yourself in hand and not to heap wrong upon wrong. Next Tuesday afternoon we are having a birthday party for your sister. Come home the day before, help your mother a little and make the little girl happy. She loves you! I am enclosing a postal order for six hundred pounds for you. You asked me for money, after all. And don't worry, Boaz, I am not deducting this from the inheritance that I am looking after for you until you grow up. You will also find in the envelope a picture of a dog by Yifat, only it came out with six legs.

Listen to me, Boaz: Let's consider your letter as if it had never been written, shall we? Call it null and void? Forget it ever existed. Your mother sends you her love, and I shall sign off despite everything with friendship and affection,

Yours,
Michel

———

To Lt.-Col. Prof. A. Gideon
Political Science Department
Midwest University
Illinois, Chicago, USA

Hi!

It's Boaz Brandstetter writing to you. You know who I am. I got your adress from my mother because Mr. Zakkeim wouldnt let me have it and from Michel Sommo I dont want any more favors. Not from you neither. So Ill be brief and come strait to the point. You gave some money to Michel Sommo for me. I found out about it from him and also from Mr. Zakkeim who told me to go and get it from Michel. But Michel wont give me the money. On the contrary. Every time Ive got into trouble he helped me but the money he takes for himself, he only left me a few pennies and he also wants to tell me what to do and what not to do. Now I am living in Kiryat Arba working and earning money in a optikal workshop but its not the place for me and its none of your bussness why. What I want is for nobody to tell me what to do and what not to do. Now: if you really gave the money to Michel Sommo then Ive got nothing more to say and this letter is canceled. But if you meant it for me then why didnt the money get to me? Thats all I want to ask.

Boaz B.

———

To Boaz Gideon (Brandstetter)   *Chicago*
% the Schulvass Family   *23.7.76*
10 Ancestral Homeland Street
Kiryat Arba, Israel

Dear Boaz,

I got your short letter. I won't be long either. You want to be on your own and not be told what you should or shouldn't do. I accept that. As a matter of fact, I wanted exactly the same thing but I wasn't strong enough. I suggest we forget for the time being about the money that is presently with Sommo. I have two possibilities for you, one in America and one in Israel. Would you like to come to America? Make up your mind and you'll get a ticket. I'll fix you up with somewhere to stay and a job. Maybe even in optics. Eventually you can also study whatever interests you. If you want to repay me the cost out of your pay here, you can. It's not urgent and it's not compulsory. But take into account that in America you'll have a problem with the language. At least to start with. Also that here nobody has cousins in the police.

The alternative is that you can have at your disposal a large empty house near Zikhron Yaakov. At present it's in poor condition,

112

but you have an excellent pair of hands. If you gradually make a start on restoring the house, I'll pay you a fair monthly wage and I'll cover all the expenditure on building materials, etc. You can invite anyone you like to live with you in the building, which is standing abandoned at the moment. There's a lot to be done there. There's scope for some agriculture. And it's not far from the seaside. But you'll be free to do only what you want.

Whether you decide to come to America or to go to the house in Zikhron, all you have to do is to see a lawyer by the name of Roberto di Modena. He is in Jerusalem, in the same office as Mr. Zakheim, whom you know and visited once. Pay attention: Don't go to Zakheim. Go straight to di Modena and tell him what you have decided. He has already had instructions to implement your decision at once, either way. You don't have to reply to me. Be free and strong, and if you can, try to judge me fairly too.

Your Dad

———

A GIDEON MIDWEST UNIV CHICAGO

HAVE MADE THE REQUISITE ARRANGEMENTS FOR BOAZS
INSTALLATION IN THE PROPERTY THERE WERE SOME FORMAL
DIFFICULTIES WHICH IM SEEING TO I GAVE HIM THE SUM YOU FIXED
FOR PRELIMINARY ARRANGEMENTS IN FUTURE SHALL PAY HIM
MONTHLY AS PER YOUR INSTRUCTIONS HE HAS BEEN IN ZIKHRON
SINCE YESTERDAY MY PARTNER IS BOILING WITH RAGE ROBERTO
DIMODENA

———

GIDEON MIDWEST UNIV CHICAGO

MACHIAVELLI DONT FORCE ME TO FIGHT YOU THE PURCHASER IS
NOW PREPARED TO PAY ELEVEN FOR ZIKHRON PROPERTY

UNDERTAKES TO EMPLOY BOAZ THERE ON MONTHLY WAGE YOUR
AGREEMENT REQUIRED INSTANTER CONTINUE TO CONSIDER MYSELF
YOUR FRIEND THE ONLY ONE YOUVE GOT DESPITE BITTER
HUMILIATION MANFRED

———

PERSONAL ZAKHEIM JERUSALEM ISRAEL

ZIKHRON PROPERTY NOT REPEAT NOT FOR SALE ROBERTO REPEAT
ROBERTO HANDLES ALL MY AFFAIRS KINDLY HAND OVER ALL PAPERS
TO HIM GO ON TRYING YOUR LUCK WITH SOMMO YOU POOR MANS
IAGO WILL YOU TRY TO HAVE ME PUT AWAY ON MOUNT CARMEL
YOUR GRANDCHILDREN ARE STILL IN MY WILL WATCH OUT ALEX

———

Ilana Sommo   1.8.76
Tarnaz 7
Jerusalem

Ilana,

You say I don't understand anything. It's always been the same
story: Nobody can understand you. So be it. I am writing this time
only because of Boaz and because of Michel and Yifat. Michel
phoned me last night and told me that Boaz is leaving Kiryat Arba
and going to live by himself in the ruined house in Zikhron. So
Alex had decreed. I begged Michel not to try to interfere. I promised
that Yoash would go to Zikhron at the weekend to see what's going
on and how we can help. Maybe you'll admit now, if only to
yourself, that you made a mistake when you got in touch with Alex
again.

I'm wasting my words. You've got the urge once again to play
the tragic heroine. To star all over again in a new performance.
Even though Alex is stealing the show this time too. If you can't
manage any other way, the two of you, why don't you get up and
go and look for him in America? Michel will rise to the occasion

114

and make an excellent job of bringing Yifat up by himself. In time he'll find himself a woman from his own circle. Boaz will have an easier time too. And we'll do the best we can to help from here. You'll finally be completely redundant, if that's your secret wish. Because what's the point in going on with this reversal of the old refrain "My heart's in the east, and I'm in the furthermost west"?

It goes without saying that I'm not trying to persuade you to go. On the contrary. I'm writing to beg you to try to think again. To take yourself in hand. Try to tell yourself that Boaz doesn't need you. As a matter of fact, there's not one of us he really needs. Just try to understand that if you don't stop yourself now, Yifat will grow up exactly the same. Not needing anybody. What is it that drives you to throw away everything you have for the sake of something that doesn't and can't exist?

Of course you can reply sarcastically. Tell me not to stick my nose in. Or not reply at all. I only wrote because it is my duty to try to stop you, even if there's not much chance. So that you won't cause even more suffering to those you are still dear to.

I suggest you bring Yifat here to Beit Avraham for a week or two's rest. You can work in the storerooms for four hours a day. Or spend the mornings at the pool. You could help Yoash in the garden. After lunch we can take the children for a walk to the fish ponds or to the pine woods. Yifat can be fitted into the crèche. In the evenings we can sit on the lawn with neighbors and drink coffee. Michel is also invited, at least for the weekends. And I promise not to tinker with what according to you I can't understand. If you like, I'll listen and say nothing. If you like, we'll go to the macramé class or the classical-music group. From here everything will look a little different. And I also suggest that at this stage Yoash and I take charge of contacts with Boaz. What say you?

Rahel

———

115

Professor A. Gideon   *Jerusalem*
Political Science Department   2.8.76
Midwest University
Chicago, Illinois, U.S.A.

Dear Alec, genie and bottle both,

Don't go on writing to me via Zakheim. Your baldheaded troll
no longer amuses me. Just write to me by mail. Or come out and
show yourself. Or call for me to come to you—I'm still waiting for
an invitation to your wedding with air ticket enclosed. Just say the
word and I'll come—I'll even bring you a faded bouquet of flowers
from Jerusalem. It's nearly a month now since you were planning
to take some little secretary by storm, and I still haven't heard the
wedding march. Or have you lost your charms? Your masculine
battle scent? The fortune you inherited from your father? Your
dazzling world fame? Your hypnotic aura of death? Has all that
really rusted like tin armor? Did the beauty turn you down? Or
perhaps you still haven't learned how to propose to a woman without
your father's help?

I only got around to reading your letter at one o'clock this
morning. It lay waiting for me all day, hidden in my handbag, like
a viper, between my handkerchief and my lipstick. In the evening
Michel fell asleep in front of the television as usual. During "Sermon
for the Day" I woke him up, so he could watch the midnight news.
Yitzhak Rabin, in his opinion, is not a Jewish prime minister at all
but an American general who just happens to speak a little broken
Hebrew and is selling the state to Uncle Sam. Once again the non-
Jews are ruling us and we are kowtowing to them. Whereas he
considers me to be the most beautiful woman in the whole world.
So saying he kissed me on the forehead, stretching on tiptoe. I bent
down before him to undo the childish bows in his shoelaces. He
was tired and half-asleep. His voice was cracked from smoking.
When I put him to bed and tucked him in he said that the most
mysterious psalm in the book is the one that begins "To the Chief
Musician, on a remote, mute dove." He delivered a sort of sermon

on the words *remote, mute.* He called me his "mute dove." And while he was still talking he fell asleep, lying on his back, like a baby. Only then did I sit down to read your catalogue of woes, to the sound of his peaceful breathing mingled with the chorus of crickets in the wadi that divides us from the Arab village. I translated word for word your darts of vicious wit into agonized cries of pain. But when I got to the sword of Goliath and your dying dragon I wept inside. I couldn't go on reading. I hid your letter under the evening paper and went out to the kitchen to make myself lemon tea. Then I returned to you, and at the window there was a sharp Muslim moon cloaked in seven veils of mist.

I read and reread your concentrated seminar, the carnivorous plants, Bernanos and Ecclesiastes and Jesus, those who live by the sword shall die by the sword, and here a shivering chill took hold of me too. Just like you on the night of the sirens in Chicago. Even though here in Jerusalem it is a clammy, slightly milky summer's night, with no lightning, no storms on lakes, only distant barking on the shores of the desert.

I am not up to taking issue with you. Your razor-sharp brain always works on me like the barking of a machine gun: a deadly accurate burst of facts, inferences, and explanations from which there is no recovery. But nevertheless, this time I will answer back. Jesus and Bernanos were right, while you and Ecclesiastes may perhaps deserve only pity. There is happiness in the world, Alec, and suffering is not its opposite but the narrow passage through which stooping, crawling among nettles, we reach the silent clearing in the forest bathed in lunar silver.

You probably recall the famous statement at the beginning of *Anna Karenina*, in which Tolstoy, donning there the cloak of a calm village deity and hovering over the void full of benign toleration and loving kindness, declares from on high that all happy families resemble one another, while unhappy families are all unhappy in their own way. With all due respect to Tolstoy I'm telling you that the opposite is true: Unhappy people are mainly plunged in conventional suffering, living out in sterile routine one of five or six threadbare clichés of misery. Whereas happiness is a rare, fine vessel, a sort of Chinese vase, and the few people who have reached it have shaped and formed it line by line over the course of years, each in his own image and likeness, each in his own character, so that no two happinesses are alike. And in the molding of their happiness they have instilled their own suffering and humiliation. Like refining gold from ore. There *is* happiness in the world, Alec, even if it is more ephemeral than a dream. Indeed in your case it is beyond your reach. As a star is beyond the reach of a mole. Not "the satisfaction of approval," not praise and advancement and conquest and domination, not submission and surrender, but the thrill of fusion. The merging of the I with another. As an oyster enfolds a foreign body and is wounded and turns it into its pearl while the warm water still surrounds and encompasses everything. You have never tasted this fusion, not once in your whole life. When the body is a musical instrument in the hands of the soul. When Other and I strike root in each other and become a single coral. And when the drip of the stalactite slowly feeds the stalagmite until the two of them become one.

Think for example what it is like at precisely ten past seven on a summer evening in Jerusalem. The ridges of the mountains touched by jets of sunset. The last light starting to dissolve the stone-lined side streets as though stripping them of their stoniness. The sound of Arab pipes rising from the wadi with a prolonged moan, beyond joy or sorrow, as though the soul of the mountains were straining to lull their body to sleep and depart on its night journey. Or a couple of hours later, when stars come out over the Judaean desert and the silhouette of the minaret stands erect among the shadowy mud huts. When your fingers feel the rough weave of the upholstery, and outside the window an olive tree shines silver as it receives a gift of light from the table lamp inside your room, and for a moment the boundary between your fingertip and the material fades and the toucher is the touched and also the touch. The bread in your hand, the teaspoon, the glass of tea, the simple, speechless things are suddenly ringed with a fine primordial radiation. Lit up from within your soul and lighting it up in return. The joy of being and its simplicity descends and covers everything with the mystery of things that were here even before the creation of knowledge. The original things that you have been banished from eternally, exiled to the steppes of darkness over which you wander howling at a dead moon, roaming from whiteness to whiteness, searching to the edges of the tundra for something lost long since, even though you have forgotten what it was you lost or when or why: "His life is his prison while his death is limned to him as a prospect of paradoxical resurrection, a promise of miraculous redemption from his vale of tears." The quotation comes from your book. The wolf howling in the darkness at the moon on the steppe is my own contribution.

The love was also my contribution. Which you rebuffed. Have you ever loved anybody? Me? Perhaps your son?

Lies, Alec. You have never loved anyone. You conquered me. And then you abandoned me, like an objective that has lost its value. Now you have decided to launch an offensive against Michel to wrest Boaz from him. All these years you saw your son as nothing more than a sort of meaningless sandhill, until you received information from me that the enemy had suddenly seen some value in that sandhill and was trying to hold onto it. And then you summoned your forces for a lightning assault. And won again, almost as an afterthought. Love is alien to you. You don't even know the meaning of the word. To destroy, to smash, to shatter, to flatten, to wipe out, to mop up, to screw, to terminate, to annihilate, to expunge, to incinerate—these are the measures of your world and the moonscapes among which you roam, with Zakheim as your Sancho Panza. And that is where you are now trying to banish our son as well.

Now I'll reveal something that is bound to cause you pleasure: Your money has already begun to corrupt my life with Michel. For six years Michel and I have been struggling, like two survivors of a shipwreck, to build a rough hut for shelter in some corner of a desert island. To make it warm and light. I used to get up early in the morning to make him his sandwiches, fill his blue plastic thermos bottle with coffee, fetch his morning paper, pack it all in his worn briefcase and send him off to work. Then I would get Yifat dressed and feed her. Do the housework to the sound of music on the radio. Take care of the garden and the potted plants on the veranda (various kinds of herbs that Michel grows in old crates). Between ten and twelve, while the child was still at the crèche, I would go out to shop. Find the time occasionally to read a book. One of my neighbors would come in for a chat in the kitchen. At one o'clock I would feed Yifat and warm up Michel's meal. When he got in I would serve him cold mineral water in summer or hot chocolate on a cold day. During his private lessons I would retreat to the kitchen to peel vegetables for the next day, bake a cake, wash the dishes, read a little more. Serve him Turkish coffee. Listen to a concert on the radio while doing the ironing, until the child woke up. After his private lessons, when he settled down to his marking, I would send her out to play in the yard with the neighbors' children and stand at the window watching the mountains and the olive trees. On sunny Saturdays in winter, when Michel had finished reading his way through two newspapers, we would go for a walk, the three of us, in the Talpiyyot woods, on the hill of the High Commissioner's Residence, or to the foot of Mar Elias Monastery. Michel was good at inventing amusing games. He did not stand on his dignity. He would mimic a furious billy goat, a frog, a speaker at a party meeting, and the two of us would laugh till the tears ran. When we got back, he would fall asleep surrounded by the weekend supplements in his threadbare armchair, the child would sleep on the rug at his feet, and I would read one of the novels that Michel always remembered to borrow for me at the city library. Even though he used to tease me for my "frivolous reading," he never forgot to bring one or two home for me each week on his way back from work. Nor did he ever omit to buy me a small bunch of flowers every Sabbath eve. Which he would hand to me with a funny little French bow. Sometimes he would surprise me with a handkerchief, a bottle of scent, some picture magazine he thought I might find interesting, which he himself would inevitably end up consuming from cover to cover, reading passages aloud to me.

At the end of the Sabbath it was our custom to go out on the veranda, sit on deck chairs, and eat peanuts while watching the sunset. Sometimes Michel would start to tell me, in his warm, scorched voice, about his time in Paris. He would describe his wanderings among the museums "tasting the delights of Europe," depicting the bridges and boulevards in pseudo-modest terms, as though he himself had designed them, joking about his poverty and his degradation. Sometimes he would amuse Yifat with animal fables and tall stories. Occasionally, when the sun went down, we would decide not to turn on the light on the veranda, and my daughter and I in the dark would learn from him his strange family songs, tunes in which guttural joy almost verged upon wailing. Before bedtime, pillow fights would break out among us, until the time came to put Yifat to sleep with a fairy tale. Then we would sit on the settee, holding hands like children, and he would lecture me on his views, analyze the political situation, let me share his visions, which he would quickly dismiss with a wave of the hand, as though he had merely been joking.

So, like people slowly saving a nest egg, we built up our meager stock of happiness evening by evening. We shaped our Chinese vase. We feathered a love nest for mute doves. In bed I initiated him into ecstasies he had not imagined in his wildest dreams, and Michel repaid me from his reserves of silent, fervent adoration. Until you opened up the windows of heaven on him and flooded him with your money, like an airplane spraying a field with poisonous pesticides, and at once everything began to wither and fade.

At the end of the school year Michel decided to resign from his job as a teacher of French at Isaac's Tent school. He explained to me that the time had come for him to "escape from bondage to liberty" and that he would soon demonstrate to me how "the moss on the wall would flourish like the cedar in Lebanon."

His new-found wealth he has decided for some reason to entrust to Zakheim and his son-in-law.

Ten days ago we were even privileged to receive a visit from the Etgars. Dorit, Zakheim's daughter, a bustling Tel Aviv beauty, who called Michel "Micky" and me "darling," led her tubby little

121

husband along on a lead; he was polite and nervous, and was wearing a tie, despite the heat, and frameless spectacles, and had a Kennedy haircut. They brought us a present of a wall-hanging featuring monkeys and tigers, which they had bought on their last trip to Bangkok. For Yifat they brought a windup doll with three speeds. Our flat did not suit them; no sooner had they arrived than they begged us to join them in their American car, which looked like a pleasure cruiser, and treat them to a "nice, wholesome tour round the pedigreed, nontourist Jerusalem." They took us to lunch at the Intercontinental Hotel. Evidently they had completely forgotten about the problem of kosher food: Michel was too shy to mention it, and invented a stomach upset. In the end all we ate there was hard-boiled eggs and cream cheese. They talked between themselves about politics, about the prospects for the opening up of the Sinai and the West Bank to private enterprise, and Zakheim's daughter tried to involve me in a discussion of the "just unbelievable" price of a Saint Bernard puppy and the equally unbelievable cost of keeping one in Israel. The bespectacled young man insisted on beginning every sentence with "Let's say that," and his wife classified everything under the sun as either "frightful" or "just fantastic," until I wanted to scream. When we parted they issued an invitation to us to spend a weekend with them in their house in Kfar Shmar-yahu, with a choice between the sea and their private pool for swimming. Afterward, when I said to Michel that as far as I was concerned he could go and stay with them as often as he liked but without me, my husband replied, "Let's say that you'll think it over."

And then a week ago I learned, by accident, that Michel is selling our flat (with the unfinished extension) to one of his cousins, with whom he has signed a contract to purchase a new home in the restored Jewish Quarter in the Old City. Perhaps because I did not manage to look surprised, Michel teased me by calling me "Vashti." He has also rejoined the National Religious Party, and simultaneously decided to take out a subscription to the newspaper *Haarets*.

Every morning he sets out for his new business, the nature of which is not clear to me, and he returns late in the evening. Instead of his invariable sports slacks and checked jacket, he has bought himself a pale blue lightweight summer suit in Dacron, which makes him look to me like a sharp secondhand car salesman in an American movie. No longer do we sit outside on the veranda to watch the twilight on Saturday evenings. No longer do the three of us engage in pillow fights before bedtime. Religious land dealers come to call after the Melave Malka and the formal conclusion of the Sabbath. Leaning over to serve them coffee I catch a whiff of cholent and gefilte fish. Self-satisfied types who feel obliged as a matter of politeness to praise my looks to him and to me the biscuits I bought at the supermarket. Making a fuss of Yifat with crude grimaces, puzzling her with the twittering they produce in her honor. Michel orders her to sing or recite for them and she obeys. Afterward he hints to me that we have both done our job. And then he confers with them for a long time on the veranda.

I put Yifat to bed. Shout at her for nothing. I shut myself away in the kitchen and try to concentrate on a book, but every now and again a gust of greasy laughter intrudes on me. Michel chuckles too, but in a strained way, like a waiter who has gone up in the world. When we are left alone he devotes himself once more to my education, trying to teach me about building plots, grants, Jordanian property laws, loans, working capital, bonuses, financial securities, gross incomes, the cost of infrastructure investments. The self-confidence of a sleepwalker has descended upon him; he has no doubt at all that you are going to bequeath to him (or make over to him in your lifetime) all your money and property. Or to me. Or to Boaz. At any event he sees your money as virtually at his disposal already. "And as it is written, those engaged in fulfilling a pious mission can come to no harm." As for you, he believes that "it has been decreed from on high" that you will try to atone for your sins through his agency, by means of a "significant" donation to the rebuilding of the Land. He doesn't mind which of us you choose to give the money to; "We, with God's help, shall use it for

Torah, commandments and good deeds, and as we continue to invest it in the redemption of the Land so shall it prosper and multiply." Last week he boasted to me about a glass of tea he had drunk in the Parliament canteen with a deputy minister and a director general.

Furthermore, he has made up his mind to have driving lessons. And to buy a car soon, so that he can be, as he put it, "my cabbie." And meanwhile his oddlings, the Russian and American youngsters with the strange gleam in their eyes, who used to sneak in in gym shoes to whisper with him in the yard, come less often than they used to. Maybe he meets them somewhere else. A complacent arrogance informs his new gait. He no longer plays the fool or mimics frogs and goats. Instead he has adopted a humorous mannerism from his brother the politician: interspersing his speech with Yiddish words that he deliberately distorts. He has even changed his brand of after-shave; the new smell wafts around the flat even when Michel isn't here. Last week he was privileged to be invited to take part in some sort of mystery tour in the vicinity of Ramallah, in which your Moshe Dayan was also involved. Michel came back bursting with self-importance and secrecy, and as full of enthusiasm as a schoolboy. He would not stop worshiping the "ideological astuteness" of Dayan, who "looks as if he stepped straight out of the Book of Judges." He deplored the crying waste of the fact that at the moment his new hero has no government position. He boasted about how Dayan had suddenly fired a tricky question at him and how he had answered without the slightest hesitation, as he put it, "on the spot, straight from the hip," that "through stratagems thou shalt acquire a land." And earned a smile from Dayan and the comment "sharp fellow."

"Michel," I said, "what's happening to you? Are you going out of your mind?" He clasped my shoulder in an uncharacteristic "one of the boys" sort of way, smiled, and replied tenderly, "Out of my mind? No, not at all. Out of my shame and poverty! Let's say, Madame Sommo, that one of these days you'll be living here like the Queen of Sheba. Your food, your raiment, and your marital dues I shall not diminish, even if you do not recognize the source of the allusion. It won't be long before my brother himself comes to us to ask favors, and he shall not find our bounty deficient. As it is written, 'the meek shall inherit the earth.' "

I could not resist shooting just a little dart at him: I asked what had become of his Europa cigarettes all of a sudden, why had he taken to smoking Dunhill? Michel was not put out. For an instant he looked at me, amused, and at once shrugged his shoulders, chuckled "Women!" and went to the kitchen to make us a meal of hamburgers and fried potatoes. And suddenly I hated him.

So, you have won again. With a single move you have demolished our little cottage, smashed our Chinese vase, and dragged out of the depths of Michel a grotesque little Alec in a cheap popular edition. Meanwhile, like a circus juggler, you simultaneously sent Zakheim to hell with a kick of your heel at the same time as your breath was plucking Boaz from our enfeebled grasp and wafting him all the way to Zikhron, where you planted him with extreme precision right on the square that you had designated for him on your campaign map. And all this you did without even bothering to emerge from your thick cloud. Like a deadly satellite. All by remote control. Just by pressing a button.

These last lines I have just written with a smile. Do not hope this time for another suicide attempt, like those that brought you eventually to a dry snigger and the "stomach-pump drill." This time I shall introduce a little variety. I shall reward surprise with surprise.

Here I shall stop. I'll leave you in the dark. Go stand at your window. Hug your shoulders. Or lie awake on the couch in your office between the two metal file cabinets and wait beyond despair for a grace that you do not believe in. But I do believe.

Ilana

———

Notes by Professor A. A. Gideon written on little cards.

176.   Whereas his sense of time is utterly two-dimensional: Past and Future. In his tormented mind, the previous, the original, glory, that was destroyed by the forces of defilement, and the promised glory, which will be reestablished with "the renewal of the days of old," after the Great Purge, are constantly reflected one in the other. The goal of his struggle is this: to be liberated from the grip of the Present. To raze it to its very foundations.

177.   The denial of the Present is a clock for the denial of the self: The Present is perceived as nightmare, as exile, as "eclipse," because the self—the focus of the sense of the Present—is experienced as unbearable depression.

178.   And in fact his sense of time is not two-dimensional but one-dimensional: the paradise that was is the paradise that will be.

178a.   The Present is therefore an unclean episode, a blot on the canvas of eternity; it must be erased (with blood and fire) from existence and even from memory, so as to do away with any barrier between the radiance of the Past and that of the Future, and to make possible the messianic merging of these two radiances. The distinction must be drawn between sacred and profane, and the profane (the Present, the self) must be entirely removed. Only thus will the circle be completed, the broken ring repaired.

178b.   The time before birth and the time after death are identical. It involves: Abolition of the self. Abolition of the whole of reality. Abolition of life. "Exaltation."

179. The realization of the ideal: The noble Past and the glittering Future converge and crush between them the impure Present. A sort of awesome, eternal timelessness descends upon the universe; its essence is above life, outside life, diametrically opposed to it. "This world is an antechamber before the world to come." "My kingdom is not of this world."

180. The ancient Hebrew language expresses this in its deep structure: it has no present tense. Instead it has only a participial form. "And Abraham *sitting* in the entrance to the tent." That is to say, not "Once upon a time Abraham sat," or "Abraham used to sit," or "At the time of writing these words Abraham is sitting," nor at the time of reading them, but like the stage directions of a play: "Every time the curtain goes up, we see Abraham sitting in the entrance to his tent." For all eternity. He sat, he sits, he will sit forever and ever in the entrance to that tent.

181. But, paradoxically, the desire to destroy the Present in the name of the Past and the Future embraces its own contradiction: the eradication of all tenses. Freezing. Eternal Now. When the days of old are renewed and the Kingdom of Heaven is established, everything will stop moving. The universe will stop dead. Movement will cease and the horizon too will move farther away. A perpetual present tense will hold sway. History, like the poets, is banished from Plato's ideal Republic. And Jesus' and Luther's and Marx's and Mao's and all the rest of them. And the wolf shall dwell with the lamb—not in a temporary truce but once and for all: the same wolf, the same lamb. Without a rustle or a breeze. The annihilation of death resembles death in every respect. The mystical Hebrew expression "the end of days" means just that: the end of days. Literally.

182. And yet another paradox: The elimination of the base Present in favor of a noble Present in which Past and Future meet also signifies the end of the struggle. The age of eternal peace and happiness. In which there is no need for fighters, for martyrs leading the way, for saviors and messiahs. In the kingdom of redemption there is therefore no place for a redeemer. The victory of revolution is its destruction, like the fire of the enigmatic Heraclitus. The liberated City of God is not in need of liberators.

183. The solution: to die on its threshold.

184. And so, with foam-flecked lips, he fights against the whole world of the Present in the name of Past and Future which he is sworn to turn to Pastless Futureless Present. An inherent contradiction. And so he is doomed to exist in a constant climate of terror, persecution, and suspicion. Lest the Present has outwitted him. Lest he has fallen into a snare or delusion. Lest the agents of the Present have succeeded in infiltrating, or penetrating in disguise, the heart of the camp of salvation. His punishment: the perpetual dread of shades of treachery on all sides. Elusive shades of treachery even within the cellars of his own soul. "The Devil slips in everywhere."

———

To Rahel Morag   4.8.76
Kibbutz Beit Avraham
Mobile Post, Lower Galilee

Dear Rahel,
    I ought to listen to what you say, and change. Break with the past. Become a loving spouse and housewife. Iron and cook and clean and sew. Take pleasure in my husband's achievements and

see in them my own happiness. Start making curtains for the new flat that we're moving to in the winter. Be content from now on with his warm smell, the smell of black bread and cheese and pickled olives. The smell of talcum powder and pee in the child's room at night. And the smells of frying in the kitchen. This gambling with "everything I have" is pointless. One mustn't play with fire. No knight on horseback will come to take me away. And if he does I won't go. If I did I'd only wrong them all once more and bring suffering on myself. Thank you for reminding me of my duty now and again. Forgive me for all the insults I've hurled at you without cause. You were right because you were born being right. From now on I'll be as good as gold. I'll put on my dressing gown and clean the windows and mosquito nets. I'll know my place. I'll prepare bowls of nuts for Michel and his guests. I'll see to it there's always enough coffee. I'll go with him myself to choose a nice suit for him instead of the blue one. I'll keep track of the housekeeping money. I'll put on my brown dress and go with him to social events he is invited to. I won't embarrass him. When he wants to speak, I'll shut up. When he gives me a hint that I should speak, I'll always talk sense, and charm all his acquaintances. Maybe I'll join his party. I'll start to think seriously about buying a carpet. Soon we'll have the telephone: he's already been moved up the waiting list, thanks to his friend Janine's brother. There'll be a washing machine too. And then a color TV. I'll go to Kfar Shmaryahu with him to stay with his business partners. I'll write down telephone messages for him on a little pad. I'll protect him from being disturbed. I'll shelter him tactfully from people asking favors. I'll go through the newspapers for him and mark items that could be interesting or useful for him. Every evening I'll wait for him to come home, serve him a good meal, run him a hot bath, and then I'll sit down to listen to the story of his day's successes. I'll report to him in general terms about the news of the kid and the house. I'll take care of the water and electricity bills myself. Each evening I'll put a freshly starched and pressed white shirt at the head of his bed for the next day. Every night I'll service him. Apart from nights when he has to sleep away from home for his work. Then I'll stay in by myself and study the history of art by correspondence. Or take up painting in watercolors. Or varnish the chairs. I'll reach such expertise in Oriental cooking that I may even get to be in his mother's class. I'll relieve him of the burden of worrying about Yifat, so that he can devote himself to his projects. His wife like a fruitful vine around his house. Her price is above rubies. The king's daughter all-glorious within. The years will slip by, and Michel will go from strength to strength. He will prosper in all his doings. I will hear his name on the radio. I'll stick pictures of him in an album. Every day I'll dust his souvenirs. I'll take it on myself to remember the celebrations and birthdays of all the tribe. Buy wedding presents. Send letters of condolence. Represent him at circumcisions. Check the inventory of the linen and make sure he always has clean socks. So life will flow in peaceable, respectable channels. Yifat will grow up in a warm and devoted home and in a truly stable atmosphere. Not like Boaz. When the time comes, we'll marry her to the son of a deputy minister or a company chairman. And I will be left alone. When I get up every morning I will find the house empty, because Michel will long since have gone out. I'll have coffee and tranquilizers, give instructions to the daily help, and go into town to spend the morning looking through the shops. When I get back I'll take a Valium or two and try to sleep till evening. I'll leaf through books of pictures. I'll dust the knickknacks. And every evening I'll stand waiting at the window; perhaps he will come. Or at least send an assistant to fetch a clean jacket and announce that he won't be long. I'll make some sandwiches for his driver. I'll delicately evade troublesome questions on the telephone. Keep away from busybodies and cameras. In idle moments I will sit and knit a sweater for a grandchild. I'll water the pot plants and polish the silver. Perhaps I'll take a course in Jewish thought, so that on Saturday nights I can surprise his guests and him with apposite quotations. Until they move on from small talk to serious conversation. And then I'll sneak away on tiptoe to the kitchen and sit there till they leave, choosing recipes from kosher cookbooks. Perhaps I'll finally join some politicians' wives' committee for deprived children. I'll learn to get involved. I won't be a burden. And I'll discreetly regulate the quantity of salt in his food in accordance with the doctor's instructions. As for myself, I'll go on a strict diet, so as not to embarrass him with an excess of aging flesh. I'll exercise. I'll take vitamins and tranquilizers. I'll dye my hair when it goes grey. Or take to wearing a head scarf. For his sake I'll have a face-lift. But what shall I do about my bosom when it starts to sag? What shall I do about my legs when they swell and get covered with a network of varicose veins and burst blood vessels? What shall I do, Rahel? You're clever and knowledgeable and you must have some advice for your little sister, who promises to behave nicely and not to play with fire. Take care of yourself.

Ilana

Regards to the children and Yoash and thanks for the invitation.

———

GIDEON MIDWEST UNIV CHICAGO

FORGIVE YOU AND WILLING TO MAKE A FRESH START PURCHASER OFFERS TWELVE NOW FOR ZIKHRON PROPERTY WILL LET BOAZ STAY SAY YES AND I WITHDRAW RESIGNATION WORRIED ABOUT YOUR HEALTH MANFRED

———

PERSONAL ZAKHEIM JERUSALEM ISRAEL

NEGATIVE ALEX

———

GIDEON MIDWEST UNIV CHICAGO

I WONT LEAVE YOU MANFRED

———

PERSONAL ZAKHEIM JERUSALEM ISRAEL

REPORT ON BOAZ DITTO SOMMO MAY COME OVER IN FALL DONT
PRESS ME ALEX

———

Prof. A. Gideon   9.8.76
Midwest University
Chicago, Ill., U.S.A.

Dear Alec,

Yesterday morning I went to Haifa to visit your father in the
sanatorium on Mount Carmel. But on the way, on a momentary
impulse, I got off at Hadera and got on a bus to Zikhron. What
could I want from our son? I didn't try to imagine how he would
receive me. What I would do if he threw me out. Or made fun of
me. Or hid from me in some abandoned storehouse. What would
I say to him if he asked why I had come?

Try to see the picture: a blue-white summer's day (not blazing),
and me in jeans and a thin white blouse, with a straw bag hanging
from my shoulder, looking perhaps like a student on holiday, standing hesitantly before the rusting iron gate fitted with rusting padlocks
on rusting chains. Underneath my sandals the old grey gravel scrapes;
thistles and weeds are growing through it. Wasps are buzzing in the
air. Through the twisted ironwork I can see the great house in dark
Zikhron stone. The windows gape like toothless jaws. The tiled roof
has collapsed, and from inside the building, like a flame, shoots an
unruly mass of bougainvillaea, which meets the honeysuckle clinging to the outside walls.

I must have stood there for a quarter of an hour or so, my eyes searching unconsciously for the bellpull that used to be there a thousand years ago. Not a sound was heard from the house or the yard, except the soughing of the wind in the crests of the old palm trees and a different, fainter, whispering in the needles of the pines. The gardens in front of the house were smothered by brambles and couch grass. Overgrown oleanders, flowering as red as pirates, had completely buried the ornamental fish pool, the fountain, and the mosaic terrace. Here there once stood strange shapeless stone sculptures by Melnikoff. Presumably long since stolen. A faint smell of decomposition reached my nostrils. A panic-stricken field mouse shot past my feet like an arrow. And who was I waiting for? Perhaps for the uniformed Armenian servant to come and open the gate for me with a deferential bow?

Over the years the town of Zikhron has moved closer to your house but it has not quite reached it. Down the slope stood modern houses embellished with tasteless turrets. Their ugliness seemed to relieve somewhat your father's pretentious architecture. Time and ruin have bestowed a certain charm on the melancholy ogre's castle.

An unseen bird startled me for an instant with a noise that sounded like barking. Then the silence returned. To the east I could spy the Hills of Menasseh, wooded, flickering with passing flashes of capering green radiance. And to the west, as grey as your eyes and shrouded in mist, the sea stretched from the edge of the banana plantations. Among these plantations flashed the fish ponds of the neighboring kibbutz, against which your father waged a fierce crusade until you and Zakheim succeeded in defeating and confining him. An unfamiliar hand had painted on the rust of the gate the old-fashioned warning PRIVATE PROPERTY / STRICTLY NO ADMITTANCE / TRESPASSERS WILL BE PROSECUTED. This warning too had faded in the course of time.

How deep the silence of the place was! The emptiness. And all at once I was overcome with sadness for things gone that can never be brought back. A sharp longing, as piercing as a physical pain, for you and for your son and for your father. I thought about the childhood you spent on this gloomy estate, without a mother, without brothers or sisters, without a friend except your father's little rhesus monkey. Your mother's death one winter's night at three in the morning, when she was inadvertently left alone in her bedroom, which you showed me once, a boxlike attic room with a view of the sea from the window. The day nurse had gone home, the night nurse had not arrived, while your father had gone off to fetch a boatload of iron girders from Italy. I remembered her face in the sepia Russian-style photograph that always stood, flanked by two white candles, on a bookcase in your father's library, with a vase of everlasting flowers in perpetual attendance behind it. No doubt they have all perished—the photograph, the vase, the candles, and the flowers.

The memory of the photograph brought back to me the smell of tobacco, sadness, and vodka that always surrounded your father and his many rooms. It was like the smell of the sea and the desert that our son exhales now. Am I really your disaster? Or is it the other way around? Has disaster made its home in you and was it hopeless of me to try to bring back what could not be brought back and to put right what could never be put right?

I started to walk along the fence until I found a gap, and by bending down managed to force my way through the barbed wire. I circled the house at a distance through a thicket of wild vegetation. Again I was startled by the barking bird. Thistles as high as my shoulders pierced my clothes and my skin as I forced my way through them to reach the rear courtyard. Beside the garden shed in the shade of the twisted eucalyptus in which you built a tree house as a child I found a cracked bench. Scratched and dusty I collapsed onto it. From the house came silence. A pigeon flew in at one window and out another. A snakelike lizard darted under a heap of stones. At my feet a dung beetle struggled to push its tiny ball. The barking bird sounded a stone's throw away but I could not see it. A pair of wasps locked in a life-or-death struggle or in furious copulation traced a winding line in the air before landing with a thud on the bench. Crash landing? Reconciliation? Fusion? I did not dare lean over them. The place seemed deserted. Had Boaz disappeared again? I was seized by panic. There was a faint smell, tinged with scents of eucalyptus. I made up my mind to rest for a few minutes longer and then to leave.

In front of the shed I noticed a rusty plow in a heap of rotting sticks. There was also a dismantled rake. And a pair of large wooden wheels half buried in the ground. Among the debris I discovered the garden table around which we once sat, joking, drinking iced pomegranate juice from shapely Greek goblets and nibbling olives. What was left of that old table? A broken slab of marble resting miraculously on three tree stumps, stained green with pigeon droppings. Overhead feathery clouds traveled dreamily eastward. A thousand years had passed since that summer day when you brought me here for the first time to show me off to your father or to impress me with his magnificence. On the way here, in your arrogant army jeep with the antenna and the machine-gun mount, you had already jokingly warned me not to fall in love with your father. And he did indeed stir a kind of vague maternal tenderness in me: he was so like an overgrown dog, a giant dog, not very clever, baring his teeth to amuse and barking tumultuously and wagging not just his tail but half his body, pleading for an affectionate caress, dancing to make friends, leaping off with great commotion and returning to lay at my feet a twig or a rubber ball.

Yes, I did become fond of him. Affection, you know, maybe you've heard about it? Even though it has nothing in common with your area of specialization? Look it up in the dictionary, or in an encyclopedia. Try looking under A.

I found his crudeness touching. His clumsy advances. His melancholy masquerading as merriment. His rough voice. His appetite. His old-fashioned courtly manners. His tempestuous attentiveness. The roses he made a great fuss of presenting to me. The role of Russian landlord that he overacted. I was enchanted by my power to gladden his boisterous bareness, as though I were soberly participating in a child's excited game. And you were green with envy. You never stopped fixing the two of us with your icy inquisitorial stares. In the catacombs of your imagination, as in a Dürer drawing, no doubt you were thrusting me into his arms. And slaying us both with your dagger. Poor, miserable Alec.

Limp, caressed by the sea breeze, I sat on that bench and recalled another summer, our summer in Ashkelon after the '67 war. The improvised raft you constructed out of wooden posts tied together with rope, without using any nails. The *Kon-Tiki*, you called it. You told Boaz all about Phoenician seafarers who sailed to the end of the world. And Vikings. And Moby Dick and Captain Ahab. The voyages of Magellan and Vasco da Gama. You taught him to tie sailors' knots, your steady hand guiding his little fingers. And then the panic of the whirlpool. The only cry for help I have ever heard you utter. And then those fishermen. Your strong arms carrying me and the boy ashore under your armpits, like a ewe and a lamb, from the fishermen's boat. The tears of defeat I thought I saw in your eyes as we escaped from the sea and you deposited us with the last of your strength on the sand. Unless it was just sea water, running down onto your face from your hair.

From the direction of the wing came a woman's voice in a melodious question. After a moment your son answered her in his quiet bass with four or five words, which I could not make out. How precious to me is his slow voice. How like yet how unlike your own. What should I say to him if he discovered me? Why had I come here? I was content with the sound of his voice. At that moment I made up my mind to slip away unnoticed

But in the yard two girls in sandals appeared, one, wearing shorts, dark and round, her nipples showing dark beneath a damp T-shirt, and her comrade slender, petite, sprouting like a cornstalk from her long dress. With hoes, they began to attack the couch grass, bindweed, and squirting cucumber that spread at the foot of the steps. They spoke to one another in soft, melodious English, and did not notice me at all. I still hoped to vanish unseen. From a window of the wing came an aroma of frying and the smell of green eucalyptus branches burning. A little goat came out of the house, followed closely by Boaz himself, holding the string: he was sun-tanned, even taller than when I had seen him last in Jerusalem, his luxuriant mane tumbling down like molten gold below his shoulders and licking at the curls on his chest, barefoot, and naked apart from tiny blue bathing shorts. Mowgli the wolf boy; Tarzan king of the jungle. The sun had bleached his eyelashes and eyebrows and the yellow bristles on his jowl. He secured the goat to a branch and stood with his arms folded and a shadow of a smile on his lips. Until one of the girls raised her glance and gave a Red Indian yell. Her comrade threw a small stone at his chest. At that moment the dauphin turned his head and caught sight of me and blinked. He slowly scratched his head. Slowly your amused, cynical smile appeared on his face and he remarked calmly, as though identifying a common bird: "Look, Ilana's here."

After a moment he added, in crude English, "This is Ilana Sommo. *My beauty mother.* And these are Sandra and Cindy," he continued. "Two more beauties. Anything the matter, Ilana?"

I stood up and went toward him. After two steps I stopped. I stood like a confused schoolgirl, twisting the strap of my straw handbag. With my eyes on a level with his chest, I managed to mutter that I had just stopped off, that I was actually on my way to visit Rahel in Beit Avraham, and I didn't want to be a nuisance.

Why did I lie to him from my very first words?

Boaz stuck his finger behind his ear, scratched himself again unconsciously, pondered for a while, then said: "You must be thirsty from the journey. Cindy will fetch you some water. *Cindy, bring water.* But it's not cold, because we don't have electricity. We didn't have any water, either, but yesterday I discovered the pipeline to the national park among the thistles and I fitted a tap to it. How's the little one? Still as flirtatious as ever? Still eating candy? Why didn't you bring her with you?"

I said that Yifat was at the nursery. Michel would collect her and take her home. And that they both sent their greetings. This too, of course, was a lie. To cover it up or out of embarrassment I held out my hand to him. He bent over slightly and squeezed it unhurriedly. As though weighing a chick. "Here. Drink. You look

137

parched. I got hold of these two lovelies at Pardes Hanna Junction. They were volunteers on some kibbutz or other, but they've finished now and they were hiking around, so I brought them here to help build the country. Tell Sommo it's okay, he needn't worry, they're both more or less Jewish."

I drank some tepid water from a tin mug that Cindy brought me.

Boaz said: "We're eating some pigeons soon. I catch them in the upstairs rooms. Today you're my guest. There's bread and salted fish, and I've got some beer, but it's not cold either. *An omelette, Sandra, for guest.* What's up? What's so funny?"

Apparently I had smiled unconsciously. And I stammered an apology for not bringing any provisions with me. I would never make a good mother, I said. "That's true," said Boaz, "but it doesn't make any difference." And he placed his hand on my hip and steered me toward the house. He held my body carefully but firmly. When we came to a broken step he said: "Watch out, Ilana."

He himself stooped as we went through the doorway. The inside of the house was cool and dark, with a smell of coffee and sardines. I raised my eyes toward him, startled by the thought that this magnificent man had come out of my body and fallen asleep at my breast. I remembered the diphtheria that almost killed him when he was four, and the complications with his kidneys just before our divorce, Alec. The kidney you were intending to donate to him. I couldn't explain to myself what demon had brought me here. I couldn't find a word to say to him. And there was your son, saying nothing, watching my embarrassment, inspecting me without embarrassment, patiently, with a faint curiosity, resting like a sated wild beast.

Eventually I muttered stupidly: "You look very well."

"But you don't, Ilana. You look offensed [*sic!*]. But then, you always do. Sit down here for a moment. Have a rest. I'll make some coffee on the camp stove."

So I sat down on a packing box that your son cleared for me with a kick of his bare foot (there were cucumbers, onions, and a screwdriver on it). In the midst of the disorder, on the filthy, sunken flagstones, I could discern the signs of the strange bridgehead Boaz was gradually establishing there: a blackened frying pan, some oil-cloth, a bag of cement, a couple of pots and a battered coffee pot, cans of paint and brushes, some old mattresses on which the girls' backpacks and his kit-bag were scattered among a muddle of building equipment, ropes, and cans of food and jeans of his and theirs and a bra and a transistor radio. In a corner of the room lay a tent or a folded tarpaulin. There was also an improvised table: an old wooden door, with peeling paint, propped up on a couple of drums. On this table I could see dark rolls of metal, and among them a pot of jam, candles with matches, cans of beer, some empty, some full, a large book entitled *Light and the Lens*, a kerosene lamp, and half a loaf of brown bread.

I asked him if everything was all right, if he was short of anything. And at once, without waiting for his reply, I heard myself bursting out and asking if he was still angry or bitter.

A secretive, regal smile gave his sunburned face an air of suffering and forgiveness, an expression that for a brief instant re-minded me of his grandfather.

"No, not bitter. Anyway, I'm against being bitter at fucked-up people."

I asked him whether he hated you. And at once I regretted it.

He said nothing. Scratched himself as though in his sleep. Went on fiddling with the sooty coffeepot on the gas burner.

"Answer me."

He said nothing. Made a broad gesture with his hand, palm facing upward. Clucked twice.

"Why should I hate him? I don't hate him. I'm against hating. What I think is like this: I have nothing to do with him. It's a pity he left the country. I'm against people leaving the country while it's got troubles. Even though I quite fancy traveling myself—and I will as soon as the country gets out of trouble."

"And why did you agree to accept this house from him?"

"Why should I care about taking money from him? Or from

139

Michel? Or from both of them? Either way nobody ever earned that money by hard work. It just grew on trees. So they might as well give some of it to me. No problem. I happen to have something to do with the money, what's more. Here, the water's boiling. Let's have a cup of coffee. Drink this—you'll feel better. It's sugared and stirred. What are you looking at me like that for?"

What was it that provoked me to reply that I was superfluous? That I wouldn't mind dying. That they'd all be better off that way.

"*Yallah*. Cool it. That's enough of that bullshit. Yifat is barely three years and a month old. What's all this about dying? Have you been hit on the head? You oughta take up voluntary work. Looking after new immigrants. Knitting hats for the troops. Are you short of things to do? What's your trouble?"

"It's . . . it's just that everything I've touched has gone horribly wrong. Can you understand that, Boaz?"

"You want the truth? No, I don't. But that don't signify much, 'cause I'm a bit soft in the head. But what I do understand is that you're not busy enough. You don't do anything, Ilana."

"How about you?"

"It's like this. Right now I'm here with these two chicks, making them work and giving them a good time, eating, working a little, fucking, looking after his house for him in return for monthly wages, and doing the odd repair job too. In another month or two there's going to be one less ruin in this country. Why don't you move in too? It's better than dying. There are too many people dying in this country anyway. Killing and dying the whole time instead of living it up. Whichever way you look, the whole place is full of wise guys riding tanks. Today we're starting on a vegetable garden. You can stay. You won't be in my way at all and I won't get in yours. You can do whatever you want to here, you can bring Yifat, you can bring whoever you want to. I'll give you work and food. Crying again? Life is not handling you gently enough? Stay as long as you want. There's no shortage of work here, and Cindy plays the guitar to us in the evenings. You can do the cooking. Or how about taking care of the goats? There's going to be a shed for them soon. I'll show you how."

"May I ask you something?"

"Ask ahead—it don't cost anything."

"Tell me this: Have you ever loved anybody? I don't mean . . . sex. You don't have to answer."

He said nothing. Shook his head from right to left, in the negative, as though in despair at my stupidity. And then, sadly and gently: "Of course I have. Do you mean to say you've never even noticed?"

"Who?"

"You, Ilana. And him. When I was just so big and I thought of you as parents. Your shouting and fighting used to drive me crazy. I thought it was all because of me. How could I know? Every time you committed suicide and they took you away to the hospital I wanted to murder him. When you screwed with his friends I wanted to poison them. Instead I used to beat up anyone who came within range. I was an idiot. Now I'm against beating people up unless they do it to me first. Then I just hit back a little. Now I'm only in favor of working and taking it easy. I only care about myself and the country."

"The country?"

"Sure. Are you blind or something? Can't you see what's going on? These wars and all the bullshit? Quarreling and killing all the time, instead of living it up? Eating their hearts out and then shooting and planting bombs. I'm against the situation. I happen to be quite a Zionist, if you must know."

"You're *what*?"

"A Zionist. Wanting everyone to be okay. And for everyone to do just a little for the country, even something really tiny, just half an hour a day so they can feel good and know that they're still needed. If you don't do anything, very soon you start getting into trouble. Take you and your husbands for instance. Not one of the three of you knows what it means to really live. You just fuss all the time instead of doing something. Including that saint and his mates from the territories. They're living off the Bible, living off politics, living off speeches and arguments, instead of living off life. It's the same thing with the Arabs. They've learned from the Jews how to eat their hearts out and how to eat each other and how to eat people instead of ordinary food. I'm not saying the Arabs aren't bastards. They are, and worse. So what? Bastards are still human beings. Not shit. It's a shame for them to die. In the end the Jews will finish them off or they'll finish the Jews off or they'll finish each other off and there'll be nothing left in this country again except the Bible and the Koran and the foxes and burned ruins."

"What'll you do when they call you up?"

"Oh, they'll manage without someone like me. Substandard and all that. So what? I don't give a damn. Even without the army I'm going to do something with my life: at sea, perhaps, or maybe in optics. Or else I'll start a commune here in Zikhron for the loonies. They can make things grow instead of making trouble. So there'll be food for the state. A commune of nut cases. The first thing I did was burn the shit those chicks brought with them. I'm against getting stoned. Better to work all day and live it up at night. Crying again? Did I say something wrong? I'm sorry. I wasn't trying to get on your nerves. Sorry. Don't forget you're not the first mother whose had a nut case for a child. At least you've got Yifat. Only don't let Sommo fill her head with his Bible and his bullshit."

"Boaz."

"What?"

"Have you got some time now? A couple of hours?"

"What for?"

"Come to Haifa with me. Let's go and visit your grandfather. You remember you've got a sick grandfather in Haifa? The one who built this house for you?"

He said nothing. Suddenly he moved his massive hand like lightning, and landed a gorilla blow on his naked chest, brushing the squashed horse fly to the ground.

"Boaz?"

"Yes. I remember. Just. But what's all this about going to visit him all of a sudden? What do I need from him? Anyway, whenever I go out, even just here in Zikhron to buy building stuff, either I get on people's nerves or they get on mine or a fight starts. Tell you what: You tell him from me that if he's got anything saved up he can send me some money too. Tell him the idiot takes from anyone who's giving. I fancy building a really serious telescope. Something straight out of the movies. So at night from here you'd be able to watch the spaceships flying over the country. And the sea with no water that's up there on the moon; maybe you've heard about it. If only people took a little more notice of the stars and that, they'd take less notice of the hassle they get the whole time. And after that, we'll see. Perhaps a yacht. We're not short of a plank or two. We'll be able to cruise on the sea. It clears all the bullshit out of your head.

"Right, food's ready. Look, over there behind the window; there's the tap I fixed yesterday. Go and wash your face and let's forget about all the soul-searching. Your make-up's got all smudged. I had Cindy crying last night too. Never mind, it rinses out the soul. *Sandra. Put food for my mother, also.* No? Leaving? Had enough of me? Because I said 'fuck' and all that? That's the way it is, Ilana. There's a bus stop two hundred yards from the back gate. So go out that way. Maybe it might have been better for you if you'd never come—you were okay when you arrived and now you're leaving in tears. Wait. I found these coins down in the cellar. Underneath the old man's boiler. Give them to Yifat and tell her they're from me, Bozaz [*sic!*], and I'm going to eat her little nose. Don't forget you can come back whenever you want to and stay as long as you like. Free as air."

Why did you do it, Alec? Why did you plant him in that ghost-ridden house? Was it really just because you were dying to beat Michel at his own game? To tear the fine web of affection that was beginning to join my little man and that overgrown savage? To push your son back into the jungle? Like a prison guard separating a pair of convicts who strike up a friendship in their cell and putting them in solitary confinement. "As after a plane crash," you wrote in your neon light letter, "we analyzed together, by correspondence, the black box of our lives.

We deciphered nothing, Alec. We only exchanged poisoned arrows. My lust for revenge is slowly ebbing. Dead and done for. I'll give up. Just let me be in your arms. Resting my fingers on the nape of your neck. Smoothing your tousled grey hair. Squeezing a little blackhead occasionally on your shoulder or in the corner of your chin. Sitting beside you in the wind-lashed jeep, careering along a remote mountain road, getting a thrill from your driving, which is as aggressive as a sword thrust yet as careful and precise as a good tennis shot. Sneaking up behind you with bare feet and sinking my fingers in your hair as you sit bent over your desk in the early hours of the morning, glowing in the electric aura of your desk lamp, decoding with surgical precision some savage mystical text or other. I'll be your wife and servant. *La commedia è finita*. From now on, thy will be done. I'm waiting.

Ilana

———

Notes made by Prof. A. A. Gideon on little cards.

185. Faith out of loss of faith: the more his faith in himself is destroyed, the stronger grows his feverish faith in salvation, the more powerful his urgent need to be saved. The redeemer is as mighty as you are tiny, worthless, of no account. Henri Bergson says: It is not true that faith moves mountains. On the contrary, the essence of faith is the ability no longer to notice anything, not even mountains moving in front of your eyes. A kind of hermetic screen, absolutely fact-proof.

186. In proportion as he loses his self-esteem, his raison d'être, the very significance of his life, so there is magnified, exalted, glorified, and sanctified the justification of his religion, his people, his race, the ideal he has clung to or the movement to which he has sworn allegiance.

186a. To assimilate entirely, therefore, the *I* within the *We*. To shrink to a blind cell within a gigantic, timeless, omnipotent, sublime organism. To blend to the point of self-denial, to the utmost limit, in the nation, the movement, the race, like a drop in the ocean of the faithful. Hence: the various kinds of uniform.

187. A man minds his own private business as long as he has business and as long as he has privacy. In their absence, for fear of the emptiness of his life, he turns feverishly to other people's business. To straighten them out. To chastise them. To enlighten every fool and crush every deviant. To bestow favors on others or to persecute them savagely. Between the altruistic zealot and the murderous zealot there is of course a difference of moral degree, but there is no difference in kind. Murderousness and self-sacrifice are simply two sides of the same coin. Domination and benevolence, aggression and devotion, repression and self-repression, saving the souls of those who are different from you and annihilating them: these are not pairs of opposites but merely different expressions of man's emptiness and worthlessness. "His insufficiency to himself," in the phrase of Pascal (who was infected himself).

188. "For want of anything to do with his empty, sterile life, he falls on the necks of others or reaches for their throats" (Eric Hoffer, *The True Believer*).

189. And this is the secret of the surprising similarity between the charitable maiden who labors night and day for the outcasts of society and the ideological brigand, the head of a secret service, whose life is utterly dedicated to the elimination of rivals, or aliens, or enemies of the revolution: their modesty. Their making do with little. Their sanctimoniousness, which can be sniffed from afar. Their habit

145

of secret self-pity, and hence their radiation of megawatts of guilt feelings. The shared hostility of the maiden and the inquisitor toward anything that might be taken for "luxury" or "self-indulgence." Dedicated missionary and bloodthirsty purge-master: the same gentle manners. The same flowery politeness. The same smell of undefined sourness emanates from the two of them. The same ascetical style of dress. The same taste (trite, sentimental) in music and art. And, in particular, the same active vocabulary, characterized by hackneyed flourishes, affected modesty, avoidance of all vulgarity—*toilet* instead of *lavatory*, *pass away* instead of *die*, *solution* instead of *annihilation*, *purge* instead of *slaughter*. And, of course, *salvation, redemption*. The shared slogan: "I am only a humble instrument." (I am an "instrument," therefore I am: "cog"—*ergo sum*?!)

190. Torturer and victim. Inquisitor and martyr. Crucifier and crucified. The mystery of the mutual understanding, of the secret fellowship that frequently grows up between them. The interdependence. The covert mutual admiration. The ease with which they are able to exchange roles with changing circumstances.

191. "Sacrificing private life on the altar of sacred ideals" is nothing more than a desperate clinging to ideals when private life has died.

200. In other words: with the death of the soul the walking corpse turns into a totally public being.

201. "The sanctity of duty": a convulsive grasping of any life raft that floats within reach. The nature of the life raft almost incidental.

202. "Purging oneself of all trace of selfishness": a selfish survival stratagem, verging on blind instinct.

———

Prof. A. Gideon   *Jerusalem*
Midwest University   13.8.76
Chicago, Ill., U.S.A.

My dear Dr. Strangelove,

At this moment in time it is not clear to me whether I am fired or not. Our purchaser is prepared to pay you thirteen for the property in Zikhron, swears that that is his final offer, and threatens to withdraw if he has not received a positive answer within a fortnight. As for poor Roberto, I have almost managed to persuade him to return your files to me of his own free will. Apparently he is beginning to realize what sort of customer he is dealing with. While I, for my part, have decided to wipe away the spittle and carry on: I shall not abandon you to your lunacy or allow you to bring calamity on yourself. Apparently you suspect me of selling you to Sommo, but the truth is the contrary: All my efforts have been directed to buying him for ourselves, and to put a bridle on him (in the form of my son-in-law Zohar). And in the meantime, in accordance with the instructions you sent me in your last cable, here is a summary of the latest news: It transpires that Baron de Sommo is buying himself a fancy apartment in the refurbished Jewish Quarter in the Old City of Jerusalem. All the evidence points to its being a bargain deal between him and one of the members of his tribe. In addition to which he is learning to drive and making plans to buy a car. An expensive suit of clothes he has now (although when he is wearing the alarming object he has selected, I regret bitterly ever having advised him to buy one). His Jewish Fellowship organization he has recently converted into a sort of reconnaissance unit or security guard in the service of an investment company called Tentpeg that he and Zohar Etgar have set up in partnership with a group of pious investors and with some discreet backing from Paris, anent which I shall report to you once I am convinced that you have returned to your senses. The joint financial handle of this Tentpeg is held, of course, by Zohar (with my Holy Spirit illuminating it from on high). The various devout partners take care of the ethical side of the business, that is to say, they have managed to convince the revenue authorities to recognize them as a sort of orphanage, brackets "charitable status."

Meanwhile, our Sommo is starring in the role of foreign minister. He is involved in expert lobbying. He is swimming around in the corridors of power like a fish or a seaweed. Spending his days and his nights in the company of party hacks, MPs, secretary generals, and director generals. Circulating in and around his brother's court, expounding Jewish love to the officials of the Military Administration, planting the longing for redemption in the Ministry of Trade and Industry, causing messianic stirrings among the staff of the Israel Land Authority, preaching, beseeching, cajoling, quoting Holy Writ, spreading a thick cloud of guilt feelings, with one hand upon his heart and the other around his interlocutor's shoulder, sweetening the whole thing with Biblical honey, dusting it with homilies, seasoning it with a pinch of gossip, rolling up permits and certificates, and, in sum, tirelessly paving the way for the Last Days and also speedily consolidating our investments to the south of Jerusalem. At the head of the third chapter of your excellent book you quote an epigram from Jesus of Nazareth, who admonished his disciples to be simultaneously "as cunning as vipers and as innocent as doves." On the basis of this specification Sommo might be promoted to the rank of senior apostle. Soon, according to information from our good friend Shlomo Zand, he is intending to set out on an urgent mission to Paris with his French passport, and I'll wager that he will return home laden with goodies. The final outcome will be that, thanks to him, we—that is, you and I, Alex—shall receive a double invitation to Paradise because of our part in the redemption of the land.

I am writing this in the hope that you will soon give me a little sign, and I will harness your dormant cash to these chariots of the gods. And I will undertake to steer Sommo in such a way that he will do for you in the present what I did for your father in the good old days. Think it over carefully, my dear friend: If your old Zakheim has not rusted entirely, then you simply have to rely on his intuition and climb onto this new wave without delay. In this way we can kill three fine birds with one paltry million: we harness Sommo to us, make your Gulliver's fortune (if you have definitely made up your mind to appoint him your crown prince), and also get our hands on Lady de Sommo. Because Zand reports to me that while Napoleon is advancing toward the pyramids, signs of restlessness are appearing in Desirée, who has begun to take an interest in the possibility of going back to work in the same bookshop where she made her living in those fiery two years of hers, after the prince left and before the frog arrived. If I have read your mind correctly, then this development is playing straight into our hands. Would you like me to book her a ticket and send her to you *prontísimo*? Or should I wait until I am quite sure that she's ripe for it? Would you like me to send Zand to sniff out what's going on in Zikhron? And the main thing, Alex: Will you let me sell that ruin that brings in nothing and costs you a fortune in taxes, and use the money to hammer in a little Tentpeg of your own? Please, send me a one-word cable: "Affirmative." You won't regret it.

Take good care of your body and your nerves. And don't hate your only real friend, who is waiting for a sane answer from you and signs off now anxiously but affectionately—

Your miserable
Manfred

———

PERSONAL ROBERTO DIMODENA JERUSALEM ISRAEL

FORBID YOU TO LET YOUR PARTNER MEDDLE IN MY AFFAIRS FIND OUT AND REPORT AT ONCE WHO HIS PURCHASER IS KEEP PAYING BOAZ ALEXANDER GIDEON

Professor Alexander Gideon   15.8.76
Political Science Department
Midwest University
Chicago, Ill., U.S.A.

Dear Alec,

From Zikhron I traveled on to Haifa. A strong, strange smell, a heady mixture of pine resin and Lysol, pervaded the sanatorium on Mount Carmel. From time to time the moan of a ship's siren floated up from the harbor. Trains hooted and fell silent. The gardens lay in rustic tranquillity shrouded in gentle sunlight. A couple of old women were dozing on a bench, shoulder resting on shoulder, like a pair of stuffed birds. An Arab male nurse who was pushing a patient in a wheelchair slowed as I passed and eyed me lasciviously. From a corner of the garden rose the croaking of frogs. And in an arbor of thick vines I finally found your father, sitting alone at a white-painted metal table, with his shock of prophetic white hair waving slightly in the breeze, his unkempt Tolstoyan beard flowing down over a stained dressing gown, his face brown and shriveled like a dried fig, with a teaspoon in his hand and a cake on a plate and a half-finished glass of yogurt on the table in front of him. The blue eyes sailing away toward the blue of the sea. His deep, calm breathing stirring the spray of oleander that he was fanning himself with.

When I pronounced his name he deigned to turn and look at me. He rose slowly, majestically, from his seat and bowed to me twice. I held out a bunch of chrysanthemums I had bought at the Central Bus Station. He handed me his oleander spray, drew the chrysanthemums to his chest, carefully inserted one of them into the buttonhole of his dressing gown, and unhesitatingly planted the rest of the bunch in his yogurt glass. He called me Madame Rovina, and thanked me for finding the time to come to his funeral and even bringing flowers.

I laid my palm on the back of his broad hand, which was crisscrossed with a fascinating network of delicate blue blood vessels and blotched with patches of brown pigmentation, like a landscape of rivers and hills, and asked him how he was. Your father fixed me with his hard, piercing eyes, and his enchanting face darkened. Suddenly he chuckled as though he had seen through my little scheme but had decided to forgive me. Then he turned serious, frowned, and demanded that I tell him if there is any pardon for Dostoevsky; how was it possible that such a man of God "could beat his wife all through the winter and then get drunk and play cards like a beast while his baby is dying?"

Here he was apparently shocked at his own bad manners. He snatched the chrysanthemums out of the yogurt glass, hurled them disgustedly over his shoulder, pushed the glass toward me, and asked me if I would care for some champagne. I raised the glass to my lips—there were petals and dust floating on the murky liquid—and pretended to take a sip. Meanwhile your father wolfed down the remains of his cake. When he had finished it I took out a hankie and brushed the crumbs from his beard. He responded by stroking my hair and declaiming in tragic tones: "The wind, *krassavitsa*, the autumn wind, all day long stealing into gardens. Ho, and its conscience is not clear! It knows no rest! Banished! And in the night they start to ring the big bells. Soon snow will be falling, and we—*dayosh!*—will ride on." Here he lost his way. He fell silent. He gaped slightly, with a cloud of sadness on his face.

"And your health is all right, Volodya? The pains in your shoulder have gone?"

"Pains? Not me! I don't have pains—he does. I heard tell that he's alive, that he talked on the radio even. If I was in his place I would marry a wife and immediately make her have a dozen babies."

"Whose place, Volodya?"

"You know, that little fellow, whats-his-name. That one. The little brother. Binyomin. The one who used to wander around in front of the Arab village of Budrus with the first flock of sheep from the settlement. Binyomin, they used to call him. Described to the life in Dostoevsky! Even truer than he was in *realia*! I was in *realia* also, but as a swine. We had another one there—Sioma. Sioma Axioma, we used to call him. He was one in million. Not one ounce of swine in him. He came from my hometown. Shirky. Minsk Region. *Realia* could not forgive him, and it killed him with love for woman. He took his own lovely soul with my revolver. Could I do something to stop him? Had I the right to? Would you offer him, dear lady, one goblet of woman's love? He would repay you with crimson and turquoise. Generously he would repay you. His soul for one single goblet! Half? Quarter? No? Well, then! Never mind. It is not necessary. Do not give. Every human being is— one planet. There's no way through. Just twinkling far away whenever there are no clouds. *Realia* itself is swine. May I offer you one flower? In memory of that poor miserable one. One flower for ascent of his soul? Dostoevsky killed him, with my revolver. Anti-Semite he was! Despicable! Epileptic! He crucifies Christ at least twice on every single page, and still he accuses us. He beats the Jews murderously. And perhaps he is right, dear lady? I am not talking about Palestine. Palestine is—another song. What is Palestine? *Realia?* Palestine is dream. Palestine is *cauchemar*, but still is dream. Perhaps you have deigned to hear of Lady Dulcinea? Well, Palestine is like her. In the dream, myrrh and frankincense, but in *realia* swinery! Misery of swines. And in the morning—'behold it was Leah!' What Leah? Malaria. Ottoman Asia. I was just little boy, little boy catching sparrows. I used to sell them two for a kopeck. I loved to wander by myself on the steppe. So: dreamily strolling in the meadows. And all around—terror! Forests! And muzhiks, with, whatdyacallem, not boots—leggings. That is our Palestine back in Shirky. The stream is Palestine too. And I can swim in it. And one day, there am I as young boy wandering between forest and meadow, and suddenly right in front of me out of the ground up pops little peasant girl. With braid. A swineherd, begging your pardon. Maybe fifteen years old. Well, I don't ask her how old she is. Up she pops and without a word she starts to hoist up—begging pardon—her skirt. And beckoning with her finger. Not one goblet of woman's love—one whole river. Take and it shall be given to you. And I am only young stripling, my foolish blood boiling, and my brain—begging his pardon—fast asleep. Would I lie to you, madame, in the middle of my own funeral? No. Lying is totally contemptible. All the more so before open grave. In short, I do not deny, my dove, I lay hands on her in that field. And for that sin I am sent to Ottoman Asia. 'Flow on, Jordan . . .' My father himself smuggles me out in middle of night, so they will not hack me to death. And there, in Palestine—wilderness! Graveyard! Fear! Foxes! Prophets! Bedouins! And the air all ablaze! Take another sip; it will do you good. Drink to memory of women's love. On the way, when I am still on ship, I throw my tefillin straight in sea. Let fishes eat and grow fat. And I will explain this to you also: Short while before we reach city of Alexandria, I have one big row with God. Both of us screaming at each other half the night there on the deck. Maybe we overdo it. What does He want from me? That I should be his little *zhid*. And that's all. Whereas I for my part, I want to be one great swine. And so we quarrel, until comes the night watchman and kicks both of us off that deck in middle of the night. That is how He loses me and I lose Him. Such a secondhand, grumpy, sour God. So. He stayed up there all alone like a dog muttering in his mustache, and I stay down here, one swine among swines. And so we part. And what do I do? *Na,* tell me what I do with the gift of life? What do I spend it on? Why do I sully it? I smash teeth, I cheat, I steal, and, above all, I hoist up skirts. Filthy swine in every way. And now, begging your pardon, dear lady, it is not quite clear to me why you deigned to come and see me today. Are you sent by Binyomin? He has been horribly punished. And who by? By the fair sex! Only because he was such a nonswine. They broke his heart at their pleasure but they did not let him beat a path to their bodies. Even before the shadow of a touch he would faint with embarrassment. So much he suffered that his pure soul departed. And by means of my own revolver! Is madame maybe familiar with the location of the city of Simferopol? There was a terrible battle there. The boys were dying like flies. And who does not die loses God. Does not know what is up and what is down. Gives up God for the sake of women's love, but women they do not find. Women in the Land of Israel are rare then. Perhaps five or six between Rosh Pina and Kastina. Perhaps ten, if you count Baba Yagas. But a *barishnya*—not to be found. The boys, after the discussions, they lie down each one on his mattress and they dream of brothel of Odessa. And this because God tricks us. He never comes to Ottoman Asia. He stays behind in attic of synagogue in Shirky, lying there and waiting that Messiah should come. In Land of Israel there is no God and there is no love of women. So everybody gets screwed up. And those that go under bridal canopy? Well, of course, in the morning—behold it is Leah. They are ringing the village bells again far away in the distance. Soon it will start to snow, and we will ride on our way. Can the good lady understand me? Can she pardon me? Forgive me? She is alone and I am alone in that field, and she hoists up her skirts and with her little finger she beckons to me and I lay my hands on her. Therefore I am smuggled to Zion. I am first Jew to extract honey from bees. First since Bible times. Malaria passes me over and I hoist up skirts, like a demon! I am first Jew to hoist up skirts in Palestine since Bible times. Assuming Bible is not legend. For that I am punished in Simferopol. One horse falls on top of me and breaks my legs. In Tulkarem they blow off my head. I get them in the teeth. Much blood spilled. Does madame know? My life is no life at all. Great tearfulness I have until day of my death. And yet once I also loved a woman. Even I forced her to go under bridal canopy with me. Although her heart did not desire me. Perhaps she desired some poet? Whereas I—how should I put it?—from navel up I was in love, singing serenades, offering handkerchiefs and flowers, but from navel down a swine from the land of swine. Hoisting skirts left and right in fields. And she, my beloved, my wife, she sat all day long at her window. She had little song: 'Yonder, where the cedars grow. . . .' Do you happen to know this song? Permit me to sing it in your honor: 'Yonder, where the ce-dars grow . . .' Beware of these songs, dear lady. They are written by angel of death. And she, on purpose to punish me, she ups and dies on me. Just to be contrary. She leaves me and goes up to God. She does not know that He is one swine also. She jumps out of frying pan into fire. Give me your hand. Let us be off. The watch is ended. The Jews built themselves a land. It is not the right land, but they built it anyway! It is all askew, but they built it anyway! Without God—but they built it anyway! Now let us wait and see what God has to say about it all. Well, that is enough now: two kopecks I should give you for your sparrows? Two. More than that I will not pay. My whole life has been battle and defilement. I soiled the gift. Skirts and punched teeth. So why should I give you money? What have you done with your own gift of life? One flower I will give you. One flower and one kiss on the lips. Do you know what is my secret? I have never had anything. And what about you? What brings you to me? What have I done to deserve this honor?"

When he finally stopped and his eyes roamed from me toward the view of the bay finding in the blaze of sunset, I asked him if there was anything he needed. If he wished me to see him back to his room. Or to fetch him a glass of tea.

But he only shook his magnificent head, and muttered: "Two. More than that I will not pay."

"Volodya," I said, "do you remember who I am?"

He withdrew his hand from mine. His eyes brimmed with tears of sadness. No, to his shame he had to confess that he could not remember, that he had omitted to inquire who the lady was and why she had asked if he would agree to see her. So I settled him back in his chair, kissed him on the forehead, and told him my name.

"Of course." He smiled with childlike cunning. "Of course, you are Ilana. My son's widow. At Simferopol they were all killed. Not one of them was left alive to observe the beauty of the fall. Soon the snow will start and we—*dayosh!*—we shall ride on. Out of this vale of tears! Away from rotting generals who drink and play cards while the women are dying. And who are you, my lovely lady? What is your name? And your business? Abusing the male sex? And for what purpose did you request that I should grant you an audience? Wait! Do not tell me! You came about the gift of life. Why did we defile it? Why did we curdle our mother's milk? You may have done, madame, but not me. Me, my revolver—down the drain. I threw it away and that is the end of that. So, may God be with us, and may we rest in peace. *Liu liu liu.* Is that one cradle song? Or deathbed song? So, be off with you now. Go. Only this do for me: Live and hope. That is all. Look at the beauty of the fall in the forest before the snow. So? Two kopecks and that is all? I shall even give you three."

With these words he rose, bowed low before me, or rather bent down and picked up one of my chrysanthemums, dirty with dust and yogurt, and delicately proffered it to me: "Only do not get lost in the snow."

And without waiting for an answer or saying good-bye he turned his back and strode toward the building, as upright as an old Red Indian. My audience was at an end. What more was there for me to do but pick up my sticky chrysanthemums, put them in the trash can, and take the bus back to Jerusalem?

The last of the daylight was still glimmering in the west between serrated clouds on the sea horizon as I sat on the half-empty bus on my way back from Haifa. The memory of his brown hand, gnarled like a volcanic slope, would not leave me: how like yet unlike your own stiff, square hand. I had an almost tangible feeling that his hand was resting on my knee all the way from Haifa. And I found its touch consoling. When I got home, at quarter to ten in the evening, I found Michel asleep on a mattress at the foot of Yifat's bed, fully dressed and with his shoes on. His glasses had slipped onto his shoulder. I woke him in alarm and asked what had happened. It transpired that in the morning, after I had left, when he had dressed Yifat and was on the point of taking her to the nursery, on a sudden suspicion he had taken her temperature, and it turned out he was right. So he decided to call and cancel at the last minute the meeting he had arranged with the deputy minister of defense, a meeting for which he had been waiting for almost two months. He took Yifat to the clinic and waited for an hour and a half before the doctor examined her and pronounced that she had "a slight ear infection." On the way home he stopped at the pharmacy and bought some antibiotics and ear drops. He made her some chicken soup and mashed potatoes. By cajoling and bribery he managed to get her to drink some warm milk and honey every hour. At midday her temperature rose, and Michel decided to call a private doctor. Who confirmed his colleague's diagnosis, but charged Michel ninety pounds. He sat till evening, telling her one story after another, and then he managed to make her eat a little chicken and rice and afterwards he sang to her, and when she was asleep he went on sitting beside her in the dark with his eyes closed, measuring her breathing with his stopwatch and singing hymns. Then he dragged a mattress in for himself and lay down at the foot of her bed in case she coughed or her bedclothes fell off while she was asleep. Until he fell asleep too. Instead of thanking him, admiring his devotion, kissing him and undressing him and making it up to him in our bed, I asked irritably why he hadn't telephoned for help to one of his innumerable female in-laws or cousins. Why had he canceled his appointment with the deputy minister? Was it really just to make me feel guilty for going away? Was any means justified to cause guilt feelings? What the hell made him think that he deserved a hero's medal just for spending a single day in the home that I was stuck in for the whole of my life? And why did I have to report to him on where I had been? I wasn't his maid. And while we were on the subject, it was high time he realized how I despised the way the male members of his community and his family treated their poor wives. I refused to give him a report on where I had gone and why. (In my blind fury I had overlooked the fact that Michel had not even asked. No doubt he was intending to ask me and tell me off, and I was merely anticipating him.) Michel listened in silence as he made me a salad and poured me a Coke. He switched the water heater on so that I could take a shower if I wanted to. And made our bed. Eventually, when I stopped, he said: "Is that it? Have we finished? Shall we send a dove out to see if the water has subsided? We've got to wake her up at one o'clock to give her her medicine." As he spoke he bent over her and touched her forehead lightly. And I burst into tears.

In the night, while he slept, I lay awake, thinking of the rhesus monkey which was your only childhood friend inside the fences of the empty estate, and which you and your father dressed as a waiter, with a bow tie, and trained to serve a tray of pomegranate juice. Until one day it bit you in the neck, and you still carry the scar. The Armenian servant was ordered to shoot it, and you dug its grave and wrote an epitaph. And since then you have been alone.

And I thought about the fact that you never asked to hear about my childhood, in Poland and here, and that I was too ashamed to tell you about it. My father, like my husband, was a schoolteacher. We lived in a cramped apartment, whose gloominess even on summer days is engraved on my memory as the gloom of a cavern. There was a brown clock on the wall. I had a brown coat. From the ground floor rose the smell of the bakery. The narrow street was paved with stone, and streetcars ran along it every now and again. At night there was my father's asthmatic coughing fits. When I was five we received a permit to go to Palestine. For seven years we lived in a wooden hut by Nes Ziona. Father got a job as a plasterer in a building cooperative, but he never lost his short-tempered teacherly manner until he was killed falling from a scaffold. My mother died less than a year later. She died of a children's disease, measles, on the festival of the trees, Tu Bishevat. Rahel was sent away to be educated in the kibbutz where she still lives, while I was enrolled in an institution of the Working Women's Council. After that I was a platoon clerk in the army. Five months before I was discharged you were put in charge of the platoon. What was it about you that caught my heart? To try to answer the question I'll write down here for you our son's ten commandments, in random order but in his own words: I. Pity them all. II. Take more notice of the stars. III. Against being bitter. IV. Against making fun. V. Against hating. VI. Bastards are still human beings, not shit. VII. Against beating up. VIII. Against killing. IX. Not to eat each other. X. Cool it.

These halting words are the exact opposite of you. As far as the stars are from a mole. The icy malice that radiated from you like a bluish arctic glow and made the other girls in the battalion hate you to the point of hysteria was what caught my heart. Your air of indifferent mastery. The cruelty that you exuded like a scent. The greyness of your eyes, like the smoke from your pipe. The murderous sharpness of your tongue at any hint of opposition. Your wolfish glee at the sight of the terror you spread. The contempt you could emit like a flamethrower, and shoot like a searing jet at your friends, your subordinates, or the gaggle of secretaries and typists who were always petrified by your presence. I was drawn to you as though bewitched from muddy depths of primeval female subservience, ancient servitude from before words existed, the submission of a Neanderthal female whose survival instinct and fear of hunger and cold make her throw herself at the feet of the roughest of the hunters, the hairy savage who will tie her hands behind her back and drag her, captive, to his cave.

I remember the crisp hail of military words that you fired from the corner of your mouth: Negative. Affirmative. Roger. Rubbish. Full stop. Scram.

You delivered this barrage almost without parting your lips. And always on the verge of a whisper, as though you were sparing not only with words but also with the use of your voice and your face muscles. Your predator's jaws, which on rare occasions bared your lower teeth in a bitter, condescending grimace that served you as a smile: "What's going on here, sweetie? Nothing better to do than sit on the stove and warm your holy places at the army's expense?" Or: "If you only had in your head ten percent of what you've got in your bust, Einstein himself would sign up with you for evening classes." Or: "That inventory report you drew up for me looks like a recipe for strudel. Why not write me a report instead about what you're like in bed. Maybe there at least you're good for something?" Sometimes your victim burst into tears. And then you would ponder, look at her as at a dying insect, and hiss: "All right, give her a candy, somebody, and explain to her that she's just been saved from a court-martial." Then you turned on your heel as

159

though on a spring and slipped pantherlike from the room. And I, driven by a blind impulse, used to provoke you sometimes, despite the danger or because of it. I would say, for example, "Morning, sir. Here's your coffee. Perhaps you fancy a little belly dance with it?" Or: "Sir, if you're really dying to see what I've got underneath my skirt, don't bother to peep, just give me the order and I'll draw up an inventory report for you on everything there is to see there." Every wisecrack of this kind cost me confinement to barracks or loss of leave. Several times you punished me for insolence. Once you made me spend twenty-four hours in the guardroom. Next day— do you remember?—you asked: "Well, have you got rid of your urge, cutie?" I smiled provocatively and answered: "On the contrary, sir. I'm all aflame." Your wolfish jaws gaped as though to bite, and you snarled through your teeth: "Do you want me to teach you what to do in a condition like yours, sweetie?" The girls started to snicker. They had giggles behind their hands. And I gave as good as I got: "Should I wait for an order to report, sir?"

Until once, one rainy winter night, you offered me a lift into town. A thunderstorm accompanied the jeep along the coast road, we were battered by sweeping rain, and you subjected me to the ordeal of your icy silence. We drove for half an hour without exchanging two words, our eyes fixed hypnotically on the rhythmic struggle of the windshield wipers against the deluge. Once, the jeep skidded, traced a loop on the road, and without saying a word you managed to regain control of the steering wheel. Twenty or thirty kilometers later you suddenly said: "What's up? You suddenly been struck dumb?" And for the first time I imagined I caught a hint of hesitation in your voice and was filled with childish glee. "Negative, sir. I simply thought you were working out a plan for the conquest of Baghdad in your head and I didn't want to disturb you."

"Conquest, sure, and how! But what's all this about Baghdad? Is that your pet name?"

"Tell me something, Alex, while we're on the subject of conquests. Is it true what the girls say, that you've got a bit of a problem in that department?"

You ignored my daring to call you by your first name. Looking as though you were about to punch me in the face, you turned toward me and hissed: "What problem?"

"You'd better keep your eyes on the road. I don't want to get killed with you. Rumor has it in the platoon that you have a problem with girls? That you've never had a girl friend? Or is it maybe just because you're wedded to your tanks?"

"That's not a problem"—you chuckled in the darkness—"that's the solution."

"Then it might interest you to know that the girls are of the opinion that your solution is our problem. That what we ought to do is pair you off with one of us who will volunteer to sacrifice herself for the sake of the others."

In the half-light of the jeep as it tore through the curtains of rain, by the beat of your foot on the accelerator, I could sense the pallor spreading on your face. "What's going on here?" you asked, struggling unsuccessfully to conceal from me the tremor in your voice. "What is this, a panel discussion on the commanding officer's sex life?"

And then, at the first traffic light as we entered Tel Aviv from the north, you suddenly asked dejectedly: "Tell me something, Brandstetter, do you . . . really loathe me?"

Instead of replying, I asked you to stop the jeep after the traffic light, and pull off the road. And without another word I drew your head to my lips. As I had already done a thousand times in my imagination. Then, maliciously, I burst out laughing and said that I could see that you really did have to be taught everything from scratch. Because apparently you'd never even managed to kiss. And the time had come to show you which was the butt and which was the trigger. That if you would just give the order, I'd put you on an intensive training course.

And indeed I found you a virgin. And clumsy. And stiff. You didn't even manage to pronounce my name without stammering. When I got undressed, you averted your gaze. At least six weeks passed before you allowed me to leave the light on and look at your naked body: slim, youthful, as if your uniform was part of your flesh. You were very strong and timid, and my caresses seemed to tickle you. They made you shudder. The hairs on the back of your neck stood on end whenever I ran my hand up and down your back. Every time I touched your manhood it was as though you got an electric shock. Sometimes in the crux of pleasure I burst out laughing, and you immediately recoiled.

And yet also the wildness of your desperate craving during our first nights, your overwhelming desire, which could not be extinguished but would flare up anew almost as soon as it was gratified. Your orgasms, which were wrenched out of you with a piercing roar, like someone being shot with a hail of bullets. All this set my senses in a whirl. I was unquenchable too.

Every morning, during office hours, my loins would melt at the sight of your taut body in the uniform that you used to starch and press ruthlessly. If my eyes happened on that spot that I tried so hard not to look at, where the zip of your trousers met the buckle of your military belt, my nipples stiffened. Our secret was kept for a fortnight. Then dumbfounded gossip erupted among the secretaries and typists.

Slowly our nights were enriched. How happy I was in my heart of hearts about the experiments I had had before you. You were an eager pupil, and I an enthusiastic teacher. Almost until dawn we used to drink each other like a pair of vampires. Our backs were covered with scratches and our shoulders with love bites. In the mornings our eyes were so red from lack of sleep it looked as though we had both been crying. In my little room, at night, between one surge of desire and the next, you used to lecture me in that resonant bass voice of yours about the Roman Empire. About the battle of the Horns of Hattin. About the Thirty Years' War. About Clausewitz, von Schlieffen, De Gaulle. About what you termed the "morphological absurdities" of the Israeli Army. I could not understand it all, but I found a strange fascination in the troop movements, the bugles, the standards, the cries of the dying Romans that you conjured up between my sheets. Sometimes I would climb on top of you in mid-sentence and make your lecture tail off in a grunt.

Then you gave in and agreed to go with me to the theater. To sit in a café with me on a Friday afternoon. Even to go swimming. I went off with you for long weekend trips to remote valleys in Galilee. We slept in your German sleeping bag. Your submachine gun, cocked and in a safe position, was by your head the whole time. Our bodies amazed us. Words hardly existed. If I asked myself what was happening, what you meant to me, what would happen to us, I did not find the shadow of an answer, only my feverish desire.

Until one day—it was after I'd finished my military service, six months or so after the night of the jeep and the lightning, and of all places in the shabby restaurant of the gas station at Gedera— you said to me suddenly: "Let's talk seriously."

"About Kutuzov? About the battle for Monte Cassino?"

"No. Let's talk about us."

"While on the subject of excellence on the battlefield?"

"While on the subject of changing the subject. Be serious, Brandstetter."

"Yes, sir," I said, as though teasing, and suddenly, belatedly noticed a tormented film over your eyes, I said: "Has something happened, Alec?"

You shut up. For a long while you eyed the cheap plastic salt shaker. Then, without looking at me, you said that you did not think you were "an easy man." Perhaps I tried to answer, but you laid your hand on top of mine and said: "Give me a moment, Ilana, don't interrupt. This is difficult for me." I said nothing. And you fell silent again. At the end of your silence you said that you lived "all your life apart, in the inner meaning of the word." You asked whether I understood. You asked what I could see in "such a . . . stiff man." Without waiting for an answer you went on hurriedly, with a slight stammer: "You're my only friend. Of either sex. And my first. You're also . . . Shall I pour you some beer? Do you mind if I . . . talk a little?" You poured out the rest of the beer for me, absentmindedly drank it yourself, and told me that you intended never to marry. "A family—you know I have no idea how to handle all that. Are you hot? Do you want us to leave?" Your dream was to be a strategist. Or something like a military theoretician. And not in uniform. To leave the army, go back to the university in Jerusalem, take a second and a third degree, "and in fact apart from you, Brandstetter. That is . . . up to the time you raped me . . . girls weren't exactly my territory. Nothing doing. Even though I'm a big boy of twenty-eight. Nothing. That is . . . apart from . . . sexual urges. Which actually gave me quite a lot of trouble. But apart from the urge . . . not a thing. I've never managed to . . . to make friends. Or to study up on romance. As a matter of fact, I haven't even made friends with men particularly. Don't get me wrong. In the intellectual, or professional, area I do have a sort of . . . circle. More or less. A group of like-minded people. But as for emotion and all that . . . it always made me feel pressured. I used to ask myself why I should start having feelings for strangers. Or for strange women. Until I . . . met you. Until you took up with me. The fact of the matter is that even with you I felt under pressure. Only, there's something between us, isn't there? I can't define it. Maybe we're . . . two of a kind."

Then you talked about your plans again: to finish writing your doctoral thesis by 1964, and then work on a theory. War studies. Perhaps something more general, a thesis about violence in history. In all periods. Look for a common denominator. Maybe reach something like a personal solution. That is, a personal solution to a fundamental philosophical problem. So you said, and you continued for a little longer; then suddenly you shouted at the waiter that the place was swarming with flies, you started killing them, and you shut up. You asked for my "reaction."

And I, for the first time with you, used the word *love*. I said to you, more or less, that your sadness was my love. That you had aroused an emotional ambition in me. That you and I, the two of us, perhaps really were two of a kind. That I wanted to have a child with you. That you were a fascinating person. That if you would marry me, I would marry you.

And that was the night, after that conversation in the filling station at Gedera, that your virility let you down in my bed. And you fell into a panic and desperate shame such as I have never seen in you ever, either before or since. And as your anxiety and your embarrassment grew, so your organ shrank at my fingers' touch until it was almost swallowed up in its lair, like a little boy's. And I, close to tears of joy, covered your whole body with my kisses and cradled your handsome, crew-cut head all night long in my arms, and I kissed you even in the corners of your eyes, because you were as precious to me that night as you would have been had I given birth to you. Then I knew that we were fused in each other. That we had become one flesh.

It was a few weeks after that that you took me to see your father.

And by the autumn we were married.

Now you tell me this: Why have I written to you about these long-forgotten events? To scratch at old scars? To reopen our wounds for no reason? To decipher a black box? To hurt you all over again? To arouse your longings? Perhaps this too is a scheme to catch you once again in my net?

I plead guilty on all six counts. I know no extenuating circumstances. Except perhaps for one: I loved you not despite your cruelty; I loved the dragon itself. And those Friday evenings when we used to entertain five or six Jerusalem couples, high-ranking army officers, clever young university lecturers, promising politicians. You used to serve the drinks at the start of the evening, exchange some witticisms with the female partners, and curl up in a corner armchair in the shade of your bookshelves. You followed the political discussion with an expression of suppressed irony, but without participating. As the discussion heated up, the faint wolf grin gradually spread on your lips. You stealthily kept the glasses topped up, and went back to concentrating on filling your pipe. When the discussion was at its height and they were all tearing one another limb from limb, shouting and red in the face, you would choose your moment with the precision of a ballet dancer, and interject softly: "Hold on. I'm sorry. I don't follow that." The hubbub would die down at once and all eyes would fix on you. Lazily drawing out the syllables, you would say: "You're all moving a little too fast for me. I've got a really elementary question." And then you would shut up. You would concentrate on your pipe for a moment as though you were alone in the room, and then, out of the thick cloud, you would deliver a short Katyusha salvo at your guests. Demanding definitions of the terms they had been using carelessly. Laying bare with an icy chisel certain latent contradictions. Drawing in a few sentences some clever logical lines, as though tracing geometrical shapes. Directing a devastating rejoinder to one of the lions in the room, and surprising all of us by backing the opinion of the weakest intellect present. Setting up a compact argument and fortifying it with a preventive bombardment against any possible rejoinder. And concluding, to the general stupefaction, by indicating a possible weak point in your own argument, which no doubt had escaped everyone's notice. In the ensuing silence you would turn to me and command: "Lady, these good people are too shy to tell you that they want some coffee." Then you would start fiddling with your pipe again, as if to say that the break was over and it was time to resume the really serious business. I was enthralled by the frost of your polite ruthlessness. The moment the door closed behind the last departing couple I would wrench your neatly pressed best shirt out of your corduroy trousers and thrust my fingers into your back, into the hair on your chest. Only the following morning would I clear up and wash the dishes.

Sometimes you got in at one o'clock in the morning from maneuvers, from a brigade-level field exercise, from a night vigil of taming some new tank (what were you getting in those days? British Centurions? American Pattons?), with eyes red from the desert dust, powdered bristles on your face, gritty sand in your hair and the soles of your shoes, your salt sweat stiffening the shirt on your back, and yet as brisk and lively as a burglar inside a safe. You would wake me up, demand some supper, take a shower without closing the door and emerge dripping wet because you hated drying yourself. You would sit down in an undershirt and tennis shorts at the kitchen table and devour the bread and salad and the double omelette that I had prepared for you in the meantime. Far from sleep you would put some Vivaldi or Albinoni on the record player. You would pour yourself some cognac or a whisky-on-the-rocks, sit me down in my nightie in an armchair and sink into the chair opposite, put your bare feet up on the coffee table, and start lecturing me with a kind of repressed, derisive rage: denouncing the idiocy of your commanding officers; tearing to pieces the "mentality of the Palmach mob"; sketching the appearance of the theater of war toward the end of the century; thinking aloud about "the universal common denominator" of armed conflicts as such. And suddenly you would change the subject and tell me about some little woman soldier who had tried to seduce you earlier that evening. Interested to know if I was jealous. Asking jokingly what I would say if you had allowed yourself to be seduced into "opening a quick packet of field rations." Interrogating me offhandedly about the men I had had before you. Demanding that I grade them "on a scale from one to ten." Curious to learn if it happened that some stranger occasionally caught my fancy. Asking me to give a "stimulation rating" to your superior officers and comrades, our Friday evening guests, the plumber and the greengrocer and the postman. Eventually, at three o'clock in the morning, we would clamber into bed or collapse onto the rug, emitting sparks, my hand on your lips to prevent the neighbors from hearing your roars, your hand on my mouth to muffle my shrieks.

Limp, drowned in pleasure, aching, dizzy with exhaustion, I would sleep next day till one or two in the afternoon. In my sleep I could hear your alarm clock going off at six-thirty. You would get up, shave, take another shower—this time in cold water. Even in the winter. You would get into a clean uniform that I had starched and pressed for you. Swallow some bread and sardines. Gulp down some coffee without even sitting down. And then: the slamming of the door. Your leaping down the steps two by two. The sound of the jeep starting. That's how the game began. The shadow of a third person in our bed. We would conjure up some man who happened to have caught my fancy. And you impersonated him. Sometimes you impersonated both of you, yourself and the stranger. My role was to give myself to you both alternately or simultaneously. The presence of the strange shadows pierced us both with a searing jungle thrill that wrenched from my belly and your chest screams, oaths, pleas, spasms the like of which I have never encountered elsewhere except in childbirth. Or in death.

By the time Boaz was two our hellfire was already burning with a black flame. Our love had filled with hate. Which consumed everything yet continued to masquerade as love. When you discovered that snowy January evening, coming back from the university library with a raging fever, that lighter on the bathroom stool, you were overwhelmed by a lunatic glee. You roared with laughter, like hiccoughs; you punched me until by a battering cross-examination you dragged out of me every detail, every jot and shudder, and without undressing me you fucked me standing up as though knifing me, and during and after you didn't stop interrogating me more and more and again you mounted me on the kitchen table and your teeth dug into my shoulder and you slapped me with the back of your hand, like punishing an unruly horse. So our life began to flicker with the glimmer of a will-o'-the-wisp. Your demented fury, whether I was obedient or not, whether I seemed to you sick with desire or whether I seemed indifferent, whether I described what had been done to me or stayed stubbornly silent. You would disappear from home for days and nights on end, shut yourself up in that hole in the wall you rented near the Russian Compound, conquering your doctorate as though taking enemy fortifications by storm, and without warning you used to descend on me at eight o'clock in the morning or three in the afternoon, lock Boaz in his room, extract a detailed confession from me, and exhaust in me the torrent of your lust. Then began the suicides, with tablets and with gas. And your alliance with Zakheim and your savage war against your father and the accursed house in Yefe Nof. Our tropical hell. A parade of dirty towels. Stinking socks of grinning belching men. The reek of garlic and radishes and shish kebab. Hiccoughs from Coca-Cola or beer. Choking on cheap cigarettes. Sourness of sticky lustful male sweat. Their trousers lowered to their ankles, not troubling to take off their shirts; some were even too slovenly to remove their shoes. Their dribble on my shoulders. In my hair. Spunk stains on my sheets. Murmured obscenities and hoarse lascivious whispers. Their lecherous, meaningless endearments. And afterward, the ludicrous search for their underwear, lost in the bedding. The jocular arrogance that descended upon them once their desire was satisfied. The absentminded yawns. The invariable glance at their watches. Crushing me as though in me they were vanquishing the whole female sex. Like avengers. Or as though they were scoring points on some masculine league table. Or clocking engine hours. Only very rarely there came a stranger who tried to listen to my body and produce a tune. Or a youth who managed to make me feel a fleeting compassion beyond my lasting disgust. And you with your tide of desperate hatred. Until I became repugnant to myself and to you and you divorced me. At the bottom of my make-up drawer I keep a note in your handwriting. Zakheim handed it to me the day of our decree, when the court declared that henceforth we have no claims on each other. You had written down four lines for me from a poem by Alterman: "You are the sadness of my balding head, / The melancholy of my aging claws: / You'll hear me in the plaster of your walls, / And in the nightly creaking of your floors."

That is what you wrote in the courthouse and sent to me via Zakheim. You did not add a word of your own. For seven whole years. Why have you returned now like a phantom to the window of my new life? Go away to your own hunting grounds. Go away to the frost of the stars in your black-and-white spacecraft. Go away and never come back. Not even in dreams. Not even in my body's longings. Not even in the plaster of the walls and the creaking of the floors. Go away from the woodcut and the cowl. Why not cross the snowbound wilderness, knock at the door of the first hut, and ask for light and warmth? Marry your bespectacled secretary. Or any of your admirers. Take a wife and make a home. Make sure there's a real log fire in winter. A little garden. Roses. A dovecote. Perhaps you will have another son, and when you get home from work in the evening you can sit down with him at your black desk, cut out pictures for him from the *Geographical Magazine*, touch his hair and mess it up with gum. Your wife will run her hand over your tired brow. Massage at night your neck muscles, strained from writing and loneliness. You can put a record on. Not Vivaldi or Albinoni—perhaps some pensive jazz. There will be a rainstorm outside. Water rushing in the gutter. From the next room you will catch scents of talcum powder and shampoo, bedtime smells of the child. You will both lie there in your bed, listening to the roar of the wind through the tight-closed window. Each reading a book. Or else you will talk to her, in a whisper, about Napoleon's campaigns. Soon the light will go out and her fingers will start wandering among the curls on your chest. You will close your eyes. Then I shall come too and slip between you like a rustling. And in the darkness you and I will laugh together without making a sound. My genie and my bottle.

It is now almost six o'clock in the morning. I have been writing to you all night. I will have a shower, dress, and make breakfast for my little girl and my husband. There is happiness in the world, Alec, and suffering is not the opposite of it, it is the thorny path along which we have to creep on our bellies to that forest clearing, bathed in a fine lunar silver, which is calling to us and waiting. Don't forget.

Ilana

———

GIDEON MIDWEST UNIV CHICAGO

FOR YOUR ATTENTION ALEX LEGALLY BOAZ IS A MINOR AND UNDER HIS MOTHERS CUSTODY YOUR ACTION COULD BE INTERPRETED AS KIDNAPPING SOMMO IS CONSIDERING CRIMINAL PROCEEDINGS

AGAINST YOU PERHAPS HE WILL RECONSIDER IF YOU AGREE TO SELL
THE PROPERTY SUGGEST YOU CLIMB DOWN ZAKHEIM

—

GIDEON MIDWEST UNIV CHICAGO

MY PARTNER IS EXERTING PRESSURE IN VARIOUS DIRECTIONS
SITUATION DELICATE FOR YOUR CONSIDERATION ROBERTO
DIMODENA

—

PERSONAL DIMODENA JERUSALEM ISRAEL

OFFER THE SOMMOS AND ZAKHEIM ANOTHER FIFTY THOUSAND IN
MY NAME IN RETURN FOR AN UNDERTAKING TO LEAVE BOAZ IN
PEACE IF YOU WANT ILL RELEASE YOU ALEX

—

GIDEON MIDWEST UNIV CHICAGO

LET ME SELL THE PROPERTY AND ILL GUARANTEE BOAZ CAN STAY IF
YOU REFUSE HE IS LIKELY TO GO TO JAIL DONT FORGET HES
ALREADY GOT A SUSPENDED SENTENCE ROBERTO IS LEAVING YOU
STOP PLAYING THE FOOL AND ACCEPT HELP DONT REFUSE YOUR
ONLY FRIEND OTHERS ARE ONLY WAITING FOR YOUR DEATH AND
THE INHERITANCE DONT BE CRAZY USE YOUR FAMOUS BRAINS FOR
ONCE IF I DIE OF AN ULCER ITLL BE YOUR FAULT MANFRED

—

PERSONAL ZAKHEIM JERUSALEM ISRAEL

FORGIVE YOU ON CONDITION YOU STOP NAGGING INSTEAD OF THE
ZIKHRON PROPERTY AUTHORIZE YOU TO SELL YOUR CLIENT THE

HOUSE AND PLOT IN MAGDIEL ILL KNOCK THE BREATH OUT OF YOU IF YOU TRY ANY MORE CLEVER TRICKS FINAL WARNING ALEX

———

GIDEON MIDWEST UNIV CHICAGO

I HAVE RETURNED YOUR FILES TO MY PARTNER NO HARD FEELINGS ROBERTO DIMODENA

———

GIDEON MIDWEST UNIV CHICAGO

EVERYTHING ARRANGED BOAZ IN MY DEVOTED CARE AM KEEPING SOMMO FED BUT ON A TIGHT REIN TAKE CARE OF YOUR HEALTH MANFRED

———

SOMMO TARNAZ 7 JERUSALEM

HAVE DECIDED TO CHANGE MY WILL YOU RECEIVE ONE QUARTER AND THE REST GOES TO BOAZ ON CONDITION YOU AGREE TO LEGAL TRANSFER OF CUSTODY TO ME UNTIL HE COMES OF AGE YOUR DECISION SOONEST PLEASE ALEXANDER GIDEON

———

MR. GIDEON MIDWEST UNIVERSITY CHICAGO

WITH ALL DUE RESPECT SIR BOAZ IS NOT FOR SALE HIS MOTHER IS RESPONSIBLE FOR HIM AND I AM RESPONSIBLE FOR HER IF YOU DESIRE HIS WELLBEING AND ALSO PARTIAL ATONEMENT FOR YOUR TERRIBLE SINS THEN PLEASE BE KIND ENOUGH TO SEND ME A DONATION FOR THE REDEMPTION OF THE LAND AND RETURN THE BOY TO OUR SUPERVISION MICHAEL SOMMO

172

GIDEON MIDWEST UNIV CHICAGO

HAVE SOLD MAGDIEL TO SOMMO REPRESENTING HIS PATRON
MILLIONAIRE FANATIC FROM PARIS TO EXCHANGE WITH FRENCH
MONASTERY AGAINST LAND IN WEST BANK MY SONINLAW IS IN ON
DEAL TOO THEY ADVISE INVESTING YOUR READY CASH WITH THEM
FOR PURCHASES IN TERRITORIES THATS WHERE THE FUTURE LIES
YOU SHOULD LEARN A LESSON FROM YOUR FATHER IN HIS GREAT
DAYS AWAITING INSTRUCTIONS MANFRED

To Ilana Sommo   *Beit Avraham*
Tarnaz 7   17.8.76
Jerusalem

Dear Ilana,

Your letter saddened and hurt me. Who does not dream occasionally of taking off, flying away, and getting singed on some
faraway flame? There's no point in your making fun of me: I didn't
invent the fixed choice between fire and ashes—I have my own
closed circle. Maybe I'll tell you something. About half a year ago
I was taking my turn at cleaning the clubroom. It was morning,
and raining, and a young boy I didn't know, a volunteer from Iceland
or Finland, with glasses, dark skin, wet hair, wrapped up in his
thoughts and floating on a cloud of cigarette smoke, was sitting by
himself in a corner writing an airmail letter. Apart from "Good
morning" and "Excuse me" we didn't exchange a word. It was totally
silent, with grey rain at the windows. I washed and rinsed and dried
the floor even underneath his feet and emptied and wiped and gave
him back his ashtray, and for an instant he smiled at me wistfully,

173

sardonically, compassionately, as though he knew the whole truth. If he had said, Sit down, if he had waved his hand, nothing would have stopped me. I could have forgotten everything. But I couldn't. On every side there lurked the giggles, the petty humiliations, the remorse, anxiety about smelly armpits, fear of the buckles, the embarrassment, the zip fastener, the wet floor, the buttons, the coarse string bra, the morning light, the open door, the cold, the curtains that had gone to the laundry, the smell of chlorine, the shame. Like a fortified wall. I haven't told a soul apart from you and in fact I haven't even told you and in fact there's nothing to tell. And Yoash was away on reserve duty in the Golan Heights and at quarter to ten I had to take Yiftah to his appointment with the dentist. There was nothing at all except the pain of realization: like a fortified wall. Like an irrecoverable loss. That evening I painted the veranda furniture white, to surprise Yoash when he got back. And I made the children some homemade chocolate ice cream. And in the night I ironed and ironed, until the broadcasting shut down and the radio went on whistling and the night watchman went past my open window laughing and said, It's late, Rahel. There's nothing to tell, Ilana. Go and work part time in your bookshop, while Yifat's at nursery school. Enroll in a correspondence course. Buy yourself some new clothes instead of the brown dress that I realize from your letter you really hate. Call me a hedgehog if you like. Don't answer if you like. Yoash is working nights in the cowsheds and I'm tired and the sink's still full of dirty dishes. I'll stop here. Your sister,

Rahel

Actually I meant to write to you for another reason: to tell you that Yoash was in Zikhron yesterday for a couple of hours; he helped to fix wire netting in the chicken run, gave some agricultural advice, and came away with the impression that Boaz is doing very well in the commune he is setting up. Next time we'll book a car in advance and take the children. There's no reason why you and Michel and Yifat shouldn't visit him sometimes.

———

Notes made by Prof. A. A. Gideon on little cards.

258. And all of them, each in his own way, begin by destroying
the institution of the family. Plato. Jesus. The early communists. The Nazis. The militarists and also the militant
pacifists. The ascetics and also the orgiastic sects (both ancient and modern). First step to redemption: elimination of
the family. Severance of all the intimate connections between people in favor of total integration in the "Revolu-
tionary Family."

261. The self—the focus of suffering. Redemption—annihilation
of the self. Complete absorption in the masses.

266. Crime—guilt feeling—need for absolution—dedication to
an ideal—more guilt—another crime committed in the pursuit of the ideal—more need for absolution—redoubled at-
tachment to the ideal—and so on and so forth. A vicious
circle.

270. And so, suddenly or gradually, life is worn down, flattened,
emptied. Esteem takes the place of friendship. Self-negation
replaces respect. Obedience instead of participation. Sub-
jection instead of brotherhood. Enthusiasm takes the place
of emotion. Shouts and whispers substitute for speech. Suspicion instead of doubt. Torture instead of joy. Repression
instead of longing. Mortification instead of meditation. Be-
trayal instead of leavetaking. The bullet instead of an argument. Slaughter instead of dissension. Death instead of
change. Purging crusades instead of death. "Immortality"
instead of life.

283. "Let the dead bury the dead"—the living will bury the living.

284. "Those who live by the sword shall die by the sword"—until the Messiah arrives with a whirling sword of fire in his hand.

285. "Thou shalt love thy neighbor as thyself"—at once, or we'll fill you full of lead.

286. "Thou shalt love thy neighbor as thyself"—but if self-hatred has already eaten into you, this commandment is loaded with deadly irony.

288. And what of the promised resurrection? It is always without the body.

290. As for your soul, it will merge totally with the other souls. Be soothingly reabsorbed in the general reservoir. "Be gathered into the bosom of the nation." Or into the heart of the departed forefathers. Or into the cauldrons of the Race. Or into the treasure chambers of the Movement. Where it will serve as the raw material of a new, purified casting. Anaximander's *apeiron*. The Jewish "bundle of life." The Christian melting pot. Peer Gynt's button molder.

291. And the body? It is nothing more than a transient nuisance. A vessel full of fetid humors. A source of depression and infection. A cross we have to bear. A trial we have to undergo. A punishment we are doomed to suffer so as to be released from it in the "world which is all-good." A block of present pollution interposed between the abstract purity of the past and the abstract brilliance of the future.

292. Stripping off of corporeality: to annihilate the body. Whether gradually, by self-mortification, or by a single redemptive blow, on the altar of some impending salvation.

293. Hence: "Dust unto dust."

294. Hence: "Viva la muerte"—meaning "Long live death."

295. And once again Pascal: All the evils in the world derive from the fact that we are unable to remain quietly in a room. Our futility comes and destroys us.

———

Michel Sommo
Tarnaz 7
Jerusalem

Hi there Michel Im riting this to you from Zikhron. I dont mind if Ilana reeds it to but you reed it first. I expect your angry with me and think Im ungreatful and that you treeted me 100 percent right and I mukked up your plans and arranged thru America to be here in Zikhron. If your furious at me then just through this letter in the trash and dont reply only dont start preeching to me again. Your not G-d Michel and Im not youre fool. And anyway to spend your time telling each other what to do and what not to do in life is stupid. Thats my opinion sorry. But this letter is not to change you anyway Im against changing people. So what is it for? Its for Ilana.

Listen Michel. In my opinion Ilana is getting into trubble. We saw it in her when she came to visit. 100 percent normal shes never been, but now she dropped down maybe below 50 percent. My sudgestion is that she and Yifat should come hear to Zikhron for a bit and work around the house or in the vedgetable garden and have a rest from your relidgusness. Dont be angry Michel you no your a lovely good person the only trubble is youve got this obseshun that everyones got to be exactly the same as you and anyone who isnt like you you think their not really a human being. You think Im a hoodlum you think Ilanas a baby you think the arabs are animals. Im begining to be scared your going to think Yifats a little girl made of plasticine that you can bend and twist anyway you like, and then 90 percent sure Yifatll end up in trubble to and youll blame everyone except yourself. All the favors youve done to Ilana and me and the country Michel they arnt good enough unless you let evryone live there own life. Take Kiryat Arba were you sent me its a very nice place with a view and everything the only trubble is its just not the rite place for someone like me thats not relidgous and dont belive that what the state needs is to keep conkering the arabs and take their places away from them. In my opinion we should leave them alone and they should leave us alone. But thats not why Im riting to you. My sudgestion is that Ilana and Yifat should come hear for a while to have a rest from youre domination and from all the crazes in Jerusalem. Ive fixed up a really nice clean room for them with some furniture and all and Ive got six people working here to get things strait and Mr. Zakeim who used to interfere with me at first has improved, now hes arranged water and electricity permits from the council and out of the money from America Ive bought sprinklers and plants and tools and chickens and the whole business is starting to take shape including a telescop on the roof thats nearly finished. Let her come with Yifat shell be comftable here. 5 stars. We work all day then we go for a swim in the sea then in the evening we have a little sing then in the night Ill take good care of them for you. Weve got a big kitchin here and I dont mind having a kosher section for them if thats what Ilana wants. Ive got nothing against it. Free and easy. Its not Kiryat Arba hear evrybody does what they feel like as long as they work hard and treat each other OK and not be a nuisance and not preech.

What do you say, Michel? Ive ritten this to you because in youre house your the boss and you make the decisions but I dont mind if Ilana reeds it to. And now Ill close with thanks and respect because when alls sed and done your not a bad sort of guy Michel. I must say that Ive lerned something from you personally, not to hit, not to pick up crates even tho at the start all sorts of cops and inspectors used to come nosing around interfering and making trubble I never touched anyone and thats thanks to you Michel. All my best to Ilana and a little pinch to Yifat. Ive made swings and a slide and a sandbox and evrything for her here. And for Ilana Ive got work. Everythings lovely here now like a little kibbutz even more because here nobody meddles in anyone elses affares. Your also invited to come and visit and if you feel like making us a donation why not? you can. No problem.

With appreciation and thanks,
Boaz

———

To Boaz Brandstetter   *By the grace of G-d*
Gideon House   *Jerusalem*
Zikhron Yaakov (South)   *19 Av 5736 (15.8.76)*

Dear Boaz,

Your mother and I read your letter twice in quick succession and couldn't believe our eyes. I am hastening to reply to each point in order. First of all I must tell you, Boaz, that I am not angry because you are so ungrateful (you write it with "grate," not "great," you GREAT nincompoop!). But there isn't enough room on the paper to correct all your spelling mistakes and the defective syntax. It is not for me to finish the task (as the rabbis put it)!

And why should I be angry with you? If I took the trouble to be angry with everyone who wronged me or was ungrateful to me I should spend my whole life in a black rage. The human race is divided, Boaz, into those who take shamelessly from others and those who give without counting the cost, and I have always, ever since I was a child, belonged to the latter section, and I have never been angry with those who belong to the former section, nor have

I envied them, because the percentage of unfortunate people is much higher there than down here in our group, and the reason for that is that to give without counting the cost brings pride and joy whereas those characters who are accustomed to take brazenly from others are condemned by Heaven to disgrace and emptiness: grief and shame combined.

As concerns you, I have done my bit to the best of my modest ability for your mother's sake and for yours, and of course for the sake of Heaven, and if I have not had too much help from on high, who am I to complain? As it is written in the Book of Proverbs: "A wise son rejoices his father, and a foolish son is his mother's sorrow." Your charming father is not entitled to rejoice, Boaz, and your poor mother has already had enough sorrow from you. As for myself, I have a measure of partial satisfaction. It is true that I was hoping to lead you in a different path, but, as it is written, "Whither a man desires to go, thither he is led." So you are longing now to become a farmer and a stargazer? Why not? Do the best you can and we will not be ashamed of you.

We were deeply touched by other points in your letter, the first of which was when you write that I have been a hundred percent okay with you. You have judged me kindly, Boaz, and this I shall not forget: as you know, we have a good memory. However, if only it were true! For your information, Boaz, I frequently torment myself in my bed at night over the thought that I may have had some part or responsibility (unwittingly!) in your youthful sins and misdeeds, which I shall not mention here. It may well be that right from the start, from the moment I was privileged to marry your dear mother, it was my sacred duty to keep you on a short rein instead of accepting it in silence when you kicked over the traces and shrugged off the twin yokes of Torah and worldly occupation. I should have afflicted you with scorpions until you returned to the straight and narrow path. Whereas for my sins I was afraid to be firm with you in case you went away. I took pity on your mother's tears and spared the rod. Perhaps I did wrong when against my better judgment I allowed you to waste your school years in a highly questionable secular institution where they did not have the good sense to teach you even so much as to read and write and observe the commandment to honor your father and your mother. Instead I took the easy way out. I did not instill in you Torah and commandments and good deeds and I turned a blind eye to your idiocies, on the principle "out of sight, out of mind." Even though you, Boaz, have never been out of my mind. Not for a moment. Perhaps I even made a mistake when I went three times to see Inspector Almaliah to beg for mercy on your behalf? Perhaps it would have been a blessing for you to have learned your lesson the hard way, to have understood through the backside if not through the head that there are rewards and punishments, that there is justice and there is a Judge? And not to have got into the habit of thinking that everything is permissible in life? That the life of a Jew consists just of having a good time, as you wrote to me extremely foolishly. I shall return to this important point in what follows. I confess my sins today, Boaz, in taking pity on you and still today not overcoming my feelings of pity because of the suffering you received in your childhood from that wicked man. As it is written, "Is Ephraim my dear son? is he a pleasant child? for since I spoke against him, I do earnestly remember him still: therefore my bowels are troubled for him" (Jeremiah, chapter 31, verse 20). This verse precisely describes my feelings toward you. Perhaps against your best interests?

But it seems that for all this my prayers have been heard and they are watching over your steps a little in Heaven. Your dear famous father schemed to lead you into evil ways, to make you leave Kiryat Arba and go to that ruin and commit seven abominations there, and behold the hand of Providence intervened to turn his evil scheme to good ends. I have noted with satisfaction what Mr. Zakheim told me, that together with some other young Jewish men and women you are fulfilling the commandment to restore the fatherland and bringing forth bread from the earth in the sweat of your brow. Very well done, Boaz: a marked improvement! I have the impression that you are laboring uprightly according to the laws of the state even though to our sorrow you are apparently continuing to transgress against a number of scriptural prohibitions and stubbornly persisting in remaining a spiritual dunce. If only at the very least you would observe the Sabbath Day and be a bit more particular about the rules of chaste behavior. I write this not by way of preaching but only as it is written: "Faithful are the wounds of a friend" (Book of Proverbs, chapter 27, verse 6). Don't lose your temper with me—just as I am restraining myself (with difficulty!) from losing my temper with you. All right, Boaz? Is it agreed? We'll still go on being friends?

And one more thing I want to tell you about your sins, which are the product of the times we live in and fall under the heading of a common woe: As long as the laws of the state continue to be more lenient than the laws of Scripture, the Messiah, whose footsteps we can already clearly hear, must wait outside on the doorstep. He cannot enter our homes. All right let's leave all that to wiser people than ourselves and in the meantime I shall be satisfied with very little: you just observe the laws of the state and we shall thank G-d for that and count our blessings. And more specifically about your giving up throwing crates and so on and so forth: It is your own good or bad deeds, Boaz, that will determine your destiny, and of your good actions, which will be accounted to your credit on the day of reckoning, we take note with deep love and satisfaction.

When I was your age I lived in poverty and want and I had to work hard to pay my way through school, just like all my brothers and sisters. Our father, who was disabled, was a ticket-seller on the Métro and our mother (Heaven spare you this!) was a cleaner in a Jewish hospital. I was a cleaner too: every evening at five o'clock, as soon as I came out of the lycée (where the children still used to get beaten!), I used to run straight from class to work till midnight. There was a concierge, a Jew from Rumania, who let me change out of my school uniform and into my working clothes, which I carried around with me in my satchel. And then I used to clean staircases. And you must remember that I was not a hulking great hero like you but a skinny weakling who could even be fairly described as undersized. However, I was as stubborn as a mule and even a rather embittered character. I won't deny it. Bullies were attracted to me, and sometimes they used to beat me up viciously. And I, my dear Boaz, I used to take it and restrain myself, take it and grind my teeth, and from shame and embarrassment I told nobody at home. "There are no problems at all," this was my motto. When it got out at school that I worked as a cleaner my charming friends began to call me Ragbag (believe me, Boaz, it sounds even worse in French). Then I found another job, wiping tables in a café, and there they called me Ahmed, because they took me for a little Arab. The truth of the matter is that that is the only reason I started to wear a skullcap. The faith came to me much later. At night I used to sit for another hour or two after midnight on the lavatory seat—excuse me—because we lived six of us in a room and a half and that was the only place where I could put the light on after everyone else was asleep and do my homework. I had only five hours left every night to sleep on my mattress in the kitchen and to this day I still haven't told even your dear mother how sometimes instead of sleeping I used to lie on that mattress sobbing with hatred and anger. I was full of resentment against everyone. I used to dream of being rich and respected and settling my scores with life. I used to tease cats in the yard, and sometimes in the street I used to let the air out of the tires of parked cars at night. I was a wicked, bitter child.

And so my situation was likely to turn me too, Boaz, into a negative element, but one Saturday I went with two friends from the same street, Prosper and Janine (you know both of them: Mrs. Fuchs and Inspector Almaliah), to a meeting of the Betar youth movement with an emissary from Israel. Believe me, it might just as easily have been the communists (perish the thought!) or something worse still, Heaven forbid, but the hand of Providence decreed that it would be Betar. From then on I was a new man; I never cried again in my life and I never did any harm again to any human being or even to a cat. Because I understood then, Boaz, that life was not given to us to have a good time but to give something of yourself to others and to the nation. Why? Because giving endows you with real stature even if you are only five feet five and lets you hold your head up even if you are only a ragbag. It is a tree of life to those who hold fast to it. Whereas if you live as you wrote to me only to have a good time, then you are an insect, not a man, even if you are as big and beautiful as Mont Blanc itself. Better you should spend your whole life as a hair or a fingernail of the Jewish people than be that wretched insect. That is my creed in a nutshell, Boaz. And you must somehow understand this, in your heart if not in your brain, in Zikhron Yaakov if not in Kiryat Arba, in secular life if not in religion, so that there will be some chance still that your good deeds will outweigh the bad ones, which as you know are already quite heavy. The gates of repentance stand ever open, they never close.

And since I have mentioned your bad deeds, I cannot pass in silence over your arrogance and impertinence: where, tell me, did you get the cheek and the presumption to write of your mother that she is (save the mark!) "not normal"? How did your hand not tremble? What, are you yourself normal? Are you? Go and look in the mirror! You wild beast! So remove your shoes please before you speak of your mother! Although I suppose you walk around barefoot there like an Arab.

And on another matter. I am aware that your dear father has started now to pay you something as a monthly wage. Take note that everything he gives you is yours anyway, not his, since for seven years he behaved as cruelly as a raven toward your dear mother and yourself and denied both of you your keep and damages for the sorrow and shame that he had maliciously caused you. What he sends you now is barely the gleanings of his field, the crumbs from his table, nothing more. But I am not attempting to provoke a son against his father, Heaven forbid. Why did I mention the money? Only to point out, my dear Boaz, that this time you should not waste it on dubious pleasures, and I shall not point out examples from the past, etc., but invest it in the restoration of the ruins that he left behind him and in setting up an agricultural settlement. That is why I said that we could not believe our eyes on reading your letter, despite the mistakes and the impertinence, and that is also why I have seen fit to enclose herewith a postal order for the sum of two thousand five hundred pounds. And so from now on I shall give you something every month on condition that you commit yourself on your word of honor to start learning to read and write and perhaps also to desecrate the Sabbath less? That makes in round figures thirty thousand pounds per annum from now until you grow up. You won't have to accept any more money from that evildoer. Is it a deal, Boaz?

Something else on the credit side, something incomparable: It would seem that you have begun, instead of causing suffering, to love your neighbor as yourself. To what do my words allude? To the childish suggestion in your letter. Childish, but deeply touching even so. You are still unworthy to receive your mother and sister as your guests—first you must improve yourself and prove yourself—but we were moved by the suggestion nonetheless. I could almost write, echoing the words of Scripture: "This was the boy for whom we prayed." Only you still have a long way to go from evil to what is right in the sight of the Lord, and up to now you have only climbed a step or two. That is the truth, Boaz, and I don't care if you get angry and call me domineering or if you go on hurling ugly lies at me such as that I subjugate your mother or that I feel hatred, Heaven forbid!, toward the Arabs or toward Jews whose eyes have not yet been opened.

Have you gone mad, Boaz? When have I ever sinned against your mother? To what are you alluding when you claim that I "dominate her"? Or you? Have I tied anybody up with a chain? Whom have I wronged? Against whom have I raised my hand? Or a crate? On whom have I brought suffering? Doubtless in the heavenly ledger there are a few black marks inscribed against the name of Michael Sommo. I am not saying there aren't. After all I am only an average sort of man and a very ordinary Jew. But to say about me that I have done wrong? To anybody? Even a small wrong?

You have done me an injustice, Boaz. It is lucky that I am not one of those people who take offense easily, and all is forgiven.

If I were you I would at least beg forgiveness for the sin you have committed against me by slandering me.

And believe me, by the way, when I say that even for the Arabs, whom you have accused me in your letter of wishing ill, I sincerely wish that they may live in peace according to their faith and their customs and that it may be granted to them speedily to return to their homeland just as we have returned to ours. Except that we left their lands naked and empty-handed and even igno-miniously, whereas I am suggesting that they leave here with their dignity and wealth and without our plundering so much as a hair or a shoelace from them. I am even offering to pay them good money in exchange for the property they seized by the sword in our land. It follows *a fortiori* that a man like me would not dream of hurting a hair on the head of a Jew, even if he were the greatest sinner alive. So why are you barking at me? And then you have the cheek to ask me not to preach at you, and to proclaim proudly that "it is wrong to change people"! Something new!

What do you mean? Are people perfect? Are you yourself perfect? Take even the chosen people: Is there nothing left to change? Nothing to put right? Rubbish, Boaz. We are all bound to try to influence each other for good. To link arms lest we fall by the wayside. Every human being is definitely his brother's keeper. And of course every Jew is!

As for your mother and sister, perhaps we shall all come to see you for a short visit, but only on condition that you start coming up to Jerusalem again for the Sabbaths. You are the one who went away and therefore it is up to you to take the first step toward us. In a few months' time we are moving to a nice spacious flat in the Jewish Quarter of the Old City and we shall keep a room ready for you for whenever you want it. That's one thing. But that they should come and stay in that ruin you received from your father? Among characters who may very well all be angels, but I don't know them or their families? What's up? Are you trying to rescue your mother and sister from my clutches? Still, I forgive you—your intentions were good.

And now for the dangerous opinion you wrote to me—that the important thing in life is to have a good time. I was shocked; I won't conceal it. Apparently it is from your wise-Alec father that you get this poison that you then try to proclaim to me in broken Hebrew. This idea, Boaz, is the source of all sin, and better you should flee from it as from a plague. The important thing in life is to do what is right. It is really very simple. And don't let your father and other wise guys of the same kind start tricking you into believing that right is a relative matter, that nobody is competent to distinguish between right and wrong, that A's right is B's wrong and vice versa, that it depends when and where, and all those clever sophistries. We have heard more than enough. We have nothing to do with that alien philosophy, which is all just flowers and no fruit, as the sage said, and poisoned flowers at that. Have nothing to do with that pollution. I tell you, Boaz, that that man is not yet born, including Arabs and sinners, who does not know in the depth of his heart what is right and what is wrong. We all know it right from our mother's womb. From G-d's image in which we were made. We know very well that to do good to others is right and to do bad to them is wrong. With no clever arguments. That is the whole Torah on one leg. Of course, there are unfortunately certain professional scoffers who play the sophist or the innocent and say: Bring proofs. Very well then, why not—there are proofs in plenty. For example, I gather from you that you have built yourself some kind of telescope there and that you gaze at the stars at night. Well, take a really good look through your equipment, and your heart will start singing songs of praise to the Creator for all his wondrous works, and you will see the proof with your own eyes. In the starry vault, Boaz, in the seven heavens arching over our heads, what do we behold? What is inscribed in outsize letters upon the skies?

So, you are silent now? Very nice indeed. Pretending the stars are nothing more than optics and astronomy. Playing the dunce. Very well then, I shall tell you what is written up there: Order! Plan! Purpose! That is what is written in the skies. That every star shall travel precisely in its own allotted path! And more than this, it is also written that there is a purpose in life. That there is a Ruler and a Guide, Justice and Judge. That we, like the host of Heaven, must always keep our watch and do the will of the Creator. Star or worm, it makes no odds, all of us were created with a purpose and all of us must follow our allotted path.

It is true that in the firmament we may also read the following: "When I consider thy heavens, the work of thy fingers, the moon and the stars which thou hast ordained, what is man that thou art mindful of him, and the son of man that thou visitest him?" In other words, that we are very small, that the foot or so by which you are taller than I is as unimportant as a garlic skin, but on the other hand it is also written in the sky that we were created in His image and that everything came into being at His word.

If you look upward with all your soul and with all your might you will observe with your own eyes that the heavens do indeed declare the glory of G-d: "He spreadeth forth the heavens as a curtain, He putteth on light as a garment." And he who looks with the eyes of the heart knows what is permitted and what is forbidden and what is human nature. No matter how clever we try to be, we still know it perfectly. We have done every since we ate of the fruit of the tree of knowledge, whose full name in the Bible is the tree of the knowledge of good and evil. Even your father knows—so it goes without saying that you do, O vinegar son of vinegar! So pay attention to the stars and to your conscience and thus you will turn to the Covenant and not turn aside after the evil inclination nor be like a star straying from its course or like a drifting leaf.

You may perhaps be interested to hear from me, if you have not already heard it from Mr. Zakheim, that I have given up being a teacher and I am now engaged almost day and night in the commandment of redemption of the Land, together with some comrades from the Jewish Fellowship, who have dedicated themselves to our revival, and whom you have met at home in Jerusalem or in Kiryat Arba, and there are also some new friends. We even have three reformed sinners, including one who grew up in a left-wing secular kibbutz but has now grown out of all that entirely.

Would you like to come for a few days without any obligation on your part and see with your own eyes? Perhaps your Jewish spark will catch fire? Soon, G-d willing, I am going to Paris on a matter of redemption of land, and when I return we shall meet. If you wish to join us you will be most welcome; we shall forget all about your running away from Kiryat Arba and not ask too many questions. You could have an interesting and important job, as security man for instance. You will learn a little Torah and also be a blessing. Only say the word and I will fix something up for you: thank the Lord I have many new connections and new possibilities in plenty.

And in the meantime do not hesitate to write me letters, even with mistakes. You are as dear to me as a son. I am enclosing some collages that your sister made and said, "Send them to Bozaz." And I also wanted to let you know that the letter you sent us made your mother burst into tears, and not tears of shame but tears of relief. She will add a few lines below. We miss you and we are praying that you will always choose the good path. Don't be embarrassed; let us know if there is anything you need, including a little money, and we'll see what we are able to do.

Yours affectionately,
Michel

P.S. Think carefully, if you accept the offer attached to the check. If not, never mind—you can keep the money this time anyway. If you do, as I have said you will receive the above-mentioned sum from me monthly. Will you think it over, Boaz? Use your brains? Your mother wants to add a few lines.

———

Dear Boaz, I haven't read what Michel's written. I read your letter to him because you said I could. I think it's all wonderful, what you're doing in your grandfather's house. You're better than any of us. I can't come with Yifat without hurting Michel. And in any case my hands are empty. I have nothing to contribute. What can I do if I've failed? I've failed in everything, Boaz. Failed utterly. Except that even a woman who's a failure, even a woman who's not normal, can love. Even if it is a miserable love.

You don't hate me and I'm amazed how it can be. What wouldn't I give for the chance, which I can't have, to give you something. At least to darn your clothes and wash your underwear. You don't have to answer. If you can, try not to despise me. You are better and purer than any of us. Take good care of yourself. Mother.

———

Michel and Ilana Sommo
Tarnaz 7
Jerusalem

Hi there Michel and Ilana and sweet Yifat

I got your letters and the money. Its a pity your worrying and making such a fuss about me. Im 100 percent and theres nothing to worry about. Your argumints give me a heddache Michel and Ive decided to give all that up. About 60 percent of what you wrote I quite agree with apart from the quotations and that, and about 30 percent I didn't understand at all what do you expect from me? Your a lovely person Michel but your all mixed up with your relidgion and your politics. Its really good that your going to Paris for a while you should take advantidge of it and have a really good time enjoy yourself and take a brake from all your redemshuns? For your informashun the stars dont say anything and naturaly they dont preech and that. They just make you feel very quiet in your sole its really special. I'm taking riting lessons from one of the girls here and on Saturdays we hardly work anyway so Ive accepted the money. And for your informashun I bought a spray and a mower. If you can please send me some more because we urgently need to buy some sort of small tractor otherwise we cant really get on. Ilana your OK only you know what? drop the tears and the feelings and

190

that and start really doing something. Im putting some peecock feathers in the envelope for Yifat because we were given a peecock by an old lady and it walks around in the yard. Bye now and all the best.

From Boaz B.

———

To Prof. A. A. Gideon   *Jerusalem*
Summer Program / Political Science   20.8.76
Princeton University
Princeton, New Jersey, U.S.A.

My dear Alex,

If by some chance you have calmed down, concluded the thunder-and-lightning phase, and entered on a period of bright spells, you can find at the conclusion of this letter an interesting idea for your consideration. If, on the other hand, you are still boiling at your Manfred, pouring out your fierce rage on the trees and stones, wallowing in self-pity in your father's best Tatar tradition, then I must ask you to sit back and listen patiently to my apologia.

It isn't difficult for me to guess what you are thinking of me right now. In fact I'm almost inclined, just for the hell of it, to write out for you the case against me. Old Manfred will appear in the role of "poor man's Iago," as you put it (although "rich man's Iago" might be more appropriate?), a kind of Heidelberg Machiavelli, who betrayed your father for you, you for your sensational ex-wife, her for her sweet husband, until he finally completed his circle of villainy by betraying Sommo—with you again. Zakheim Iscariot squared. It's not surprising you've got black smoke coming out of your nostrils and ears. I haven't forgotten your fits of temper as a child: first you used to pull your hair out and smash your expensive toys, then you used to fix your teeth in the back of your hand until a kind of bleeding clock appeared. As far as I'm concerned you can go on producing such clocks. Or open the thesaurus and hurl all the insults you find there at me in alphabetical order. Go right ahead, be my guest. I am practiced in all the Gudonskian repertoire of the last three generations and I'll be delighted to give as good as I get. I only want you to remember, my dear, at least in the back of your mind, that had it not been for my wise foot on your faulty brakes, you would long since have been stripped naked, relieved of all your worldly goods, and sent off to die like a dog in the nearest poorhouse.

Moreover, Alex, had it not been for this same terrible Manfred all your father's property would have melted away between his senile hands and been squandered ten years ago on some project to de-salinate the Dead Sea or set up a Yiddish university for the Bedouin tribes. I was the one who pried the property and most of the money for you from the Tsar's claws, and smuggled the booty out safe and sound under the noses of all the Bolshevik ambushes laid for you by the various tax authorities. All this I now remind you of, O best beloved, not to earn a belated commendation from you for bravery under fire, but to establish this fact as a basis for an oath on my word of honor: I have not betrayed you, Alex, despite the hail of reproaches and insults you do not stop showering me with. On the contrary, all along the way I have stood humbly at your right hand maneuvering to the best of my ability to rescue you from emotional blackmail, devilish schemes, and above all from your own latest lunacies.

Why did I do it? An excellent question. I have no answer. At least not an easy one. With your permission I shall set forth the facts of the present plot, so that at least we can agree upon the sequence of events. At the end of February, like thunder out of a clear sky, you suddenly instructed me to sell the property in Zikhron so as to finance Rabbi Sommo's crusade. I admit that I saw fit to play for time, in the hope of cooling off your Robin Hood caprice. I took the trouble to collect and set out for you the information required for a reconsideration. My hope was to coax you down with delicacy and tact from the nut tree you had climbed. As a token of gratitude you drenched me with a flood of reproaches and insults such as would delight your father himself if he could only remember who you are, who I am, and who he is himself. As for the saintly Manfred, he wiped your spittle off his face and religiously carried out your instructions: sell up, pay up, and shut up.

I confess without any shame: at this point I permitted myself to cut a few corners. I displayed initiative under heavy fire, and decided on my own to sell another of your properties to pay that protection money, but I saved Zikhron for you. I must have been under the influence of prophetic inspiration: you have to admit that I managed to foresee with amazing accuracy your next twist. Before I could say "mad Gudonski" you had changed your mind and were clinging to your property in Zikhron as if your life depended on it. Hand on my heart, Alex: if I had executed your original instructions in February or March and sold the Winter Palace, you would have wrung my poor neck, or at least plucked out my few remaining hairs.

And what princely thanks did I get, Marquis? You stood me against the wall and fired me. Just like that. Kaput! Anyway, I accepted the verdict and withdrew from managing your affairs (after thirty-eight years of unconditional devoted service to the glorious House of Gudonski!). I even felt relieved. But before I could finish my cigarette you sent an urgent cable to say that you had changed your mind again, craved my forgiveness, and needed, more or less, my emotional intensive care. And what did Magnanimous Manfred do? Instead of sending you to hell with all your whims and lunacies, he got up and dashed the very same day to London, where he sat at your feet for a night and a day and took a concentrated bombardment of fire and smoke from you ("Fink," you called me, before you decided to promote me to the rank of Rasputin). And when eventually you managed to cool down somewhat, you issued a new set of orders: all of a sudden you wanted me to detach the Beauty from her Beast, and "buy the gentleman lock, stock, and barrel, no matter what the price." Why? No reason. "Decree of the king in council" and that's that.

And so, having received a proper dressing down, dear Manfred returned to Jerusalem with his bald head bowed and his tail between his legs, and began to pull on the strings. However, in the midst of all this he had an inspiration. Apropos of the taming of the Shrew, why not fix a halter on Sommo's saintly snout, tether him with a little rope, so that your father's fortune, instead of being wasted on founding a Fonivezh Yeshiva in Halhoul or a Chortkov Shtibl in Upper Qalqiliya, would be intelligently invested in solid real estate. So much for my sin and my crime. And bear in mind that the fortune in question was as much soaked in Zakheim's blood and sweat as it was the fruit of the Tsar's visions. It would appear that to my misfortune I have a sentimental bond with the orphaned wealth of the various generations of the Gudonski family. I have invested the best years of my life in building it up, and I do not get any kick out of demolishing it with my own hands. Once, in 1949, when I was the deputy military attorney, I managed to get a reduced sentence for a soldier by the name of Naji Santos, who had removed a hand grenade from his base, claiming that he had spent a year and a half writing the whole Book of Psalms in tiny letters on it in India ink. Apparently I too am becoming something of a Santos.

And so I sealed my nostrils carefully with a clothespin and descended deep into the masses. I burst my ulcer in a titanic effort to train Saint Sommo to be a Jesuitical fanatic instead of a Kamikaze fanatic. And believe me, my dear Alex, when I say that this was a very doubtful pleasure: so numerous were the missionary sermons that I was forced to swallow that I really should have charged your account by the yard.

And thus, while you were still cursing me and firing me and the Rabbi was saving my soul, I managed to tie Sommo hand and foot to my son-in-law Zohar Etgar and to turn him, if not through one hundred and eighty degrees, at least through ninety, give or take a degree. With the result that at this moment in time your hundred thousand are heeding the commandment to be fruitful and multiply, and very soon they will be two hundred thousand.

And now you will ask why I had to bother. Surely I could

simply have said to myself: Look here, Manfred, if your crazy Count has really got a fancy to hang a gold ring in a pig's nose, just pocket your commission quietly and let him jump off the roof. At this point Tender Feelings enter the picture. Zakheim Iscariot may not turn his nose up at the thirty pieces of silver (or more), but he has no desire for some reason to hand his lord over to be crucified. Nor does good Manfred wish to be a party to the exploitation of orphans. We were friends, you and I. Or so I thought. When you were seven or eight, a strange, gloomy child who made statues for rhesus monkeys and tried to bite himself in the mirror, the undersigned had already placed his sharp wits at the service of your father's visions. Together the two of us built an empire out of nothing. It all began in the roaring thirties. The day will come, my learned client, when I shall finally sit down and write my sensational memoirs, and you will discover how I wallowed for your father's sake in the filth of degenerate Arab effendis, in foul British beer, in the Bolshevik phrases of nasal officials of the Jewish Agency—and all so as cunningly to add acre to acre, stone to stone, pound to pound, everything that you received from me on a silver tray, gift-wrapped and tied up with a blue ribbon. Take it or leave it, chum; I couldn't stand the thought that you would waste it all on fixing a golden mezuzah on every Arab ruin in the territories, on tying tefillin on every Godforsaken Arab hill, on all that idolatry. On the contrary, before my mind's eye there opened up the attractive prospect of using Sommo to renew our days as of old, to purchase at rock-bottom prices parcels of land in places where no white man had yet set foot, to hitch our wagon to this messiah's donkey and do for you in the present twice as much as I did for your father in his day. That is the case for the defense, Alex. There are only one or two odd points left.

By efforts verging on martyrdom I set Sommo on the (relatively) straight and narrow path. I turned the black Pygmalion into a Zionist real-estate dealer, and attached Zohar to him in the role of safety pin. I hoped that in the course of time you too would calm down, sober up a little, and authorize me to mount in your name the new wagon I had built. I was confident that when the sound and the fury were over you might at last begin to behave like a true Gudonski. I was planning that your money plus my brains plus Sommo's armor-piercing cousinhood plus Zohar's dynamism would make all our fortunes and we would live happily ever after. In a nutshell, to quote the diminutive Moses, all in all I was trying to bring forth sweetness from the strong. And that's all there is to it, mate. That was the only reason I associated myself with the Sommo-Paris axis, and plugged into the Toulouse deal. That was the reason I begged you to agree to exchange your ruin in Zikhron, which doesn't bring you in a penny and only gobbles up property tax, for a foothold in Bethlehem, where the future lies. Take note, Alex: our Bolsheviks are on their last legs. The day is not far off when this country will be in the hands of Sommo & Zohar and their ilk. And then land in the West Bank and the Sinai will be released for urban development, and every clod of earth will be worth its weight in gold. Believe me, sweetheart, for a lot less than this your father would have sent me a little Mercedes and a case of champagne for my birthday.

And what did you do, darling? Instead of inscribing Manfred in the Golden Book, instead of offering thanks thrice a day to your father for bequeathing you not only his throne but also his own private Bismarck, instead of the Mercedes and the champagne, you fired me again. And you cursed and swore at me in your cables like a drunken mujik. And what's more, you heaped your new lunacy on me: buying Boaz from them. As it says in Shakespeare: "My kingdom for a horse" (but not for an ass, Alex!). And this after all you forced me to do in your divorce suits? Why Boaz all of a sudden? What for? What's the big deal?

For so it seemed good to you. "Le Roy le veult," and that's that. The Frenchified Russian aristocracy from North Binyamina Region smashes crystal goblets, and we the servants have to pick up the pieces submissively and scrub the stains off the carpet.

When I carried out my humanitarian duty of delaying the execution a little in case you reconsidered your mad orders, you fired me again and hired Roberto in my place. Just as you threw your father in the bin, just as you threw Ilana and Boaz on the scrap heap, just as now you have decided to throw yourself in hell: like throwing away a pair of old socks. After thirty-eight years of service! Me, who built the whole Duchy of Gudonski out of nothing! You've heard of how the Eskimos throw their old people out in the snow? Well, even they don't spit in their faces as well. Roberto! That will writer! That maître d'!

And then, lo and behold, dear Uncle Manfred, that great-souled avatar of King Lear and Pere Goriot, determined, despite the blow, to remain at his post. To turn a blind eye to his dishonorable discharge. "Here I stand, and can do no other." In the military court of appeals we once had a case of a soldier who had refused to operate a mortar on the grounds that he had personally signed for the shells.

And in the meantime you bought Boaz, shook off Roberto, and turned to me again pleading that we start afresh. You know, my genius, there's method in this madness. First you trample (Ilana, Boaz, me, even Sommo), then you apologize, you grovel, you shower with money and excuses, you mollify and attempt to purchase retroactive absolution. And even to beg for mercy. What is this: folk Christianity? "They that shoot in tears shall bandage in joy?" "As you have murdered, so shall you bind up?"

And at once you imposed a new task upon me: to lay my hands on the monumental child on your behalf and at your expense, and to assist him to set up a sort of hippie colony on your father's abandoned land. (By the way, that Gulliver is evidently fashioned of passably good materials, albeit totally demented, even by the standards of the Gudonski family.) Manfred, your unconditional lover, once more gritted his teeth but discharged your lunatic instructions. Like a cobra dancing to a fakir's pipe. He betook himself to Zikhron. He pleaded. He paid. He lubricated. He pacified the local police. Evidently I still have some sort of little gland that goes on secreting a kind of affection toward you and constant anxiety about your health. If you will permit me, I shall remind you that even the great Shakespeare himself did not let Hamlet, in the mass-stabbing scene, casually run through his faithful Horatio. In my humble opinion, it is not I who owe you an explanation, but your lordship who owes me at the least a formal apology (if not a case of champagne). And by the way, you also owe me money: I invest some two hundred fifty dollars per month in your Goliath as per your orders. But you deigned to forget (since when do you have a head for trifles?) that you have no ready cash here. On the other hand you now have, thanks to me, a great pile in your William Tell account, following the Magdiel-Toulouse deal. It's not very nice to descend from the sublimity of moral stocktaking to the banality of the financial vale of tears, but I would still ask you not to forget. And don't wave your famous will at me again with the sweet item for my grandchildren: old Manfred may be a bit doddery, but he is still far from being senile. Nor has he volunteered in the meantime for the Salvation Army.

Or perhaps he has joined up after all, without noticing it? Unknowingly joined the motley ranks of holders of the Legion of Honor for rescuing Alexander the Wretched? Otherwise how to explain his peculiar devotion to you and all your successive whims?

Go fuck yourself, Alex. Go and get married to Sommo, adopt your ex-wife as your mother, her hoodlum as a rhesus monkey, and Roberto as your adjutant. Get lost. That's what I should have said to you once and for all. Go and donate your trousers to the Union of Reformed Nymphomaniacs for Judaea and Samaria, and get the hell off my poor back.

The sad thing is that sentimentality is constantly getting the better of my pure reason. Antediluvian memories tie me to you like a pair of handcuffs. You are stuck in my soul like a rusty nail without a head. And apparently I am stuck in you too, somewhere among the cogwheels you are equipped with instead of a soul. I wish you'd explain to me one day over a glass of whisky how your black magic works on us. How do you manage to manipulate us all, over and over again, including foolish Uncle Manfred? In 1943, when I was still a little second lieutenant in the British Army, I was called out in the middle of the night once to Montgomery's field HQ in the Cyrenaica desert, to translate some German document for him. Why is it that in your presence I always feel as I did then, with him? What is there about you that makes me jump to attention? Time and time again I click my heels (symbolically) and whisper submissively "Yessir" to all your whims and insults. What is the spell that binds us all to you, even from beyond the Atlantic?

Perhaps it is the mysterious combination of ruthlessness and helplessness.

I can see before my eyes your supine form reclining on the leather sofa at the Nicholsons' house in London the night of our last meeting (even though you are back in America now, if not in Ceylon or Timbuktu). Your patrician features fixed in a brazen effort to conceal your pains from me. Your fingers curled around a teacup as though at any moment you might hurl its contents in my face or smash it over my head. Your voice was clear and cold, and your words like lead soldiers. Every now and again you closed your eyes slowly, as though you were a medieval castle raising its drawbridge and dropping the portcullis. While I was waiting for you to deign to take notice of me again, I looked at your back, stretched stiffly on the sofa, at your blank, pale face, at the expression of bitter disgust etched permanently around your lips, and just for a moment, as though peering through the firing slit of a tank, I could discern the child I remember from forty years ago: a large, pampered child, a decadent boy emperor who might at any instant signal to his servants with a lazy nod of the chin to chop my head off. Just like that. As a little nocturnal diversion. Because I had stopped interesting him.

That is how you looked to me at that moment in London. And I experienced a mixture of submissiveness and a vague paternal compassion. Physical awe combined with a sudden urge to rest my fingers on your brow. As when you were a child.

Your gladiator's body, which had become so skinny and bony, your expression of a tortured prince, the power of your grey eyes, the radiance of your tormented spirit, the icy shield of your iron will. Perhaps it was this: your fragile savagery. Your defenseless tyranny. The childish wolfishness which gave you the air of a wrist watch that had lost its glass. That is how you mesmerize us all. Arousing even in a man like me an almost womanly feeling toward you.

Even if you explode I shall not restrain myself this time from writing that at that meeting of ours in London you stirred a sort of sympathy in me. As though I were a peeling old eucalyptus that had all of a sudden surprised itself by producing figs. I was sorry for you. For what you have done with your life and for the way you are now planning your death. Surely you developed the disease like a deadly, sophisticated missile that you targeted on yourself (I have an inner certainty that you can command the choice, whether to stifle the illness or submit to it entirely). Now you will chuckle dryly to yourself, twisting half your mouth, and maybe make a note that Manfred the villain is dancing unctuous attendance on you once more. But Manfred is worried for you. For that strange child of solitude who, forty years ago, used to call him Uncle Malfrend and climb up on his lap and feel in his pockets and sometimes find a chocolate or a piece of chewing gum. Once we were friends. And now I too am a monster. Albeit only a carnival monster. When I get up every morning and shave I see in front of me in the mirror a bald, ugly, wrinkled satyr, dragging his ugliness from day to day so as to bestow his money when the time comes on his precious grandchildren. What is precious to you, Alex? What makes you get up every morning? What looks back at you out of the mirror?

We were friends once. It was you who taught Uncle Malfrend how to ride a donkey (a spectacle that ought to have been immortalized by Chagall!), and I taught you to cast on the wall a whole theater of animals created from the shadows of our fingers. During my frequent visits to your home I sometimes used to read you a story when you were in bed. And we used to play a card game I can still remember: it was called "Black Bear." The object of the game was to arrange everybody in pairs, the male dancer with the ballerina, the tailor with the seamstress, the farmer with the farmer's wife; only the black bear had no partner. The player who was left with the bear was the loser. Every time, without exception, I was the loser. More than once I was obliged to resort to complicated maneuvers to insure that you won without discovering my renunciation, because otherwise you would have been seized by a fit of terrifying rage—if you had lost or, even worse, if you had suspected that victory had been given to you as a gift. You would have started to smash, throw, and tear, accused me of cheating, bitten the back of your hand till the blood came, or gone into a dark depression and crept away like an ichneumon to hide in the darkness of the narrow space under the staircase.

On the other hand, every time I lost a game you would go overboard—according to some strange code of justice—to compensate me. You would rush to the cellar to fetch me a cold beer. Or make me a present of a marble or a basket of white snails that you had industriously collected in the yard. You would climb on my lap and slip one of your father's cigars into my jacket pocket. And once, in the winter, you slipped into the closet and scraped the mud off my galoshes. Another time, when your father was roaring at me at the top of his voice and cursing me in Russian, you caused a short circuit with a broken iron so as to plunge the house in darkness in the middle of his thunder and lightning.

And then in forty-one I volunteered for the British Army. For five years I wandered from Palestine to Cairo, Cyrenaica, and Italy, from Italy to Germany and Austria, from Austria to the Hague and from the Hague to Birmingham. All through those years you remembered me, Alex. Every two or three weeks the gold soldier Malfrend would receive a package from you. From you, not your father. Candy, woolen socks, Hebrew newspapers and magazines, letters containing sketches of imaginary weapons. In return I sent you postcards from all the places I visited. I collected stamps and banknotes and sent them to you. When I came back, in forty-six, you vacated your room for me. Until your father rented me my first apartment in Jerusalem. And I still have standing on my bedside table a photograph from April of forty-seven: good-looking, sad, and a little violent, you are standing like a dreamy wrestler holding one of the poles of the canopy at my wedding. Seven years later, when Rosalind was killed, you and your father invited little Dorit to spend the whole summer at Zikhron. You built her a hut of branches, with a rope ladder, in one of the pine trees and captured her heart forever. When you went to the university in Jerusalem, I gave you the key to my apartment. When you were injured in the back in the raid north of the Sea of Galilee, you stayed with us again for a fortnight. It was I who prepared you for your examinations in German and Latin. Then came your meteoric wedding, and soon afterward your father began dispersing his fortune to all sorts of charitable funds and handing out checks to confidence men who assured him that they were representing the ten lost tribes of Israel. Until he sent his Circassians on a night raid on the neighboring kibbutz, and then the two of us got together and decided to plan a coup. We have not forgotten, you or I, the eleven lawsuits I conducted on your behalf before we managed to extricate the property and put the Tsar away. Nor will you ever be able to forget everything I did for you during your divorce suits. I have set down these brief notes to tell you that Uncle Malfrend has been carrying you on his back ever since your childhood, while you were establishing your world-wide reputation and your book was being translated into nine languages. You for your part paid for Dorit and Zohar's honeymoon in Japan and even opened a generous savings account on the birth of each of my grandchildren. Was this merely a calculated, cold-blooded investment? I'd be grateful if you'd enlighten me. And if you would confirm in writing, at least between curses and insults, that what I have written here really happened. Otherwise I shall be compelled to infer that one of us is already decrepit and sees things. Are we friends, Alex? Answer me yes or no. Just to set the record straight. And the main thing: send me a sign and I'll invest the proceeds of Magdiel in purchasing the meadows of Bethlehem. Take care of your health and let me know how I can help.

Uncle Malfrend
Keeper of the Signet

PERSONAL ZAKHEIM JERUSALEM ISRAEL

DEDUCT WHAT YOU ARE OWED FOR PAYMENTS TO BOAZ FROM MY
ACCOUNT TAKE ANOTHER TWO THOUSAND AS A TIP AND STOP
WAGGING YOUR TAIL ALEX

———

GIDEON SUMMER PROGRAM PRINCETON NJ

I AM A MONUMENTAL FOOL AND YOU ARE A LOST CAUSE IVE TAKEN
FIVE THOUSAND AM SENDING DETAILED ACCOUNT ROBERTO REFUSES
ABSOLUTELY TO RESUME MANAGEMENT OF YOUR AFFAIRS REQUEST
URGENT INSTRUCTIONS ABOUT TRANSFER OF YOUR PAPERS MAYBE
YOUD BEST HAVE YOURSELF INSTITUTIONALIZED VOLUNTARILY
BEFORE THEY PUT A STRAIT JACKET ON YOU MANFRED

———

PERSONAL ZAKHEIM JERUSALEM ISRAEL

YOUR RESIGNATION NOT ACCEPTED YOU ARE AUTHORIZED TO
CONTINUE MANAGING THE PROPERTY ON CONDITION YOU KEEP
YOUR MEDDLESOME NOSE AND PAWS TO YOURSELF IM LEAVING
YOUR GRANDCHILDREN IN MY WILL THE DEVIL KNOWS WHY ALEX

———

GIDEON SUMMER PROGRAM PRINCETON NJ

MY RESIGNATION STANDS IM THROUGH WITH YOU REPEAT REQUEST
INSTRUCTIONS RE TRANSFER OF PAPERS MANFRED ZAKHEIM

203

PERSONAL ZAKHEIM JERUSALEM ISRAEL

MANFRED CALM DOWN AM GOING INTO MOUNT SINAI HOSPITAL NEW
YORK FOR A WEEK FOR RADIOTHERAPY MY ESTATE TO BE SHARED
AMONG MY SON HER DAUGHTER AND YOUR GRANDCHILDREN DONT
LEAVE ME NOW THINKING OF COMING BACK TO ISRAEL PERHAPS
AFTER TREATMENT CAN YOU ARRANGE ME A QUIET PRIVATE CLINIC
WITH FACILITIES FOR CHEMOTHERAPY YOU HAVE A FREE HAND IN
MANAGING MY PROPERTY ON CONDITION YOU STAY WITH ME DONT
BE CRUEL ALEX

———

GIDEON MOUNT SINAI HOSPITAL NEW YORK

FURTHER TO MY PHONE CALL YESTERDAY EVERYTHING ARRANGED IF
YOU DECIDE TO COME INCLUDING EXCELLENT CLINIC PRIVATE
DOCTOR AND NURSE HAVE INSTRUCTED ZAND TO DROP SOMMOS AND
BOAZ AM INVESTING YOUR CASH IN TENTPEG BUT NOT TOUCHING
REAL ESTATE UNDERSTAND YOU DONT WANT ME TO TELL ILANA OR
BOAZ ABOUT YOUR CONDITION DORIT AND I LEAVE FOR NEW YORK
AT THE WEEKEND TO BE WITH YOU FAILING OTHER INSTRUCTIONS
WITH YOUR PERMISSION A BIG HUG MANFRED

———

PERSONAL ZAKHEIM JERUSALEM ISRAEL

THANKS DONT COME NO NEED UPDATED WILL ON ITS WAY I MAY
COME OR NOT FEEL FINE AND BEG YOU TO GIVE ME A BREAK ALEX

———

SOMMO HOTEL CASTILLE RUE GAMBON PARIS

MICHEL DONT BE ANGRY IVE GONE TO ZIKHRON WITH YIFAT I HAD
TO YOULL UNDERSTAND FOR YOUR SAKE ILL TRY TO KEEP SABBATH
AND EAT KOSHER NO NEED FOR YOU TO CUT SHORT YOUR TRIP
BOAZ SENDS AFFECTIONATE GREETINGS AND TELLS YOU TO ENJOY
YOURSELF AND NOT WORRY LOVE YOU ILANA

———

MRS SOMMO GIDEON HOUSE NEAR ZIKHRON YAAKOV ISRAEL

ILANA GO HOME WITH THE GIRL AT ONCE OR ILL GET ALMALIAH TO
FETCH YOU WITH A PATROL I HAVE TO STAY HERE A FEW MORE
DAYS ON A MATTER VERGING ON LIFE AND DEATH I FORGIVE YOU
ON CONDITION YOU GO HOME TODAY I HAVENT WRONGED YOU SO I
DONT DESERVE THIS FROM YOU IN GREAT SORROW MICHEL

———

To Mrs. Janine Fuchs   *August 31, 2335 hrs.*
Lemon St. 4
Ramat Hasharon

Dear Janine,

It's two days now that I've tried to get you on the phone and
this evening I came to your house personally and found everything
closed and locked. From the neighbors I discovered that you've
taken an organized holiday in Rhodes, supposedly flying back El
Al from Athens in the early hours. Since I have to be in Eilat on
official business, I've decided to slip this under your door in the
hope that you'll find it. It's in the matter of our mutual friend
Michel (Sommo). Michel went to Paris on a certain matter of public
interest (and also to visit his parents, who are living now near his
sister in Marseille). When he returned the day before yesterday he

came upon a very bad situation following on the step taken by his wife on her own initiative, who has gone with her little girl to stay with her son by her previous marriage, who is living in an abandoned building between Zikhron Yaakov and Binyamina. And now it turns out that approximately one day before Michel's return her first husband (the scholar who emigrated to America) also turned up there. You can imagine the shock to Michel and the unheard-of shame to our friends the Sommo family because of this dishonorable situation, that she is cohabiting with her first husband, causing tongues to wag and refusing for the time being to return home to Michel, whose world has collapsed in ruins around him.

I went there yesterday with Michel's elder brother and two more friends to talk to her, but what do you think? She refused to see us! And so we went back to Jerusalem empty-handed and sat there in grief and despondency with the whole family until half past three in the morning and then we came up with the following plan: that Michel should register a formal complaint against her for taking the girl away from home without his consent, which is verging on kidnapping.

The sad thing is though that Michel is suffering from a terrible depression and insists like a mule that he will never issue a criminal complaint against his wife. He would rather die, he says, what's done can't be undone, and even worse things of the same sort. He seems to me completely shattered and even quite desperate. And you see without a formal complaint from him my hands are tied. His brother and the cousins were thinking of going there and taking a rash step which I don't even want to mention in writing, but I talked them out of it with great difficulty.

In short, dear Janine, seeing as how you and Bruno have good personal relations with all the various parties, that is to say with Michel and with Ilana and with her son Boaz who was living with you for a while after I got him out, and seeing as Bruno served in the army at one time under the first husband and knows him from then, perhaps it would be worth the two of you going and trying to talk to them? Before heaven forbid a public scandal breaks out with the newspapers and all sorts of unpleasantness and disgrace, which will be a terrible blow to Michel and the whole Sommo family. I beg of you in the name of family and friends in the strongest possible terms. We are all pinning our last hopes on you!

If you consider it would be any use me joining you (in plain clothes), of course I am prepared to go there with you as soon as I get back from Eilat. Just leave a phone message for me at Tel Aviv District HQ under the name Chief Inspector Almaliah, and they'll pass it on to me at once. But you know what, maybe it would be best not to waste any more time but for you two to go there directly as soon as possible? Also Janine please call Michel without delay because he's in a very bad way and talk to him, tell him not to do anything foolish and not to listen to bad advice. Thanking you and hoping you will succeed and of course as always in friendship,

Yours,
Prosper Almaliah

Mr. A. Gideon	*By the Grace of G-d*
Gideon House	*Jerusalem*
Zikhron Yaakov	*Eve of the Holy Sabbath*
	8th Elul 5736 (3.9.76)

BY HAND

Dear Sir,

This letter will be delivered to you by special messenger before the commencement of the Sabbath, so that we are giving you approximately thirty hours to ponder and consider the state of your soul, since on Sunday morning at nine-thirty a.m. some friends of mine will be arriving to fetch my little girl, Madeleine Yifat, and bring her home, whether politely and respectfully or by other means, depending on your own behavior. As for the poor woman who is also dwelling under your roof, she must face her own fate. How can I behold her face when my heart is empty within me? According to what the Rev. Rabbi Bouskila kindly explained to me last night, her status is still in need of clarification: she may very well be in the position of a woman who is forbidden both to her husband and to her paramour, and expelled from both worlds. At all events my present demand concerns only my daughter, Madeleine Yifat, over whom you have no rights, responsibilities, or claims under either religious or state law, and consequently it would be better for you to return her peacefully on Sunday morning and not compel us to resort to other means. You have been warned, sir.

[Signed] Michael (Michel-Henri) Sommo

P.S.: For the life of me I cannot understand how you can have acted so disgracefully. Or so cruelly. Even among the heathen or in gangs of brigands and robbers you would not find such behavior! Have you heard, sir, of the Prophet Nathan? About the sin of King David with Bathsheba? Or perhaps in these days our modern professors are dispensed from having to know what is in the Holy Scriptures?

It is three days and four nights now that I have been roaming the streets of Jerusalem, with mourner's stubble on my cheeks—for how can I shave? Roaming the streets and asking myself: Are you a Jew or are you an Amalekite? Are you a human being created in G-d's image, or are you, Heaven forbid, some kind of a demon? All the wrongs you have done in the past against the woman and the boy are as driven snow compared to your latest outrage. Even the men of Sodom and Gomorrah would not have received you in their midst! Not content with maltreating your wife and casting off your son, you could not keep your unholy paws off the poor man's ewe lamb and spilled my blood as well!

The truth is that I have doubts whether someone like you, a confirmed evildoer and rogue imbued with the spirit of Belial, possesses any fear of Heaven or even any conscience. Apparently not. I have heard people talking about you here in Jerusalem, and saying that you are a great devotee of the Arabs. According to your "views" this is apparently the Land of Ishmael, promised by Heaven to the seed of Ibrahim, the land that Musa spied from the distance and over which Daoud ruled, and we Jews have no business here at all. In that case perhaps you might consider me as an Arab? Perhaps you could treat me according to the fine principles you adopt toward them? Would you have taken away an Arab's wife? His daughter? His little ewe lamb? No doubt you would have written newspaper articles about it and organized demonstrations and signed petitions and moved Heaven and earth if someone had dared to do such a thing even to the least of the Arabs! But we are as outlaws, our lives are unprotected, a disgrace to our neighbors and scorn and derision to all those around us. We are already in the Days of Penitence, Mr. Gideon, and it would be better for you not to forget that there is One Who dispenses retribution to the arrogant, One before Whom there is neither laughter nor levity. Or am I living in error? Perhaps, Heaven forbid, there is nothing in Heaven? No judge and no justice? Perhaps the world is really an ownerless property?

The truth is that right from the outset I had a suspicion that your heart harbored evil schemes. From the moment you and that wretched woman began to correspond with each other all of a sudden beyond the bounds of natural behavior. From the moment your checks began to descend upon us like bounteous rain. At times my entrails tormented me with fear in the night, lest you were spreading a net at our feet to trap us. What is happening? Have you suddenly got a new heart within you? Or is this Satan dancing before us? Why is he showering all this money upon us? Perhaps when all is said and done he is lying in wait to snatch the poor when he pulls in the net, as it is written in the Book of Psalms? But I said to myself, perhaps my duty is to stand the test. Not to fall into suspicions. To give you the benefit of the doubt and open the gates of repentance before you. Too pure of eyes to behold the evil, that is what I was, instead of nipping this filthy scheme in the bud.

Or did I also sin? Were my eyes blinded by greed?

I confess today that I transgressed against the verse "Thou shalt not be excessively righteous." And now Heaven has punished me sevenfold. To teach me a lesson, not to give my back to the lash nor to turn the other cheek. Which is not the way of Judaism, but to do to the evildoer what the Passover Haggadah says we should. Now I have paid my penalty and you are merely the whip with which I am scourged. For five or six years Michael Sommo was allowed to hold his head up, for five or six years he was permitted to stand upright as a father and a husband and a human being, and now he is called to repay his debts with interest and to return to being nothing. To return to the dust from which he had the impudence to attempt to raise himself.

This evening at the beginning of the sunset I went to the Talpiyyot woods and stood there for a while. I lifted up my eyes to the hills to see from where my help would come, where was Sommo and where were the hills. The hills were silent and did not bother to give me an answer to age-old questions such as how long shall the wicked rejoice? or shall the judge of the whole earth not do justice? Instead of replying the hills wrapped themselves in darkness. Who am I to complain? Rabbi Bouskila advised me to accept suffering with love. He reminded me that the aforementioned questions remained unanswered even when they were asked by greater and better men than I, thousands of years ago. The hills wrapped themselves in darkness and paid no attention to me. And I stood there a little longer, I marveled that the wind could bother to caress someone like me, I was astonished that the stars could show themselves to such a worm-and-not-a-man, until it began to be cold. Then I understood, vaguely, that Sommo is very small. That his sorrow is like a passing shadow. That he is forbidden to investigate what is too wonderful for him. So that if for a moment I pondered on the ways of Providence, if for a moment I was sick of life and hoped for death, if I even harbored the terrible thought of killing you with my own hands, after a moment I regretted it and submitted. By the time the moon came out I had calmed and silenced my soul. My days are like a shadow and I shall wither like grass.

But what of you, sir? How can you not be afraid? Where will you lift up your eyes? And your hands full of blood?

The truth is that you may be a great champion of the Arabs and a hater of the Jews, but you have shed Arab blood like water during the wars and perhaps even between them. Whereas I, the so-called chauvinist and extremist, have never shed blood in my whole life. Not a single drop. And I have never caused an Arab hair to fall to the ground, despite the fact that both I and my forefathers received our fill of insults and spitting and worse. I have not caused harm or distress to Jew or gentile; I have merely contained myself and said nothing. But what happened? You are considered a great humanitarian, showing compassion and making concessions, whereas I am considered a cruel zealot. You are considered a man of the world and I am considered narrow-minded and limited. You are considered the peace camp and I am considered the vicious circle of bloodshed. And how does this slander come to take wing? Because you and those like you are apparently worthy of praise, whereas I and those like me apparently deserve only silence. No doubt it is because you have shed so much Arab blood that you have become such a blood-shedder. And how we admired you and those like you when we were young! How we looked up to you out of the depths! Such heroes! Such demigods! The new lions of Judah! But why should I argue with you and recount my humiliation to you. You must give me back my child on Sunday morning, and after that—go and burn in hellfire. Perhaps you will read all this with mocking laughter, imitating my accent, chuckling at the mentality, and she will rebuke you and tell you to stop, that it's not nice to laugh at the poor man, but even she will not be able to suppress her smile. What is lost is lost.

King David was not only prevented from building the Temple. He was also reminded by Heaven of the innocent blood he had shed. But this punishment did not console those whose blood had been shed. Doubtless the Sommos of the days of King David were not content with their lot. We are chaff before the wind. Doormats underneath your feet.

Relatives, friends, and acquaintances come and sit with me from morning till evening to offer their condolences. They enter with bowed heads as into a house where there is a corpse, squeeze my hand, tell me to be strong and of good courage. I am like a mourner, except that my heart does not allow me to rend my garments for her. Perhaps there is still a shadow of doubt? And I give her the benefit of this doubt, of course on the conditions that I shall stipulate for her and in accordance with the legal decision of Rabbi Bouskila. But you shall return the child on Sunday morning and not an hour later; otherwise you may compel me to take desperate steps. I have even thought of standing outside your gate day and night with a placard: "A shameful deed has been done in Israel!" Relatives and friends of ours speak of even more fateful steps against you. It may be Heaven that stays my hand. That I do not sink to your level.

All day long my brother's dear wife stays in the house with me. She has left her own children and come to be with me in my sorrow. She serves the guests with cold soda water, savories, and black coffee, empties the ashtrays, reproaches me with "Eat, eat," and I heed her and eat my bread with a tear. Good people strive all day long to distract my mind from my ordeal. They talk to me about the government, about the Agranat Commission, about Rabin and Kissinger and Hussein. I pretend to listen to them to the best of my ability. Even Mr. Zakheim has called. He spoke smooth words and proposed himself as intermediary. Why do we need intermediaries? Only give me back the girl, and after that you must stand and face your own fate. And the woman must face her own fate too. Yesterday evening when the last guest had left, my brother arrived clutching a bottle of brandy; he hugged and kissed me, and sadly said: "We should never marry with them. They are infected with something that we neither understand nor know; we should remain among our own, avoiding their contact and their contagion." So he spoke, and then he took his wife and left. I too went out to wander around the streets. I went up the hill to watch the sunset and to ask forbidden questions. The only answer I received was the whispering of the trees. Perhaps it is all a mistake? Perhaps the Garden of Eden and Noah's Flood and the Binding of Isaac and the Burning Bush never existed, but were merely allegory? Perhaps the great sages erred in their identification, and the ancient Jerusalem is not here, or the Biblical Land of Israel, but somewhere completely different? Beyond the hills of darkness? Could a mistake like that not happen? Do scientists never make mistakes? Perhaps that is why it befell that there is no G-d in this place?

When the moon came out from behind the hills I came home. I have no dealings with the moon, lest my instincts get the better of me and I despair of life or strangle you, sir. And when I got back to my empty home what had I left to do but pour myself a glass of the brandy that my brother had left behind, turn on the television, and sit in the dark watching the lithe and lissom detectives with their pistols chasing some criminal in the land of Hawaii in America? In the midst of the leaping and the shooting, in the midst of the chase, I stood up and left them. They needn't do me any favors. Let them flicker on their own in the dark. I went out instead on the balcony to see if the world was still standing and the moon still submitting itself with pieces of silver despite the shameful deed that had been done in Israel. Passers-by went past on the sidewalk, each going home to his wife and children, and my eyes followed their shadows: perhaps I could find where to take my disgrace?

Eventually the street was empty and I went back indoors and found that in Hawaii in the meantime everything had come to a happy ending. Perhaps I should take my little girl and go and live in Hawaii?

I sat in the kitchen facing her apron on the hook, counting the footsteps of the neighbors next door and also upstairs, leafing aimlessly through the Book of Psalms for comfort. Even though it would be more appropriate for me to be reading the Book of Job instead. Why had my heart been proud? Why had I married a woman of superior birth? Why had I aimed so high? With dimming eyes I studied the text, "May those who seek my soul be ashamed and disgraced, may those who plot my evil turn backwards, may their way be dark and slippery, for they have set a snare for me in vain, they have spread their net in vain for my soul, thy justice is like the mighty hills, thy judgments the great deep" and so on.

What profit is there for me in such texts when my heart is dead within me? What is done is done and the crooked cannot be made straight. The shame is mine, not of those who seek my soul. Abandoned like a tamarisk in the wilderness. My path is strewn with darkness and slippery places and thou seest thy world in thy life. And why? A deep abyss. What sin have I committed against you, sir? What good was it to Uriah the Hittite if in the end the king was punished somewhat? Even now after the passage of three thousand years we read and revere the psalms of David son of Jesse, whereas the lamentations of Uriah never existed. Or else they did exist but they have been forgotten and even the memory of them has perished. The Lord preferred Abel and his offering, but for Cain and his offering He had no respect. What good was it to Abel? Abel is dead and Cain lives on and the mark on his brow gives him immunity and nothing stops him from becoming rich and famous and enjoying every pleasure.

I got up and walked around the room, I opened a closet and there were her dresses. I went to the bathroom to wash my face and there were her cosmetics. I passed the girl's bedroom and there was a bear looking at me. It was the bear that your son brought after Passover as a present for my daughter. Will you return her, sir?

Why should I plead with you? The land has been given over to the wicked. You are the salt of the earth, you have the property and the power, you have the wisdom and the judgment and we are dust under your feet. You are the priests and Levites and we are the drawers of water. You are the glory of Israel and we are the mixed multitude. He chose you and sanctified you as sons of the All-Present, while we are stepsons. To you he gave the splendor and the grace and the tall stature—all the world is astonished at you—to us lowly spirit and low stature and barely a hair's-breadth divides us from the Arab. Perhaps we should offer thanks for the privilege that has fallen to our lot of hewing your wood and shame-facedly eating the leftovers of your meals and living in the houses that you have grown tired of and doing all the work that you have grown to despise including the building of the Land and occasionally to marry your castoff wives when you deign to permit us to drink from the well that you have spat in and to try to acquire your ways and so perhaps to please you. Be it known to you that one like myself, a simple ordinary Jew, is prepared to pardon and forgive. But not now, sir—only after the cup has passed over you all and you have received your just desserts. When you have beaten your breasts and confessed your sins. When you return from your evil ways and come back to serving the country instead of destroying it and caring only about enlarging your own private property, and even slandering the country before the wider world. I don't give a fig for your world fame or for the cheap praise: you brought Israel into disrepute in the book you wrote for the gentiles and which I have not read, nor would I dream of reading it; it was enough for me to read what was written about it in the evening paper: "the Zionist obsession"! How could you? How did your hand not tremble? And in English too? A festival for our enemies?

When I was a young man I worked as a waiter and there were some customers, including Jews, who mistook me for a little Arab. They would call me Ahmed—and after everything the Arabs had done to us. That is why I came to live here, full of faith that in Israel we would all be brothers and the Messiah would come to rule over us. And how did this country receive an idealistic young man who came, for your information, from the Sorbonne? Builder. Night watchman. Cinema ticket seller. Regimental policeman. In a word, the tail of the fox. A perfect ass all my life and now thanks to you, Mister Professor, an ass with horns on his forehead if you can imagine such a creature. Or a dog who has been deprived of the bone he found under the table.

But I said, in my haste, why not? On the contrary, I shall spread my wings over his son as well. He cast out and I shall gather in. He trampled down and I shall raise up. I shall be as a father and teacher to your son, and so I shall repay evil with good and also save a soul of Israel, perhaps even two. I was simple. Or foolish. It is true that it is written "Happy are they of the simple way" and it is also written "God guards the foolish," but it seems that these verses are not to be taken literally. Whoever wrote them was not thinking of Sommo but of someone better. "The way of the unjust prospers," "the land has been given over to the wicked"—these are the verses that actually prevail. And I accept the verdict. Only let me have the girl back. You have no rights over her.

And what are your rights, anyway? That you were a war hero? The violent sons of Zeruiah and the wicked Ahab were also great heroes. And between wars, what did you do to the state? Defile it? Sell it for a mess of pottage? Feast on it?

That is why your time is up. Your bells are tolling. It is after midnight now, early Friday morning, and here in South Jerusalem you can hear the bells. The kingship has passed, sir. Soon it will be given over to your neighbor, who is better than you.

I never said I was spotless. Perhaps I sinned in offering my hand to a woman who was destined for someone superior to myself. She is taller than I, and beautiful, and who am I anyway? All the years that I was married to her your impure shadow never left us. However hard I tried to ignore it, I could hear you laughing at me out of the darkness. And now apparently Heaven has decided to punish me. Or else, Heaven forbid, there is no G-d in this place? He has moved to Hawaii? The truth is that this letter is mixed with a quarter of a bottle of brandy that my brother left and also two tranquilizers that I found in a drawer. Hers. Where there was also an old photograph from the newspaper showing you wearing your uniform with all sorts of badges of rank and decorations and as good-looking as a heavenly being.

Better I should stop now. I have already written too much. In the morning my brother-in-law will come with his Peugeot truck to collect this letter and take it to you in Zikhron. I shall walk instead to the Western Wall to say midnight prayers, although who knows if prayers that come from someone like me make any impression up there. Probably only a bad impression. But there is no bad without good: "the left hand wounds and the right hand heals," as it is written. Now that I have nothing left in this world, I shall dedicate myself from now on to the great task of redeeming the

Land, and let me be avenged in this: that despite you and the likes of you it still will be redeemed. Until Sommo's meed of suffering is complete and he is called to ascend on high to rest from all his labors and be done with it. Perhaps even in the world to come they need cooks and RPs, so that you may still see me saluting you at the barrier, though I don't suppose you'll notice me. One more thing: would you try at least this time to behave considerately toward her? with some compassion? Do not abuse her further, for she cannot take any more suffering.

And you will return my daughter to me without causing any trouble. I shall sign with cold contempt,

M. S.

—

Mr. Sommo   *Gideon House*
Tarnaz 7   *Zikhron Yaakov*
Jerusalem   *Saturday, 4.9.76*

Dear Mr. Sommo,

I. Yesterday your brother-in-law brought me your disturbed letter. Your suspicions are groundless. Nobody has deceived you. However, I understand your sensitivity well, and in a sense it is not alien to me either. As a matter of fact, it was your wife who decided of her own free will to stay here for a few more days and look after me until I go into the hospital (soon) for radiotherapy, when she will naturally return to you at once. I should hope that you, Mr. Sommo, would not be harsh with her on her return. At the conclusion of your letter you indicated that she "cannot take any more suffering," and I agree with you. I therefore have no alternative but to return your own request: treat her kindly.

II. It seems I shall not be leaving Hadassah Hospital. A year ago I contracted a cancer of the kidneys and I have had two operations. The growth has now spread in the abdomen. The doctors in New York saw no sense in a further operation. My condition is fairly miserable, and from this you may deduce that there is no foundation for your jealous fantasies and no point in going as far as Uriah the Hittite. Or Hawaii. It is sufficient to go back a few years. As you know, I married Ilana in September 1959, more by her choice than mine. After a few months she became pregnant and had Boaz by her own decision: I did not see myself as cut out to be a father, and I told her so from the start. Then our life together became complicated. It became clear beyond any doubt that I was causing her suffering. Which is perhaps what she wanted (I am not an expert in this subject). Out of weakness of character I delayed our separation until September 1968. The divorce was vicious on both sides, and on mine even petty: my behavior was dictated by hatred and vindictiveness. Then I left the country. I severed all contacts. I learned of your marriage in a roundabout way. And at the beginning of this year I received a request for help from her, or perhaps from both of you. For reasons not clear to me, but that sprang perhaps from the development of my illness, I saw fit to comply. Now with the termination of my life there are one or two things that I have begun to regret. That is why I came back to Israel last week (without advance notice) to see Boaz and to stay in the house in which I grew up. I found Ilana here, and she chose to treat me more or less in the role of nurse. I did not invite her to stay here, but I did not see any reason to send her away again. Moreover the house really belongs to Boaz, even if officially it is still registered in my name. The relations between us, Mr. Sommo, are not the relations between man and wife in any conventional sense. If you require it, I shall draw up an affidavit for your rabbi testifying to your wife's innocence.

III. I have given instruction in my revised will to take good care of the future of both Boaz and your family. If you do not waste the money on messianic investments, etc., your daughter will therefore be sheltered from the poverty and want with which you yourself were afflicted, and of which you gave such a highly colored description in your letter. By the way, the little girl seems to me to be both gentle and generous: early this morning, for instance, while the whole commune here was still asleep, she came and sat on the edge of my bed, invented a kind of medicine for me (kerosene and mulberry leaves, apparently), and made me a present of a dead grasshopper in a plastic bag. In exchange she demanded (and received) three paper boats. We had a short philosophical conversation about the nature of water.

IV. As for the rest of your complaints, both those addressed to me in the second person singular and those you chose to frame in the second person plural, and of an ideological or political tendency, I can only plead guilty to the majority of the accusations. On condition that I am first given an opportunity to remove certain emotional exaggerations, which I am inclined to ascribe to your anger or your accumulated bitterness. In simple language, Mr. Sommo, not only do I consider you a better man than I am—there would be nothing particularly remarkable about that—but I consider you a good man. Full stop. I have been discovering your excellent qualities during the past year, and especially the past few days, both from Ilana and from Boaz, and also, indirectly, from a concentrated study of your daughter (she has just come into my room again, tapped out her name on my Baby Hermes, and this time gave me half a dozen ants in a cup and invited me to a dance. I was obliged to decline, both because of my illness and because I have never managed to learn to dance).

V. Even though you feel, to quote your words, "cold contempt" for me, I feel a certain esteem for you, leaving aside our differences of opinion. And I hereby apologize for the trouble that my existence causes you.

VI. You are right to accuse me of arrogance. Unlike you, Mr. Sommo, I have always tended to look down on people, either because stupidity was so widespread wherever I have been or because for some reason ever since I was a child people have looked up to me. Now that I hardly manage to achieve real sleep, nor am I completely awake, it seems to me that this was a mistake. Attentiveness and hesitancy characterize my present relationship with those around me here (even though I am not certain that they are aware of it). If only there were more time left, I might suggest that you and I should try to meet someday and see each other from roughly the same height. We might not find it boring. Only, as you pointed out in your letter with a penetrating intuition, my time has indeed run out, Mr. Sommo. The bell really is tolling for me.

And I am not talking about metaphoric bells but real ones. Boaz has fixed up in an upstairs room a kind of chime made of bottles suspended from the ceiling. Every gust of wind from the sea produces a desolate, repetitive tune. Sometimes it drives me out of my bed of planks. Last night, with the help of a walking stick that Boaz made for me, I managed to get up and make my way downstairs to the darkening garden. The eight young people who are staying here have pulled up the thistles and couch grass, scattered goat dung (whose piercing smell brings me back something of the smells of my childhood), and dug the ground up. In place of the exotic strains of roses that my father used to cultivate here there are now beds of vegetables. Ilana has volunteered to make scarecrows (it seems to me that the birds are not particularly impressed). While your daughter waters them twice a day with a watering can that I sent someone to buy for her in the town.

Among the flower beds, beside the restored marble pool now restocked (with carp instead of goldfish), I found two wicker chairs. Ilana brought out coffee for herself and an infusion of mint for me. If you are interested in the details, we sat together with our backs to the house and our faces toward the sea until it got dark. We exchanged only necessary words. Ilana may have been shocked by the pallor of my sunken cheeks. And I no longer find anything to say to her, except that her dress is pretty and her long hair suits her. I cannot deny that during our marriage it never occurred to me to speak to her like that. Why should I? Do you, Mr. Sommo, compliment her on her dress? Do you expect her to praise your trousers?

She covered my knees with a blanket. And when the wind got up I spread it over her knees too. I noticed again how her hands have aged, even though her face is young. But I didn't say a word. We sat in silence for about an hour and a half. Far away, near the goat shed, your daughter was laughing and shrieking because Boaz was hoisting her up on his shoulders, his head, and then onto the donkey. Ilana said to me, Look. And I said, Yes. Ilana said, Don't worry. And I said, No. With this we returned to our silence. I had nothing to say to her. Do you know, sir, this is how she and I use language now: No, Yes, It's cold, The tea's good, I like the dress, Thank you. Like two small children who can't speak. Or like the shell-shocked soldiers I saw after the war in a rehabilitation center. I am lingering over this detail so as to stress once more that your suspicions are absurd. Between her and me there is not even a real bond of words. On the other hand, I had an urge to write you these pages. Even though I have no idea what the reason is. Your letter, which may have been intended to hurt me, did not. On the contrary, it pleased me. Why should that be? I have no idea.

At seven o'clock the sun set and a slow twilight set in. The sound of a mouth organ came from the kitchen. And a guitar. And smells of baking. (They bake their own bread here.) And at eight o'clock or a little later a barefoot girl brought us a kerosene lamp, pita still warm from the oven, olives, tomatoes, and yogurt (also homemade). I forced myself to eat a little so that Ilana would eat too. And she nibbled without enthusiasm so as to encourage me. At a quarter past nine I said, It's getting chilly. Ilana said, Yes. And she said, Let's go in. And I said, All right.

She helped me up to my room, out of my clothes (jeans and a sweatshirt with a picture of Popeye the Sailor-man), and onto my bed of planks. As she left the room she extracted a promise to call her if I had any pain in the night. (Boaz has rigged up a rope by my bedside. If I pull the end it rings the tin mugs he has tied at the head of her bed on the ground floor.) But I did not keep this promise. Instead I got up and dragged a chair and sat on it for several hours by the darkened window, whose panes have been mended with bandage tape. I was trying to absorb the night and to check what the moon was doing to the Hills of Menasseh to the east. This was how my mother used to sit during her last summer. Can you imagine to yourself what it is like to toss three hand grenades into a bunker full of Egyptians? And then burst in with submachine gun spraying, amid shrieks, howls, and groans? To get splashes of blood and brains on your clothes, your hair, your face? And have your shoe sink into a burst stomach, which emits a viscous bubbling?

I sat at the window until two o'clock in the morning and heard the sound of Boaz's commune. Around the glowing embers of their bonfire in the garden they were singing songs which were unfamiliar to me. A girl was playing the guitar. Boaz himself I did not notice, nor did I hear his voice. Perhaps he had climbed on the roof to be alone with his telescope. Perhaps he had gone down to the sea. (He has a little raft, made without a single nail, which he carries on his back to the coast three miles away. When he was a child I taught him to make a *Kon-Tiki* from balsa tied with string. It appears that he has not forgotten.)

At two o'clock the house was wrapped in darkness and deep silence. Only the frogs continued. And some faraway dogs. And the answer from the dogs in the farmyard. The fox and the jackal, with which the place was infested when I was a child, have disappeared without trace.

I sat beside that window until the early hours, wrapped in a woolen blanket like a Jew at his prayer. I imagined I could hear the sea. Although probably it was nothing but the wind in the palm trees. I pondered on the complaints in your letter. If I had more time left I would take you out of your sentry box. Make a general of you. Give you the keys. And go and philosophize in the desert. Or perhaps take your job at the cinema. Would you like to change places with me, Mr. Sommo?

And around me the little hippie commune carries on its routine, even in the daytime, as it were in whispers, on tiptoe. As if I were a ghost that had emerged from the cellar and nested in the rooms of the house. And rooms there are in plenty. Most of them are still abandoned. Fig and mulberry branches grow through their windows. I find it charming the way Boaz officiates here—no, not officiates; exists—in the role of first among equals. I enjoy their singing in the kitchen or when they work or around the bonfire in the farmyard into the middle of the night. The strains of the mouth organ. The smoke of their cooking. Even the peacock that marches around like a brainless, arrogant supreme commander among the troops of pigeons in the passages and staircases. And the telescope planted on the roof (I want to climb up there. I want to ask Boaz to invite me for a little star trek. Even though I have almost no understanding of the host of heaven, except as an aid to desert navigation at night). The principal difficulty is that the rope ladder is now beyond my strength. I get dizzy easily. Even during my attempts to move by myself between the bed and the window. Apart from that, Boaz avoids conversation with me, except for Good morning, How are you, What do you need from the shop in town. (This morning I asked for a table to place my Baby Hermes on so that I could write this letter. An hour and a half later he brought up a table he had made for me out of packing boxes and eucalyptus branches, with a slanting footrest. And he also bought me on his own initiative an electric fan.) Most of the time he works apparently in the jungle that covers what was once the gardens: hacking at roots, sawing branches, removing rocks, carrying baskets of stones on his bare shoulder like Atlas the Titan, digging, pushing wheelbarrows of manure. Or standing in the wing mixing cement and gravel and sand with shovel and hoe, pouring the concrete onto a network of iron rods that he has interlaced, to lay a new floor. Sometimes I spy him at the end of the day high up in one of the old eucalyptus trees that my father planted here fifty years ago, hanging in a hammock that he has fixed up for himself at a height of twenty-five feet, and to my surprise reading a book. Or counting the clouds from close up. Or speaking to the birds in their own language.

Once I stopped him outside the toolshed. I asked him what he was reading. Boaz shrugged his shoulders and replied reluctantly: "A book. Why?"

I asked what book.

"A language book."

Namely?

"Grammar Made Simple. To finish with spelling and all that."

Is it possible to read a "language book" as though it were reading matter to pass the time with?

"Words and that"—he granted me his slow smile—"is like knowing people. Where they come from. Who's related to who. How each one behaves in all sorts of situations. And in any case"—pauses; sends his right hand on a long journey around his large head to scratch his left temple, an illogical and yet almost regal gesture—"in any case, there's no such thing as 'passing the time.' Time just doesn't pass."

Doesn't pass? What did he mean?

"How do I know? Perhaps it's the opposite: we pass in time. How do I know? Or else time passes people. Do you feel like sitting down and helping me sort some seeds? They're in the shed. In the shade. Only if you want to do something. Or maybe you could fold up empty sacks?"

That was how I was introduced, more or less, into their work roster (half an hour or so every morning, sitting down, if the pains are not especially bad. And sometimes I doze off there).

The girls who live here: two or three Americans. One French. One who looks to me like an Israeli schoolgirl from a good home, perhaps on a romantic escape from her family, perhaps "fulfilling herself." Or maybe as an alternative to suicide? All of them seem to be his mistresses. Maybe the boys too. What does a man like me understand of all this? (When I was his age I was still a masturbating virgin. I imagine you were too, Mr. Sommo. I was even a virgin when I married. Were you, too, sir?) Boaz, as far as I can estimate, is close to six feet five and must weigh at least two hundred pounds. Yet he is lithe and feline, walking around all day barefoot and naked aside from a sort of faded loincloth. His dull golden hair descends in waves to his shoulders. His soft blond beard, his half-closed eyes, his lips, which do not close but hang slightly open, all give him the look of Jesus in a Scandinavian icon.

And yet he looks dreamy. Not quite here. And silent. Despite his physical size I do not find him at all reminiscent of my father, who was thick and bearlike. But, rather, somehow, of Ilana. Perhaps in the softness of his voice. Or his long, supple strides. Or his drowsy smiles, which strike me as childish and shrewd at the same time. "Are you going to restore the fountain, Boaz?" "Don't know. Maybe. Why not?" "And the weather vane that used to be on the roof?" "Maybe. What's a weather vane?"

From the window of my room: rows of onion and green pepper. Hens wandering around and pecking, as in an Arab village. A few mongrel dogs that were attracted here from far away and found food and affection. Eucalyptus trees. Cypresses. Olives. Figs and mulberries. Then the overgrown fields. Red roofs on the hill opposite, five hundred yards away. The Hills of Menasseh. Woods. And a mist or slight haze on the eastern horizon. Even the bottle chimes in the upstairs room where, forty-one years ago, my mother died seem precise and on target. Even though the only target of their strange sounds is me. If you have conjured up the image of a robbers' den in whose half-light your wife cavorts day and night in the arms of a cruel demon, the simple truth is that there is no half-light: there is either harsh summer light or darkness. As for the demon, he dozes most of the time under the influence of painkilling drugs he brought with him from America. (Apart from them, his Baby Hermes, pajamas, and pipe, everything is still packed in his suitcases, which are stacked in a corner of the room. Even the pipe serves for biting rather than smoking—smoking makes him feel sick.) And when he is not asleep? He lies on his bed of planks and stares. Sits at the window and stares. Sorts some seeds in the cool shed in the yard until his strength gives out. A deposed demon serving out his sentence. Fuzzy from pills. A polite, quiet demon, making an effort not to become a burden, and almost pleasant-mannered. Perhaps like his father, who changed from a bear to a lamb in his sanatorium on Mount Carmel.

Or dragging himself around a little, leaning on his new walking stick, wearing the sandals his son has made him from strips of tire and string, faded jeans and a child's shirt with Popeye on it, padding gaunt and threadbare from room to room. From entrance to hall. From the restored wing to the garden. Stopping to talk to your daughter. Trying to teach her to play five-stones. Strapping his wrist watch on her. And continuing on his way to count and catalogue to himself the shades of his childhood and his adolescence. Here he reared silkworms. Here he slaughtered and buried the parrot. There he ran (and subsequently blew up with gunpowder taken from cartridge cases) the electric train his father brought him from Italy. Here he hid once for two days and a night after his father kicked him. Here he used to come to masturbate. There he conquered with pins and arrows the map of western Europe. Here he burned a live mouse in a trap. And here he displayed his member and groped, half fainting, the crotch of the Armenian servant's grand-daughter. Here he helped the Martian invaders to land, and here he secretly tested the Israeli atomic bomb. There he cursed his father one day and received a fist in the nose and lay bleeding like a pig. And here he hid the fine sandals he found among his mother's effects (and two days ago he actually discovered their rotten remains under a loose floorboard). There he shut himself up with Jules Verne and conquered desert islands. And here, in the low space under the back stairs, he huddled and wept unseen for the last time in his life: when his father killed his rhesus monkey. For this was the house where he grew up. And now he has come back to die here.

Perhaps like this: At twenty to eight, after the setting of the sun and before the extinction of the flickering fire brands on the sea horizon. And, of all places, on the broken bench at the beginning of the slope, close to the edge of the cliff, facing the orchard, which has grown into a subtropical forest but which Boaz has begun to restore to its original state. There is a mound of stones at the spot where the well used to be. Not a well really, but a water hole, which his father dug here once to collect rain water. Ilana sitting beside him. Both his hands, growing cold, held between hers: for there are times when she and I, like two shy children, silently hold hands. You have a generous spirit and will not think any the worse of her for that.

And so, while I am writing the pages that are before you, I am gradually becoming inclined to obey my son, who told me yesterday, in his even, indifferent voice, that instead of moldering in Hadassah Hospital, where they could probably do nothing to help me, I'd be better off staying here and catching (as he put it) some peace.

Didn't my presence bother them?

"You pay."

Did they want me to try to be useful in some way? Could I give some sort of classes? or lectures?

"But nobody here tells anyone else what to do."

Do? But I do virtually nothing here.

"That's the best thing for you: sit quietly."

I shall indeed stay. Quietly. Will you be generous and let them both stay a little longer? Day by day I shall entertain your daughter. I shall make her a shadow-monster theater with my fingers on the wall. (It was Zakheim who taught me. When I was six. Or seven.) I shall continue to exchange views with her about the nature of fire and water and what lizards dream about. She'll make me medicines from mud, soapy water, and pine cones. And day by day, with the evening breeze, I shall sit with Ilana on the bench to listen to the rustling of the pine tree.

It is a question of only a short time.

And you are fully entitled to refuse and demand their instant return.

By the way, Boaz suggests that you come and join us too. As he puts it, you can contribute the benefit of your experience as a construction worker, on condition you do not try to make everybody eat kosher food. That is what Boaz says. What do you think?

If you demand it, I shall send them without delay to Jerusalem in a taxi and not grumble. (What right have I to grumble?) You know, sir, my death seems quite reasonable. Don't mistake my meaning: I am not talking of a death wish or anything like that (there is no difficulty about that: I have an excellent handgun given to me once by a Pentagon general), but another kind of wish entirely: not to exist at all. To cancel my presence retroactively. To make it so that I am not born. To pass from the outset to some other mode:

a eucalyptus, for example. Or a bare hill in Galilee. Or a stone on the surface of the moon.

By the way, Boaz has allocated to Ilana and Yifat the best part of the house: he chose to put them on the ground floor, in the semicircular room that looks out through French windows at the roofs of the kibbutz below us, at the banana plantations, the coastal strip, and the sea. (Sea gulls before dawn. Deep brilliance at midday. Bluish clouds every evening.) Once this room housed my father's grandiose library (I never saw him open a book). Now they have painted it a sort of penetrating psychedelic blue. An old fisherman's net adorns its high ceiling. It contains, besides four beds covered with army blankets and a peeling, cracked chest of drawers, a pile of sacks of chemical fertilizer and several drums of gasoline. Some enamored girl has painted over an entire wall the image of Boaz, naked and radiant, striding with closed eyes over a calm patch of water.

Instead of walking on the water, he is passing my window at this minute, sitting on the small tractor he has recently purchased (with my money). Trailing a disk harrow. And your daughter, like a little monkey, is sitting in his lap with her hands between his on the wheel. By the way, she has learned to ride the donkey almost by herself. It is a very young, docile donkey. (Last night, in the dark, I mistook it for a dog and almost stroked it. Since when do I stroke dogs? Or donkeys?) Once, near Bir Tamadeh in the Sinai, a stupid camel got into my firing zone. It walked slowly along a low ridge at a range of two thousand yards. Slightly above the barrel we were using as a target. The gunner fired two shots at it and missed. The loader asked to have a go and he missed too. Entering the spirit of competition, I got down into the gunner's seat and fired, and I missed as well. The camel stopped and calmly assessed the spots where the shells had landed. With a fourth shot I took its head off. And I could see clearly through my binoculars the jet of blood that shot up to a height of a yard or two. The decapitated neck went on turning this way and that, as though looking for the severed head, when it turned backward and sprayed the hump with blood, like an elephant spraying himself with his trunk, and eventually with graceful slowness the camel folded its slender front legs, folded its hind legs, knelt down and lay on its belly, laid its gushing neck in the sand, and froze thus on the ridge like a strange statue, which I vainly tried to blow up with another three shells. Suddenly from the dead area there sprang a Bedouin waving his arms, and I gave orders to stop firing and clear out.

There is the sea breeze stirring the chimes again. I stop and leave the Baby Hermes alone to ask myself whether I am out of my mind. Why am I pouring myself out before you? Why should I write a confession for you? Is it a sick desire to appear ridiculous to you? Or, on the contrary, to receive absolution? From you? And in general, Monsieur Sommo, what is the foundation for your blind confidence in the existence of a "supreme Providence"? atonement? rewards and punishments? or grace? Where did you scrape it from? Would you kindly offer some proof? Work a little miracle? Turn my walking stick into a snake? Or your wife into a pillar of salt, perhaps? Or else get up and admit that the whole thing is just foolishness, stupidity, narrow-mindedness, deception, abasement, and fear.

Zakheim describes you as a cunning, ambitious fanatic, although not without Jesuitical talents and fine political instincts. According to Boaz you are nothing but a well-meaning nuisance. Ilana, in her customary style, attributes to you more or less the holiness of the Archangel Gabriel. Or at the very least the halo of a secret saint. Even though, in a different mood, she detects a Levantine side in you. You have even managed to arouse a certain curiosity in me.

But what is holiness, Mr. Sommo? I have wasted some nine years of my life on a futile quest for a reasonable and more or less unemotional definition. Perhaps you will approve of me and agree to enlighten me? For I still have no idea. Even the dictionary definition of holiness strikes me as empty and shallow, if not essentially circular. And I still have a kind of need to succeed in deciphering something. Even though my time has run out. But even so: holiness? Or purpose? And grace? What does a wolf understand of the moon at which it howls with its neck extended? What does a moth understand of the flame into which it hurls itself? Or a camel-slayer of redemption? Can you help me?

But no sanctimonious sermonizing, you hypocritical fart, who dares boast to me that you have never shed a drop of blood. That you have never touched a hair of an Arab's head. That you are redeeming the Holy Land by licking it. Driving all the aliens out of it by means of charms and spells mixed with my money. Purging the patrimony of our forefathers with pure olive oil. Fucking my wife, inheriting my house, saving my son, investing my fortune, and then showering me with Biblical expostulations at my moral turpitude. You wear me out. You irritate like a mosquito. You have nothing new to offer me. I have long since finished with your sort and turned to more complex types. Take the money and run well out of my range.

As for me, what can I offer you except my dying soon? You hope in your letter that "the cup my pass"—well it really is "passing," in fact it is nearly empty. You accuse me of stealing the "poor man's ewe lamb" and the crumbs of your meal. But in reality I am the one who is now picking up crumbs from under your kosher table. You threaten me that soon I shall have to "stand and face my fate," but the fact is that I can hardly stand at all. You can hear bells, but the bells are right here, above my head. What more do you demand, sir? To eat of the sacrifices of the dead?

And apropos of sacrifices of the dead, dear Zakheim values me at roughly two million dollars. So that even after deducting Boaz's half, your share is definitely not petty cash. You will be able to ride around in a limousine from your "first step of redemption" to the next one. Zakheim and his yellow-headed daughter are threatening to drop in this week: he has decided to take me "by force if necessary" to Jerusalem in his car for my radiotherapy at Hadassah, and on the same trip to return to you your lost sheep. I, however, while writing these pages, have finally decided to stay here. What do I need to look for in Jerusalem? To expire amid dribbling prophets and barking messianic lunatics? I am staying with my son. I shall fold sacks to the end. Sort radishes. Wind old lengths of string. Perhaps I shall send for the clown who was my father from Haifa: we can hold a family billiards marathon until I drop dead. Will you let her stay with me a little longer? Please? Maybe you will be given an extra coupon for your collection of good deeds?

Boaz tells me, with a twist of the lips somewhere between boredom and contempt, that one of his mistresses here once used to pour water on the hands of an old guru in Wisconsin who was able, she claims, to heal malignant diseases by means of bee stings. And I, to my surprise, amused myself this morning by thrusting a stick into the beehive. But Boaz's bees, being as distracted and worn out as I am or as peace-loving as he is, buzzed all around me but refused to sting. Maybe the odor of death that clings to me repelled them. Or else perhaps they do not deign to cure those of little faith?

So here we are again, inadvertently, with my old obsession: turning every stray bee into the bearer of a theological question, only to attack it with gritted teeth and squash it, together with its question. To derive a new question from its hollow death. And hurry to shatter the new question with a direct shot. For nine years I have been wrestling with Machiavelli, taking Hobbes and Locke limb from limb, unstitching Marx at the seams, burning with desire to prove once and for all that it is neither the selfishness nor the baseness nor the cruelty in our nature that turns us into a species that destroys itself. We annihilate ourselves (and shall soon wipe out our entire species) precisely because of our "higher longings," because of the theological disease. Because of the burning need to be "saved." Because of an obsession with redemption. What is the obsession with redemption? Only a mask for a complete absence of the basic talent for life. This is the talent that every cat is endowed with. Whereas we, like the whales that dash themselves against the shore in an impulse to mass suicide, suffer from an advanced degeneration of the talent for life. Hence the popular urge to destroy and annihilate what we have so as to hack a path to regions of redemption that have never existed and are not even possible. To sacrifice our lives cheerfully, to eradicate other people ecstatically, for the benefit of some vague false magic that seems to us to be a "Promised Land." Some kind of mirage that is considered "superior to life itself." And what on earth has not been considered superior to life itself? In Uppsala in the fourteenth century two monks slew ninety-eight orphans in a single night and then did away with themselves, all because a blue fox had appeared at a window of their monastery as a sign that the Virgin was waiting for them. Therefore: to cover the ground over and over again "with a carpet of our split brains / like white roses"? a carpet destined for the pure footsteps of some unlikely savior (according to the poem by a local fanatic, who certainly succeeded in fixing himself a fine brain-spill from twenty pistol bullets that the British landed in his skull). Or in a different local variation: "For peace is but mud / so renounce soul and blood / for the sake of the glory concealed." What concealed glory, Mr. Sommo? Are you out of your mind? Take a look at your daughter sometime: that is the only hidden glory. There is none other. It's a shame to waste words on you. You will murder her. You will murder everything that moves all around. And you will call it "birth pangs of the Messiah" and acceptance of divine judgment. You may even outdo me, and manage to commit murder without shedding a drop of blood. You will boil in olive oil and mutter thrice "Holy."

I have just had a short lunch break. A girl by the name of Sandra came up to my room barefoot and, smiling as though moonstruck, set before me an aluminum teapot full of a fragrant infusion of herbs and a plate covered with another plate. A hard-boiled egg cut in half. Some olives. Slices of tomato and cucumber. Onion rings. Two slices of homemade bread spread with goat cheese flavored with garlic. And honey in a miniature bottle. I nibbled and sipped and poured myself some more. This Sandra went on standing there in her djellaba, watching me with unconcealed curiosity. Perhaps she had instructions to count my bites. And yet, as though afraid of me, she stayed near the door. Which she had not closed behind her.

I decided to try to hold a simple conversation with her. Even though as a general rule I haven't the slightest idea of casual conversation with strangers. Where was she from, if she didn't mind my asking?

Omaha, Nebraska.

Were her parents aware of where she was and what manner of life she was leading?

It was like this: her parents were not exactly her parents.

Meaning?

Her father's second wife and her mother's new husband had given her some money to go off and see the world, on condition that she promised to come back at the end of a year and go to college.

And what was she contemplating studying?

She didn't know yet. In any case, she was learning a lot here.

What, for instance? Introduction to primitive farming?

To understand herself. A little. And also to get some idea about the Meaning of Life.

Would she be kind enough to enlighten me? What was this Meaning?

But this, in her opinion, "should not be put into words."

Then perhaps she would give me just a general idea? A hint?

"That's something you have to do for yourself? Isn't it?"

She has a bizarre habit of ending every sentence with a question mark. Not as though it were a question but as though she were surprised by her own words. I stood by my request to be given at least a slight hint of the meaning of life.

Embarrassed. Blinking. And smiling as though pleading with me to give up. Very pretty. And shy. Unbelievably childlike. Blushing and shrugging her shoulders when I suggested she sit down for a moment. And she stayed there, my son's mistress, or one of my son's mistresses, standing in the doorway, like a deer which can sniff pursuit. Flight makes her skin quiver. One more word and she'll be gone. But I persist:

"Where should one begin, Sandra?"

"I think: just at the beginning?"

"I think: maybe as far back as your memory can reach?"

"As far as my circumcision, is that far enough? Or do I have to think back even further?" (I was tired of these banalities.)

"To where they first humiliated you, right?"

"Humiliated me? Wait a minute. Sit down. I happen to be one of the humiliators. Not one of the humiliated."

But she refused to sit. They were waiting for her downstairs. Boaz. And the friends. Today they were looking for volunteers to open up the choked well. The water hole.

"So maybe we can talk later? And by the way, maybe you could do with some money? Don't get me wrong. Well? Can we talk a bit this evening?"

"Possibly," she said in surprise, avoiding the financial approach. And after another dreamy reflection she asked cautiously: "What is there to talk about?"

And she picked up the dishes, my almost untouched meal, and minced out of the room (still, she kindly left me the teapot and the honey). Outside, from the dark passage, she added in English: "Never mind. Be at peace? Can't you?"

A half-wit. Or maybe drugged. A few more years and the Russians will come and eat them for breakfast.

But in any case: where *is* the beginning?

My first childhood memory is an image of a scorching summer's day, bathed in the bitter smoke of eucalyptus shoots being burned farther down the yard. Touched with the haze of a khamsin. A thick cloud of flying ants—or perhaps it was locusts?—land on the child's head, shoulders, knees, in his shorts, on his bare feet and fingers busy demolishing molehills. Or, with a sliver of glass that he had found in the garden and used to focus the sun's rays, setting fire to pieces of paper from a cigarette pack (Simon Arzdt?). A dense shadow fell upon him and blotted out the world. His father. Who stamped out the fire. And flashing rage like the Biblical Jehovah hit him over the head.

And the garden: what did not grow in it? Squill and wood sorrel in their season. Cyclamen and lupins and groundsel at the end of the winter. White daisies. And poppies. Cassidony. All these were despised by the father, who purged them all in favor of his rose beds, the exotic rare strains that he ordered from the Far East and perhaps from the Andes. And there were insects and creeping things and lizards and upside-down cathedrals of spiders' webs, and tortoises and snakes, which the child caught and imprisoned in cans and jars in the cellar. Occasionally they would escape and hide in cracks in the stone or make off to nest in the house. And the silkworms that he collected in the thick of the mulberry tree, hoping to make butterflies, and invariably all that ever came out were some malodorous rotten stains. The samovar in the dining room was a shaggy, panting devil. The china dinner service in the glass-fronted cabinet was like motley soldiers in battle array. The bats in the roof were rockets guided from some far-off place. In the library stood a squat brown radio, in which in the dark a devilish green eye glowed on Vienna, Belgrade, Cairo, and Cyrenaica on the glass wave-band indicator. And there was a gramophone with a handle and a horn that would sometimes erupt into ecstatic opera accompanied by his father's bellowing. Barefoot, bent double like a burglar, the child used to creep into corners of the house and the garden. Build himself from mud, under some rusty tap, cities and villages and bridges, forts, towers, palaces, which he took pleasure in destroying by aerial bombardment with pine cones. Faraway wars raged in Spain, Abyssinia, Finland.

Once he fell ill with diphtheria. Between sleeping and waking with a high fever he half saw his father coming into the room naked to the waist, with unruly grey curls on his broad brown chest, and stooping over the nurse. Then there was moaning and pleading and desperate whispering before his fevered slumber once more drowned the memory between fragments of dream.

On late summer mornings, like this Saturday morning, Arab peasants used to arrive from the village on the coast. With their docile donkeys, with their dark robes, with a hubbub of guttural entreaties, with whiskers aquiver, they would undo their wicker baskets. Bunches of dark muscatel grapes. Dates. Animal manure. Greenish-purple figs. A faint female smell used to pervade the house and linger after they had gone. The father would chuckle: These fellahin are better than the Russian mujiks; they don't drink, they don't swear, they're only filthy, and they steal a little, children of mother nature, but if we let them forget their place they're liable to cut throats.

Sometimes the child would wake up early in the morning to the sound of camels braying. A caravan from Galilee or the desert bringing building stones. Or sometimes just watermelons. From his window he could see the softness of their necks. Their expression of contemptuous sadness. The delicate line of their legs.

At night from his room at the end of the second floor he could catch sounds of hilarity when his father gave a party. British officers, Greek and Egyptian merchants, real-estate agents from Lebanon (apart from Zakheim, hardly a Jew ever set foot here), they would gather in the salon to spend a male evening together, drinking, joking, playing cards, sometimes erupting into drunken sobs. The room was paved with fine marble tiles (which were all stolen during the years of desolation. Boaz is laying floors of grey concrete instead). And there were soft, low Oriental sofas covered with embroidered cushions. Strangers used to shower the child with costly, complicated toys. Which did not last long. Or bonbonnieres. Which he had always detested (but two days ago he sent for a couple from the shop in the town to spoil your daughter). A wily, inquisitive, elusive boy, peeping and vanishing like a shadow, always devising little schemes, bitter and proud, wandering around by himself summer after summer on the empty paths of the estate. Without mother, brother, or friend, apart from his rhesus monkey, which his father killed and on whose grave the child erected a sort of hysterical mausoleum. Which is also a ruin now, where your daughter is keeping a tortoise. It was Boaz who found it for her.

And in the nights: the silence of the nights. Which was no silence at all.

The house stood alone. Some two miles separated its northern window from the last building in the town. On the edges of the orchard stood five or six workmen's huts that his father had built from corrugated iron and cement blocks to house the Circassian laborers that he brought from Lebanon or Galilee. Dim and dull in the night their voices rose in a song that had only two notes. In the darkness foxes barked. The jackal poured out his heart in lamentation in the stony wilderness of thistles bristling with mastic trees that extended all around the house. Once a hyena appeared beside the toolshed in the light of the full moon. His father fired at it and killed it. In the morning its corpse was burned at the bottom of the slope. Four empty rooms, a corridor, and six steps separated the child's room from his father's bedroom. Even so, he could sometimes catch the sound of a woman groaning. Or soft wet laughter. Each morning he was awakened by the sound of crows and pigeons. An uncompromising cuckoo used to repeat each morning a fixed insistent slogan. And it is still here: repeating. The very same slogan. Or perhaps its great-grandchildren have returned to teach Boaz what his father has forgotten. Occasionally wild ducks flew past in arrowhead formation. The storks camped and moved on. Are you able, Mr. Sommo, to tell the difference between a stork and a wild duck? Between a jackal and a fox? Between a poppy and a cassidony? Or only between sacred and profane, or between two evening papers? No matter. Possibly your daughter will.

Until the age of four or so the child did not learn to speak. Perhaps he did not make a particular effort. But by the age of four he could kill a pigeon with a stone and suffocate moles with smoke. And he could also harness a two-wheeled cart to the donkey (tomorrow I shall teach your daughter, if Boaz has not anticipated me).

Hours upon hours, all alone, he used to fly overseas (Atlantis, Shangri-la, El Dorado) on a swing that the Armenian servant fixed up for him in the garden. At the age of seven he erected a lookout post with a rope ladder in the top of a eucalyptus tree. There he used to climb with his rhesus monkey, peep over the Great Wall of China, and check on the travels of Kublai Khan. (Its remains are still visible from my window now, while I am writing. One of Boaz's oddlings is lying there, naked, shaven-headed, playing a mouth organ. A fragmented, wistful tune reaches me intermittently.)

Ten barren years that child, the tallest of the lot but skinny and bony like a Bedouin, served in Monsieur Markovich's class in Zikhron. Always on the last bench. Punctiliously fulfilling his obligations but nevertheless separated from them all by a ring of persistent loneliness. Reading alone in silence. Reading even in the breaks. Memorizing the pages of the atlas. And once, in a fit of rage, he picked up a chair and broke Monsieur's nose. Such outbursts of fury, rare but bloodily violent, earned him a kind of aura of danger. Which never left him all his life. And inside which he always seemed to be fortifying himself against the general stupidity.

As soon as he was nine he began, on his father's orders, to travel to Haifa twice a week for private boxing lessons. When he was ten his father taught him to dismantle and assemble a handgun. Very soon they were having shooting contests in the lower extremities of the farmyard. His father also decided to initiate him into the mysteries of the use of the dagger; a collection of curved daggers—Bedouin, Druze, Damascene, Persian—occupied half a wall in the library. Do you know, Mr. Sommo, how to use a dagger? Perhaps we should have a little duel?

And the wide, coarse house, built like a drunkard's wager, like a wild, extravagant gesture. Of local stone. Almost black. Edged with a different stone brought from Mount Hebron or the Shouf Mountains. With high walls and raging illogicality. Twisting passages, spiral staircases transferred from Jerusalem convents, storerooms, secret hiding places, entrances that only led to other entrances. And a secret tunnel through which you could pass, stooping, from the cellar underneath the wing and emerge in the pavilion in the garden (now it is blocked with earth).

When you come and visit one day, after I am gone, I expect Boaz will treat you to a guided tour. You will be able to see it with your own eyes and pronounce the appropriate benedictions. Perhaps by then they will have unblocked the tunnel, just as they are now clearing out the water hole, which was erroneously considered a well. By the way, my father bought Boaz a mountain in Tibet, which is officially called Boaz Gideon Peak. Perhaps I shall get in touch with that firm of Italian crooks and buy your daughter a mountain too.

How shall we explain the urge that took hold of me to write my childhood memoirs for you? Can you find me a verse for that? Or a fitting little homily? A tale of old-time rabbis? Perhaps I was moved by what you wrote of your own childhood. Or by the contempt you nurse for me. Or perhaps again I was motivated by my instinct for tidiness, the need to leave some sort of report in reliable hands? Has Ilana told you about my passion for tidiness? Which always amused her? Has she shared with you, Mr. Sommo—or may I call you by your personal name, Marcel, I believe? Michel?—other amusements from the time of her first marriage?

Ever since my childhood I have always insisted on putting everything in its proper place. My work tools, screwdrivers, saws, files were all arranged on a cork board in my room, like a little museum. My toys were sorted and stored according to their type and country of manufacture. To this day my desk in Chicago is permanently set out ready for the CO's inspection. My books are arranged in order of height like a guard of honor. My papers are perfectly filed. In the Yom Kippur War, in the bitter fighting over the seam between the two Egyptian armies, I was the only Israeli officer who went on the assault shaved and with a freshly starched shirt. In my bachelor apartment, before and after Ilana, the sheets were arranged in a wardrobe as though in the cross of a gunsight, and the records were in alphabetical order. Behind my back in the army they used to call me "Right Angle." Ilana used to laugh aloud every time she saw my shoes lined up on the shelf. Has she told you about it? Has she told you about our nights? About my war wound? About the destruction of Khirbet Wahadneh? How do you see me, Marcel—as a villain, or as a ridiculous villain?

But what do I care. Since when do I bother about what the Regimental Police think of me.

And in any case, Mr. Sommo, Michel, you ought to take care. Even an old sick snake can still bite for a finale. I may still have a drop left in my poison gland. Why not reveal to you that your beautiful wife climbs upstairs to visit me at night? That she sneaks into my bedroom in her nightdress when the rest of them are asleep. Boaz's scout torch trembles in her hand and makes pale blisters tremble on my plaster-peeling wall. She removes the blanket from me. Slides her palm over my belly. Her lips in the darkness plow the thinning hair of my chest. Perhaps she is trying to extract a drowsy coitus from me. Perhaps she succeeds. I cannot report with certainty: my waking resembles a dream, and my sleep is a holding defense. Perhaps all this only takes place in my fantasies. In hers. And in yours, Marcel.

Why not set Zakheim on you? I can still manage to alter my will. Divide the whole lot between the Protection of Animals and the Council for Reconciliation with the Palestinians. I'll smash you, my friend, if the spirit takes me.

But there isn't any spirit. My evil powers are abandoning me together with my thinning hair and my sunken cheeks and my lips which are withdrawing into my mouth leaving only a vicious slit.

Now that the viciousness has gone.

Why should I trample you?

You have suffered enough. Now it is my turn to pay and yours to receive compensation. You won't refuse, will you? I shall undertake to be your messiah. To bring you out of slavery to freedom and from poverty to great wealth. As it is written in your holy books, Thy seed shall rise up and inherit the gate of his enemies.

Set your mind at rest, Marcel: your wife is faithful to you. No nocturnal sorties and no deathbed coitus. Except in the imaginations of the three of us. Where neither tanks nor Sparks of Redemption can penetrate. Even your little daughter does not forget you: she has just come into my room and decided to promote my electric shaver to the rank of telephone (which we don't have here) and uses it to report to you in half-hour calls to Jerusalem on the development of her relationship with the goats, the geese, and the peacock. Have I already mentioned that Boaz has found her a tortoise?

I shall conclude, dear sir. Never fear. Cain is dying and Abel will inherit. It is not only in Hawaii that right wins out in the end. Your old theological question, how long will the wicked rejoice, preceives in the case before us a simple concrete answer: until September or October. At the very latest—December.

And then, as it is written in your scriptures, "Man and beast shall be saved, and thou shalt make them drink of the stream of thy delights."

I have no telephone in this house, and therefore, to make sure you do not get up in the meantime and run off to Hawaii, I have asked Boaz to jump on his bicycle and call a taxi from Zikhron. For forty or fifty dollars (how much is that nowadays in Israeli pounds?) the driver will surely agree to take this letter straight to your home in Jerusalem and hand it to you the moment the Sabbath ends. I am a little tired, Michel. And there is some pain. So I shall conclude here. Enough. The taxi driver will have instructions to wait until you have written me a reply and bring it straight back to me tonight. What I am asking of you is this: Do you still insist on your right to have the two of them back at once? If so, I shall send them tomorrow morning and that's that.

On the other hand, if you agree to leave them here a little longer, you receive half my inheritance. And you also receive the bonus of a first-rate good deed. Think fast and decide. I shall be waiting for your reply via the taxi driver tonight.

Take good care of yourself, chum. Don't learn anything from me.

A. G.

———

Mr. A. Gideon
Gideon House
Zikhron Yaakov

By the Grace of G-d
Jerusalem
Conclusion of the Holy Sabbath
9th of Elul, 5736 (4.9.76)

To be delivered personally by special messenger

Mr. Gideon,

By the driver you sent, who is kindly waiting here in my home drinking a cup of coffee, I am returning to you a few lines in reply to your letter of this morning. First of all I must ask you to pardon and forgive me for the harsh and unnecessary insults I cast at you in my letter of two days ago, not knowing you were unfortunately desperately ill and in fact on your deathbed. It is written in our texts, "A man should not be blamed for words spoken in grief," and when I wrote to you I was in the grip of a very great grief.

And now we are on the threshold of the Days of Awe during which the gates of repentance and compassion are opened wide. Therefore I suggest that Ilana and Yifat should come back home tomorrow morning and you too should come at once and without delay to receive the appropriate treatment at Hadassah Hospital. And I suggest that you stay with us as our guest, Alexander. And that Boaz should come too of course, because his sacred duty now is to stay close to his father and tend him on his sickbed. By virtue of your remorse and your suffering and your heroism in the sanctification of the Name on our battlefields, and with the help of the divine Mercy, I believe you will be healed. Until then you must stay here with us. Not with Zakheim, not in a hotel, and I don't care a fig what all sorts of people of uncircumcised heart say behind our backs. Tomorrow morning I am going to explain the whole affair to the Rev. Rabbi Bouskila, whose eyes will doubtless see to the heart of the matter. And I shall ask him to receive you for a meeting as soon as possible and he will not withhold his blessing, which has already done many wonders for the seriously ill. Apart from that I've also phoned a cousin of my sister-in-law who works in Hadassah in Oncology and I've fixed it up so you'll get special treatment there and they'll do everything possible for you, over and above.

One other thing, Alexander. As soon as the driver finishes his coffee and goes back to you with this letter, I'm going to the Western Wall to pray for you there and put a note between the stones that you should recover. It's the days of mercy now. Please be kind enough to tell Ilana and also Boaz this very evening that we've forgiven each other and that I forgive Ilana and I'm sure that Heaven will forgive all of us.

With best wishes for the New Year, and for a perfect recovery, and without a thought for any anger there may have been in the past,

Michael (Michel Sommo)

———

To Michel Sommo   *Thursday, the 21st of October '76*
Tarnaz 7
Jerusalem

My dear Michel,

It's been raining since the night. There was a grey light in the windows this morning. And on the horizon out to sea sharp lightning is capering silently, without any thunder. The doves that were cooing until yesterday are silent today as though stunned. The only sound that crosses the falling water is the occasional barking of the dogs. The big house stands once again deserted and extinguished, its entrances, its rooms, its cellars, and its attic, all handed over again to the old ghosts. Life has retreated to the kitchen: Boaz lit a nice big wood fire there this morning. Around this fire they are sitting or lying on their mattresses, inactive, drowsy; for hours on end they have been saddening the empty house with the guitar and their low drawn-out songs.

Boaz dominates them almost without words. Wrapped in a cape he has made himself from a lambskin he is sitting in a corner of the kitchen, cross-legged, silently stitching sacks. No task is beneath his dignity. Last week, as though sensing the early arrival of the rain, he swept the chimney and filled the cracks with cement. And today, all through the morning, I was also among them. While they were playing the guitar and singing I peeled the potatoes, churned the butter, and pickled some gherkins in vinegar with garlic and parsley. Dressed in a wide black embroidered Bedouin dress that I borrowed from a girl called Amy, with a checked kerchief around my head, like a Polish peasant woman from my childhood. And with my feet bare like theirs.

It is two o'clock in the afternoon now. I finished my work in the kitchen and went to the abandoned room where Yifat and I were staying at the beginning, before you sent and took her away from me. I lighted the kerosene heater and sat down to write you these pages. I hope that with all this rain you and Yifat have put a straw mat down. That you've remembered to put some plastic pants on her under her flannel trousers. That you've made fried eggs for the two of you and removed the skin from the cocoa. And that you and she are constructing a model airplane for her doll that really cries or sailing in the ottoman where we keep the bedclothes in search of the winged dragon. Then you will run her bath, blow bubbles with her, comb each other's hair, dress her in warm pajamas, and sing her "The Sabbath Bride." She will mumble into her fingers and you will kiss her and say Little Miss Empty-Vessels-Make-Most-Noise, no getting out of bed now. And turn the television on and with the evening paper on your lap watch the news in Arabic and then a comedy and the news in Hebrew and a nature film and a drama and "Today's Scripture Reading" and perhaps fall asleep in your stocking feet in front of the set. Without me. I am the sinner and you have to serve the sentence. Haven't you handed her over to your sister-in-law? To your cousin and her husband? Haven't you ruled a line under her and started a new life? Or perhaps your astonishing family has already found you a partner, a pious dumpy docile creature with a covered head and thick woolen stockings? A widow? Or a divorcee? Have you sold our apartment and gone to live in that Kiryat Arba of yours? Silence. Not for me to know. Cruel Michel. Poor Michel. Your dark hairy hands grope at night between the folds of the sheets for my body that is not there. Your lips seek my breasts in a dream. You will not forget me.

A dim, sensual smell filters in from outside. It is the smell of raindrops touching the heavy earth that has been roasted by the sun all summer long. A whisper passes through the leaves of the trees in the garden. There is cloud on the forested hills to the east. This letter is pointless: you will not read it. And if you do you will not answer me. Or you will answer through your brother, who will demand again, insistently, that I stop tormenting you and remove myself once and for all from your life, which I have made into a hell. And he will write that by my bad deeds I have forfeited all my rights to the child and there is divine justice and a Judge and the world is not a moral no man's land.

Soon a girl will pass my window stooping in the rain, with a sheet of canvas covering her head and shoulders. Sandra or Amy or Cindy, on her way to feed the animals. The dogs will follow her. Meanwhile there is nothing but the sheets of rain at the window. No sound penetrates from outside except the conspiratorial whispering of the pine trees and the palms at the touch of the sodden wind. No sound from within either, since the singing and music have stopped in the kitchen. A little stream is running down the slide that Boaz built for Yifat. And from upstairs there reaches me the echo of his rhythmic footsteps. The tapping of the walking stick that his son made for him. With strange strides he measures over and over again the three empty yards between the wall and the door in his new place in the attic. Three weeks ago he told Boaz suddenly to take away the bottle chimes and to move all his things to his mother's old bedroom. In the bare wall, with its plaster peeling, he found a rusty nail on which he hung the remains of her sandals, which he had dug out from underneath a loose floorboard in the wing. In a chest in the cellar he discovered her sepia photograph, blotched with damp stains. And he set it up on his table. Although without the candlesticks and everlasting flowers with which his father used to surround this same photograph in the old library.

And now she looks at us with her dreamy Russian eyes, with her braid wound like a garland around her sad face, and a shadow of a faint smile hovering perhaps around her lips. Alec speaks to her in a grumpy childish voice, like a spoiled boy who is not content even for a moment. And I am unable to calm him. What I am trying to say is that I have moved in there too. Only to take care of him at night: he often wakes up in a panic. He sits up in bed and starts to mumble vague orders, as though continuing his nightmare. And I hurry to get up from the mattress I have put at the foot of his bed, give him an herbal infusion to drink from the thermos bottle, thrust a couple of pills between his lips, and hold his hand until he drops off to sleep again and settles into a painful, interrupted snoring.

Is your face glowering with jealousy? Is hatred darkening your eyes? Do not cast a stone at me. It must be written somewhere in one of your holy books that I am fulfilling a commandment? Performing an act of mercy? Will you not open for me those gates of repentance? Each morning I shave him with his battery-operated shaver. I comb what's left of his hair. I dress him, put on his shoes and tie the laces, and then gently help him to sit down at his table. I put a bib on him and feed him a soft-boiled egg and yogurt with a spoon. Or a mush of cornflakes. I wipe his chin and his mouth. At the time of day when you are finishing your coffee, folding up your morning paper, and going to lower the side of the cot, make a perfect imitation of a cock crowing, and say, "Bonjour, Mademoiselle Sommo, arise, renew your youth like a lion for the service of the Creator." And if she asks about me? Have I gone a long way away? And if she wants to know when I'll return? When shall I return, Michel?

On days when it's not too cold I generally sit him in the easy chair that Boaz has fixed up for him on the veranda for half an hour, put his dark glasses on him and watch over him while he dozes in the sun. Sometimes he asks for a story. I recite from memory chapters from the novels you used to bring me from the lending library. He now has a faint, absentminded curiosity to hear about other folks' lives. Tales that he, like you, always used to regard with utter contempt: Le Père Goriot, Dickens, Galsworthy, Somerset Maugham. Maybe I'll ask Boaz to buy a TV. We are on the electricity grid now.

Boaz looks after him with a sort of submissive attentiveness: he has fitted shutters on the window, replaced a windowpane, put a lambskin rug down for him in the toilet; he takes care of buying the medicines for him at the pharmacy in Zikhron, fetches a fresh bunch of mint every day to drive away the sick smells, all in tense silence. He stubbornly avoids all conversation, beyond Good morning, Good night. Like Friday with Robinson Crusoe.

Sometimes we spend the best part of the morning, he and I, playing endless games of checkers. Or cards: bridge, rummy, canasta. When he wins he beams with childish glee, like a pampered child. And if I win he starts to stamp his foot and complain to his mother that I cheated. I manipulate our games so that he is nearly always the one who wins. If he tries to fool me, to put back on the board a piece I have already taken, or deal himself an extra card, I slap his hand and stand up as if to leave the room. I let him plead and promise that from now on he'll be good. Twice he fixed me with a strange look, smiled with silent madness, and asked me to take my clothes off. Once he asked me to send Boaz to the public telephone in Zikhron to call the minister of Defense and the chief of staff, both of them old acquaintances of his, and tell them to come urgently on a matter I must not know about but which brooked no delay. And another time he surprised me in a different way: he delivered a well-organized, terrifying, brilliant, and totally lucid lecture on the way in which the Arab armies would defeat Israel in the nineties.

But for the most part he says nothing. He breaks his silence only to ask me to take him to the toilet. This is a complicated and painful business, and I have to help him with everything, like changing a baby.

Toward midday he generally feels a little better. He gets up and walks around the room obsessively putting everything in its right place. He folds up my clothes, which are draped over the back of a chair. Puts the cards away in their box. Pounces on a piece of paper. Removes the empty glasses from the room and leaves them on the bench in the hallway. Takes great pains to get the blanket perfectly straight, as though this were a base for new recruits. Scolds me for leaving my comb lying on the table.

At midday I feed him mashed potatoes or rice pudding. I make him drink a glass of carrot juice. Then I go down and work for an hour or two in the kitchen or one of the storerooms, taking down with me the dirty dishes from the bench in the hallway and the accumulated dirty laundry. And he starts on his daily walk between the wall and the door, tapping with his stick, always following the same route, like a caged animal. Until four or five o'clock, the beginning of twilight, when he gropes his way with his stick downstairs to the kitchen. Boaz has made a kind of day bed for him, a sort of cat's cradle on a framework of eucalyptus branches. He huddles in this, close to the fire, wrapped in three blankets, silently watching the girls preparing dinner. Or Boaz studying grammar. Sometimes he dozes off in his cradle and sleeps painlessly on his back with his thumb in his mouth, his face at peace, his breathing slow and regular. This is the easiest time for him. When he wakes up it is pitch dark outside and the kitchen is lit by yellow electricity and the log fire in the grate. I feed him. I give him his pills with a glass of water. Then he sits in his cradle, resting on a heap of cushions that Boaz has made from sacks stuffed with seaweed, listening to the guitar until close to midnight. One by one, or in pairs, they get up, say good night to him politely from a distance, and leave the room. Boaz bends over him, picks him up carefully in his arms, and carries him silently upstairs to our attic room. Softly he lays him down on the bed and goes out and closes the door.

As he leaves I arrive. Bringing a thermos bottle for the night and the tray of medicines. I turn the kerosene heater around. I close the shutters that Boaz has fixed up for us. I wrap him in his blankets and sing a few lullabies. If he considers that I have sung sloppily, repeated myself, or finished too soon, he turns to his mother and complains. But at times a sharp flash, a rapid, sly flicker, flares up and dies in his eyes and the wolfish smile passes for an instant across his lips. As though to hint to me that despite everything he is still running the game, and that of his own free will he chooses to play the fool a little so that I can play at being a nurse. If pain brings out a sweat on his high pale forehead, I wipe it with my hand. I run my fingers over his face and through the remnants of his hair. Then his hand between mine and silence and dozing and the bubbling of the kerosene every few moments on its way from the tank of the heater to the wick that burns with a blue flame. As he dozes he sometimes whispers woefully: "Ilana. Wet."

And I change his pajama trousers and the bottom sheet without getting him up. I've become an expert at this. I have spread oilcloth over the mattress. And at one o'clock in the morning he stirs, sits up in bed, and asks to dictate something to me. I sit down at the table, switch on a light, and take the cover off the Baby Hermes. I wait. He hesitates, coughs, and finally mutters: "It's not important. Go to sleep, Mother. You're tired too."

And he curls himself up in his blanket.

In the silence of the night he says after a couple of hours, in his low inner voice: "You look good in that Bedouin dress." Or: "It was a slaughter, not a battle." Or: "Hannibal should have acquired naval supremacy first." When he finally gets to sleep I have to leave the wall light on. I sit and knit to the sound of the dogs barking and the wind sweeping the darkened garden, until my eyes close. In the past four weeks I have knitted him a sweater, a hat, and a scarf. For Yifat I have knitted a pair of gloves and a cardigan. I shall knit something for you too, Michel: a sweater. White. With stripes. Who irons your shirts? Your sister-in-law? The cousin? Your dumpy arranged match? Perhaps you have learned to launder and iron Yifat's clothes and your own by yourself? Silence. No answer. Exile. As if I never existed. I am unworthy of all the Biblical punishments you have all condemned me to. What will you do if I turn up tomorrow afternoon on your doorstep? With a suitcase in my right hand, a plastic bag over my shoulder, a woolly teddy for Yifat, a tie and after-shave for you, I'll ring the bell and you'll open the door and I'll say, Here I am, I'm back. What will you do, Michel? Where will you put your shame? You'll slam the door in my face. They'll never come back, our Saturday mornings in the simple flat, the sparrows chirping into our late sleep from the branches of the olive tree at the open window. Yifat, in her pajamas with the pattern of cyclamens, creeping in with her dolly between the two of us under the blanket to make a cave with pillows. Your warm hands, half-awake before your eyes have opened, groping blindly in my long hair and her tousled curls. The morning kiss we all three bestow, ceremoniously, upon the bald plastic doll. Your custom of bringing us a glass of orange juice and a cup of strained cocoa in bed on Saturday mornings. Your habit of sitting Yifat on the marble shelf next to the basin in the bathroom, lathering her cheeks and yours with your shaving cream, and having a toothbrushing race with her while I make breakfast and the sparrows squeak outside as if the happiness were more than they could bear. Our Sabbath walks to the wadi at the foot of the monastery. Grace after meals on the balcony performed by the Sommo Trio. The great pillow fight and animal and bird fables and the rebuilding of the Temple in toy bricks on the mat with the Chamber of Hewn Stone made of dominoes and colored buttons from my sewing basket representing priests and Levites. The Sabbath afternoon rest amid a scattering of evening papers on the bed and the armchair and the mat. Your repertoire of Parisian stories and the imitations of singing *clochards*, which made us both weep with laughter. And fill my eyes even now, as I remember and write. Once Yifat took my lipstick and colored a map of the ten tribes of Israel that hung above your desk, a gift from an evening paper to its readers, and in your fury you locked her outside on the balcony "to ruminate on her actions and mend her evil ways" and stuffed your ears with cotton wool lest your heart be softened at the sound of her faint weeping and you forbade me to take pity on her because of the text "He that spareth the rod hateth his child." But when her weeping suddenly stopped and a strange silence descended, you rushed outside and cuddled her and folded her tiny body deep inside your sweater. As though you were pregnant with her. Won't you take pity on me too, Michel? Shan't I be folded into the warmth of your hairy womb, underneath your shirt, when my punishment is complete?

On the eve of New Year, a month ago, you sent your brother-in-law Armand in his Peugeot truck to take Yifat to you. By way of Rabbi Bouskila you informed me in writing that you had initiated divorce proceedings, that my status was that of a "rebellious wife," and that you had begun to raise loans so that you could repay "that tainted money of yours." At the beginning of the week Rahel and Yoash were here: they came to talk me into hiring a lawyer (not Zakheim) and insisting on my right to know what you have done with my daughter, demanding to see her, not just giving her up. Yoash went down with Boaz to look at the water pump, and Rahel put her arm around my shoulder and said, "Lawyer or no lawyer, Ilana, you have no right to ruin your life and abandon Yifat." She volunteered to go to Jerusalem and talk you into agreeing to a reconciliation. She demanded to speak to Alex face to face. She suggested enlisting Boaz for the round of shuttle diplomacy that she was apparently planning. And I sat facing her like a clockwork doll whose spring has run down and said nothing except "Just leave me alone." When they had gone I went up to Alec to make sure he took his pills. I asked him if he would agree to letting you and Yifat come here at Boaz's invitation. Alec smiled wryly and asked if I was thinking of holding a little orgy here. And he added, "Sure, sweetie; on the contrary, there's no shortage of rooms here and I'll pay him a hundred dollars for every day he agrees to stay." Next day he suddenly told us to send urgently for Zakheim. Who arrived two hours later, red and puffing, in his Citroën from Jerusalem and received a cold rebuke and instructions to transfer another twenty thousand dollars to you at once. Which you apparently decided despite everything to accept, taint or no taint: because the check was never returned. Alec also told Zakheim to put the house and the land around it in Boaz's name. Dorit Zakheim received a gift of a little plot near Nes Ziyyona. and Zakheim himself, the next day, two cases of champagne.

"Are you or are you not his wife?"

"Yes. And yours too."

"And the child?"

"With him."

"Go to him. Get dressed and go. That's an order."

Then, woefully, in a whisper: "Ilana. Wet."

Poor Michel: right to the end he has the upper hand. I am in his hands, your honor is underneath his feet, and even the halo of the victim deserving of pity is filched from you, because he is dying, and is placed on his own balding head. I saw the noble note you wrote him magnanimously inviting us all to stay with you and instead of weeping I burst out laughing suddenly and couldn't stop myself: "It's creeping annexation, Alec. He's got the impression that you've weakened, and that the time is right to annex us all under the wings of his presence." And Alec twisted his lips in the grimace that serves him as a smile.

Every Sunday I go with him in a taxi to Haifa, to the hospital, where they treat him with chemotherapy. Meanwhile they have stopped the radiotherapy. And, surprisingly, there is an improvement in his condition: he is still weak and tired, he still dozes most of the day and lies half-awake at night, his mind is muddled by drugs, but he has less pain. He manages now to spend two or three hours walking between the wall and the door. To make his own way with the help of his stick to the kitchen in the evening. I allow him to stay there until they disperse to their rooms, close to midnight. I even encourage him to converse with them to distract his mind. But once, last week, it happened that he failed to control himself and he wet himself in their company. He couldn't be bothered or forgot to ask me to take him to the toilet. I told Boaz to take him straight up to our room, I cleaned him up, I changed him, and the next day, as a punishment, I forbade him to come downstairs. Since then he tries harder. Before the rain that started falling yesterday he even walked by himself a little in the garden. Tall and gaunt in his patched jeans and a ridiculous sweatshirt. When he misbehaves I don't hesitate to hit him. For example, when he slipped away from me one night and climbed up to the observatory on the roof and on the way back slipped and fell off the rope ladder and lay stunned in the hallway until I found him. I beat him like a puppy, and now it is clear to him that he does not have the strength to climb stairs, and he lets Boaz carry him up to our room every evening in his arms. You have taught us all compassion.

And what about you? Do you take time off from your work of redemption and fetch Yifat from the nursery at half past one? Do you sing to her in your scorched voice "For the food which Thou hast given us," "Behold thou art fair," "Mighty in kingship"? Or perhaps you have planted her in your brother's family, packing all her clothes and toys in the brown suitcase, and left for the rocky hills of Hebron? If you come and bring her I'll forgive you, Michel. I'll even sleep with you. I'll do whatever you ask for. And even what you're too shy to ask for. Time is passing and every day that slips by and every night is another hill and another valley that we have lost. They will not return. You are silent. Avenging and resenting and punishing with all the rigor of your silence. You have compassion for all Israel, for ancient ruins, for Boaz, for Alec, but not for your wife or daughter. Even about the divorce proceedings you saw fit to tell me through your rabbi. Who informed me in your name that I am a rebellious wife and henceforth I am forbidden to see Yifat. Am I too unworthy for you to demand an explanation from me? For you to impose a penance on me and show me the way of repentance? That you should write me a Biblical curse?

Boaz says: "The best thing for you to do, Ilana, is to let him finish being angry out there. Let him work it all off on his religious chums. Then he's bound to cool down and give in to you whatever you ask."

"Do you think I wronged him?"

"Nobody's any better than the next person."

"Boaz. Frankly. Do you think I'm mad?"

"Nobody's more sane than the next person. Do you feel like sorting some seeds?"

"Tell me: who are you making that merry-go-round for?"

"For the little one. I mean, when she comes back."

"Do you believe?"

"Don't know. Maybe. Why not?"

This morning I hit him again. Because he went out on the balcony without my permission and stood in the rain and got wet. There was an expression of total idiocy on his tortured face. Had he decided to kill himself? He smiled. Replied that the rain was very good for the fields. I grabbed him by the shirt and dragged him indoors and slapped him. And I couldn't stop myself. I beat on his chest with my fist and knocked him down on the bed and went on hitting him until my hand hurt, and he didn't stop smiling, as though he was enjoying making me happy. I lay down next to him and kissed him on the eyes, on the sunken chest, on his forehead which is spreading upward thanks to his falling hair. I stroked him till he dozed off. And I got up and went out on the balcony myself to see what the rain was doing to the fields and to wash away the pain of my longing for you, for the smell of your hairy body, the smell of bread and halva and garlic. For your voice cracked from smoking and your bold moderation. Will you come? Will you bring Yifat? We'll all be here. It's nice here. Wonderfully quiet.

Take the ruined fish pool, for example: it's been mended with cement and now there are fish in it once more. Carp instead of goldfish. The renovated fountain replies to the rain in its own language: it doesn't gush, it drips. And all around, the fruit trees and the ornamental trees stand in the grey silence in the gentle rain that falls on them all day. I have no hope, Michel. This letter is pointless. The moment you identify my handwriting on the envelope, you will tear the paper to shreds and flush it down the toilet. You have already mourned for me. All lost. What is there left for me except to accompany my obsession to his grave?

And then to disappear. Not to exist. If Alec leaves me some money I'll go abroad. I'll rent myself a small room in a big faraway city. If loneliness gets the better of me I'll give myself to strange men. I'll close my eyes tight and taste you and him in them. I can still manage to stir bashful glances of desire in the three odd youths who wander around here among all the girls who are twenty years younger than I. Because Boaz's commune is slowly expanding: every now and then another lost soul drops in. And the garden is cultivated now, the trees in the orchard have been pruned, new saplings have been planted on the slope of the hill. The pigeons have been evicted from the house and installed in a large dovecote. Only the peacock is still entitled to roam at will in the bedrooms, hallways, and staircases. Most of the rooms have been cleaned out. The electricity has been rewired. We have about twenty kerosene heaters. Bought? Or stolen? Impossible to tell. Instead of the sunken tiles, concrete floors have been laid. An aromatic wood fire burns in the grate in the kitchen. The small tractor stands in a corrugated-metal shelter and all around it are various attachments: sprayer, mower, cultivator, disk harrow. It wasn't a waste to send Boaz to an agricultural school. He purchased all these things with the money his father gives him. And there are beehives and a goat shed and a little stable for the donkey and coops for the geese, which I have learned to look after. Even though the hens still wander around the yard, pecking among the plants as in an Arab village, with the dogs chasing after them. Opposite my window the wind stirs the tatters of the scarecrows that Yifat and I put up in the vegetable garden before you sent to take her away from me. Does she ask if she can come back? Does she ask after Boaz? Or the peacock? If she complains of earache again don't rush to give her antibiotics. Wait a day or two, Michel.

The bougainvillaea and wild oleander have been cleared away from the house. The cracks in the walls have been filled. There is no more scampering of mice across the floor at night. Boaz's friends bake their own bread; its warm, guttural smell fills me with longing for you. We make yogurt too and even cheeses from the goats' milk. Boaz has made two wooden barrels and next summer we shall have our own wine. On the roof stands a telescope, and on the night of the Day of Atonement I was invited to climb up and look through it and I saw the dead seas that extend over the surface of the moon.

Low, stubborn, even, the rain continues to fall. To fill the stone water hole in the yard, the pit that Volodya Gudonski dug and his grandson cleared and restored and which they erroneously call a well. The storehouses, sheds, and shelters are full of sacks of seed, sacks of organic and chemical fertilizer, drums of kerosene and oil, pesticides, cans of engine oil, hoses, sprinklers, and other irrigation equipment. Yoash sends *The Field* every month. From here and there they have collected old furniture, camp beds, mattresses, bookcases, wardrobes, a mixed multitude of household and kitchen utensils. In the refurbished workshop in the cellar he makes tables, benches, easy chairs for his father. Is he trying to say something to Alec with his two huge hands? Or is he also bewitched in his own way? In a niche dug out underneath the rusty boiler they discovered the treasure chest that Alec's father hid there. All that was left in it were five Turkish gold coins, which Boaz is keeping for Yifat. For you he is reserving the job of builder, because I told him that during your first year in the country you worked as a construction worker.

The bottle chimes tinkle on the ground floor, because Alec's bed of planks, his table and chair and typewriter have been taken up to his mother's old room, which has a window and a little balcony looking out over the coastal strip and the sea. He doesn't write a thing, nor does he dictate to me. The typewriter is gathering dust. Books that he asked Boaz to buy for him in the shop in Zikhron stand arranged by height, like soldiers, on the shelf but Alec doesn't touch them. He is content with stories I tell him. Only the Hebrew dictionary and grammar are open on his table. Because in his lucid hours, in the afternoon, Boaz sometimes comes up: Alec is teaching him spelling and basic syntax. Like Friday with Robinson Crusoe.

When he leaves, Boaz stoops slightly in the doorway, as though bowing to us. Alec takes up his stick and starts measuring the room with his rhythmic steps. The tire-and-string sandals that Boaz made for him make a padding sound. Sometimes he stops, surprised, bites his dead pipe, and bends over to adjust the angle of the chair to the table. Sternly straightens his blanket. Or mine. Removes my dress from the hook on the door and hangs it in the packing box that serves us as a wardrobe. A slightly stooping, balding man, with fine skin; his appearance reminds me of a Scandinavian village pastor, on his face a strange mixture of mortification, meditation, and irony, his shoulders sloping downward, his back bony and stiff. Only the grey eyes seem cloudy and damp, like the eyes of a confirmed alcoholic. At four o'clock I take him up an herbal infusion, pita fresh from the oven, a little goat cheese that I made myself.

And on the same tray a cup of coffee for myself. For the most part we sit and sip in silence. Once, he spoke up and said, without a question mark at the end of the sentence: "Ilana. What are you doing here."

And he answered for me: "Embers. But there are no embers."

And then: "Carthage is destroyed. So what. And had it not been, what then. The trouble is quite different. The trouble is there's no light here. Wherever you go you trip."

At the bottom of his suitcase I found the pistol. I gave it to Boaz and told him to hide it.

There's not much time left. It's already winter. When the big rains come the telescope will have to be dismantled and brought down from the roof. Boaz will be obliged to give up his solitary wanderings on Mount Carmel. He will no longer vanish for three or four days, to measure the wooded valleys, to explore abandoned caves, to startle night birds in their holes, to lose himself in the thick tangles of the vegetation. He will no longer go down to the sea to float alone on a raft made without a single nail. Running away? Pursuing? Seeking astral inspiration? Groping in empty expanses, a gigantic inarticulate orphan, after some lost bosom?

One day he will go off on his rambles and not come back. His friends will wait for him here for a few weeks, then they'll shrug their shoulders and vanish one by one. The commune will disperse. Not a living soul will remain. The lizard, the fox, and the viper will reinherit the house and the weeds will return. I shall be left alone to watch over the death pangs.

And then? Where shall I go?

When I was a little girl, the daughter of immigrants struggling with the remains of her comical accent and alien manners, I fell under the spell of the old pioneer songs, which you don't know because you came here late. Tunes that brought me dim yearnings, a secret female longing even before I was a woman. To this day I tremble when they play "In the land the fathers loved" on the radio. Or "There was a lass in Kinneret." Or "Upon a hill." As if they are reminding me from a distance of vows of loyalty. As if they are saying there is a land but we have not found it. Some jester in disguise has crept in and seduced us into loathing what we have found. Destroying what was precious and will not return. Led us on with a will-o'-the-wisp until we strayed deep in the swamp and darkness descended upon us. Will you remember me in your prayers? Please say in my name that I am waiting for mercy. For myself and for him and for you. For his son. For his father. For Yifat and my sister. Say in your prayers, Michel, that loneliness, desire, and longing are more than we can bear. And without them we are extinguished. Say that we tried to receive and return love but that we have gone astray. Say that they should not forget us and that we are still glimmering in the darkness. Try to clarify how we are to get out. Where is that promised land.

Or no. Don't pray.

Instead of praying build David's Tower out of toy bricks with Yifat. Take her to the zoo. To the cinema. Make her your fried eggs, take the skin off the cocoa, say to her, "Drink, Little Miss Empty-Vessels." Don't forget to buy her some flannel pajamas for the winter. And some new shoes. Don't hand her over to your sister-in-law. Think sometimes how Boaz carries his father in his arms. And how about the evening, when you come back from your travels? Do you sit in your stocking feet in front of the television until tiredness gets the better of you? Fall asleep fully dressed in the armchair? Chain-smoke? Or instead do you sit at the feet of your rabbi studying Torah with a tear? Buy yourself a warm scarf. From me. Don't catch cold. Don't get ill.

And I'll wait for you. I'll ask Boaz to make a wide bed of planks and to stuff a mattress with seaweed. Wide-awake and attentive we'll lie with our eyes open in the dark. The rain will beat at the window. Through the treetops a breeze will pass. High thunder will move in the direction of the hills to the east and dogs will bark. If the dying man groans, if the cold brings on a shivering fit, we can hug him, you and I, from either side until we warm him between us. When you desire me I'll attach myself to you and his fingers will slide over our backs. Or you can attach yourself to him and I'll caress the two of you. As you have always yearned to do: to be joined to him and to me. To be joined in him to me, in me to him. For the three of us to be one. For then from without, from the darkness, through the cracks in the shutter shall come wind and rain, sea, clouds, stars, to close in silently on the three of us. And in the morning my son and my daughter will go out with a wicker basket to dig up radishes in the garden. Don't be sad.

Mother

———

To Mr. Gideon   *By the Grace of G-d*
and Mrs. (in reply to her letter to me)   *Jerusalem*
and to dear Boaz   *4th of Marheshvan 5737 (28.10.76)*
Gideon House
Zikhron Yaakov

Greetings!

Thus it is written in the psalm, "Bless the Lord, O my soul" (Psalm 103): "The Lord is merciful and gracious, slow to anger, and plenteous in mercy. He will not always chide: neither will he keep his anger forever. He hath not dealt with us after our sins; nor rewarded us according to our iniquities. For as the heaven is high above the earth, so great is his mercy toward them that fear him. As far as the east is from the west, so far hath he removed our transgressions from us. Like as a father pitieth his children, so the Lord pitieth them that fear him. For he knoweth our frame; he remembereth that we are dust. As for man, his days are as grass: as a flower of the field, so he flourisheth. For the wind passeth over it, and it is gone; and the place thereof shall know it no more. But the mercy of the Lord is from everlasting to everlasting upon them that fear him. Amen.

Michael Sommo

ABOUT THE AUTHOR

Amos Oz was born in Jerusalem in 1939. At the age of fourteen he joined Kibbutz Hulda, where he lived, taught, and wrote for many years. A veteran of the 1967 and 1973 wars, Oz has since been active in various efforts seeking reconciliation with the Arabs. He now lives in Arad, Israel.

James Joyce, Marcel Proust, Thomas Mann,
E.M. Forster, Isak Dinesen, Albert Camus, Günter Grass,
V.S. Naipaul, Doris Lessing, Gabriel García Márquez,
Wole Soyinka, Salman Rushdie, Primo Levi, among many others:
VINTAGE INTERNATIONAL is a bold new line of trade paperback books
devoted to publishing the best writing of the twentieth century
from the world over. Offering both classic and contemporary
fiction and literary nonfiction, in stylishly elegant editions,
VINTAGE INTERNATIONAL aims to introduce to a new generation
of readers world-class writing that has stood the test of time
and essential works by the preeminent
international authors of today.